FORGOTTEN THINGS

STEPHEN MULLANEY-WESTWOOD

To
Laura,

Blessings,

Forgotten Things

This novel is a work of fiction; all characters and events are either fictitious or used fictitiously.

ISBN-13: 978-1514303269
ISBN-10: 1514303264

Front cover art Copyright © Ed Org used with kind permission.

Additional silhouette figure art Stephen Mullaney-Westwood. Child model Draven Westwood.

Websites at time of going to press:

www.mullaneywestwood.com

www.edorg.co.uk

Also available digitally.

Stephen Mullaney-Westwood

For all the good folk

Stephen Mullaney-Westwood

Here in cool grot and mossy cell
We rural fays and faeries dwell
Tho' rarely seen by mortal eye
When the pale moon ascending high
Darts thro' yon' limes her quiv'ring beams
We frisk it near these crystal streams
Her beams reflected from the wave
Afford the light our revels crave
The turf with daisies broider'd o'er
Exceeds we wot the Parian floor
Nor yet for artful strains We call
But listen to the water's fall
Would you then taste our tranquil scene
Be sure your bosoms be serene
Devoid of hate devoid of strife
Devoid of all that poisons life
And much it vails you in their place
To graft the love of human race
And tread with awe these favour d bowers
Nor wound the shrubs nor bruise the flowers
So may your path with sweets abound
So may your couch with rest be crown'd
But harm betide the wayward swain
Who dares our hallow'd haunts profane

William Shenstone

Stephen Mullaney-Westwood

THE FIRST CHAPTER

The tale I now impart may appear too incredible to believe, but it is important that you try to understand. Stories and folklore do not spread so vast without seeds of truth, and these roots have been growing here since the dawn of man.

I know how easy it is to forget where it began, where we came from, what it is really all about. We are afraid of the monthly bills through the door, those vices and creations of the human race, but there are true ancient threats much more worthy of that fear.

It isn't about your towns, your concrete jungles, your high finance businesses; all of that which never used to exist. I am talking now of the real world, that of nature; the prettiness of flowers, the wildness of fern and bush, the vastness of the trees, the truth of earth, grass and dirt. That is where our bodies will ultimately lie and rot, that is where we end, and some seem to forget, that is from where we begin.

* * *

I was the impressionable age of twelve when my parents relocated us to Cornwall, to what I expected to be the slower paced life of desolate moors... and woodland...

A beautiful place, certainly, but recounting these memories for you now is sure to be bitter sweet.

I sit here as my grandfather once did, speaking into an old cassette player that could care less about my stories and philosophies on life. But perhaps you will, perhaps you already know how much it matters... How every small thing is needed to make the bigger picture.

I remember noticing how the fog would often not lift till mid-afternoon, and even then it was only to reveal how dark the clouds were. If it didn't rain the mist itself could soak you cold, and in the woods, it felt like it was always raining. When the mist was low like that, I only had to walk under those trees to hear the sound of gentle rain as it dripped down from leaf to leaf and feel the drops upon me sink through my hair and wet the top of my head.

I would look up to the patches of grey sky, through the twisted maze of tangled branches, in awe of it all, feeling smaller than I was, and feeling that my place in the world was even smaller. I liked that though, the sense of being so grounded. The woods soon became my place.

Martin, however, could always be found wandering the coastal paths around the town. He was a true loner, more content to be in his own company, though somehow I found a way into his life. I don't think that he truly wanted to spend so much time alone, but he had never met anyone that he could relate to. I would like to think that I became that peer, that he found in me the intelligence his maturity craved for, and a familiar childlike soul that appealed to the twelve year old innocence he desperately clung to.

Martin never seemed to be truly 'happy' and it was strange really, for a twelve year old boy to be so deep and into himself, yet I soon became the same. Things can change you.

I remember how Martin's green eyes hardly ever looked up over his thick eyebrows. Through the framing of dark childish straight hair, those eyes spoke of years far surpassing the twelve he had lived. His shoulders dipped with the weight of an imagined sad and troubled existence. But in time he became my best friend, and I understood him better than anyone.

We were both the quiet, thinking types, but I had the drive; I had the childish curiosity and the abandon that comes with not knowing enough about life to see fear in every step. Martin lacked that, and from the moment we met, he worried me.

Trudging over the moist, soft and mossy ground, I would head towards the coast, knowing well his fixation with the sea. I soon realised how much he was fascinated by it, and how his humbled fear was its true allure.

I would sometimes watch him from a distance. I would see how he had strayed off those safe trails, trodden down by the ramblers that would visit there every summer, and how he would push closer to the edge. He would stand; a mere step from the plummet onto jagged rocks and the froth of white kicking waves below. It seemed to speak to him. And the Earth roared on its constant lament, heard by any who cared to listen.

He was definitely a strange boy, Martin: too small, too pale, hair too dark, mood so often subdued. Thinking of him now, knowing that I may never see him again, grips me cold in my heart. He was the best friend I ever had.

I'm not sure which part of our souls finds such attraction in rugged cliff faces with waves breaking white against them, but for some primal reason we do. Smelling the salt and feeling the spray as you stare down at the thrust and tumble of the crashing foam so far below... I guess it makes you stop and take notice what you are part of. There is the ocean, alive and calling out as it always has been, for all time. Never for a second, does it stop. I found it as beautiful as Martin did, yet it frightened me far more.

I preferred to spend my time in the woods. I felt that I understood them more than the sea. Looking back on it now, as of course I was a child then, I understand my longing to be there in that ancient space. They were a secret belonging only to me, a place where I could forget that anything else existed. Within them was a wise knowledge which felt much less relentless than the oceans, wild yet calmly rooted.

I grew to know them, and they knew me. Whilst they forever changed, they were always familiar. I felt part of them, part of all that nature, that whole earthiness. Within them was a true kind of magic, of new beginnings, the knowledge of all life.

Before my family had moved to Cornwall we had lived in a town where the best I could get to woodland were the purposely-planted trees in the park which stretched in a row to each side of the well used pathway. I would climb them sometimes; although they were so regularly clipped back that the first branch was often too high to reach; and I would be scolded for the green stains which invariably smeared my jeans. My parents always preferred me to play inside where it was safer, and cleaner. But not every spirit is so easily tamed, and my head was forever in the clouds, praying for something to happen.

Perhaps you should be careful what you wish for.

There was not much to do in that Cornish village other than wander the countryside, but that suited me fine. I have always been able to amuse myself, and the woods soon became a place of wonder and adventure, even though to most people they were just a forgotten undergrowth of rotting trees. As it turned out I was right; they were much more than that.

Martin, Josh and I were the only kids of our age in the village, so we just fell into friendship, even though Josh was very different to both of us.

You had to walk to the furthest point of the village to get to his house, not that it was particularly far, and not that anything would stop you. There was little chance of bumping into another living soul, and even less chance that anyone would speak to you. People would silently look up, check that you were not a stranger, clock that you were 'just a child' and then return to their tasks. It was, I think, the quietest place to live in the whole world, ostracised from all others and surrounded by miles of countryside.

It was too quiet really; it had a strange atmosphere, as if it held some secret and no one dared to speak lest it get let out. Even the few cars which drove through seemed to lower the sound of their engine noise as they passed. There was a deafening hush and a grey washed out tone to everything, a place that seemed forever asleep, no matter how much was happening. Birds that sang muffled songs and footsteps that failed to break the silence. It truly felt as though I were dreaming, yet if I was, I have still not woken up.

Back then Josh's house appeared to be huge and incredibly posh. It was not adjoined to any other, and reminded me of dolls houses with the typical symmetrical layout of windows and the door in the centre. His mother or father would always answer the bell with a courteous yet challenging manner and Josh would soon come barging passed them, pulling on his coat with a big smile on his face. No matter what upbringing he was having with his 'well to do' family, he was still a twelve year old boy and airs and graces were only for Christmas dinner and the occasional trips to church.

He was energetic, and possibly a little too enthusiastic, but he would always stick by us, and he had been looking out for Martin over the last few years. He was a big lad for his age, all muscle mind, and much more assured of himself than either of us. If Martin was the brains, and I was the imagination, then Josh was certainly the brawn.

I admit that he definitely had his place in our 'gang' and due to his competitive nature, and of course his rich parents, he would always come up with the goods. It was Josh who supplied everything we used to make our camp in the woods, and Josh in fact who undertook most of the manual work it involved.

That camp is still a fond memory from my childhood, despite all that happened. I can remember the plans I had for what to do with it, drawing pictures and making up names. It still reminds me of what it feels like to be a kid and feel like you have so many possibilities. I think, as you get older, it is the amount of possibilities which scare you.

It was late May when we moved there, and with school closed for half term I had a week, at least, to become accustomed to my new surroundings. I had yet to meet Martin and Josh but I had always enjoyed exploring places on my own. It was one of the good things about having moved; that I could find some new adventures. And I certainly found one.

The house, it was explained to me, would be left to us by my grandfather on my mother's side. It was the house that she had lived in as a child but had not been back to since. Grandpa was still alive and living there, though not fit enough to look after himself after suffering a stroke. His mind was certainly still sharp, however, and he had voice enough to say that he would 'not go to no 'ome'.

I had never even met Grandpa Finn until then, and had no idea what to expect. I had seen some old pictures and had received birthday and Christmas cards from him and his late wife, but that was really all I knew. I think that was the only thing scaring me; that there would be someone else living there that I had no choice but to share my home with.

We had to drop everything in order to re-locate there, travelling miles from all that we knew to the seemingly idyllic seaside of Cornwall. I had no say in it but then my parents did not have much choice either. It was a huge upheaval, abandoning everything, but I took it well. The life I had before the move was not exactly overwhelming, living in a town where the only adventures to be had were trips to over-sized shops and the thrill of avoiding certain 'dodgy' areas.

I relished the idea of starting afresh, and had sat staring in wonder as we travelled by car to the views of empty fields and over roads cutting through deep dark woodlands on either side. I watched with wide eyes as houses made way for trees and sheep and cows became the populace. I could hardly believe that I would actually be living there, and this was not just a country holiday.

My father seemed fine about it all. His work was no problem as the firm he worked for had premises near the new location. He took his career seriously. Everyone joked with him that his job was incredibly boring and he always had the same answer to it; he said 'It's actually very high class. I find special homes for special people.' What that really meant was 'expensive homes for people with far too much money'.

But he didn't really look like a typical estate agent. When he was not all suited up for the office he actually looked quite modern with dark hair I did not inherit, quite long but neatly brushed back behind his ears. He fell into his free time with blue jeans and bright white T-shirts and although he certainly did have a serious side, he was often making some smart joke or other.

It was actually my mother who seemed the most put out by the move. Even then I could not help but notice how uneasy she seemed to be. I felt that perhaps she begrudged looking after her father, or that they did not actually like each other too well. But with excitement taking hold of me, I found all else fairly easy to ignore.

When we eventually pulled up onto the small gravel driveway I was out of that car as soon as we had stopped. I wanted to see everything- my new house, my new room, and all the interesting countryside which surrounded us.

That dream cottage looked instantly strange to me though, not quite built right. Standing askew in the sunshine it had a real lived in feeling, it had a past. It was certainly much older than the clean lined semi-detached house we had just left. All the houses I was used to looked the same, but this was different, this had real character.

Of course my imagination kicked in, thinking that it might be haunted, and although scared by that prospect, I was also incredibly excited by it. The four wood framed windows visible at the front were all differently sized and not quite straight. The door was up a stone step, with a roofed porch way casting the entrance into shadow. I also noticed, and was suitably intrigued, that there was an iron horseshoe nailed to the middle of that painted olive green door.

The garden was somewhat typical of an older person's home with tidy flower beds on either side of the path and well trimmed grass, all a little too perfect. I knew my mother would like it. I was more taken by the high slanted roof that I had to tip my head to see properly, and the fact that the roof itself had a small window in it.

I looked from the house to my parents. My father was next to me, and looking very pleased with himself, but my mother still seemed anxious, and was standing well back. She did not say much, but it had been apparent the whole time. There had been reluctance in every box that she packed.

She took a deep breath and went towards the door, while my attention went back to surveying my new home.

"Yep," my dad said, addressing me and looking up to the roof I was still staring at, "that's got to have a good loft in there. I might even be able to make a room out of it."

And then both my father and I returned to Earth with the sound of a formal, female voice addressing my mother.

"Hello, you must be Ann."

Looking over at the door I saw a slim lady in grey, who I now know to have been Grandpa's nurse. My mother was slowly walking into the house on the woman's tail, and so we had to follow suit. By now though, the trepidation had returned as I knew that I was soon to meet my grandfather for the first time. Children do not enjoy formal greetings, and I also knew the importance of this one.

I was the last in, and trailing very much behind, looking around the hallway with my eyes, yet keeping my face lowered to the ground. In front of me the three adults moved through a side door into the lounge room, blocking my way and any early view I would have had of my grandfather. I looked only at the rather dark hall with its brown carpet and the old fashioned wallpaper which I knew my mother would want to change.

Some boxes of our possessions were stacked in a corner; I recognised them and the writing on the outside. Ahead was the staircase leading up to lighter things; my new room, and my own boxes... I wanted to fast forward the next few moments.

But I was trapped there for a while, and the closed door to my left radiated a quiet, thick atmosphere. I had mused, that if any room was haunted, then perhaps it was that one.

"Hi Dad," my mother's voice came, holding within it an emotional and childlike quiver. I looked towards the source. Perhaps I was not the only one feeling anxious about this part. "How are you feeling? Mary here says you are doing ok after your stroke, just your legs are bad, is that right?"

She sounded as though she were addressing a child, even I noticed that in her voice.

"Motor control my Annie, and ataxia too." It was my grandpa. The gravelly voice of an old man I had yet to meet, frail but still low and masculine. "Don't worry, I know all the lingo, and yep I 'ad a stroke but I ain't gone soft in the 'ead!"

I liked him already; he was telling off my mum! I would have sniggered but I was a little afraid of him myself. I think at this point I held my father's hand, even though I had perhaps not done so in years. We were moving into the room ourselves though I stayed behind my father's legs still only allowing my eyes to look about me.

The room seemed predominantly orange, sunlit, and long rather than wide. I remained hidden yet I also kind of wanted to see my grandpa. I was of course intrigued, frightened, mixed with suppressed excitement. Childhood tends to be like that.

"Stroke's a bloody funny word for it really. I ain't been given a gentle pat like a dog.

"But I'm still 'ere ain't I? I ain't no stock and those elf arrows 'ave only knocked me down, not made me fall. I ain't givin' in that easy. Finn still stands, well, at least, I sit!"

The old man certainly still had his humour. He had been through a lot with the recent loss of his wife, and his own decline in health; only to now be forced into sharing his home with us. Even then I remember feeling awkward about it, invading his home like that, moving his possessions to make room for our own. A lifetime of memories being cast out, as though we were hurrying him to his end.

The fact that he had not gone insane with grief could only be put down to a peaceful acceptance that you must garner at that age. I guess you simply come to understand that you have nearly had your time, and that it is the natural order of things. As a boy, death was the horror stories and ghostly tales which I loved to read. I knew that, for Grandpa, it could be reality at any time.

"Anyway Annie, nice to see you too. How was the journey?"

"Fine Dad... long. I think we could all use a cuppa."

And then at last I set eyes on him, daring, as I did, to let my curiosity get the better of my fears.

My first thought was that he looked somewhat like a goblin.

His skin was very tanned and sprinkled with liver spots. I noticed these mostly on the shining crown of his bald head, surrounded with straggly, wispy white hairs. There he sat on a brown and worn arm chair, both arms rested to each side in a white shirt rolled to the elbows. He was very thin yet somehow seemed to still have muscle, like he was made of nothing but sinew.

Although I tried to take in what I saw, I had little time, as his icy blue and very round eyes spotted me peeking out from behind my father and his face seemed to animate and light up as if I was the best thing he had seen in years.

"Ahh," he forcefully yet musically exclaimed, "this

must be young Adam?"

My natural reaction was to shrink back behind the leg of my father, but I felt his palm push me forward to stand in the clear space in front of my grandfather.

"Say hello to your grandpa Adam," he said.

There is something about age that is scary for a child. He wasn't exactly ancient, but to see a man who had obviously deteriorated over the course of years, yet still knew more about the world than I could ever hope to, certainly engaged a natural recoiling. Though for some reason I was warming to his whole presence already. He looked more like a cartoon character than a real person, and I think I amused myself with thoughts like that quite a lot when I was young.

"Let's get a look at ya boy," he smiled with yellow teeth.

I thought at first that he might grab me if I moved too close, rationally to ruffle my hair like so many old people like to do, or irrationally to gobble me up like some ogre from a fairy tale. So I crept slowly forward, shuffling step by step, taking in the view of a man so old he could die at any moment, or already was, and was in fact an animated corpse.

Before I was too uncomfortably close, and before I could make up for him any more frightening personas, he outstretched one of his arms and held out a thinly skinned hand so that I could see every thick raised vein. And then, looking right into my wide eyes, with his equally open and definitely resembling my own, he said:

"Pleased to meet ya master Adam."

Taken aback, and after a pause, I shook his hand like a gentleman.

"We will be friends young lad, I just know it. There's many a tale I can tell ya of this 'ere place."

I stood there, looking into his wise eyes, old yet sparkling with life, and I felt a smile creep into the corners of my mouth. My mother was giving him a disapproving look and slowly shaking her head, to which Grandpa gave me a firm wink of an eye. It was a moment which seemed frozen in time and is now forever imprinted on my memory.

The moment was broken with Mary bringing in the tray of tea and I was soon being jostled onto a seat upon the sofa.

"Good old Mary," Grandpa said, "She's been lookin' after me well."

And there we sat with much tea sipping and munching of soft Viennese whirls which I too was thankful for. But the pleasantries soon began to make way for adult chat while I lost myself in thought as I looked about the room.

To the left of the brown fabric sofa we sat on, Grandpa was seated on his old seat which held the greasy imprints of many a day spent there. Another, much cleaner arm chair to Grandpas' was on the right where Mary now sat. And behind her a large window let light flood in yet seemed to stop at the dark wood rectangular coffee table in the middle. A beige brick fireplace in front of us had a three bar electric fire stuck unceremoniously into the chimney breast. Above it the clock ticked my life away.

Grandpa was sitting in his own little shadow with that being his space, his clutter of things on another almost matching but small table beside him. There was a cassette player, pens and books, and what I recognised to be a white paper bag which would contain sweets of some kind.

My glance kept catching sight of him peeking over a raised tea cup, to my mind, only pretending to be listening.

The talk had turned to that of Grandpa's needs, the

nurse explaining things so that my mother could take over his care. Stuff about money and bills and the upkeep of the house. It was conversation I had no part of and was far too grim for me to have any interest in. I remember noticing how my legs seemed too short as they hung over the sofa, and I felt very much the child.

Yet I believed that Grandpa was uninterested in all of it as well. Maybe at his age you grow bored of acting mature and just want one last play before you leave the world. Perhaps at his age you finally realise none of that 'adult stuff' is really worth a damn.

"Well, is it time for me ta give you the tour?" Grandpa announced, putting down his tea cup noisily upon its saucer beside him.

"No need for that Dad, don't trouble yourself."

"Where's the trouble?" he answered, sounding annoyed with Mum again. "Can't sit on me arse all day. Not good for me, is it Mary?"

Mary was back in the kitchen at that point which adjoined the lounge through an open door behind Grandpa's seat. He had purposely raised his voice so that she heard.

"Anyway you lot, how ya like it so far?"

"Nothing's changed much Dad. The pansies out front are lovely."

"Ah, if you say so. I been keepin' 'em for Hilary, but I can't do it now. She was a good woman but don't think she quite understood what nature's all about... like you Annie, didn't want to 'ear what I 'ad to say. She liked it 'just so', spent hours out there tending it, keepin' it tidy the way peoples like. The love in idleness out there, they was 'er babies, not my choice. The best garden is still out back, I'll shows ya... Adam'll love it."

I just caught sight of my mother's rolled eyes before Grandpa took our attention; struggling back and forth in his seat to stand up. He was huffing and puffing with a determined look on his face, despite many exclamations from Mum and Dad to not worry about it.

Soon my mother was over with him on one side and Mary on the other, arms under his own to lever the old man from his chair without him falling back down. He staggered on his slippered feet, the legs within his baggy brown trousers seeming to have little width and barely any strength. He tottered like a flicked spring for a few moments, concentration straightening his face and then giving way to a huge grin.

"There you are," he said, "no problem at all!"

"Hmm. Come on then let's see this garden... I don't suppose it's changed."

The adults began to move towards the back door of the room, and I jumped to my feet after them. I was still feeling impatient to see my room and the rest of the house, but the garden would be nice to see as well. Grandpa was obviously going to 'give us the tour' as best he could but he was needing help to walk as every step forward he seemed to fall a little back. I felt bad for him, but in my head, that was just how old people were.

The kitchen was not very exciting to me but the opposite door led outside, and the sun was still shining. There was his garden. Ahead I could see exactly what Grandpa meant, and it lightened my mood immensely.

There was a stone, tended area at the front ending at a short red-bricked wall, and beyond that, everything exploded into life. Things grew everywhere, almost completely wild, and I thought it was wonderful!

A metal archway led to a tiled path which cut a clearing through that main garden. I was heading that way while my mother had obviously decided to stay where she stood.

"Remember all this Annie?" Grandpa asked, but there was no answer.

All around the outer sides a fence was keeping the

garden enclosed, but nature was doing its best to break free and was bursting out in every direction. Grandpa had allowed the trees there to do as they pleased with one in the far right corner towering well above the height of the cottage. Tangled branches met twisted vines and bramble lowering boughs into green bushes, ferns and a cornucopia of plants and flowers. There were no patches of bare dirt where plants had been clipped and trained. Flowers in tens of different colours, heights and variations mixed with one another until there was no start or end to any of it.

Walking along the path was like stepping into an enchanted forest. I was skipping down the little path like Dorothy on her way through Oz. Yet I was alone in my appreciation. No one was speaking, no one was saying how I felt in my head about how glorious this was and how it was the best garden I myself had ever seen. I wondered if I should be thinking that way at all.

I looked behind me and no one was even following me. I saw Grandpa though, looking down the path to where I stood holding his hips in quiet tribute to all that nature had done there. Mary was close, hands poised as though he were sure to soon fall. I know that it meant a lot to him to show his garden to me, and that I loved it like he did.

I began tottering back as my own moment seemed wasted on only myself. Grandpa smiled with closed mouth, eyes squinted and a white thick eyebrow raised.

I saw that my mother had not gone any further and I found her expression hard to decipher. As an adult now myself I know exactly what was going on. She thought that the garden was a complete mess, and perhaps even a little unsafe. There she was doing the only polite thing she could do in the position she found herself in, admiring the foxglove flowers which had been planted against the side fence, before the wall.

Grandpa shuffled behind her, stumbling a little with Mary clasping tightly onto his arm. He was still smiling to himself as he spoke some words I will always remember.

"Faery fair and faery bright, come and be my chosen sprite!"

That is what he said, that is what he sang at my mother, and with it she turned and gave him a look of complete confusion and distaste.

"What are you on about now Dad?"

They gave one another a hard look, but my mother's was the hardest.

Time seemed, for a moment, to be still.

"The beds could do with some weeding," my mother said, breaking the silence, "I'll help do that."

"Weeds?" he scoffed in a rhetorical question. "No such thing. Weeds is just plants, with a different name."

My mother looked despairingly at him.

"Anyway, I knows what you're doing Annie, you's not lookin' at weeds, you's lookin' for faeries."

"Here we go!" she announced, but the humour in her voice was for show, her face gave away a real emotion behind it, with venom in her eyes. She had lost patience. "Don't you start teaching Adam your silly stories; that's all we need. He's already obsessed with ghosts as it is. In this family there is no such thing as the supernatural, ok?"

"Got it!" he grinned. "Nope, no supernatural. I agree, 'cause supernatural is just natural we's don't understand. Ha! Nothing in this world is unnatural, if it was, it wouldn't be 'ere."

He looked at me as he spoke his last words, and he gave me another one of his winks. I was lost a little, and was now occupied by staring through a little window in the old garden shed.

"We best get some stuff unpacked," my dad spoke at

last, taking his cue to save my mother from Grandpa's wayward logic.

"Yes you're right Thom. Excuse us Dad, there is a lot for us to do upstairs."

And Grandpa, defeated, gave one firm nod.

Upstairs were our bedrooms and one little box room. Box room was the right term for it as it happened, for that was where most boxes of our possessions had been stacked up. Grandpa now had his bedroom set up downstairs, in the room I had initially been weary of. The house did have an old feel to it, but it was not as creepy as I had thought. In all honesty, I was probably pleased. I would no doubt have found it quite hard to sleep in a haunted house.

My new room was what, of course, I was most excited to see, and I had been waiting too long.

With my bed already in place and my white wardrobe at the other end, the room was quite small, but it was the window to which I went straight towards. I crawled up onto my bed so that I could look out of it.

To see the view of nature out there rather than next door's yard was really quite amazing. A great open field bordered by a little uneven stone wall, the sea somewhere in the distance, just about visible. And, with nose to the glass and eyes turned to the far right, I could see the beginnings of a decent sized wood.

That wood. We have a love hate relationship, me and that place.

I remember staring at it for some time and I imagined being there, dreaming of exploration and adventures. And as my mind wandered, the wood seemed to draw closer, to show more of itself to me, filling my view as if it wanted me to know it.

I was intrigued, wooed. I was suddenly desperate to go there and truly see it for myself. Yet, I also felt a little strange. I know I did feel it and that it is not just my memory filling in an emotional portent. I was sure those woods were creeping forwards, pulsing in the waning light.

I drew myself from them and sat on my knees upon the bed thinking and trying to shake away the slight unease. My room was quite dark despite the spring sun, and also a little cold, but the disquiet was within me.

As with most childhood fancies however, it was momentary. Soon enough normality returned as always and I went on to thinking of simpler things that perhaps a kid should be thinking of. I decided that my room could do with brightening up, perhaps with a poster from the film 'Ghostbusters' which I had enjoyed at the cinema the previous year. And I began to unpack my things.

But I never did really decorate that room and I remember that I already felt different, that I was already beginning to change. My mind kept travelling through the countryside, and thinking about Grandpa. I did not really want to waste time taking old things out of boxes and placing them in this new life. For some reason none of them seemed important.

It was my first day in a new place and I wanted to be able to look back on it and say that I had done something, seen something. I wanted to explore all that I had seen from the window; those landscapes usually reserved for postcards and artist's canvases. Admittedly the mist made the sea the same colour grey as the sky, and the fields seemed soggy and a little miserable, but it was my home now. It held even more fascination due to its imperfections. I wanted to go out there and see what my new world had in store.

So suddenly I sprang to my feet, and ran down the stairs, bumping into my mother as I reached the bottom.

"Where are you going in a hurry?"

"I want to have a look outside Mum, at the woods and that, can I?" I was obviously speaking urgently, and had not planned my pitch. And then, after a pause of about two seconds, I changed my tone, "Just for a little while?"

She had actually seemed quite happy, but now her face dropped. A few words from me and the unease had returned. I had no idea what was wrong so I just stood there, looking imploringly at her.

Her cheek was smudged with something black, and her ash blonde hair was matted, dust and dirt from all the removal boxes. She looked pretty though; my mother was always pretty.

"Have you unpacked those boxes yet?" my father asked, coming into the hallway where I still stood poised on the last step. He had obviously heard that a parental decision was in process and was doing his usual trick of trying to seem masterful, when I knew perfectly well that he was a pushover.

My mother managed to pull herself together, now in view of her husband.

"He wants to go out," she told my dad. "I don't know Adam, it's getting late already." She seemed overly concerned.

"Let him go out," I heard a voice from the living room, the voice of my grandpa. It gave me hope. I had an ally.

And then followed a conversation of voices raised so that they could be heard, between my parents and the non present entity of my grandpa to whom my mother spoke with eyes to the sky.

"Dad I'm not happy with Adam going out on his own in... in a strange place."

"This place may be strange but there's less to 'urt 'im in the fields than on roads and streets."

"Dad please, it's getting late and anyway, I'm making

dinner soon."

"Not dark for an age yet. It's spring. Good light for at least an hour."

"But he's on about going to the woods." And that anxiety showed itself, choking her voice.

"He wants to see bats Finn," Dad added while I stood there awaiting my fate, "he's bats about them."

"Ha-ha Dad," I sarcastically mocked. For a moment the mood was light.

"You won't see no bats out that way," Grandpa's disembodied voice answered, sounding more serious. "The bats know better than go to those woods."

"See?" Mum looked back stiffly at me, and at my father. Her eyes were searching. "It's not safe."

Despite speaking the words quietly, Grandpa had heard.

"Ah poppycock. It's safe enough, nothing happens if you just abide by the rules. Nature has its rules you know."

"Oh just let him go for half an hour," my father spoke up on my behalf. "He's bound to want to see his new haunts, get away from all this for a while."

My mother was trying to find another excuse and her eyes were daggers at my dad, yet she gave in. I knew that I would get my own way eventually but the fight had gone on longer than I expected. "Ok, but please don't go too far, and don't get lost."

Dad silently raised a finger and went over to where the coats were hanging on hooks by the door. He rummaged through his work bag before bringing out his latest gadget; a mobile phone.

"Here, take this, and like Mum said, don't be gone too long, if you are I'll be calling you back!"

I stared at the phone looking huge like a brick in my tiny hand, but they really were that big back then. Dad was lucky to have one and it was only supposed to be used for his job, allowing his boss to chase him up all the time. My mother always got annoyed with it, and said we'd be lucky if it worked anyway.

I felt very grown up though, to have such a thing. Then I quickly thanked him and went to leave, my hand on the door handle.

"Careful of those piskies!" the crackly voice of my grandfather came again from the lounge room to my left, and stopped me dead in my tracks.

I heard my mother make an overly loud hushing noise at him, which actually sounded angry. And when all that had finished, it made me move even faster to get out.

I wanted to go everywhere. I was impatient to know every corner of the place and was looking around frantically as soon as I stepped outside, not knowing where to start. But it was obvious really, to turn to my right where the fields began, and to walk towards those woods.

I climbed over the long wooden gate and started to trudge onwards, looking back up at the cottage and at my new bedroom window. I was not there, in that room, I was here, alive, and breathing air which had begun to cool as the sun made its final attempts at survival. The chill was coming from the great open space that was the sea.

I was not used to the coastal wind and was surprised at how it took my breath away in a sudden gust and then left to return the stillness. The day had been fairly warm, but it was not so now, it had turned its thoughts towards darker, colder things. The night wanted to be known.

In the distance I saw the woods which from my window had weaved their spell upon me, and lured me into that barren field. There stood what should have been a mere mass of innocent trees, but their numbers made a whole of those individuals, making them become something much, much more. The woods were a living breathing organism, imposing, inviting, which moved both towards me and away.

After a time of staring, thinking and challenging my wits, I set to walking straight ahead until the field became lost to undergrowth. It wanted to stop me, maybe it wanted to warn me, yet I went on, pushing through the bushes of bramble. I lifted my feet higher and squashed down its defences; I lowered my head to its attacking spindled twigs. And finally I fell into its heart, and to its softer side, to a barely visible, but certainly once used, footpath within the wood itself.

Nowhere is undiscovered, not anymore. What we think of as wild unspoilt countryside is more often farmland or is preserved for public walks. That place had a trail all along its outer edge but it was obvious that no one ever went there now. It was overgrown and quite inhospitable. It was a discovery as far as I was concerned, it was mine.

I had not really seen anything quite like it before. The trees were grown by their own volition, there by their own desire and left alone to lead their own existence. They had stood undisturbed, probably for decades, and here I was, awakening them... awakening something.

It should have been quite silent. As I stood there in the shadowy stillness I should have heard only the song of birds, the breeze through branches. As I walked the sounds should have been only my feet upon cracking twigs, the brush of plants against my jeans.

But I swear there was more. An indistinct sound was growing louder in my mind, if not truly in my ears. It was heavy upon me, thicker than the thickets themselves.

As birds periodically flapped in the leaves above, as things buzzed and flew about me; the woods themselves seemed to whisper, seemed to live. I cannot truly put my finger on it or quite remember exactly the sounds even as sounds, but I knew it then, I knew clearly. The woods were not simply at peace.

I pushed on, away from the once trodden path, enthralled by the sights which befell me. I left the surrounding banking of exposed twisted tree roots, stepping over nature's debris as I walked.

The beauty of it had a thousand expressions; no two steps were the same. Branches dipped and rose, mosses and lichens grew like clothing for the trunks of the varying sized trees, and plants bright green, covered the ground of the glades.

I did not stop; the difficulties of manoeuvring through untouched nature making the adventure feel only more visceral. I was heading towards the wood's darker depths, moving carefully, pushing through areas thick with dead brown bramble, sometimes stepping on the fallen branch of a tree only to find my foot squash its rotten bark beneath my training shoe.

I went on with no real purpose, yet it had taken me, taken me over with the fever of determination, the low humming sound in my head driving other thoughts from my mind. Perhaps I was challenging it, claiming it, but I did not yet know my place. I was only a child, but the woods had no lenience for that.

I don't know why I had not stopped, but eventually I did, suddenly, abruptly. In a moment of clarity I realised how afraid I truly was of the blackness I was heading towards. And when I stopped, my confusion ceased.

I knew that I had been gone quite a while, losing track of time. It was becoming harder to see at all through the fading light and ahead of me the woods were threatening. It was time to make my way back home.

I gathered my senses, turned around and hurried back from whence I came. The distance did not seem far, but it took longer than my patience. I felt an unfounded urgency, struggling through the bushes in my sudden need to escape. An irrational panic gripped hold.

It became a fight. No sooner had I broken down one of those bramble-tentacles, another seemed to grow in its place. Although I was convincing myself to be calm, I grew ever more anxious, smashing and thrashing at the brush with total disregard to the cruel whipping of the spring loaded branches. I was thinking that I might never get out, that I was unprepared, that people like me should never go somewhere like this. My thoughts became desperate as night threatened, until eventually, and with complete relief, I broke free into the open field once more.

It was a lot lighter away from those trees. The night had begun only in those woods.

I had to get away from there; I did not know why but felt that my sanity depended upon it. Darkness was approaching; the dusk had already started the clock ticking.

I began my urgent steps into the field feeling the cold creeping upon me and the woods at my heel. Everything was faded in the grey hue of semi-light, almost becoming like a black and white photograph taken long ago. It was serene, lost in a timeless solitude, peaceful, yet my heart was still gripped tight.

Behind me the complete silence was touched by the distant rustling of a crow's wings against leaves, and the single voice of a seagull gliding somewhere overhead. I must have imagined the noises, I reasoned, there were no displaced sounds. Yet I knew consolation would only truly come from being far away from that place. I had to keep moving. Darkness would fall quickly now that it had begun, and I was still quite far from my home.

I sped up my steps as I walked, looking back now and then so that I could see how far I had gone. I needed to know how much distance I had put between myself and those strange woods. But on the third time that I looked round at those dark silhouetted trees, I stopped, squinted, and stared.

There were lights amongst the dark, tiny flickering specks of light like those of naked flames. I did not count them, but I remember something close to twenty of them, small enough to be merely cigarette lighters yet strangely moving in procession from the left to the right.

Perhaps people used the woods after all? Perhaps the noise and presence I felt had a simple explanation? That I thought, all this I noticed, mesmerised, but completely unconvinced of my rationality. There was something wrong, something distinctly not right. I was unnerved, a feeling that I was seeing something that I simply should not have been able to see. Open mouthed, arms limp, feet rooted to the spot.

I knew that I should have been leaving, that I should turn and run and never look back. But I was completely fixed by the vision of those tiny moving lights as they waxed and waned, somewhere in the black backdrop of trees. They almost danced while my mind was swimming. I was becoming completely lost within the moment.

Suddenly a shrill noise stopped my heart and woke me cruelly from the trance.

I quickly realised that it was my father's mobile phone sounding a high pitched ring from where it was, protruding from the pocket of my coat.

I answered it. My senses returned.

"Hello?"

The welcoming voice of my father broke through the terrible crackling sounds, "Are you coming home or what?"

"On…my…way," I answered slowly, distracted as I looked back up at those woods.

The lights were all gone.

CHAPTER TWO

It was quite dark when I finally arrived back at the cottage and the warm yellow glow lighting each window was a homely and welcoming sight. I stood on the step and knocked the door with my knuckles.

My mind was still full of questions and aroused by the odd events I had just witnessed. Waiting there I tried to compose myself well enough for it not to be noticed how frightened I had made myself. I did not want to scupper any future plans, and I only hoped that I would not be in trouble for staying out too late.

Mere seconds later my father opened the door and gave me a disapproving, yet purposely comical look. I realised then that I did not have to worry.

Dinner had just been cooked and my mother was in the kitchen busily dishing it up onto plates, my father now helping. The room felt soft and warm and somehow motherly. I already felt that it was home.

There were creamy brown cupboards fixed all around and a large floor space between surfaces, patterned with a flower design. To the left, almost in darkness, was our fold away table that was not set up for the evening, and that meant we were eating off our laps, which I much preferred.

I suddenly remembered, however, that I had seen no television in the lounge. If we were eating from our laps that usually meant watching TV and a chance to escape boring conversation. I put my head through the other doorway and looked into the living room to double check.

"Nice walk young Adam?"

Grandpa's voice made me jump, he must have had

eyes in the back of his head.

I was about to answer but my mother pushed passed me carrying a tray with Grandpa's dinner on it.

"Ah, Shepherd's pie, the food of kings!" my grandfather seemed pleased and unfazed by everything as usual. "Thank you Annie."

"Actually it's the food of Shepherd's," my dad said, smiling to himself as he came into the room and sat on the other armchair with his own food.

"Aye, so long as it ain't *made* of Shepherd's!" Grandpa cackled with a mouth full.

A long running competition of wit had begun.

I was well and truly pushed into the room now by my own dinner plate, and forced down onto the sofa to eat. And there we all sat, eating, in silence, with no TV. I really wanted to mention it, and I think, in honesty, that I needed some light entertainment to clear my mind. I was hungry, yet reluctantly eating as my stomach felt anxious after the unease of what had happened to me out at those woods.

Of course, being amongst all that nature was a new experience for me, but I had not expected to be so scared of the place. Perhaps I already felt out of my depth, a boy from the town lost in the country. But it was more than just unfamiliar. In those woods, with the darkness approaching so quickly and filling them with such deep shadows, I had been truly afraid. I could sense things there which I knew nothing about, things creeping just out of sight and watching from the bushes. And there was no doubt that I had seen those lights.

It was exciting to some degree; having an experience that was so different to my usual everyday life, seeing something so unusual; but it had also shaken me. It had challenged what I thought I knew of the world.

I would probably not rush to go back there, at least certainly not so close to dusk.

"So where'd ya go on your walk young Adam?" Grandpa asked me, breaking the silence and my mental querying.

"Yes, where did you go for three hours?" my father added loudly, and my mother joined in with the show of eyes.

I stopped eating, looking up at them all as they looked at me, half wishing that they would forget that I had not answered. I shot a glance up to the clock, confused.

Three hours?

"Did ya go as far as Old Bob's?" Grandpa added, saving me from having to directly answer my father.

"Adam has no idea what 'Old Bob's' is Dad," my mother spoke for me, my eyes darting from one speaker to the next, my mouth still full.

"You do though, don't you my Annie?" Grandpa said, a fork poised in the air as a gesture towards my mother. There was a twinkle in his eye that I had seen before, and which my mother seemed to find unwelcome. She started eating again and tried to ignore him.

I swallowed. "What is it Mum?"

She raised her eyes but gave no response. My grandfather was all too happy to oblige my question with an answer.

"Old Bob's is the wood you sees. Old Bob's is the name we gives it."

"Cause it belongs to Bob?" I asked. And although I noticed that my mother seemed for some reason uncomfortable, she did not say anything, so I was happy enough to just talk to Grandpa about it.

"Who knows whom it 'belongs to' Adam. No person can really own a bunch a trees. We calls it Old Bob's 'cause old Bob may well still be there. He may dwell beneath its depths. Apparently, time agone, Old Bob went in there and 'es never come out."

I gasped.

"Bad taste Dad," my mother said sharply, "and it's all just tales. We have them in the towns too, they're called urban legends." She sounded quite angry. I never understood why she seemed so irritated by Grandpa, at times when I found him the most agreeable. "Adam take no notice of him, and eat your dinner. Grandpa's not well anyway, it's been a long day."

"Hey you watch what you say about me my Annie." Now it was Grandpa's turn to be irritated and he sounded truly sharp for the first time. "I don't know wheres ya did your research but flights a fancy are no symptom of me stroke, or of being tired either... they's an old man knowing a thing or two."

"Hmm," my mother left it at that, disapproving as ever, but shrinking from an argument she felt was not worth fighting.

"So did ya boy?" Grandpa addressed me.

I had actually become a bit lost trying to work out what was really going on between my mother and he. I guess I had simply not seen my mother talking to her father before, and the dynamics of it were confusing.

I wasn't sure if I really believed in his little tale, but as a child you can know that something is unlikely to be true, yet want to believe in the fantastical so badly that you just go along with the whole thing. In the end you can actually convince yourself rather than let it go. Like being completely aware that it is your parents not Father Christmas who puts those presents under the tree, yet still sleeping with one eye open, hoping to catch a glimpse of him.

"I went close to the woods," I lied, and still wondering how much I could tell, my mouth went on moving without any more prompts, "I saw something."

"Oh yes?" Grandpa enquired in a voice that had raised a pitch.

He sat back in the chair and put a hand to his chin.

Old people believe that scratching your chin helps you think more clearly. He sat like that a while, breathing deeply. And then spoke, somewhat flippantly, "Not that I'm surprised," and he shuffled back his shoulders to get more comfortable, as if the subject was making him feel cosy. Sighing deeply, he then took up his usual posture of both arms on the rests then craned his head forward while his eyebrows rose. "After all," he said in what became his somewhat characteristic storytelling voice, "twilight is a magical time, one of the four hinges of the day."

And now my father became interested in the conversation once more. "Go on Adam," he prompted.

"Well, I saw some lights... in the trees."

Grandpa's face was unreadable, but I had his attention.

"What do you think that could be Finn?" Dad began chatting, "Fire flies maybe?"

Grandpa truly seemed deep in thought, and perhaps a little troubled. "You 'eard of the Will-o'-the-wisp?"

"That's just marsh gas isn't it Finn?"

"Not gas Thom... of a darker order they is. They's the foolish fires... They will make ya follow 'em. They're bad news."

"Were they ghosts Grandpa?" The only Will-o'-the-wisp I knew of was a cartoon I sometimes watched, and that featured a talking ghost.

"Oh really!" my mum could not help but exclaim, trying to stop our discussion.

Grandpa shot her a glare. "What's rattling your chains Annie? When did you become so old, and teasy?"

I held my breath when Grandpa said that, though I didn't fully understand. His voice was both serious, and playful, but I had never heard someone stand up to my mother so much.

"Dad come on," my mother also seemed a little dumbfounded and unsure how to answer. I could see my grandfather silently sniggering at the fact that he knew how to wind her up. "And my name is Ann not Annie," my mother continued. "Everyone calls me Ann these days."

"Well everyone calls me Finn, but you keep goin' on with this 'Dad' rubbish!"

She rolled her eyes and Grandpa began to laugh out loud to himself, swiftly followed by a fit of coughing. It broke the thin veil of tension that had briefly fallen.

"Oh come on ANN there's no worries. Just let ya self go a bit. You was young once young lady. Remember how we used to play marbles in the back yard? Well, I still got some-a those marbles... I ain't lost 'em all yet! I can teach all of yous a thing or two. You don't get as old as me without a bit-a wisdom."

"I'm sorry Dad. I just don't like all this talk, you know that. It's not healthy."

"Having a stroke and not bein' able to walk without 'elp, that's unhealthy." Grandpa sat forward and held a quivering finger aloft. "Being late in me seventies and on death's door, that's unhealthy. But chattin' about interesting things like ghosts 'n' wisps while we're all still livin', that is fine and dandy I assure ya. Anyway," he sat back again and looked more comfortable, "it's not ghosts you need to worry about round here." And he looked at me with his wise concentrated expression. "It's different things round 'ere that you need to worry about."

That seemed to unnerve my mother even further, so much so that she stood up and left the room without a word, yet with eyes burning into her father. She seemed to have lost her place as boss of the household. But I preferred Grandpa in charge; I imagined he and I were going to have some fun.

My own eyes were wide as though those words had been entering my brain through sight. There were a thousand visions in my imagination.

"Ok," my mother announced loudly, coming back in from a break in the kitchen. We all paid sudden attention to her, our dinner's finished, the air thick with strange conversations. "Let's change the subject. Where Dad, is your TV?"

That was very clever because I soon forgot all else and my mother retook her place as my hero.

It turned out that Grandpa actually did have a TV but it was in his bedroom, unplugged, and never used.

"You mean that wooden boxed device for rotting brains?"

To which my dad had answered. "Yep that's the one."

My father set it all up and got it playing while my Grandpa wrinkled his entire face as though holding in an outburst. He then sat back on his chair and lowered one arm over the side to grab his sweet packet. I remember then, a very loud sucking and chewing for a time, as we continued to have our brains rotted while Grandpa's teeth took a similar battering.

That night in bed, I found sleep eluding me for several hours. My brain was whirring, unable to wind down from all I had seen and heard. I had always believed, but now more than ever before, I could imagine that there was magic and mystery all around us, veiled in the cloak of every day.

I had never been interested in what was on the surface. I preferred to fill my life with things that pulled me up further from the mundane. I wanted to be in Grandpa's world, wanted to know what he knew and learn from his years of wisdom. I wanted to know what he had alluded to, yet knew that it was probably something far different to anything I could possibly imagine. The best stories are those you have not heard before, and of things you could never make up yourself.

I lay there with eyes open in tight layers of sheets and covers which seemed to be constantly cold to the touch, yet kept me warm none the less. My mind buzzed as my ears heard every tiny sound, all of which were new to me. The wind was nothing but a gentle breeze, yet it made a slight whistle as it moved through the trees outside. An owl was close; I had never heard one in real life before. And the boards of the loft were creaking.

I tried to put horrors from my mind. Thinking of that dark, empty space up there, full of dust and spiders. It had no doubt been unseen for years, living its life undisturbed, but I wondered if our presence there might have awoken something.

And more than anything I knew that those woods were there outside. I sensed their presence as keenly as I knew the glass protected me and separated me from the wild.

I could almost hear them reaching towards the cottage, scratching and tapping twig fingers against the window. I felt, even when my eyes were closed, the room growing darker as they drew closer to my new home, trying to get to me, trying to make me remember them. I half expected that when I had the courage to thrust open the curtains, instead of open fields I would see nothing but the thick of the trees right there in front of me. I would see only the blackness of overhanging branches obscuring even the light of the moon.

But kneeling on the bed still gripping the ends of the curtains I regained my breath, staring at the view ahead which I had felt such a need to check. All was as it should be. The sky was quite light grey with the moon bright above the dark green fields. To the right the woods were but shadows, safely in their place. Yet still, they haunted me.

* * *

Thankfully daylight turned the view from my window back into a benign playground once more. Time had hazed the memory of my fears and in the light of the sun I could muse that perhaps the woods were only calling to me because they actually wanted me there, playing amongst its lonely trees.

But my sleep had been unsettled and I was left feeling tired. Despite not being able to remember my dreams, I knew that I had been having them. It felt as though I had dreamt one thing after another, and I had been left with confused emotions hanging over me which had no source but to have been planted there over night in my ever active brain.

I wish that we could completely close down our minds at night, so we would at least get some peace from thoughts while we sleep. Yet perhaps dreams have some deeper part to play. Perhaps when we sleep we are learning valuable lessons. But it is also possible that when we're at our most vulnerable, things from other worlds may have an open door through which to have their fun.

My first decision that morning was to see if Grandpa was awake. I wanted to have a chat with him before my parents were there to interrupt and filter our subject matter. I ran down the stairs, a child for whom morning means that everything has woken, including my imagination, and I went straight into the lounge. No one was there.

Above the fireplace was the round, gold coloured clock with its decoration around the outer edge of leaves, ivy I believe, and I could hear it ticking quietly, the only sound in the house. It was just after seven am.

I tiptoed, in large strides, out of the room, around the staircase, and to the door of my grandpa's room which was just below the foot of the stairs. The layout of the house meant that his room was actually below my own, and it was the only room in the cottage that I had not yet seen. I had a feeling it would be worth seeing.

I stood in the dark hallway, hesitating, shivering a little in my night clothes which were just a towelling shirt and shorts, staring at the door. It was of brown wood, just like the other doors in the house, unpainted. I was stalling there, fascinated by the natural grain of the wood which ran vertically in thousands of natural lines.

I wasn't even sure if I was allowed in Grandpa's room, but I really wanted to go in, and I really wanted to speak to him; he knew things that I needed to know.

"Come in young Adam," I heard the slightly weary yet assured voice come from my grandpa. Eyes in the back of his head, and some in the hallway too.

Tentatively I pushed the door open. My mind was speaking, apologising for the intrusion, asking if I could come in, but in reality I was completely silent.

I saw him, sitting up in the bed within that semi-light, the curtained window casting a square of yellow sun on his pyjama shirt. Its top few buttons were undone revealing a bony tanned chest. On the bed next to him was a large opened book and his antiquated bedside lamp was turned on to help him read.

My head was pivoting as I looked about his room. Dust played in the shaft of sunlight which came through the gap in the curtains making a dancing smoke made of sparkling particles. Through it, the far wall was hardly a wall at all but resembled a library, made up of bookshelves stacked with various sized volumes. He had a wardrobe, which also looked very old and had a full length mirror on one door so covered in the thick dust that you would be lucky to see a reflection in it at all.

Then, next to that, and remembered with the most clarity, a table covered in a dark green and black frilled cloth with items upon it which had really caught my attention. I was staring at it all in silence.

"Kind of an altar young Adam. Do you know what an altar is?"

I thought that maybe I did, but not really, and shook my head still looking at it all with my back to him.

"It is a place where you worship," Grandpa announced. "Or, at least, you pay your respects."

It was what Grandpa appeared to be paying respects to that I had been staring at. There was a skull there, a real one. It was not a human skull, it had been from an animal, and at first I thought perhaps a dog. The head of a dog with no fur, no flesh, white, almost cream coloured bare bone, with teeth still sitting in the jaw. To think that creature had once been living and using that skull, that it had once been a head. I was fascinated.

"It is from a deer," Grandpa said. "Beautiful creatures, alive or dead. They's the faery's cattle. Found that skull myself on a walk through the woods."

I shot Grandpa a sudden look, did he mean *those* woods?

He gave me a slow nod, though I do not know to what he answered.

And that was not all that was on the altar. I went to the front of it, unafraid now to be in the room with Grandpa or to show my obvious interest in his table of curiosities.

It seemed he had gathered other things on his walks. An assortment of various sized black feathers, and some that were mostly white with black at their tips. They were displayed lying in a kind of fan design. Amongst it all were pine cones, browned acorns and withered leaves as well as some fresher green ones scattered about.

A couple of thick white candles had been used and allowed to drip wax in pools beneath them. And to the left, adjacent to the skull, was a picture frame, crudely fashioned from entwined sticks, with a photograph inside of an old lady in the sunshine of Grandpa's garden, a pretty smile on her face.

"My dear departed," he said with a sigh, "my Hilary."

I looked at Grandpa with his forced closed mouth smile, and then back at the picture.

My mum's mother had died before I was even born and I knew that Grandpa had remarried. I had never met either of his wives however, and to me it was almost as though they had never even existed, yet to Grandpa they were everything.

I was thinking deeply for a moment about the sadness caused by having known, and having lost. To a child, death seems so far removed from their lives, that it is hard to comprehend, but I was a sensitive boy, and I did spend a lot of time in my head. If I were to decipher those emotions I had back then, and turn them into an adult's philosophy, then it brings up this question: If those departed become only memories, and then those who remember also die, does that mean they are then gone forever?

I went over to him. I did not know how I was supposed to deal with Grandpa if he was upset about her loss. Without thinking, and with a natural inclination, I put my hand on his. There was a sudden connection and it felt a little strange; as though I had suddenly seen myself as an adult.

"Don't be sad," I said, though I myself had begun to feel quite mournful.

"No, not really sad young Adam," he said, though I did hear a break in his voice. "Happens to us all, death, whether we like it or not, it's part of life. I think we needs to spend more time accepting what is natural than wishing we could change the order of the world. You end up trying to make it unnatural then..."

I tried to smile and I moved my hand, glad if it was not needed.

"I miss 'er," he continued, and looked over at her photograph as he spoke, "but I won't 'ave to for long cause I'll be in the same boat. Don't know if I'll see her again then or not, but I'm certain not to miss 'er anymore after that.

"And remember Adam," he shot his head and his eyes back to me, and I met his glare face to face. "When I'm dying don't let that mother of yours take me to no 'ospital. They can give ya all the pills in the world but they can't stop ya from dying. We's supposed to die, and when I do tis on this bed me body will rest and on these creaky boards I want my ghost to walk. I couldn't stop 'em takin' Hilary and that *is* something to feel sad about.

"I'll probably get in trouble talkin' to you 'bout things like this, ya mother wants to keep you a boy. But you're a young man Adam. You can know about the world without it killing off ya innocence. She don't seem to get that. To have the innocence of a child and the knowledge of an oldie like me, that's the goal. You ain't afraid of knowledge as a child, you want it all, and why shouldn't you? I don't mind telling you about dying cause you ain't stupid enough to think I is gonna live forever. I ain't got much time left if I'm honest boy, so let's make the most of it, we can talk you and I."

Great! He wanted to talk, and I wanted to talk. And I liked how he spoke to me. It was on a level which was in no way condescending, and with only small allowance for my age. He seemed pleased that I wanted to hear his words, his stories, his knowledge. I was someone for Grandpa to speak to and I think he had a lot to say. The day had already begun.

"Yes, I wanted to ask..." but I could not finish my sentence as he raised a finger to the air which I knew meant that I must wait for him to say something important. I stopped with my mouth still open.

"I've been given rules Adam. Ya mum 'got to me' first. I probably been out of line already. I don't see why I needs to rein it in, but she's ya mum and she brings you up as she sees fit, I can't really step on 'er toes. I know she 'as her reasons for me not tellin' ya things, but they's 'er problems not ours. Anyway, if ya happen to ask the right questions..."

He waved his finger and then returned his hand flat to the bed. My brain whirled and my mouth remained agape while I tried to think around whatever my mother must have asked him to promise. I failed.

"Well, what I really wanted to know, is... what did you mean when you said 'different things than ghosts'?"

"Hmm," he pushed himself back on the headboard, which was wooden and worn. I could almost hear his mind thinking as mine was. I could also hear his breathing which was a little hoarse in his chest, and smell a minty scent about him which was somehow not quite fresh.

"That ain't the best question Adam," he admitted, mouth pursed in more thought. "Now if you were to tell *me* the answer, then perhaps I could nod when you gets it right."

His eyes sometimes seemed quite wild, and very alive, full of wonder and equally, mischief. I saw my own expression in them.

I took to his challenge. It was a good game.

I was slightly afraid to say something silly, but began to rattle off a gambit of monsters I knew from reading books, watching his head for a nod, but only seeing it slowly shake. The top candidates like werewolves and vampires were all met with that same assured shake and I was flustered to make my brain think of anything more obscure.

Unfortunately our game was brought to a sudden end with a loud knock at the door which made me jump out of my skin, and my mother entered. I had not even heard her coming, and my heart pounded as though I had been caught doing something naughty, though Grandpa did not seem startled at all. He merely looked up at her and said 'morning'.

"What are you doing in here Adam, up to no good the pair of you I bet?" And she started pointlessly shifting and tidying Grandpa's covers. She picked up his book and lay it on the bedside table.

Grandpa winked at me and then gave a clandestine point with his eyes over to the book. And I knew what that meant.

"We was just havin' a chat." Grandpa covered for us. I smiled.

"Hmm. I know your chats."

"He didn't say anything," I tried to explain defensively.

Mum threw open the curtains and the room filled with sunlight disturbing the dust all the more and making both Grandpa and I squint our eyes and recoil a little like the vampires I had recently spoken of. I got out of Mother's way up the corner near the wardrobe and tried to look at myself through the dirt on the mirror.

"Looks a bit like me don't he Ann?"

"I hope not!" she joked.

Grandpa started to chuckle.

As it happens I do look like Grandpa, if you take the years away. We have the same light blue eyes and quite rounded face. Though his own face had sunk in the cheeks and his hair was all but gone. Once he would have had that same mousy brown, almost blonde hair, though it was hard to imagine it.

I wore my hair short, because my mother made those decisions and crew cuts were the latest fashion. I didn't really like it that way and tried to avoid trips to the hairdresser, messing it up as much and as often as I could get away with it. Looking back over at my mother, I could see myself in her too.

"I knew I couldn't trust you two," she said, but she was teasing really. "What *were* you talking about?"

"Just talkin' about life, and death... mainly death!" He laughed again, more like a witch's cackle, and followed by a croaky cough.

"Thought as much."

"Ahh. I was only telling him I don't see the need in all the poncing around death. Dig an 'ole in my garden and throw me in. Don't want no tight wooden box. Let me flesh go back to the earth like it should do, let the worms 'ave their meal n my spirit live on in 'em all!"

"Dad!"

"Well..." he said in retort.

"You're being morbid Dad, and it's far too early for being morbid."

"I'm 78!"

"Too early in the morning," Mum said exhausted. "I'll get your tea. Adam, come on, breakfast, leave your grandpa in peace."

And Grandpa gave me a wink again.

We had breakfast at the kitchen table and, at length, I found a break in the dull conversation my parent's were having to say something which was obviously playing on my mind. "Is Grandpa going to die?"

"Everyone's going to die," my dad said flippantly, coming back into the room with his coat half on, grabbing toast from the toaster, a cup in his other hand. He was rushing as usual, trying to get ready for his first day at the new branch.

My mother ignored him and he was soon out the door taking the toast *and* the cup with him.

"Grandpa is old, and not that well Adam. You two seem to have hit it off though."

I realised that we had. I liked my grandpa very much.

"He's funny," I said. "He's a bit weird, but he knows stuff."

"*Thinks* he knows stuff. Well you can chat to him later. Finish up your milk. I need your help today."

And with those words the day was gone.

I had been told to unpack in my room but found myself standing in front of the closed door feeling an anxiety about going in there which, at first, I could not place. I stood, thinking, and holding my cup of still warm milk in both hands as a comfort.

As unfounded as it may be, I soon realised that my fear was of those woods. The fact that I could always see them through my window, hiding around the corner. It made it seem as though they were always going to be watching and teasing me. Plus I had not yet been told one way or another if there was something there to be afraid of.

But I would not allow something so illogical and silly to spoil my new home. That wasn't the way I wanted to begin.

I thrust the door open, half expecting, again, that the woods would be there at the window. But there was nothing. The room was fairly light in fact, and things were just as I had left them.

I had to stop this I thought to myself. I could not let it get me so wound up like that. I had to get on with things, get the boxes unpacked and make the room my own. I had to claim my territory. Those woods might have been the boss once, but now I was there, and I could not allow my imagination to lead me down paths which would stop me from enjoying the trees and woodland that I was otherwise destined to fall in love with.

I lifted the mug to my lips, staring out at the view with determined thoughts, and manfully gulped down the rest of my milk.

Seconds later, I was trying to spit it out.

It was off, thick and curdling. I felt sick, bending over, spitting and staring down at the mess I had made on the floor with a bitter foul taste in my mouth.

I swear that only moments before I had been drinking that same milk from that same mug and it was fine and fresh.

It made me feel deflated as though it were the woods to blame, that they were mocking back at me. I felt their chill and I physically shivered.

When I finally got down to the task in hand, of sorting my room, I could not help but periodically glance over at the window. It was half to see if the weather was holding, but half to check on that feeling which kept tapping at my shoulders.

By lunch time the sun had turned to grey and an hour after that the rain was pounding like fists upon the glass. The day was vanishing before my eyes and the mediocrity of everyday life was in full force, with the rain simply echoing my despondency. My spirits dampened as the fields sapped it up, a soggy unwelcoming wilderness. And the woods were no doubt using the time to regroup. They were out there, drinking the sustenance of water and growing ever bigger, higher, stronger.

But Adam Briggs was not afraid. I *would* go back there. Once the sun was out I would go over there and I would confront them. And a simple display of elemental power could only keep me away for so long.

That night I fell asleep while the adults still chatted in a muffled mumble down in the lounge. Aside from the morning chat with Grandpa the day had been a write off. I was sure that the morning would bring back the spring weather, and the key to let me out of my bedroom cell.

* * *

It actually felt quite warm in my room when I woke up. The sun had indeed decided it was time to show its face. I did not even think about those woods until I threw the curtains open to the glare of the day. But there they were, same as ever before, looking around the corner at me and then shrinking back, as though they had been secretly waiting for me to show consciousness.

Yes, I thought, today is the day; my day. But I wanted to speak to Grandpa first.

This time I went straight to his room, only to find that he was not in his bed. When an old person's bed is empty, it is hard for your brain to not skip a few scenes. But I could hear faint words spoken somewhere in the house and Grandpa's voice, somehow both tinny and low at the same time, was quite distinct. It soothed my wayward thoughts to hear it, and I followed its source.

He and my mother were fully dressed and in the garden with their backs to me. The back door, that of the kitchen, was wide open and their voices were trailing and echoing about the lounge. The clock said nine thirty; I had slept in too long.

I did not know whether to disturb them, thinking perhaps they needed time alone to speak. It had been many years since they had been in the same room.

The story I knew was that my mother left as a teenager, with her sights set on London. Knowing Grandpa as I do now, London would have been like the devil's playground to him, a world as far removed from his as you could go. I could not imagine a better place to grow up than the countryside, but maybe a child always rebels against their upbringing, no matter what it is like. And maybe a father always thinks they know better, wanting their offspring to follow in their path.

Well I was glad we were all there now.

Quietly I snuck over to the lounge's door frame, listening. I could not hear it all, but whatever they had been speaking about had now turned to chat about his garden.

"I enjoy seeing what nature has grown, not knowing what I'll see next," he was saying, as though in defence. "Things that were not blooming yesterday are today, and those from yesterday are dying away. There's a whole system out 'ere, and all the creatures thrive on it. I come out 'ere and I know I'm alive. That's its beauty. One thing I miss is going for me stanks in the wilds... can't manage it now... but at least I have all this."

Already there was warmth in my heart for Grandpa, and I was glad that they weren't arguing. Bitterness is pointless at his age, just as it is when you are a child.

Taking my leave I skulked about in the lounge for a while, thinking on whether to wait for Grandpa or to just go out.

I could see that some of the things from my old house had now been integrated into the lounge. On the mantel piece, which had previously only been home to a brown dish for keys, were five familiar gold framed photographs. They were the exact same family pictures we had up in the old place including, unfortunately, an unflattering baby photo of myself. There was also a box marked 'fragile-figurines' in the corner by the TV, indicating that my mother was planning to put up other things I'd rather never see again.

With no one else there I edged over to clearly see what Grandpa had upon the little side table.

The cassette player loaded its tapes from above, and it had a clear grey tape inside but I could not see a label. I wondered what music he was listening to on that thing.

Two books were next to that, the top one was hard backed, and looked old; as all books with no dust jacket looked old to me. I now know that it did have some age. The light blue cover had the title upon it in a darker blue print: 'The Hobbit'. And below that was a crudely drawn dragon in the same shiny blue. I love that book now, but had no idea what it was about back then. I remember thinking that it looked somehow mystical, like a book of spells, and certainly it does hold magic within it.

Underneath that book was a paper back, its black spine crumpled with white lines where it had been opened so many times and left to stretch. And behind a cup, half filled with cold tea and a small drowned fly, was his packet of sweets. It was a white paper bag with its sticky contents making darker marks on the outside of it.

I peered into it without touching and saw possibly ten glossy striped sweets, adult sweets, a type that I had not tasted before. Using pickpocket skills which I never knew I possessed, I managed to prise one out with two fingers and moved slowly backwards and quietly away.

Stealthily, with my prize sticky in my palm, father at work and my mother and Grandpa somewhere in the back garden, I tiptoed back through into the hallway.

Outside Grandpa's bedroom door I stood thinking for only a few moments before taking one look behind me and then making a quick movement into the room, shutting myself in. Then, with a certain amount of playful devilment, I popped that sweet into my mouth.

Grandpa's room was quiet as a tomb, and quite dark. If my mother had pulled the curtains open again, he had obviously closed them. I could still see the dust particles in the air, but in the semi-light they took a form that was more like a haze, and it made me feel that my eyes were blurred or that the room was in soft focus.

I was being a little naughty, perhaps, but there was something about Grandpa's room that made my heart slow and relax my breathing. There I was, secretly looking about his room, sucking one of his sweets. It made me smile, even though the sweet actually tasted a little like cough medicine, and was becoming surprisingly hot.

That room was like a place free of time or pressures. I imagined that I might take a book from its shelf and sit upon his bed for hours reading, undisturbed by life. The dust would settle over me and every surface. One hundred years would pass and all of the knowledge in those books would have been absorbed. Only then would I leave there, wiser, yet no older, and with no idea of the years that had gone on without me.

I took a side glance at that deer skull, checking it had not moved, and then very slowly I moved over to the book cases.

I was quite aghast at the size of the collection, and a collector was what Grandpa must have been. He obviously prized those books highly. I had never seen so many in one place other than at public libraries. But this selection was completely tailored to his particular taste, with a book on every possible countryside topic you might imagine. And then, even more interestingly; titles featuring King Arthur, dragons, folklore, fairy tales, religious beliefs and other great mysteries.

I allowed my finger to stroke over the curves of the books, each spine a different texture to the last, the titles embossed, indented or printed. I drank them in like an old scholar in a forgotten treasured archive.

The house was so silent. I was not used to such peace. The town was never quiet. There was always the sound of a passing car, a pet dog barking, the noise from neighbours through thin modern walls, clattering, shutting doors, talking or shouting. Here I could almost hear the dust fall and the brush of my skin rough against the surface of the books.

And then I remembered the book he had surreptitiously gestured towards. My eyes found it, still there beside his bed.

Without thought of decorum I jumped up onto Grandpa's bed, and grabbed it, kneeling then upon his covers, carefully holding my prize.

I stared for some time at the picture on the front, feeling the glossy surface of the dust cover. That picture was, in fact, a photograph of a 'U.F.O', black and white, out of focus and fuzzy.

I had never believed or had much interest in aliens and my enthusiasm waned slightly. But the book was called 'Unsolved Mysteries' so it was obvious that it featured Earthly things as well.

But was that an actual photograph? Surely if it were a real photograph then that was then evidence proving what had been seen?

At the time I did not really understand the possibility of fakery. Back then it just made me wonder if every mysterious creature ever spoken about really did have some basis in fact, but that they had always avoided the camera lens. Perhaps in a more affluent age, where owning and even carrying a camera became common place, every single mystery would be exposed and proven. Perhaps everything that was once consigned to the realm of myth would finally be accepted.

Gently and respectfully turning each page of that large book I was greeted with illustrated accounts of many high profile mysteries. There were recent artist's interpretations but also ancient wood cuts and medieval pictures of the monsters I presumed to be mere fiction. A were-man with a child dead in its mouth, maps of the world depicting where sea monsters might be found. And then a couple of photographs, questionably containing images of real life ghosts which I had seen before in my own books.

I almost skipped over the next page completely as the title 'fairies' did not interest me. But as my mind caught up and thoughts dawned on me I suddenly stopped, and I turned it back. Had Grandpa not used that word 'fairy' himself? Was there, as I knew there to be with a lot of fantasy stories, some ancient truth behind them?

It just seemed a little too far fetched. All I knew of fairies were the magical, butterfly winged, peaceful joyous beings that little girls dreamed of. They were the subject of hundreds of children's storybooks, living in gardens and granting wishes. I did not expect to see them sharing a book with the loch Ness monster and Bigfoot.

But what if? What if there was some truth in these too? What if they dwelled within those woods? I wondered what I might wish for.

At first I had thought that the photograph on the 'fairy' page was from a film, but looking again and reading the text below it, I saw that it was claiming to be real.

There was a girl, sitting in pose to the camera, with tiny winged human like creatures, no bigger than her hands, dancing about in a parade in front of her. The photograph was not in colour but it was clear, and I looked at it, deep in thought with the book opened on my lap, fingers touching the page. And I creased my brow in disbelief and wonder, looking up above me as though searching the air for answers.

I scanned the words on the page and it clearly said that the photograph was thought to be genuine and there was a story that went with it. Two girls from a place called Cottingley had apparently seen the creatures on several occasions and even spoken with them. At length they decided to borrow a camera and take the photographs. As far as the book was concerned, no one was yet to disprove the claims or the pictures.

I had to see Grandpa!

I jumped to my feet without a further thought and rushed from the room with the book in my hand. I walked into the lounge quite boisterously, as a child is want to do, and then stopped to retract my noise as I saw Grandpa now asleep on his chair.

His head was drooped to the side, with a snoring, or rather a whistling, coming only from his nose. I crept up to look at him closely, though I was not sure why. I remember noticing the dark brown spots on what was already quite a brown tanned and shiny bare head. His wrinkled eyelids were flickering, his pale thin lips pursing occasionally, but otherwise he was completely still.

"Grandpa," I whispered, my voice hardly penetrating. And then I raised it, perhaps too much, "Grandpa!"

He coughed and spluttered like a fire sparking back to life, shifting himself to his normal position as if being re-inflated, eyes squinting in my direction.

"What is it boy? Where's the emergency?"

"Look," I said, ignoring his age and his inability to be wide awake at a moment's notice, thrusting the open book onto his lap.

A little bit more coughing, huffing and puffing, and Grandpa became Grandpa again, the rust oiled away. He looked over his bulb nose at the page with forced concentration.

"Ahh getting warmer..." he said looking back up at me, half a smile and both eyebrows raised.

"Is that not it? What's in the woods... fairies?"

"Well you sees, those ain't real faeries boy." He was looking at the book, examining the page. "Real faeries couldn't be caught in no photograph. Most of the time, they's invisible, and not nearly as pretty."

I was confused all over again, and starting to think that Grandpa was just playing games with me. It did seem infantile to believe that there were little diaphanous winged people living amongst us.

He tried to sit forward a little, to look up at me with clear eyes as he spoke quite seriously:

"Fairy tales is one thing, *faeries*... are another."

But now I was despondent to think that I was still no nearer, even though he had pointed the book out to me. "I don't understand."

"You're not supposed to." Grandpa stretched himself to look around the side of his chair and back towards the kitchen. Then he recoiled back to how he sat before. "Where's ya mother? Still in the garden?"

I nodded, even though I wasn't sure.

"Ok, well listen two minutes to ya Grandpa. I knows ya excited boy, but these 'ere," and he pointed a finger straight down hard on the book and kept it there, "these ain't real. The girls they admitted it themselves, few years back. But I always knew, 'cause these ain't what they look like. They don't 'ave no wings, and they ain't sweet natured.

"I probably shouldn't talk about it, ya mother don't like it... and neither do *they*... Supposed to be unlucky. But they have many peculiar ways, you never really know where ya stands with 'em...

"To be honest they can be quite nasty. But it ain't likely to ever see 'em. You'll just know, you'll just feel, or other things'll 'appen to show them off to ya. D'you know what I mean Adam?"

I think I nodded, but I was paralysed with the dawning of this revelation. There *are* things you just know, without them being seen, without being told. His words fitted like jigsaw pieces into the puzzle my new home had set up before me. These were not childish games now. Grandpa truly believed what he was saying, and I was scared of those truths, almost wishing he would take them back.

"I don't want ya ta be scared." His voice had lightened, but his words did not. "But if you're interested, ya have to remember... We 'ave our world, they 'ave theirs. Thing is, they come n go as they pleases, we can't. We can never enter theirs boy... ever."

His last sentence sounded very forceful, and I was struck dumb. My heart was frozen to hear an adult speaking so strongly of such things. The world that made any sense was starting to shatter about me, but it was also opening up.

He looked down at the picture again, paused for a moment, and then shut the cover, resting his hand down on it, closing the book on the subject.

"Just abide by their rules if you play in their playgrounds. They is 'armless then."

Then he looked back up at me with the friendly twinkle returning to his eyes. "One thing ya should know... is we don't call 'em like in this book, fairies with an 'i'. There's many ways to spell their name, but that ain't even one of 'em. Peoples that know spell it f-a-e and maybe best not call 'em faeries at all. You'd do better ta call 'em 'the good people' or as most know 'em, 'the little people'. And forget all that you think you know about 'em... Everything's a contradiction.

"Though they 'ave as much right to be in this world as we do Adam, maybe more... Don't upset 'em. Theys been 'ere longer than us."

The air was thick with this conversation, thick with tension from a subject incomprehensible, unexplainable, unbelievable, yet I completely believed it. A few sentences from Grandpa, in that wise old man voice of his, with those eyes looking so far deep inside of my soul, and I believed it all, with every ember of my being.

"G..randpa..." I stuttered and stumbled on thoughts to find just one, single coherent question, to think of that which might trouble me the most. "Do they live in *that* wood?"

"Adam my boy," he spoke in a whisper, yet his eyes were shouting their wild excitement, "they is everywheres."

CHAPTER THREE

Grandpa had frightened me, even though he had not meant to, and even though I dared not admit it.

Although my plan had been to go back to those woods I was now considering spending the rest of the day some other way. But I was also too obstinate to just stay inside.

The most obvious choice was to head towards the sea instead. There were the coasts to explore and their beauty was stark.

From my window the ocean was too far and often obscured by the mist as well as the brow of the hill. I thought perhaps I could find somewhere to enjoy it, perhaps even some kind of beach to sit on. Somewhere close where the rocks might fall at a gradient which allowed access to that impenetrable sea.

So by those thoughts I had set myself a mission.

Walking the coastal path was perhaps a little tame compared to an exploration of the woods, but I argued that I was not a coward, I was simply being sensible, and broadening my horizons. And as I plodded on I felt my fears and doubts clearing away to blank reflections of the now. I was, as a child should be, living only in the moment that I was experiencing.

I walked over the field until all that was ahead of me was the ocean; close and cold. It had a simplistic beauty, a timeless, empty haven from thoughts. It was the edge of the world.

There was not much wind that day and the mist hung unmoving over the peaks to each side, as though the sky had sunk down onto the hills. The path which was cut into the ground like a scar was lost to it in the distance, disappearing into the white as if it might be leading me into the clouds themselves.

It was like a land of fantasy, though far ahead I could see the black specks of other people walking that same trail. I knew that at some point I might reach them, and I was not sure I liked that. I preferred to be the first to tread, the one to find, to make my own paths. Seeing other living people spoilt my moment somewhat.

I walked a while, taking in the fresh salt air and the natural scenery, feeling the late morning sun rising higher to increase its heat for the afternoon. But I soon tired of the views, which while magnificent in their own ways, were almost too cleanly cut, hiding nothing and offering no secrets. One stretch of coast could have been another.

I looked behind me from whence I came, wondering if I should head back, missing the woodland. And then, close to the edge, I saw the dark figure of a boy.

He appeared to be looking over the cliff, hunched shoulders, teetering as if a strong breeze might knock him down.

My heart leapt into my mouth thinking that he might be someone wanting to jump, to kill themselves, and I was the only one there to see it. I might have to save him. In my head I had rushed over there and held him by the arms, gently walking him back to safety. In reality I was dead still, waiting for him to go away and for that moment to pass.

I don't know how long he had been there, but I had not long to wait before he turned and slowly drifted away from sight.

I edged closer myself, looking down over the cliff to maybe put myself in his position, to see what he had seen. It was so high and steep that the sea seemed untouchable, unreachable in any way but to jump. And as the waves pushed in, and then pulled away, it was to reveal even further rocks, hiding just under the surface of the foamy water, threatening me.

The dizzy, unsafe feeling of vertigo spread from my feet up to my head and I stumbled backwards and on to the path once more. It was to stand with nothing to grip on to, nothing in front and nothing behind. Climbing trees never gave me a fear of heights like that; they always had their branched arms ready, waiting to catch your fall. I missed the trees.

But I decided that I would march onwards. I had to focus on the mission. I was sure that I would soon find an adventure to stop me from recanting my initial decision.

I trudged on, over the hills covered in rich green. High above those tall drops of prehistoric looking rock that fell so majestically into the sea, home to the huge sea-gulls which became my journey's companions. Those birds, gliding on massive wing spans around the cliff faces where no man could ever reach.

I imagined seeing those dinosaur birds flying that same stretch, just as they would have once done in a scene almost identical despite the millions of years that had passed. I felt that I could be in any time, for the sea was timeless. And that day I wore no watch, and had no care for such things.

I was walking, on and on, getting hotter and hotter, as the sun rose huge and bright over head. It was becoming a day of extremes, and the freak one day heat wave that had now begun seemed to be trying to deter me.

But I had now gone much too far to turn back, and I had no idea how far I would have to go on. Each step moved me forward to something that lay in the future. And with that philosophy I drove onwards, growing tired, yet always determined. I *would* find a way to defy the sea's reclusive intentions.

Focused, I pulled my feet to move step after step and I

thought of nothing else. Time was lost to distance, and I had no way of judging either.

Eventually, when it seemed that I could reach no higher above the level of the sea; I saw in the distance below me, the signs of life. I saw what through a haze of heat and exhaustion looked like houses, and other buildings. I saw cars and I saw people.

This time I was thankful that I was not completely alone, although I almost believed for a moment, that the whole thing might be a mirage. I had scenes from films flashing in my head, where the hero is lost in the dry heat of a desert, finally seeing his salvation, an oasis... imagined.

Then, on the wisp of the air, I was sure that I could make out the muffled sounds of chatter.

The trail dipped from then on and quite steeply too. But without any more thought, I began to descend, at times walking with my feet sideways to help me grip and not slide down the dusty path. The further I got, the more I could see of where I was heading. Slowly, it was revealed to me that I had made my journey and that I had reached somewhere that I could call my goal.

There was a pub there, and an ice-cream shop, the black text of the signs becoming more easily readable as I drew closer to the end of the falling pathway. It was a little cove where the beach was made from rocks and the sea came in, fierce and white, yet stopped far enough out to give the people there both room to sit, and a visionary spectacle.

Two flat grey rocks were jutting out into the sea and at least one person was brave, or foolhardy enough to be riding upon one of them.

All day I had not passed a single soul, they had been only ahead, or behind, and I had only myself for company. Suddenly I was there amongst the throng of people.

They had all driven there, cars parked around the back edge, but I had walked, I had made that pilgrimage. They were holidaymakers, but I was on an adventure, finding the place myself, a discovery just like those woods had been.

I had entered another world; beautiful, grandiose and so obviously scenic. But the magic was spoilt by the amount of people I had to share it with. It made the fact that I had discovered the place much harder to believe.

But I did like the fact that all of them had travelled there to see it. Admittedly a lot of them were gathered at the pub, but most were spilling out onto the benches which overlooked the scenery. I could just see through the pub windows, three or four kids gathered around an arcade machine, but I had no urge to join them.

I sat, or rather collapsed into sitting upon a small rock for a while, wishing that Grandpa was with me to share it, and I wondered if he had ever been to that place. It would have made him smile, I think, to see other people appreciating the natural beauty of things. It proved that not all adult kind are dead to dreams.

But I knew already that I would not stay there long. I was over hot, and I had walked too far. I had no idea where I actually was, but now all I really wanted was to be back home.

I had achieved what I set to do, feeling the moisture thrown up by the moving sea cooling down my blushed face. Smelling the fresh scent of salt water, trying to let it clear my head through the babble of background chattering. But no sooner had my legs begun to regain some ounce of energy, than I was back up and walking upon them. It was time to go.

I went across the bay and bought a can of cola from the shop. I ordered it in monotone, almost surprised to hear my own voice. I drank it in one gulp, trying to give my body an instant cool down. Then I took in the view for one last time before heading off.

I was not looking forward to the walk home. I was a fit young boy but the heat was a little too much and I did not relish retracing my steps. I thought that I understood the location of the place in some regards though, and thought that I could follow the road back home instead. That way I would at least see different scenery on my journey back.

It did not take long to be clear of the place and to be able to look back on the green cliffs that I had once been walking, now seeing them from behind, and seeing little houses carved into their alcoves.

The mist had risen away, but that only meant that the sun had grown even fiercer and beat down mercilessly upon me. The road surface felt hard on the soles of my feet and there was no shelter for quite some distance. I wished that I had been more prepared, or at least, kept some of the cola I had bought earlier. It was further than I thought, my legs were growing numb with fatigue, and I had no idea how far out I now was.

At length the road began to cut through some woods and I was relieved that they occasionally gave shade as they leant their branches into arches above me. Moving, flickering shadows were cast upon the dappled road. The light dipped and rose continuously as I walked, making my eyes feel blinded as they tried to adjust.

I had not stopped in my relentless march until that moment, but I had to now. My senses were overexposed and I thought that I might fall.

I took some time to compose myself, looking about my surroundings. I was pretty sure that we had travelled that road, and passed through those same woods, in the car on route to the house. I was quite pleased by the memory, and impressed by my own sense of direction.

Over the far side of the road the woods were dark and seemed to have a slight malevolence. It could have merely been that being so far from home was making me tense, but I could not help but think of Grandpa's words and warnings.

The woods on my side were much lighter than those to the left, and much more inviting. They were dense, but bright and shining in hues of green. I felt a feeling of comfort from them, and an incredible draw. It called to me in a base way that, somewhere in my soul, I completely understood.

Looking over the little fence I could see a steep drop of undergrowth heading down to a stream and the woods continuing beyond. It made me smile with the beauty. That clear moving trail of sparkling water, and the trees green with their velvet, moss covered trunks and crawling ivy. It could have been a painting it was so perfect, and it reminded me how much I enjoyed the scenery of the woods more than I did the sea. Those harsh emotions were immediately softened.

The whole journey had long begun to feel fruitless and had since become no less than unpleasant. I wanted to leave the road I had grown so tired of, in every way, and feed off the energies that were whispering to me. Seductively those trees were asking me to come, beckoning me to be with them, to gain their solace and cool in their shade. I felt the need to answer.

And so I reasoned that a small diversion to take a look, despite my encompassing lethargy, would do me more good than it would harm. It would lift my spirits to enjoy that pretty scene at close hand. And to hear the quiet trickle of the stream would be so much favourable to that roar of the ocean.

It felt wrong to have abandoned my woods for this

pointless mission. And now I truly needed the soothing embrace of the trees. The longing had become so strong that I no longer had a choice. It was a hunger and I knew that I would collapse upon the road if I was starved for another second.

I jumped over the fence, struggling down the steep hill and allowing myself to slip as I held the ground trying to quickly reach the bottom. The whole place opened out for me in vision and sound. The beauty bewitched me.

Now, finally there, the aching for it subdued and I felt a calm acceptance, yet I still longed to go in deeper. I instantly forgot all the pains in my body and my heart felt healed.

Ahead of me the trees held out their branches and dipped their leaves into the stream, making majestic archways of bright coloured greenery. The flow of water gently forcing itself through algae covered stones made the breath of the land. And then there was the one tree which had sacrificed itself to be my bridge, falling perfectly from one side of the stream to the other to allow me access into the further depths. It had become something else the moment it fell, welcomed by the ground as the plants grew all around it, enveloping it as part of their world.

I looked at it for some time with a joyous smile on my face, and then crossed over, thanking the woods in my head. I believed that the trail would still lead me to home, and that I could walk the rest of the journey through the trees.

I hardly cared about the distance anymore, as I was completely enraptured with the place. I followed the stream as close as I could get, marvelling at the way it made a little light show out of the sun's ever present rays. Yet in the thick of the forest all light was green as it filtered through the leaves, and no matter where I looked, the ground was lush and alive.

It was the most magical place and some of the most magical moments I had ever spent. And this time it really was mine as I was completely alone and I could truly believe that no one else had ever been there. It was untouched.

There was no one to judge me or my strange behaviour as I almost danced and skipped through the place like I was some kind of elf, stepping on stones that allowed me to walk on water. No one was going to see how I kept taking closer looks at the wild flowers, protruding tree roots and then looking up in awe, my arms outstretched.

I was feeling it, sensing it, following onwards along the stream as though it were now my path. And no one was there to spoil it. No one would see.

But then I saw someone.

My heart skipped and I stopped in my tracks. I was standing in the middle of the stream, balancing on one of the larger stones; when, far ahead through the trail of winding water, I saw someone jump across. It was silent, the whole moment, it made no sound, yet it was full of eerie feeling.

I was sure that I had seen it, a figure leaping, almost in flight, straight over the stream.

I had been brought back sharply to reality. Suddenly I was not the only person on Earth.

I could have felt some annoyance, and even embarrassment that my antics might have been seen, but there was a stronger, thicker feeling. The whole moment was accompanied by a disquieting, otherworldly atmosphere.

I had been staring for a while, at where it had happened, but then my mind kicked back in with strong commands, telling me to move. What if I had just seen something truly mystical? What if that creature was more preternatural than human? What if it was a faery?

I *had* to know.

I started forwards, breaking into a run, trying to get to where it had been, trying to get there quickly. I don't know where I summoned the energy from, but I simply dare not miss the moment.

I ran and I tripped, my feet constantly sinking where the stream ran deeper. I had to get out of the water and run on more stable ground, but I didn't want to lose sight of where it had been, and trees constantly rose up to bar my way. I ran with my feet now soaking in water filled training shoes. I would not stop until I caught up with it. I was panicking, almost sure that by the time I reached the spot I would not see a thing. But I was so desperate to prove it...

There was nothing; just as I had feared. Even though I could remember exactly where it had been, there was no evidence that anything had ever been there. I heard no sounds, saw no animals, and there was certainly nothing magical or untoward.

I felt everything crumble around me, and dropped onto a natural seat of moss at the water's edge where my legs could stretch down. The fatigue returned at full force. Everything ached, including, without doubt, my heart.

I sat and tried to regain my breath, feeling the cracking of my body and my mind, allowing tears to burn in their ducts. I just felt so deflated and more tired than I had ever been in my entire life. Being alone had lost its charm, and now it was only loneliness. I was sun burnt, battered, torn, and totally emotional.

I saw my body melt down over the rocks and into the stream, only hoping that it really would and that I could drift away with its tide and be taken home. Into that water I stared as I filled it with cathartic tears. I nestled my face in my hands, wishing to be whisked away.

What did I really expect? In that magical glen where all the elements of a faerie world were there in front of me; I had seen something with my own eyes, but it had meant nothing.

And then something tender came to answer my sorrow, something heard as if to try and sooth me of all other thought. I looked up in wonder, sniffing and slowing the sobs down to a stop.

What was that? I reasoned that maybe it was merely the trickle of the stream, but my ears were now becoming attuned to the sound, and although it grew no louder, it became more distinct, and it was music.

Distant, and yet somehow right there with me, the tinkling sweet notes of a melody which seemed both random and perfectly formed.

I looked about me where I sat and tried to clear my head to listen. The sounds appeared to have travelled through the trees and were now there, fading in and out as though my ears were pulsing. It was faint yet each tiny sound seemed to join, linking to the next, forming a harmony, inherently familiar, eerily drifting in the air as though carried on the breeze with every tiny gust.

I wondered if it were only within my head. Perhaps it was a ringing in my ears; white noise that my mind had assembled into strings of coherent and beautiful notes? But somehow I knew it to be more. It felt ancient, and though mere sound, completely and unnervingly alive.

I stood and looked about me, following every harmonic piece as though it were dashing about me, yet not even sure if it were there at all. I circled the spot trying to listen more intently, to catch its source. Spinning and looking up through the trees as the woods spun even faster.

I felt a need to pursue it; following the music though it whispered far from my grasp. There was nothing to follow, for it was truly all around me, faint and untouchable. Each tone was within me; running through my veins, yet also outside, in the sky, in the trees, water and earth. It came from no one place, no easier to decipher in one corner than the next; it was everywhere, and then nowhere, blown towards me then sucked away.

I really can not explain the effect it had upon me; it was so hallucinating, and overwhelming.

I knew that I was moving deeper into the woods. My hands were flailing in front of me. I parted the way blindly through the hanging branches and leaves. I was looking all around though not at my path, travelling by my instinct, in dazed fascination. My mouth was open, drinking in an experience unlike any I or maybe anyone had ever known.

And then it just stopped. It did not fade away, it did not disappear, it simply was not there anymore.

Whom or what had been playing that music so well, with such inhuman talent, I would never know. But I realised that it had truly filled my soul with an unspeakable joy and now that it was gone I felt damaged to have had such elation wrenched away from me. It had gone and my hope had gone with it.

I knew that I had to turn back, retrace my steps, and get myself home. But now drained of all adrenalin, and with my heart heavy and low in my gut, it was daunting just to begin.

It was harder than I ever could have imagined.

I was aware that it was possible to get lost in the forests. I know that I had not been taking any care to mentally note my route. But there was more to my predicament than simply straying from the path.

I should have been able to get out by simply heading in one direction, but it just went on and on. I could hear the trickling of the stream, and I knew that I could follow it back, yet I could not find the water. And whenever I tried to break the path I was blocked by impassable undergrowth.

Nothing was familiar yet I knew that it should be. Something was not right, in fact, everything was out of place. My brain went from one confusion to the next. My head was aching, it was so full of everything that had happened, weary and masked in pain, lost to anxious restlessness. I felt that I was going mad.

I am not sure how I even continued to put one foot in front of the other as I had been walking with barely a stop for most of the day. And now my desperation was not to find adventure or solve mysteries, it was a simple longing for it to end, to be comforted, to be home.

My anguish reached a pinnacle at the point when I most thought I was saved. With much relief I finally found the stream, and I knew instantly that I was close to the clearing where I had first dragged myself into. I was near the fallen tree bridge that I had used to cross over before entering that nightmarish dream. But as I stepped towards the water I saw that the bridge was no longer there. It was not because I was mistaken, but because it had vanished.

I felt the need to scream, but had not the energy to do more than whimper. It was impossible. That tree had obviously been lying fallen for years, but it was gone, and there was no trace.

I suppose I could have just trudged through the stream, or found a shallower part nearby. But of course my mind could not accept that I was in the right place, it fought against it despite knowing deep down that I was correct.

I backtracked again, and I continued to look, hope against hope, for the right way. I do not know how long I circled those same patches of woodland, thinking I was heading to a new part, only to find myself back where I had begun. Every route led to there, and none seemed to lead me away. I was going out of my mind. I was deeply worried and completely afraid.

I do not remember much else; I don't really know how long the ordeal lasted. It is possible that I really had lost my mind in there. I had spent hours travelling back and forth not daring to walk too far lest I make things worse. I think I blotted part of it out. Perhaps even more happened which then made my mind purposely forget the details? I will never know, and perhaps it is better forgotten.

At some point I broke the spell. I found myself frenziedly pushing through a patch of thorns. They scratched at me, my shirt ripping, my skin torn... But eventually I was free of my woodland captor.

I was left exhausted and bleeding through their retaliation and their reluctance to let me go, but I had escaped. I had pulled myself up an impossibly steep bank, not really knowing if it was where I had entered or not. I had scrambled up there, holding onto clumps of grass, refusing to let myself fall back. And finally I was at the peak, crawling up, over the fence and falling to my knees upon the road.

Exactly which road I had found, I did not know. I just kept on walking, hoping it was the right way. Dragging my feet as more time lapsed, hoping that I would soon see something I recognised. Cars would pass me rarely, but each one that came brought with it a wish that someone would stop to offer me help.

But I was on my own, and I saw no one until I entered a village and passed people working in their gardens. I looked at them, but they did not seem to see me, they were in a mist, they were through a glaze.

I questioned whether I was even in the real world. Perhaps I had entered some other dimension, some shift in reality. I think I knew that it was my own village, but nothing felt right, all was askew. Every corner that I thought would lead me home only led me to more road. My fatigue was in my dry throat and in every muscle, bone, and sore patch of skin.

At some point on that very road, I had finally collapsed, and I had lost consciousness.

Presently I saw faces, heard voices, and some glimmer of normality began to return.

I could not move or speak but I thanked God that I was alive. I had survived, I was still on this Earth, and I was saved.

* * *

Memories after that are lost like scenes in a movie with reels spoilt through time.

I remember only a few things. Sitting on the lid of the toilet in the bathroom of the cottage, staring at the bath as it filled with steaming water. My mother holding me, though I could hardly even see. My brain was fazing, my eyelids heavy, my body paralysed. And then my father was carrying me, wrapped in towels, into my bedroom, while my mother's voice spoke in an anxious high pitch.

Apparently I had fallen asleep in the bath, and I could have drowned. I was still not fully awake when they lifted me out of the cold water, swiftly dried me and took me to bed. I was delirious. I mumbled things but did not know what I was saying. I slept; lost to a fevered dream world.

Until noon the next day I was dead to everything. Yet

my mother was there when I woke, sitting on a chair beside my bed, looking troubled. I had been in such an unbelievable state, she said, I had been speaking such strange things. But only I had any idea of the cause, and it was far less simple than any human sickness.

Only Grandpa would know.

It was evening before I felt well enough to actually get up. I had frightened them all and we ate our dinner in complete silence. I truly believe that a single voice could have shattered me. But I needed that food. I felt sick and dizzy with such a complete lack of energy, as though all of my blood had been drained.

Everything was different. I felt altered, that I was no longer a child but an old man, broken by years of hard labour.

One of those three adults finally felt the need to speak, for one of them, this had to be explained.

"Ok Adam? What 'appened to you yesterday?"

It was Grandpa, and he was so matter of fact, interested, yet with some care about his tone.

I did not answer at first. I was eating slowly as my stomach felt it had retracted and shrunken. But the rest of my body so wanted the food.

"He doesn't have to tell us yet," my mother said, yet I knew, it was obvious, that they were all dying to know.

"I got lost," I said, my voice small. I did not know how I should elaborate. There was only so much I could tell. I saw my Grandpa's expression change, grow darker.

My mother pushed herself to ask more while remaining on a level of calm and keeping her voice low. "You were saying, Adam, while you were unwell, that you saw 'one' that they were real... Do you know what any of that meant? You were asking for Grandpa. Can you tell me Adam?"

My mother was looking at her father in a way I did not like at all. I loved my grandpa, and I saw a glimmer of hatred in her eyes. Grandpa was keeping quiet and seemed to almost be shrinking into his seat. It may have only been temporary, but I could see something was going on. I was clever enough to understand at least one part of it.

"I don't remember," I lied. "I don't know what I meant. It's nothing Grandpa has ever said." I was looking at him in the corner of my eye. I did not know if my act was completely obvious, but I knew exactly what my mother was hinting at. I only wanted to protect my grandpa. "I just got lost."

There was no more talk of the episode that night though a thousand questions were ripe in their mouths. The general consensus was that I had strayed too far from home, in a place I was yet to know, and suffered terrible sunstroke and fatigue. I was warned of the terrible things that could have happened to me, and I had to swear to be careful in future and never to wander so far.

The matter, for them, was then closed, but for me a new chapter was opening. I knew that something profound had occurred that day, and although a skeptic could argue it all away, there are some things you just know.

What I wanted now, more than anything, was to speak to Grandpa about it. I wanted to see if he could shed any light on the experience, or whether it really was that the light had gone to my head.

* * *

When I looked from my window the next morning I saw that there had been more rain and the mist was hanging low obscuring a white sun. It mystified the epic views and added foreboding to the woods which already haunted my nightmares.

My dreams that night had been plagued with twisted images of the trees themselves gripping me and dragging me down into moist earth, sucking me in, covering me in filth, burying me...

But I could not allow dreams to creep into reality. I could not let my fears, named faery or otherwise, spoil Cornwall for me.

As expected, Grandpa was awake, sitting up in bed with a book open on his lap. The sun through the closed curtains and the dim bulb from his lamp were not really conducive for reading. I wondered if he had read all of his books so many times that he did not even need to see the words anymore.

"Hi Grandpa," I spoke very quietly. I still felt a little fragile from all that had happened to me, like something inside me had died, perhaps the part of a child that believes itself invincible.

"Adam," he said formally, abandoning his book to the side and giving all his attention to my shivering frame in the doorway. "Come on in. If ya got things ta say laddie, I got ears."

He watched me softly close the door and come towards him. His head was down but his eyes were looking up, kind and patient. I knew that I could tell him all of it, but I was not yet sure if I could piece together all of my garbled memories that eloquently. I also thought that I might want to keep some for myself.

I stood by his bed and he tapped the covers beside him as if inviting a pet cat to take the space there and sleep on the warm sheets. I put one knee up to get on but then Grandpa began to fuss away the covers.

"Na get in boy, you'll catch cold."

I was slightly nervous but it *was* fairly cold in his room. Despite the temperature outside being typically spring like, his whole room was a cool shade. Perhaps my burnt, red skin had become sensitive.

Cautiously I made myself comfortable next to Grandpa, and although there was not much room in his single bed, it felt nice to be close to him, it felt cosy.

"Are you reading a book from your shelves?"

"Always," he said glancing proudly at the collection his room housed. "All the best ones have already been written. Used to get some in the library, but don't get out now. Anyways, I get the good reading from over there, or in my underground store."

He looked mysteriously at me.

"Underground store?"

I had been set up for a punch line.

"Yep, under me bed!" He started to laugh.

I smiled, cheered by his bad humour, *and* by the fact that there was a library close by.

"You can borrow any of me books any time lad. Some a them is old as I is, and the stories inside older still. I've read 'em all. Every word of those books is in 'ere somewhere," he said pressing his finger up and down hard against his forehead. "Somewhere in ya 'ead you mind... everything."

To me Grandpa had stopped talking about books a long time ago. We looked at each other then, eye to eye, attempting to exchange thoughts, and the jovial small talk came to an end.

"So what *do* you remember young Adam, 'bout Thursday?"

My mouth froze shut for a moment, and although I wanted my river of thoughts to flow out, for some reason, I would only allow it to trickle.

"There's lots of things, but not all clear. I think... I know... I saw... *something* in the woods." And there my river was trapped on rocks, because I could not bring myself to say that word which still seemed that it should be confined to children's story books.

"The little people?" Grandpa said it for me, questioningly, and avoiding the use of that less acceptable word of 'faery'.

When he said it, there was a babbling brook of understanding behind it. He was looking at me with his eyebrows raised, paused and waiting.

"I... I think I did." I felt less burdened now that it was out, my confession, there in the open. But it frightened me that it was now able to run amok. "I didn't want to say anything in front of mum and dad. I was worried I would get you in trouble because of our 'chats'."

Grandpa put his arm around me and gave a gentle squeeze. "Ya did well lad, ya mum is none the wiser." And then, with some struggle, he moved the arm back away, rather than outstay its welcome. He shuffled back against the headboard which creaked with every movement, and got himself comfortable in a position where he could look straight at me without craning his neck, and get down to serious chat.

"What'd it look like?" He said with some revelry.

I had to think, but that did not make my thoughts any clearer.

"I'm not really sure. I did see it... but I couldn't really see it properly... I couldn't quite make it out."

"Most likely was a faery then." My grandpa was relishing this chat more than ever.

"What else ya not tellin' though young Adam? Ya said you was lost... but ya can't be getting lost in Old Bobs were ya? Saying that though, if the little people are at work, ya could be getting lost in ya own back yard."

What he had said did not yet penetrate. I was busy answering, "No, I wasn't there. I found some other wood, a forest really, with a stream through it. I walked quite a long way."

"A stream ay?" He rubbed his fingers on his chin, "Water is powerful, and crossing it more so." He was thinking, and with the strain of thought his whole face seemed to crinkle. He did not say anything for a while, and then he just looked back up at me with searching eyes. It was obvious he wanted me to say some more, but I was still unsure whether I could, or whether I now even wanted to.

"It's alright," he filled in, acknowledging that I was a little uncomfortable. "I suppose you was frightened?"

I nodded, and he shuffled a little closer.

"If anything it's just that you're a stranger 'ere... Don't mean they want ta do you any 'arm Adam. But you're from the towns, the new ways... you're an impostor far as they's concerned. They're keepin' an eye on ya that's all. It'll be fine, once they know the cut of your jib..."

Again he rubbed his non-existent beard but this time with some intent. Then he stopped the incessant thinking, seeing shock fixed in my eyes. "You said enough lad?"

I think I nodded.

And then he moved up even closer to me with his head down at my shoulder so all I saw was the top of his bald head.

"You know I won't judge you boy. If ever ya need to, I'm 'ere to talk. Whether other folk believe what ya seen or not, it don't matter, 'cause it's what you seen. No one's gonna take that away. If you think you's seen 'em, then I dare say you has. Not that ya see the little people with your eyes mind, it really ain't that simple.

"Anyway, if ya wanna keep a lid on it that's fine too. But sometimes secrets can be 'ard to live a life with. It's up to you now lad, I won't be making your choices or pushing no questions."

And with his speech over, he laid a huge hand on my leg, squeezed it once, and then moved back over to his space in the bed. I could tell that he definitely wanted to know more, but he had been kind enough to give me that choice; it was completely selfless.

"So you really believe in them Grandpa?" I asked after a pause.

He backed his neck away so that his chin lowered to his chest, perhaps surprised a little to have been asked so directly after what he had just said. Perhaps it was just an exclamation to highlight his answer.

"I believe Adam, of course. One side a my family was Irish originally, and in Ireland everybody knows about the little people. I was brought up on those stories. They exist, and they live their lives. Best ta let 'em get on with it... But it's possible we may cross their paths every day 'n' never even know we 'ave."

He was sincere, I knew it. He wasn't playing games. And then to the next important question:

"Have you ever seen one?"

"*Seen*? No Adam, I ain't, not personally. Maybe 'cause I wanted to so badly, or maybe 'cause I knew it best not to. Not many 'ave. That's why they go by another name, that of 'the hidden people'. They ain't just hiding behind the bracken 'n' thorns; they is not quite in our senses, they's never easy to grasp. Parallel they are, always here, on the Earth, going about their business and up ta their tricks. But you ain't supposed to see 'em.

"I've 'eard it takes a certain kind of person, a particular frame of mind; a change in tides. It's like a radio that's 'ard to set. But I reckon if you've tuned into their frequency, you may well see 'em again.

"I don't 'ave to see to know they's about. I've been alive many years Adam, livin' 'n' workin' in these parts.

There's no doubt I been on the receiving end of the spriggans 'n' piskies."

It was exciting, but an unwelcome darkness hung over the subject, wonder mingling with apprehension.

"But Grandpa... should I really be worried about them?"

"Nah!" he scoffed, but it wasn't convincing. "I know some people would still say otherwise. But I think ya just 'ave to be wary that's all. There's many a tale about 'em, some good some... not sa good. No one really knows anything... what they are, where they come from.

"One tale says they ain't quite good enough for heaven, or bad enough for hell, so they stays 'ere with us. If ya believe any of that rubbish. The only thing you can really believe in is ya self, and the things you see and feel.

"Far as I can tell, they ain't evil so much as, I dunno... they 'ave a short fuse the little folk. We 'ave to respect 'em and be on their good sides that's all. People 'round 'ere know not to push their luck. This ain't just our world ya know; we share it with many things. Maybe they don't like the way we treat it."

He cleared his throat, ending the speech that had drifted uncontrolled by his wayward thoughts, and swiftly changed the subject back to me. "But you was in a mess when you come back the other day lad, there's no denying that."

"I was really lost. Even though I knew where to go... it wasn't there."

I did not think that my explanation made any sense but from Grandpa's reaction it was clear that I had hit a chord.

He put his hand over his mouth, rubbed his face and took a deep breath. He seemed lost for words for a moment, which was very unlike him.

"I did suspect Adam. You've got ya own story to tell

now lad."

He looked at me, checking that he had my attention, waiting for the last words to leave the atmosphere before hitting me with more. His big line:

"You was pixy-led my boy."

CHAPTER FOUR

You have to be careful what you say to a child; they take it all in.

I truly believed in all Grandpa had told me. I was strangely excited, because I was only a foolish boy seeking adventure and magic, but there was a dread to it all as well. To think of those creatures living amongst us, with lives adjacent to our own. And more importantly, that they now knew I existed.

I had gone on to ask Grandpa if all of this meant that I was special, and he had almost laughed and answered far too quickly. He said that 'No one is more special than anyone else. The world has special places, but we's all the same.'

Perhaps I was too young to really understand, to see all the intricacies in what Grandpa was trying to explain. I could not help but think that there was much more he could tell me and that he was saving the choicest morsels for another time.

I wanted every answer and I wanted to know it all yesterday. I felt that I could have shaken Grandpa just to get the information out of him faster. But perhaps I had to learn to ask the right questions. And perhaps part of the fun would be learning what those questions were.

Anyway, real proof could only come from seeing and feeling it first hand. True scientific mystery solving required field work.

Whether the subject of the little people would be more or less mysterious if I understood their true nature I did not even know. I only knew that they were now becoming very real, and in my knowledge they were losing any of the whimsy that their name used to conjure up.

Life becomes very surreal when a dream becomes reality.

I remember us sitting in silence for a while. We could almost hear one another's brains ticking, coming to terms with the conversation, until almost like a muffled explosion, the door swung open. Grandpa and I shook away the heavy burden of those filtering words as we looked up in unison to see my father enter in a shimmering cloud of disturbed dust.

"Finn..." he had begun to speak before he was fully inside, appearing to be in some hurry to say whatever he had planned to say. "Oh, hi Adam," he then said, realising I was also in the room, "feeling better?"

He only paused long enough for me to give a quick nod, then focused back to Grandpa.

"Finn, there's a bird in the garden..."

"Oh..." Grandpa kind of interrupted with an enquiring exclamation and his eyebrows raised. "In the garden you say?"

He had me fooled for a moment, and I was watching my dad's urgent expression.

"Yep, theys have a nasty habit of comin' into gardens!" Grandpa started one of his wheezy laughs and nudged me as I began to chuckle too.

"Ha-ha Finn. I hadn't quite finished. I think it might be hurt, it's not moving much."

Grandpa managed to calm himself and to speak in earnest, "Ok Thom. So what sort a bird is he?"

"It's just a pigeon."

"Just? Of course, 'cause a pigeon ain't so important as say, a more pretty bird." Grandpa was provoking my father a little now, for his own amusement.

"Could you have a quick look Finn?" Dad did not take the bait.

"Yep, sure sure, I'll go like the mail."

My dad ducked back out of the room and Grandpa carried on cackling at the same time as shuffling about in the bed as if to try and get up.

"Could've 'elped me up there Thom!" he said to himself, still rocking about but getting nowhere.

My mother then came in. She had a silver frame with her with little white plastic wheels.

"Oh no not that thing!" Grandpa exclaimed on seeing the Zimmer frame.

"You have it for a reason." And then she left it by the door, rushing over to his side of the bed when she realised that he had the intention of pushing himself up. "Hey Dad you wait till I come and help you now will you? And use the damned frame or you'll have a fall."

She was genuinely concerned and I realised that she must do that every day, that she had no choice for he could not help himself. I worried for him that he could not even get out of bed on his own. "Adam, off you scoot," she said, waving her hands towards the door.

I left slowly, and I kept looking back at the scene of my mother dutifully helping her father, a role reversed. I can guess that the poor man must have been feeling his pride shattered, putting up his facade of playful grumpiness perhaps to hide those feelings. It was a shame. Speaking with him in bed, our bodies could have been any age. We had a meeting of minds.

I had looked back bashfully, and through his struggling, he gave me a wink.

The pigeon was in the back garden, on the paving right near the house, puffed out like a ball, with its legs tucked away beneath it. The only thing moving was its neck, shifting its head about in small jerks, with grey feathers occasionally being parted by the breeze. It looked a bit of a sorry sight and I felt bad for it.

My dad was watching through the window, jerking his

own head in a similar fashion trying to see it clearly. And then my mother came in behind us.

"Has it moved yet?" she said, joining us in our watch.

"No," Dad answered, "still there."

It was quite the object of fascination for us all, standing in a row by the window, but I was more worried that it really had been hurt.

Grandpa came in eventually with the frame contraption leading him on. He pushed it begrudgingly as means to keep steady. I had never seen it before let alone seen him use it.

"Bloody thing," he mumbled as he moved slowly forwards, sliding each slippered foot about half a step at a time. "Nothing age you quicker than one a these things."

My mother turned and gave him a disapproving scowl.

He continued to mumble as he tried to lean over the frame to open the back door, becoming obviously quite agitated at the difficulty in that simple task. He was making all manner of huffs and puffs and did not seem to want our help.

"Let's take a geek at it then..."

In due course Grandpa and my mother were outside inspecting the creature.

It did not take flight which we all thought a little out of character for a wild bird; it just sat there, looking at us. But they could not see anything wrong with it and thought it seemed unharmed. So we simply decided that we should all just keep an eye on it.

My father acted very down trodden as he said that his plans were to take us all out for the day... to a little beach cove.

"So what happens if it has smashed itself on the window or something?" he asked in annoyance, "I have no intention of driving down to the vet with a bloody pigeon."

"If it's 'urt you'll 'ave to ring its neck," Grandpa said, looking right at Dad.

My father looked shocked, "Me? I can't do that," he defended.

My mum looked disgusted. "Dad that's horrible."

"It's what's kind," Grandpa answered plainly. "Worse to leave it suffering ain't it?

"In the wild poor thing would suffer 'n' die, 'cause that's nature. But it was us humans that built brick 'ouses and glass windows for 'em to fly itself into. That makes it up to us." He was holding onto his frame yet still managing to hold up a finger in emphasis.

There was silence.

"I am NOT killing anything," Dad argued. "Just 'cause I'm a man I'm supposed to be ok with that? How the hell are you supposed to do something like that?"

"Ya grab its neck," Grandpa made a fist, "and then, you ring it!" He was completely serious.

"Urgh," my mum went out of the kitchen into the lounge, obviously disturbed, and my father followed after her. I think they were quite annoyed.

"Welcome to the countryside!" Grandpa called out at them. "Here you may well 'ave to worry about things other than ya selves."

Grandpa and I looked at each other, and although I too was shaken by it all, I gave a comical shrug. We were all disturbed by it, but I wanted to be more like Grandpa.

My parents retreated to the lounge and the TV was put on, playing to dour faces as the pigeon dilemma remained a bone of contention. It was a sport program, so although my dad might have looked as though he was watching, I knew that he would really have no interest.

Grandpa decided not to let the whole subject drop.

"So," he said as an announcement, calling loudly from the kitchen so that they had no choice but hear. "What else don't you know about country livin'?"

"Dad, it isn't exactly a different world," my mother tried to douse.

Grandpa was struggling to turn himself with the Zimmer frame. Until then the argument could not even be face to face. "Ah, now that is where you are wrong, you need to remember, and start to believe that it is. Adam's the only one of ya that's realised it."

Grandpa grinned at me, and we waited for a reply, but none came. Eventually, he gave up and changed his tune. "So you going back out rambling today master Adam?"

I had not been sure before, but I *did* want to go back to Old Bob's wood. Somehow I felt it calling to me.

Most people would think the things which had happened to me were nothing but a child's imaginings; a child scaring itself. But as ambiguous as those events were; I believed in them, and so did Grandpa. I might not know exactly what I was afraid of; but the unknown, the things we do not understand; they are the true foundations of fear. I knew that the longer I kept away, the more I turned my back, the greater those unfounded fears would grow.

I nodded, and shrugged simultaneously.

"You want to play in the woods, you just do so. Don't you worry 'bout all what I said. Just go there, enjoy it, with the innocence in your heart. More importantly though, you do as I say now, strange though it will sound to you." He nodded once, and I answered as I knew he wanted me to, with a nod in return despite having no idea what he was going to say.

My mother walked back into the room and eyed us suspiciously, making us instantly hush.

"You ok you two?"

"Yep the boy's looking after me ain't ya?" He ruffled my hair.

We stood still in there as my mother began making cups of tea. She obviously felt that enough time had passed to begin again, and try to forget the attempted argument. "Want one Dad?"

"Of course," he said in an appreciative fashion. "Want a nice cup a tea Adam?" he asked me, knowing full well that children do not acquire a taste for tea or coffee till much later in life. And then, rather than ruffle my hair again he kind of playfully pushed the back of my head. He was strangely strong I thought, as he nearly had me over.

We were both patiently waiting, putting on an act until my mother had gone.

"I'll take your tea in Dad yeah?" And off she went with a tray of three cups into the lounge.

Grandpa gestured me to him with his hand and a whispered 'pssst'.

I came close so that I could hear what he had to tell me in his lowered voice. "Adam, if you're goin' back in the woods, you need to take some milk along. Put it in a bowl... you know? It's for *them*." It was strange, but I nodded.

"They like milk?" I whispered back, feeling unnerved by memory.

"Yes, it's an offering."

As everything about the little people was new and peculiar to me, I simply took the advice without further questioning. But then Grandpa made me even more bewildered. "And Adam," he continued to whisper as I moved away, and had to come back to be within ear shot. "Put some stale bread in ya pocket."

* * *

I was surprised to find no argument about me leaving the house. But I had promised to stay close and all the turmoil I had been feeling was my secret. No one but I knew what was really happening inside my mind, so I could, therefore, pretend that it was not happening at all.

Though I was sure the woods knew.

I had managed to stow away a blue breakfast bowl, an emptied drink bottle with some milk poured in, and I had put some bread into my school bag. With that protection at my side I was back on track.

Perhaps moving to Cornwall and beginning to roam its beautiful wild countryside without any of that knowledge was like being thrown to the lions. Well now I was set to tame them.

I practically marched across the moist muddy field with the sun as my beacon and ally. Walking like that cleared my head of anything but the job in hand and filled me with the confidence and strength to do that which I set out to do. I almost expected the woods to back off from my determined march but no, they stood fast.

Nearly there I stopped to catch my breath. The sun was beating harder than I had at first thought and I worried due to my past experience. There was moisture beneath my T-shirt.

I felt my will flounder.

"I'm NOT afraid of you woods!" I yelled out loud, holding my body stiff, alone in that vast empty field. I had seen enough films and read enough books to know that was a good strategy.

I could still see the village and my home behind at some distance, so I knew that I could not get lost. There was nothing to fear.

"Old Bob I'm coming in!"

Moments later I had reached the final stretch and then the fight with undergrowth began. Wrestling with the coiling twisted hedgerows which barred my way. I refused to cease in smashing at them with my arms and flattening them with raised feet, pushing thorny vicious vines aside with the weight of my body. The odd scratch meant nothing, for they would not beat me, I would beat them down.

And almost all of a sudden, I was out into that clearing as though the bushes had given way to my aggression and the woods had conceded to suck me into their enclosed protected body. I felt almost thrown into it, and stumbled as my thrusting weight no longer had anything left to push against.

"HA!"

It was almost too easy, taking only my determination, and now I was in and looking around me for any danger or further unseen attack. Perhaps I felt a little disappointed that the woods now seemed to be as benign as, reasonably, they should always have been. In the bright light of day, they were perfectly beautiful.

The sun was bright and the early afternoon shadows only added to the atmosphere of benevolence rather than causing any masquerade of menace. Natural light spread out to the ground in a hundred shafts through gaps in the labyrinth of branches above. I looked up at their intricate patterns obscuring the expanse of sky, and I span on my heel until I had dizzied myself.

As I walked on I noticed how the entire woodland floor was a wash with every shade of green and splashed with colour in a few patches of late blue bells.

All had been invigorated by recent rain and drips of water still fell through the leaves, the only sound I could hear. It was alive in every corner, and every inch had something to see that was different to its neighbour. Some parts were lighter than others, some easier reached, some overhanging and secretive.

The trees had their own personalities with their own way of being, making their own ways in the world.

Some reached incredibly tall, some were thick and strong, while others seemed to have danced as they grew, forming bending new ideals of beauty.

It was everything that I loved to see and I felt almost silly to have ever been fearful.

I did not know where or when to put down the milk, or what kind of ceremony it needed, but I wanted to get it done and so decided that meant it was time.

I felt conspicuous, taking it out of the bag, placing the bowl amongst twigs and shoots and pouring the milk. But no one was there to interfere with these moments, and it felt as important as Grandpa had stressed that it was.

So it seemed appropriate that I should say some words to announce that it was a gift. Then I remembered the words he had used.

"An offering," I whispered under my breath, staring ahead into silent, seemingly empty woodland. And then, not waiting for an answer or indeed for anything to happen, I put the empty bottle away, and moved from the spot.

The bread Grandpa had simply said to put it my pocket, and unceremoniously, I did just that. I took the slice from out of the bag and stuffed it crumbling into the pocket of my jeans.

I had no idea why he had told me to do these things, but now I know that everything he said had credence. It was not an old man making things up for his own amusement; it was from centuries of folklore which long ago were much more diligently adhered to. All I knew then was that it comforted me, and made me feel safe to be there amongst those things unseen.

I felt no real need to be afraid. The woods, almost silent and dappled with sun and shadow, appeared only serene. It certainly did not speak of any danger. But I remained on my guard, making sure to take note of each move that I made.

As I continued to walk I heard every tiny sound, every crack of twig. And yes, they did seem to be watching me, checking me out; friend or foe. There were eyes in the tree bark and in every fern bush. There were faces amongst the leaves and branches. And I expected to see something, waiting to be unnerved, but as I looked about me with darting eyes I saw nothing, nothing but what should be there, the undeniable existence of Mother Nature.

Without the effort of trying I felt the wonder, the awe and respect that I had been taught to feel. I was completely aware of the complexity, the intricate system of life and decay. I was observant, always, of how the light changed, how the sun dipped in some places more readily than others.

When the woods fell dark their age was told, a deep feeling in my soul of their ancient knowledge and their countless years of endurance out there, alone. And the age was not only of those old trees, but of the earth itself, and of something there which perhaps predated time. If it was *they* I was feeling, then it was *they* I felt with total reverence.

Perhaps I had earned the wood's respect because it seemed to be repaying me in spectacle. And it was not long before it offered me up a gift of its own.

A little way from there I found what was to be my greatest prize: the camp.

There it stood, standing proud yet forgotten. Half covered in undergrowth, reaching out to be known.

It was strange to see. A man made tower amidst everything that was natural. As soon as my eyes caught sight of it I rushed over as quickly as the unsteady ground would allow. I made haste to part the vines which tried to keep it a secret, the ivy which grew over its entrance and walls.

I could hardly believe that it was not some fantastical dream. Because for me, at that age, it was instantly a wonder.

It was like a broken turret from a medieval castle, made of old crumbling bricks that had turned white and powdery with age. The ivy crawled aesthetically up its sides amidst the branches which drooped down around it.

I wanted to go inside, through the gap where the door would once have been, but there was a certain amount of work to be done to make my way. The entrance was heavily guarded by brambles but nothing would prevent this true discovery from belonging to me.

At length I pushed my way in. Standing on the floor of leaf and dirt and realising then, that it actually formed a hexagon. It was really quite large, with a little glassless window on the far wall. Light came in a little through that aperture, but the roof, although long gone, was now formed with a shading canopy of hanging leafy boughs.

I felt a warmth there, perhaps in my heart, or soul, that it had now become my place. I loved the woods as I always should have.

Already my mind was making plans for it to be a camp, fired up with possibilities. Despite the inside being full of woodland growth, I knew that, with a bit of work, this would be my base, my look out post, and it was far better than any tree house or tent.

The woods were now filled with that childish wonder and excitement again. They were benign. They were a great maze of trees that held only adventure. The hidden people may well remain hidden and I would not feel any wrath from them henceforth.

As I was want to do, I nearly spoke aloud, and I nearly said 'thank you for this woods.' But something stopped the words before they left my lips. Strange, because in a later conversation I remember Grandpa warning me that you should never thank the faeries.

So I had finally found my place, and I set my roots. Cornwall was at last my home.

Happily I made my leave accompanied by bird song, the only sound to be heard. Occasionally my footsteps disturbed their roost and heavy wings caused unsettled commotion in the tree tops above, startling me for a moment. But it only made me realise how isolated the place was, that I could hear nothing else at all. There were no human sounds but my own. With peace like that, the volume of your own mind is deafening. And my thoughts were wild with awakening emotion.

I weaved between hanging branches, parted vines with my hands and stepped over remnants of fallen trees, not stopping for some time. And then I did, I stopped. Without really thinking first that I wished to halt my persistent steps, I had stopped dead in my tracks. Somehow, subconsciously, I had realised that I was somewhere else of note.

Given some dowsing rods and walking to that spot I am positive that they would have gone crazy with the unseen power. It seemed to fix my feet still so that I had no choice but to stand there.

I was at the foot of a truly massive tree, in a perfectly round clearing.

Perhaps I had simply seen it in peripheral vision, or at least noticed a change in the light which made me realise I was somewhere special. But I think there was much more to it than that, and I knew it then. I almost felt my breath cease in my lungs.

The girth of that tree was astounding; especially as I had always been taught that a tree's width tells of its age. It must have been ancient, probably the oldest tree there. It is possible that it was the beginning of the entire wood and of everything that surrounded it. That it had been the first, the father, spreading its seeds to make its young. And then those new trees made homes for the wildlife and birds which would have then brought more plants and more trees there. Perhaps the whole wood was now thick with its offspring.

That was it. It was the centre, the heart. And as if to stress the point further, a ring of small white mushrooms had formed in a circle around it. I looked down and could see them there, with one of my feet inside the ring, barely having avoided trampling on them.

I moved back away.

I was not sure but I thought it might be an oak tree. My early years were spent in the town so I never really knew the names of flowers or trees. I expected that Grandpa could have named them all. But you do not need to know something's name to be attracted by it, or to know its nature. I knew that it was special. It required my respect, and to think of all the years it must have weathered left me truly in awe.

It was not the highest tree of them all, but it was magnificent, and I could not help but think that it was also very climbable. I knew that I could do it, I was good at climbing, and I wanted to climb this one, this special one, nothing less.

Without further debate I leant forwards and put my hands flat on the trunk, palms against the deeply grooved, rugged bark. They began to feel strangely warm and I felt then, for whatever reason, a kind of kinship. But now I would conquer it, as man has always conquered and tamed any nature he has come upon.

I threw down my bag and, avoiding the mushrooms, gripped onto that first, lowest branch, to pull myself up. Then I began my ascent. It was easy for me, like second nature. My brief pauses were not for courage but only to plan my next move, and I was high before I realised I had even made an effort. Some children are said to be able to swim like a fish; I could climb like a monkey.

I had the sense to stop, however, when the branches became thinner, giving way to its crown of leaves. There was no way to get any higher from there, even with my climbing skills. But it was still a triumph, if not quite a victory.

Being up there on my own felt liberating. No one on earth could see me then or knew where I was at that moment. I was free. The air was clear, and the view was new and wonderful. If I was to get in trouble for stains on my jeans this time then it would definitely be worth it.

It suddenly became a sobering thought, however, that any wrong move at that point could actually kill me. I had never been so high up a tree before and looking down made me feel a little queasy. It was those thoughts which brought me, metaphorically, back down to earth.

Looking below through the jagged ladder of branches that I had just climbed up, I could barely make out the ground. I began to feel dizzy as I strained my eyes and planned my decent. When then, at a speed too quick to be sure of anything, I saw something dart into the bushes from the base of the tree trunk.

I nearly fell as my eyes followed the sudden movement. I lost one of my feet and fell forward, heavy on my shoulder, grabbing another moist branch with my hands. I swore under my breath.

My heart was in my mouth, and my shoulder hurt. But I was too concerned with finding out what I had just seen than to worry about my own well-being. I was panicking to try and get down as soon as possible yet I knew that what was there had now gone. I would never be quick enough to find out the truth.

I was not concentrating. I slipped a few more times, scratching my shin and then catching and tearing my T-shirt at the hem. I was looking at the spot where I had seen it and not really at where my hands and feet were supposed to be. I allowed myself to fall through most of the tree now, feeding my body through branch after branch, so desperate was I to get back down and prove my suspicion.

My nerves were shot. I was so sure that it had been something; I had even heard the rustle of parting leaves as it was lost into the bushes. I had seen something, and it was not just an animal. It was too large to be a rodent, and it was no bird. It had been upright, running on two legs. I was close to certain.

In fact, I was pretty sure that it had been a person. I had seen a living person come out of where the tree should be, and with lightning speed, lose itself into the woods.

My feet finally hit the sanctity of ground but there was nothing to see. The light of the clearing should have put things into perspective, but the thumping of my heart, loud in my chest, did not leave me for a second. I was spinning round, looking about, searching with eyes and ears for some clarity which might explain these events and this place to me. But no answer came.

Standing there with quivering legs, I looked that tree up and down. The mushroom ring now surrounded me as I stood at the centre of everything. I waited for my heart to gain a steady pace, and then I almost laughed, speaking to the woods, distinctly in my mind, but left unspoken.

I think if I had known the phrase, I might well have exclaimed. 'Touché!'

Yes, again the woodlands had frightened me, made me afraid but also, and perhaps even more so, they had fired up my imagination. I knew now that there was definitely something strange going on. I knew that Grandpa had told me the truth. And this time I was convinced that I had seen something.

I could still see it, firmly and clearly fixed in my memory; a little person, running on two legs, at the speed of a startled mouse.

* * *

Walking away from the woods that day I must have turned to take a look at them a hundred times. On each turn they looked exactly as they did before, while my understanding, my thoughts about them, were different every time.

Back at the cottage my mother was in the front garden, tending to the pansy flowers with a green handled shovel. Grandpa was out there too, standing proud on his own two legs, though having gone no further than to step into the sun from out of the porch way, one hand holding on to its frame.

He always wore the same clothes, white shirt, brown trousers, though now his somewhat loose slacks were held up by a pair of old fashioned braces. He was looking on his daughter as a father would, with a comforted pleasure.

Perhaps he was happy to have her there in his twilight years. He kept looking to her, then squinting up at the sky, then back to her again with a smile. And Mum looked happy too. Perhaps it was just because the sun was shining, because the view was so beautiful, the air so peaceful clean and clear. But perhaps even more importantly it was because she and her dad, my grandpa, had patched up their differences, and were not so constantly at odds anymore.

As I drew closer I tried to mask my preoccupied

demeanour. I feigned an air of serenity more in keeping with theirs by walking in assured, untroubled strides. As if to enhance the authenticity of my actions I even hummed a quiet tune.

I believed that it was working and a smile and a hello would suffice as I went up the path to the door. I did not want to disturb them, yet completely unintentionally, I disturbed something.

"Hi Adam," Mum said looking up from her work and holding a flat hand above her eyes to shield the sun. "Everything ok?" It was a simple question, with no intent. But I answered defensively.

"Yes, sure... of course." And then remembering that I had ripped my shirt at the bottom, I covered it with my arm.

I knew that I could not rely on my acting skills so I took up the humming again, continuing towards the cottage with one arm very stiff over the torn T-shirt.

On passing Grandpa my smile to him was more than genuine, yet hiding and harbouring thoughts about what had happened. It was good to know that I had someone I could talk to about it. I had no doubt that he would be interested.

So happily I increased the humming and was moments from the door when he shot me back a glance so quick and unreadable that it shocked me silent. Then he grabbed my shoulder, stopping me from moving on. We stood looking eye to eye and he began to scare me. His eyes, usually wide with an entertaining passion for stories were now glowing with some kind of frenzy.

"You go back to the woods boy?"

I tried to remain poised and did not really understand why that sounded so sharp and so much like an accusation.

"Err, yes."

His grip had grown hard and tight, his thumb pressed

painfully against my collarbone. I began to squirm against it and he reluctantly let go, but his eyes still bore into me and I did not dare to move. I had never seen him look menacing like that. He seemed to be staring into my very mind. It completely unsettled me. Suddenly Grandpa was not whom I thought and hoped that he was. He was an adult in that moment, an over bearing and dominant male. I did not understand why.

"Anything to tell me?"

I realised that my mother was coming over towards us and I did not want to be there any longer. He had frightened me, but I did not want to spoil things or get him into trouble.

"I'm done," my mother said with a relaxed sigh. "It's getting so hot now, I must get in."

Completely unaware that there had been any altercation she stepped between us both, up the step and through the door.

I was deeply unhappy right then, and I was set to turn and follow her, to run up to my bedroom and never come out.

"Ah, you can tell me later," he said. And his voice and his eyes were back to their normal Grandpa self. He was benevolent once more, as always he should be.

To some extent I began to doubt whether any of that had actually happened.

I did just go to my room for a time. I lay on my back, on the bed, staring at the ceiling and simply thinking. Mere days living in the new home and I was already more confused and awake with emotions than I had ever been in my whole life.

I could hear the woods shouting melodies outside but I practically shut my ears to it all. I did not know what to think about them, or Grandpa or anything else.

Did I hate my new home or was it the beginning of a

fantastic adventure?

I felt that it was too much too soon, yet not really enough of anything.

Later that I day I helped myself to two of Grandpa's sweets, rather than just the one. He had upset me, and that was the only revenge a twelve year old boy could think of.

When we were sitting in the lounge together I kept watching my grandpa, to see which Grandpa he was going to continue to be. And he asked me how I got on in the woods, though he must have known that I could not recount the whole story with my parents there.

I told them I had seen a circle of mushrooms.

"You didn't eat any did you?" My mother shot the question at me in sudden concern.

"No," I said back to her snidely, "I just saw them."

"Ay, Adam ya mum's right to ask," Grandpa spoke up, "there's some mushrooms that will kill ya in a blink. I knew of one woman, always made mushroom soup from the same patch in 'er garden, yet one night her and 'er husband took sick. Spent the next day in 'ospital but they couldn't save 'er. She'd not checked 'er harvest. Was about two death caps in there, and just half a one of them will rip ya guts to shreds."

"Not the right time of year for mushrooms is it?" my dad asked.

"Ah, well, mushrooms is funny things, they don't always follow rules. Bit like us folk.

"You're right though, be in autumn usually, when everything is dying off, they is coming to fruit, eating up on the decay. Sometimes they circle an area of goodness to them, they can be doing that for hundreds of years, never dying, just going back to the earth. We calls 'em faery rings. You knows about faery rings don't you Annie?"

My mother had been only half listening. "What? No Dad, I don't."

Grandpa winked at me, which always made me smile. He seemed to be back to normal but my mother looked very awkward. I had thought the subject of mushrooms to be fairly safe but it had hit another nerve.

"I think I'll go upstairs." I said.

My room was a little darker than it should be. It might have been mine now, but I was sharing it with the view from my window. Those bleak fields, the threatening sea, and the haunting perplexity of the woods... all of that was *theirs*.

I spent almost an hour lying on my bed thinking about things, staring out the window though all I really saw from that position was light blue sky. I felt older, like I had left Adam the boy back in those towns, and now I was growing up, a man of the country. And I was reaching an age where the childish abandon of acting on impulse was beginning to fall away. It seemed that I had a need to take stock of my thoughts much more frequently, but then, I *had* been given strange things to think about.

I had ceased to doubt that it was all real, I believed and I had faith in that belief, and also in Grandpa. If people can believe that there is a God without ever seeing him, without ever being able to see him, then I had faith in the faeries. Belief in God comes from your heart, and with all my heart and soul I knew that the woods were alive, and a home to more than just the animals and birds.

I heard, then, shouting from downstairs. It was my father but it was not anger so much as confounded frustration. I had not yet left my childlike energy behind, and so, although I had needed to catch up on rest, I was soon down the stairs to investigate.

He was standing in the doorway between the kitchen and the garden scratching his head, now quiet.

"What's up Dad?"

"Damn pigeon," he said. I had almost forgotten about that whole escapade. "Just flew off," he hand gestured, "not a care in the world. Wasted the whole day worrying about that thing."

"Well," Grandpa started up from the living room, and we both went back in there together. "It was a wood pigeon. He's gone back to the woods now where it don't worry about nothing.

"Maybe it just wanted to come 'n' see 'ow the other folk live, then saw better of it 'n' went back to where it belongs... Don't rightly blame it!"

And neither did I.

CHAPTER FIVE

It was Sunday, and that meant that Monday followed and school, a new school full of strangers and no friends, was but one sleep away. I did not like Sundays, they had that impending doom hanging over them like a dark rain cloud. It was hard to enjoy the day at all yet I truly wanted to.

So much had happened in that first week but I wanted more. I was not ready for that day to day humdrum of going to lessons to encroach upon the fun of freedom.

My morning chats with Grandpa were exciting, and that was the only time I was able to get him on his own. I enjoyed that connection with him. We had something in common now, we shared a secret.

I was planning to go straight to his room again that day, and I was the first to be up.

The cottage made no sound but for the usual subtle ticking of the clock, and walking slowly about the lounge, and then into the kitchen, I ruminated on the fact that I lived here now, that this was my home. Being in those rooms, alone, I could imagine that I was a grown up and that the house actually belonged to me. Grandpa's empty chair could have been my own, and his bag of sweets, which was also close to empty, were mine as well.

After a small cursory knock I found him sitting up, not against his headboard with a book, but with both legs over the side of the bed. He was in the process of pulling his Zimmer frame closer to use as leverage as I entered and I quickly knew to go and help.

"Thanks there lad, you're a good boy." He actually

sounded quite subdued, tired perhaps, of being old and being frail. "Would ya like to accompany your old grandpa into the garden?"

He had somehow managed to pull on a green towelling dressing gown and slide his feet into his slippers, presumably left in strategic places for ease. The day was certainly plenty warm enough, and I knew I was capable of making sure that he was ok. I nodded.

The front garden would have been brighter and hotter at that time, but I instinctively knew that out the back was where we were heading. That little pocket of nature he had captured between the fences was his sanctuary.

As we opened the door a flock of birds seemed to be instantly lifted up from the back trees, taking flight in unison and then one by one returning.

We stood at the doorway a while, Grandpa needing a break from concentrating on his shuffling walk, and taking in the breath of morning. The song of those birds was a backdrop of pleasant sounds which never seemed to break the peace.

"Nice ain't it?" he mused. "Spent an age in this 'ere cottage, never felt the walls were so close till now." He looked at me, paused a while, then gave a warm smile. "I want to show ya somethin' young Adam," he said, and moved himself off.

I realised that I had not even spoken a word to him yet, just observing everything, and somehow I still did not feel the need to.

I watched as he walked, or rather dragged his feet down the little slate stone path ahead of me, and I followed. He stopped briefly every few steps, moving his head slowly in every direction. I could see how much he delighted in the beauty of his home grown thicket, enjoying the sun as it illuminated all the yellows and reds of the wild flowers which grew there. It was his place.

We did not come to a permanent halt until we reached the very far fence with further trees growing up against it. I could see, as I drew closer, that these had tiny green apples, tinged with red, growing upon them. It was a simple thing, but it fascinated me. I don't think I had ever seen apples growing in a garden like that. Perhaps I believed that fruit just appeared on the supermarket shelves.

Those apple trees made the garden even more enclosed. I could not even see through them to the view that I knew would be there. Perhaps irrationally I thought that Grandpa might have grown it all that way on purpose, to obscure the field which was beyond. Perhaps *he* was hiding from Old Bob's wood.

He brought my attention to the ground with a nod. In a little alcove, tucked away in that corner, hidden from view, was a little wooden house. It was a replica, it seemed, of the cottage itself.

I might have gasped. I remember that I was very surprised, and very impressed.

It stood under the trees around it, yet still managing to catch the sunlight. Its own tiny pathway of broken slate led to the little painted door, no bigger than a couple of inches high. Its white wooden walls were weathered, its gravel garden had small weeds and dandelions growing through it, untended, but it was utterly charming and at some time, exquisitely crafted.

"Built this years ago," he said, gaining even more of my admiration for his handy work. I could hardly believe that he had constructed it himself. "Annie loved it, when she were young, but secretly I think it was more for *them* really. I've known they visit me 'ouse, the real house. It's old this place you know? Not just the cottage, but the ground where it stands, this land, it was sacred, backalong. They probably always been 'ere."

He looked about himself, but mainly, I noticed, he looked in the direction of the woods; though the garden was all there was to see.

"I seen an old map of this whole area, before the cottage was ever 'ere. It 'ad a word on it, said 'thorn', and that want no place, it were the trees. If there were thorn trees 'ere, and they were important enough to mark 'em on a map, then that spells bad news Adam. Everyone knows that you never chop a faery tree.

"So it 'as an history. It'll never be a modern 'ouse. Sticking some modern electric thing in the fireplace don't make it any less the hearth, it's still the 'eart. But I'm teachin' you best I can 'cause the old ways get lost in the end... and they's old for a reason... they've endured."

That tiny sunlit model had definitely seen time, but it had also been loved. We were both looking intently at it, with our own thoughts.

"This was one of them offerings I guess. Perhaps I was 'oping they'd go in there, use the place 'stead of me own 'ouse. But this land is thin... maybe they can't keep away long. Time passes and they start to play their tricks again."

He looked at my frozen face and smiled his warm closed mouth smile. "I ain't trying to scare you Adam, I do take measures, like the 'orseshoe at the door, made of iron, poison that is, to them. But don't you fear. Those woods is only the woods, and the little people, well, they's only the little people."

He gave me a big grin and put his hand on my shoulder, though he struggled a little when he pulled it back and I put a hand out to steady him. "You're like me, you love all this." And with that same hand he swung it around himself to gesture the garden and all its nature. He tottered a little, like my father at a Christmas party, and grabbed the metal frame tightly. "Well it's yours now ain't it?"

I had been very quiet, with words reaching my lips only to then retreat once more. I had wanted to speak to him about what I had seen, but part of me wasn't sure if the time was right. I got the impression we were going to head back inside.

But then he was looking right at me, and his face had changed. It reminded me of the way he had looked when he grabbed me, asking me about the woods. Perhaps it was that which kept those secrets close to my chest. The expression on his face was unintelligible, but it disturbed me. He rubbed his cheek, then his eyelids, as if he were attempting to alter his thoughts.

"I gotta ask ya something lad," he began, and I could tell he was uncomfortable. "Did ya do as I said, before ya went back there... did ya take milk and bread to the woods?"

I nodded, hard and expressively.

"And did ya feel safe? Nothing bad 'appen?"

I felt that it was impossible to tell him about seeing a little person now. He actually seemed concerned. "I was fine, it's nice in there. I found a camp..."

"Oh yer? That's good... and... that tune you were hummin' lad, on the way back, you never 'eard that 'song' before?"

"No," I said, quite certain of my answer. But in honesty I could not even remember what I had been humming.

"No?" He rubbed his chin, nodded slowly, and then took hold of the Zimmer frame. "Good lad."

As we started back to the house I heard my last word hang in the air. I had said 'no', clearly without thinking, and now I began to doubt myself. As we walked the tune started to resonate inside my mind. I began to remember what I had been humming. And I remembered that sweet music which had once led me so astray.

Immediately I felt a chill that was not there. And now I dare not speak up, to tell Grandpa that I had made a mistake, that it was, in fact, the song of the woods themselves... And I could never know why it scared him so.

* * *

Monday morning; the worst day and time of any week.

I was trying my best to be positive and complacent when inside I was a bag of nerves. My mind could only focus on the next few hours to come, completely incapable of living in the present. I did all the practical things that needed to be done to ready myself for school, but mentally psyching myself up was taking all of my concentration.

It was going to be such a wrench to suddenly abandon my solitary, mystical adventures for the social normality of school. For now my playground would not be trees, but tarmac. And my teachers would not be interesting, wise old men, but dull, paid, middle aged suits who smelt of coffee.

I was sitting at the kitchen table eating my cereal, and my father sat opposite reading a newspaper. He had ordered it to be delivered, catching up with events over tea and a neglected piece of cold toast. I occasionally looked up at him and was a little amused by the expressions on his face which changed as he read; interest, then disgust, then shock. It did not go unnoticed, but I was trapped in my own bubble of discomfort.

"Still talking about the miner's strike in the paper Finn," My dad called over to his side, projecting his voice to my grandpa who was seated in the lounge as usual. "That was your trade wasn't it?"

"Mining?" Grandpa called back, "For tin yes, not coal. Same thing though, still an 'orrible job, and still the boys all sticking together."

"Yes, I wouldn't fancy that job; hard work," my dad spoke loudly back, respectfully.

I was listening, because my ears could not be switched off. But the last thing I wanted to hear before my first day at school was the latest 'important' news from the paper. It did not affect me, because I was still a child, and very little of it would have affected me even if I wasn't.

"Mining was 'ard work for sure, but not so bad as backalong. My father he had a rough time. But I'm Cornish, didn't have much choice. Could've been a fisherman or a miner. I never much cared for the sea, and the Bucca-boo puts the wind up me! So I took my chances in the earth instead, like me father before me.

"Anyway, lucky to be 'ere and done with all that. I certainly ain't proud of what I did. But those poor boys deserve their rights."

Grandpa had emotion in his voice, it was a bit cracked as he spoke, but it was strange to hear and not see his face. "Don't know why you reads that thing anyway, what goods it do ya, knowing everyone's sufferin'?"

I totally agreed with Grandpa, as usual.

My father lowered the paper, looking down at it with brief contemplation. "Know thine enemy?" he said, questioning his own thoughts.

"Like that bloody woman who's running the country? Well I'd rather stick me 'ead in the sand over that one. Animals out there, like that pigeon the other day, they ain't worried about any of that so why should I? They don't know nowadays a woman can be so cold 'n' downright evil, yet still be in charge of a nation's fate.

Far as the countryside's concerned, the world's still a place of plenty. At my time a life, I needs to 'ave peace in me ignorance."

Politics meant even less to me than they did to Grandpa, yet by the tone of his voice, I could tell it actually meant more to him than he wanted to admit.

I had finished my bowl of cereal, which I realised I had eaten extremely slowly. I think my intention may well have been to draw out the morning, and my last slice of freedom. But the clock was not going to stop. My mother came into the room carrying my jacket and my bag.

"Oh no," I said under my breath, but perfectly audibly.

"Oh yes," she said. "No more putting it off or you'll end up missing the bus." She put down my things, the light green jacket and brown leather bag. She then stood in the living room doorway to address Grandpa. "And you," she said, equally bossy with her own father, "don't be so cynical. I heard what you were saying just now."

I was putting on my jacket, accepting my fate, but still managing to listen. My interest was strangely intent, but that, again, was to prolong the time before school.

"Cynical? I though it was quite optimistic considering this world is turnin' to shit."

"Dad!"

I was shocked too, and had to laugh, to which I was thrown a very disapproving glare by my mother. My dad also scowled, and I started to tie my shoelaces quickly in response.

My mother looked back in on Grandpa. "Dad, come on. There's loads of good things happen in the world, how would you even know if you don't read the papers? All the stuff Greenpeace are doing and that."

"Ah... it's all too late Annie. Patchin' up wrongs

already done. If the boat is sinking a few good buckets bailing it out won't stop the water comin' in. None a that would need doin' at all if we ain't ruined it already."

My mother huffed and stomped back passed me. She went to the cupboard and opened it forcefully. "And where's that bowl gone now?" she said in a definitely irritated voice, shutting the cupboard and then checking around the sink. She was not addressing anyone in particular but it was me that could have given her the answer.

All of that just added to the unsettled feeling already sitting in the pit of my stomach; I kept my mouth shut of course.

"What is it with this house? That's the third thing I've lost since we got here."

Although the sound was very quiet, I was completely aware that Grandpa was chuckling to himself in the living room.

* * *

Leaving the house that day was to go on another adventure, but not one of my own choice.

The fears I had then were of a much different and more likely nature. I had true concerns that I would not be accepted, that I would make no new friends and that I would get lost in those maze like corridors. I was worried about the fact that it was single sexed, that I would be surrounded by nothing but boys trying to gain the role of alpha male.

Perhaps these rural schools would be rougher, more antiquated. Perhaps the teachers at this school would be old timers with over heavy discipline; wishing it was still legal to use the cane.

My dad had said, before I left, 'you can't miss the stop, it's straight down the main road.' But I had never walked that way, and it only added to my apprehension.

I tried in vain to put it all from my mind and enjoy the new views from walking the road towards the main hub of the village. But the urge to go the way I was used to walking had been strong. I had a sudden desire to skip school altogether and imagined hiding out all day at Old Bob's and eating my lunch under the great tree.

I had, however, been brought up too well, or was just too plain scared, to 'bunk off'. As appealing as it may have seemed to hide amongst the trees rather than deal with the day at a brand new school; I was heading the way I was supposed to go.

At first, to each side of me on the road, there had been only fields, soggy and dirty. It seemed to have rained almost every night, but the sun would rise hot each morning as if oblivious. The landscape showed the evidence.

To one side was a waterlogged field full of scattered, dreary sheep. In the other, a single, miserable looking donkey. Its grey hair was darkened by the wet, its mane practically dripping over its neck. I saw it in the corner of my eye as it intently watched me pass, its head following my progress the entire way.

The main village was soon upon me; it was not far and it would have been hard to get lost, as much as I half wished I could be.

I passed quaint cottages with their twee little gardens, even more meticulously trimmed than the one in front of our house. And ahead I could see there was a crossroads, which was where the stop was. I could see it there, next to an old fashioned convenience shop which looked like someone had simply stuck a store sign to the front of their home.

I felt my steps slow up unconsciously; there was

another person standing waiting, another boy about my age. He was hardly moving, kind of rocking on the balls of his feet, and I could not make out his features from that distance. But I had seen that same small body outline before. It was easy to put two and two together fairly quickly; that he was the boy I had seen at the coast.

I was nervous to meet my first school pupil before even entering the grounds of the school, but perhaps it was a good thing to make a connection with someone my age in this place, and perhaps it would ease me into the day more gradually.

I started up my normal pace again. I was not an unsociable person, just anxious that I would not know what to say, or how to say it. Invariably I was fine meeting people, but it did not matter how many times I was reassured by experience, I still doubted my aptitude.

I think my courage kicked in the minute I saw his face. He was not the least bit threatening. I could tell immediately that he was more of a sensitive quiet child than one that would be too loud and confident. He had dark untidy hair and equally dark thick eyebrows. When he looked up at my approach he did not raise his head, just his eyes, green and soulful. I don't think he would have opened his mouth if I hadn't begun a conversation.

"Hi."

He answered, "Hello," very quietly, as though he were not used to speaking and his voice was stuck in his throat. He hardly even looked at me.

"I'm Adam," I said.

I did not have to ask if he was going to my school as he wore the exact same uniform. He also had on a scruffy burgundy coat, unzipped and overly large.

He definitely seemed to be shy and was coyly looking at me from the corner of his eye now and then.

"Martin," he announced at last, his voice gaining a little more volume. He continued to rock on his feet, in fact that movement seemed to grow in pace as he looked down at the floor, or at his newly cleaned, yet very worn shoes. His eyes rose briefly when he spoke, "You've just moved to Ash Cottage haven't you?"

I knew that it was a small village, but still surprised how quickly such gossip had reached a boy of our age. I was also intrigued to hear the name 'Ash Cottage'. There was no sign anywhere on the house and I knew our address only to be a number on the street. It felt almost posh for my home to have a name, if he was not mistaken.

"I live at number 4?"

"Yes, on the corner. Your name is Briggs." It was not even a question, and I had no idea how he knew so much.

It interested me how he had the same accent as Grandpa. I guess it was simply Cornish, but to hear it coming from such a young person didn't seem quite right or possible. He was much softer spoken though, and his voice remained on one level with none of Grandpa's more outlandish pronunciations.

"I delivered your paper today," he said, clearing up the confusion apparent in my face.

"Not mine!" I answered, "My Dad's the boring one." With an attempt at humour I thought we might be friends, but we were friends from the first second we met.

I stood back for Martin to get on the bus, and he did the same so that both of us ended up standing there waiting for the other. We both smiled, looking right at each other, a connection through British politeness.

There were some other school boys in the back seats making a noise, laughing and pushing each other, exactly what I was afraid of. I purposely did not go far on before I sat down. I took the window seat and lay my bag at my feet. There I just sat and tried to ignore everything that was going on around me, staring out of the window to the bus stop sign.

There were some older people nearer the front of the bus, and putting myself in their heads for a moment I knew that the noise was bound to be disturbing them. When you retire to a village like that, it is because you want peace. If Grandpa were there, he would no doubt tell those kids to 'belt up'.

Martin was hovering in the aisle and it took him a few moments to find the courage to ask if he could sit with me.

"Can I?"

I turned as though I had only just realised he were there, "Of course," I answered, glad that he wanted to. Perhaps he would be able to cheer me up a little.

I already liked Martin, despite the fact that he seemed quite guarded and nervous when speaking to me. Somehow he did have a calming aura to his nature. His quietness was an infectious relaxant, and I really needed that.

By the end of the bus journey, he had learnt not to be wary of me, and that he did not need to be so timid. I was the same age as him, lived in the same village and was going to the same school. But I was the one with a reason to be apprehensive. It was my first day there and I was the new boy.

"So what's it like?" I had asked Martin with a comical smirk, and he had said that it was 'fine, just a school.' But I could tell that he was being defensive. The question seemed to almost make him jump out of his skin.

I was close to certain that some of the boys in the back were making jokes about me. It could have been paranoia, but there was something about their laughter and a few of the words I picked out that made me worried. "What about the other kids?" I pressed in a whisper.

"I keep myself to myself," he said.

He never clarified what he meant, and that made me even more uneasy. The last thing I needed was to start getting bullied there. I would rather take my chances with the little people.

I had been reasonably popular at my last school. I didn't really have close friends but I had people I could speak to and I was certainly liked well enough. But now I had to start the whole popularity game a fresh, and it was not a game I really followed the rules to. I was simply myself and so far it had not got me into any trouble. But as the years of school go on, and you reach the ages of teenager, hierarchy starts to become more important. It wasn't something I was interested in, and I decided that I would simply follow Martin's example, and keep to myself.

I had been quiet for a while.

"I go to school to learn," Martin eventually continued his thread of conversation. "If I work hard enough I'll soon be finished with all of it and get on with life."

I definitely heard a hint of bitterness that could mean Martin might have had some trouble there, and he did seem particularly vulnerable. Yet his words were also very pragmatic for a boy of our age.

"Yep," I agreed, though I did like the idea of having some fun as well as learning. "School isn't forever."

He smiled at me, right at me this time, with his barriers breaking down.

"So why did you move here?" Martin changed the subject. "Where's Mr.Penrose?"

"That's my grandpa, my mum's dad, he's cool... But she needs to look after him, so we're here."

"Ahh," Martin seemed pleased. "How is he now?" With gossip obviously rife, Martin had no doubt heard that my grandpa had been taken to hospital. It was a small place and an ambulance siren would definitely have been noticed. He sounded genuinely concerned.

"He had a stroke, but he's fine, just can't walk too well."

Martin smiled again. He had a nice smile, his mouth kept closed, his lips swelling red. It made him look all the more a child, yet there was definitely a certain maturity to his conduct.

We were already destined to be close.

Having lost myself in speaking with Martin I had almost managed to forget about the inevitable destination of the bus. We had now reached the school however and the kids from the back were jostling along the thin aisle to get out first. One of them, a grinning thin boy with spiky black hair stopped the procession before our seats in gesture for us to get out ourselves.

Martin looked up at him and the boy nodded his head forward. Tentatively Martin got out from the seat and began to make his way along, and I followed.

"Thanks," I said, in respect of the courtesy, though I definitely had doubts about its authenticity.

I made my way down the aisle, the condemned, walking to my punishment. As I started down the two steps to the pavement there was a commotion and I felt a shove from behind which made me lose my footing. I was lucky not to fall flat, and Martin, standing waiting, grabbed me in order to steady me. He had real worry about his face.

I instantly knew that it was deliberate and shot my glance back at that spiky haired kid who was now contorted with his inane skull faced grin.

"Mind ya step," he said facetiously and rolled away past us with his entourage in tow. I knew without being told that I had just met one of those boys it was best to keep away from.

And so it began, the rough and tumble, the highs and lows and force fed socialness that was the secondary school system. Aesthetically drab, overwhelmingly constant, everything the woods were not. More than a few times I imagined I could be back there, sitting with the sunlight shining through the gaps in trees above me and warming my skin. The school felt like a prison from the outside world, it felt like a false manufactured reality.

I had to endure an overly formal meeting with the headmaster, lecturing me quite aggressively about school rules, conveniently forgetting that I was only twelve years old and therefore still a child.

The air of insecurity was that of an overly organised regime that threatened disruption at every turn. The timetable and complicated school map he gave me only increased my impression that I was completely out of my depth.

I was thankful for Martin, thankful that we shared most lessons with no sign of the 'ne'er-do-wells' from the bus. And later that day, I would also be thankful for Josh.

My last class was maths and Martin was not there. Basically, he was in the top form for everything but mathematics was never my strong point.

The lesson was run by one of those strict teachers I had imagined; very 'old school' in his brown tweed suit, side parted combed hair and his lack of pleasantries. I had no reason to feel frightened of him, but Mr. Jackson could make you feel that you had done something wrong even before you had.

I was neither the first or last into the lesson and a boy

seated in the middle, with big, highly styled blonde hair, looked right at me as though he had recognised me. He gave a nod, and I responded by returning the gesture although I knew that I had never seen him before.

He was not one of the boys from the bus; this I knew for a fact as that same group were sitting at the back of the class. Of course I recognised one of them; the spiky haired kid. What had my father said earlier? 'Know thine enemy.'

School was a war, and that lesson was a battle ground. As it turned out, however, although they tried their best to cause disruption from their back seated seclusion, none of them were any match for Mr. Jackson. He was on them like a hawk.

It was home time. I was relieved. I had survived. But it was then, with those kids probably feeling riled up by their inept fights with the teacher, that I got a taste of the bullying I had been afraid of all day.

I did not have my wits about me. I had my sights set on getting on that bus and getting home. I did not expect to have to check behind me, to be ready to defend myself. But I was only halfway along the corridor when I was suddenly grabbed and pushed up against the wall.

It was that spiky haired kid.

He pinned down my arms while the rest of his pack surrounded me. That ring leader facing me, too close, staring with beady ignorant eyes. He was trying to look menacing, attempting to make me feel small. And I *was* frightened of the confrontation. But I was also disappointed. I despaired at society I suppose, in my own twelve year old way. I was annoyed that I could not just get on with life without such unwelcome interference.

I think it is true that bullies are cowards. Making that first dominant move makes them feel on top. But they would only ever attack when they were in their group; and there was five of them and only one of me.

That spiky haired leader was not exactly large, but he was evil looking, as if a little damaged in the head and had nothing to lose. Those others followed him like mimicking shadows.

At that point my previous idea of spending the day in the woods made even more sense. I pretended that I was there. I imagined a host of faeries smothering those boys and pulling them all away. I moved my mind out from my body and out of the whole situation, just waiting for it to end.

"What are you doing at this school?" the leader said through gritted teeth. They always ask questions, yet they never want an answer. "You're not even Cornish, ya bloody English. We don't want ya 'ere London boy."

He shoved me, staring with his unintelligent mind ticking, pushing me harder, but I did not speak, I could not find any suitable words.

"Hey!"

A voice came, shouting at them, and I felt relieved though I could not see anything through the group of bodies. Whoever it was had caused them to disburse and I was glad that the ordeal would not be drawn out any longer. It had probably all happened in but a minute or two, but it had felt quite long enough.

The spiked haired leader let go of me and turned around to face the source of the voice. At first I presumed that the low authoritative tone must be a teacher, yet as the posse dispersed I saw it was the blonde haired boy from the last class. He was striding towards them all looking much more confident and menacing than the rest of them put together.

He was big, having a frame that was either built up through sports, or naturally grown to be two years ahead of its time. He could easily have been in his teens already, yet he was in my class. I could tell where he fit into the hierarchy, with those hyenas backing off like that, but why he was helping me I did not yet know.

"What's it to you Josh?" the ringleader said, trying to sound unperturbed by the threat. I could have rushed off at that point but I was too intrigued. I would stay and watch the show, and then meet the star, my saviour; Josh.

"This new kid ain't even Cornish," the kid went on.

"And you ain't even got a brain," Josh mocked, "So who are you to talk?"

They were right there in front of each other, Josh squaring up to the other who now looked particularly puny in comparison. He was trying to hold his ground yet I did not envisage an actual fight occurring, it would definitely have been one sided. The henchmen were standing back, just in case.

"He's got more right to be here than you have Liam," Josh explained with his thick neck craned. "His Grandfather happens to be Finn Penrose, and he also happens to be my neighbour."

There was a pause, eyeballs burning into one another, then finally Liam mumbled, backing off. "Sorry Josh, I didn't know."

"Didn't think," Josh said in a mimicked voice of stupidity, banging the palm of his hand against his forehead in gesture.

And now Liam walked away with the others at his heel, watching his back in case anything more was to happen. Josh stayed with me.

"Thanks," I sighed.

"I like any excuse to pick off that kid," he smiled at me with huge white teeth, not sounding at all menacing anymore. It had been quite an act.

"He only picks on people 'cause his father picks on him," Josh said. "But he's a waste of space. I'd feel sorry for him if he wasn't such a prat. Even if he gets through school after all his minching and causing trouble, what's he gonna do? He'll be lucky to get a job stacking shelves at Safeway. More likely to end up at her majesty's pleasure!"

I mustered a short laugh. "You know my grandpa?" I asked.

"Course... we all know Mr. Penrose. *And* I live in the house right at the end of the village... you seen it? Big white house. So I'm neighbour enough. Martin's my best mate."

It all made sense then, and I could smile for real.

"We stick together us, there isn't anyone else. Anyway, you best get home, I'll see you around."

"Yes... Thanks Josh."

So in one day I had made two true friends, and a few false enemies. I doubted that those kids would want to push their luck any further. I still didn't fancy getting the bus with them every day, but now Liam had been emasculated even more than he was being at home, I was probably safe enough. I would sit with Martin, chat only to him and keep my head down.

It was hard to get to know someone who was always so quiet. We had already spoken for quite a while, but I did most of the talking. The general impression I got was that he did not quite trust people, and was also not very well versed in the art of chat. I could tell that he was very clever though, and he was just out of practice.

We had some common interests, in reading books, and even in the idea of mysteries. But I had to slam on the breaks. It was a little early to be telling him my stories, though I really wished that I could just tell him everything.

When I arrived home that day I was in quite a good

mood, but was met with the sounds of Grandpa in the midst of a coughing fit.

I dropped my bag in the hall and rushed to his seat to check if he was alright. My mother was there already, kneeling beside him on the floor, and looked up at me as I came in. She appeared worried, but not overly so.

"You ok Grandpa?" I asked immediately and went to his other side. The coughing had a deep down rattle which sounded most uncomfortable and certainly unhealthy.

"Ah, I'll live," he spluttered, wiping his mouth with the outside of his wrist. "Well, this time I will. It's years of breathin' dust out the earth I expect."

"It's not miner's lung Dad," my mother answered, more relaxed now that the worst of his coughing was over. She turned on her scolding voice. "More something to do with smoking for thirty years I should think."

"We never knew the dangers of smokin' back then, we all did it," Grandpa argued. "Nature grew the darn plant so why shouldn't we smoke it?"

I perched on the edge of the couch, concerned.

Periodically he continued to choke and clear his throat but he was beginning to gain control of it and was looking at me. "That's rot of course, you take note boy. Not good for ya. Nature is cruel as well as kind. So just 'cause it's there don't mean it's for us to use as we see fit. Like that mushroom I told ya about. Some make a lovely meal, some kill ya stone dead."

My mother stood up from her stance beside Grandpa and came and sat next to me. She smiled warmly and put a hand on my leg.

"So how was school?" she asked.

I smiled to myself, "That was like nature too," I said, and glanced briefly at Grandpa, speaking for his benefit. "It was good and bad."

Dinner that night was on our laps as had now become usual. I was rushing my food a little, not really wanting to listen to the adult's conversations.

My father was taking the opportunity to speak about his job. He enjoyed telling us how important the next client was, how much money they were spending on a house, and how he, my father, had helped them choose it. He said that he had a 'lead' and that he could soon be making some big sales in other countries.

"Boasting again," my mother said in mock of him.

"Proud I am, not boasting," my father retaliated in good humour. He took another mouthful, chewing as if pondering something, and then gestured his fork in Grandpa's direction. "Finn... why did you say you weren't proud of working down the mines? Sounds like it was a family profession and all?"

"Hmm," Grandpa mused, his brain beginning to wind itself up before his mouth went into action. "You might not understand Thom, but us people, we 'ave forgotten respect. Whether we know it, and whether we 'ave a choice or not, we take from this world, and we don't give nothing back. It's just the age we live in."

My mother looked up from her plate as if to say something of her displeasure, but obviously thought better of it.

"It's the industrial revolution," my dad said. "It's progress!"

Grandpa looked disgruntled. "Progressing further from all that we were, 'n' what we're supposed to be," he said with a cynical tone. "We could have stopped 'progressing' an age ago 'n' we would 'ave been fine. What the world needed most was to be left alone!" He then tried to backtrack a little. "People need 'ouses of course, you're doing a decent job there Thom, not 'urtin' no one if they was there already. Wish they wouldn't keep building the bloody things though I tell ya.

"Too many peoples being born, that's the problem."

My dad laughed a little. I think he was a little embarrassed that he'd unintentionally riled Grandpa up. But he also wanted to carry on the mining conversation, despite Grandpa's diversion. "You're job was important though Finn, especially in the war."

"Ah! War," he scoffed. "Nothing important about that. They didn't use tin for weapons mind. Just as well, 'cause I don't know what would be worse, mining metal for guns or shootin' 'em myself. But those boys needed grub, so I was 'elpin' 'em survive I guess... that tin keepin' their food fresh. I wonder what'd have happened if we'd gone on strike then? They couldn't run a war like that so maybe they'd have 'ad to call it a day and come 'ome, stop the whole silly business. Humph."

Grandpa had worked himself up again, and began eating his food as if he were angry with it. My father seemed to be reining it in, words on his lips unspoken.

Grandpa looked up and pointed to me with his fork, bringing me suddenly to attention. "I'll talk 'bout mining sometime with young Adam... thinks he'll understand a bit... but it's a sore point wi' me now."

Why Grandpa should want to speak to me about it I did not know, because really I had taken no interest. Those sort of conversations were too much like a school history lesson, and school itself had turned my world secular enough already.

* * *

I missed those morning chats with Grandpa. I was getting to know Martin, and it was nice to be able to have a conversation with someone my own age, but I still counted the days to the weekend. For some reason,

I saw Grandpa as my closest equal.

I was set to have much less time to myself in the next couple of months and there was so much I felt that I wanted and needed to do. I had big plans, adventures to go on, things to see. It's strange that time appears so short when you are a child, even though in reality that is when time is most on your side.

In my mind, every weekend was fully booked.

"I should probably have taken you for a haircut Adam," my mother said one morning, "before you started at school. I'll take you on Saturday."

"No!" I had not realised how forcefully I was going to say that word before it left my lips. I think it shocked my mother and it shocked me a little too.

I never wanted to go in to town. It was quite odd that I had lived right in the thick of a much larger and noisier place my whole life, but now going into the hub of the streets made me feel completely out of my comfort zone. I was more frightened by crowds than I was of the trees. Such a short time living in the country and I already felt that was where I belonged. Brought up in the town, but a country boy in my heart and soul.

I really thought that I would never leave it.

"Ok, ok..." my mother tried to calm me, not realising that threatening to cut my hair would panic me so.

"What's the problem Samson?" my father joked from behind his paper. I did not understand the reference, and was more concerned with fighting my corner for two specific reasons: I did not want to waste any of my precious weekend going to the town or the hairdressers, and I did not want to look like just another school yard thug. The cropped cut that my mother seemed to always want me to have was no longer 'me'.

"I'm growing it," I explained.

My father laid his paper on the table and took a long

look at me, then smiled. Looking back at his wife he had decided to join my side. "Well... he's a trend setter Ann. It's the age."

I had not stood up for my own beliefs so strongly as that before. Perhaps things were changing. I had found out quite a lot about myself in that last couple of weeks. I had learnt to be alone with my own thoughts more, and to have more thoughts of my own. I had met challenges and had been brave in my facing of them. I had entered a world more ancient and more powerful than any man, and had stood my ground.

I was finding a proper foothold in life.
I was finding my place.

CHAPTER SIX

My place in the school was now becoming secured.

I almost longed for that bully Liam to single me out, one to one, just so that I could put him in his place as well.

No more would I put up with anyone making me feel small.

But despite the issues of the first day that gang of would be bullies did little more than make the odd remark, and I knew that they would not challenge me again. Perhaps they knew that I was now more confident, or perhaps they were simply threatened by Josh; for he and I were now firm friends.

Josh was an 'all rounder', good at a lot of things yet academically just doing enough to get through. He excelled at sports, not surprisingly, and yet he had little interest in them. He was actually very good with his hands and could probably have become a good tradesman of some kind, but his father was a businessman and there were definitely pressures on him to follow suit. His family were financially well off, and as far as I could tell it was a happy enough home.

I enjoyed his company, though he was not the same as Martin or I. He could still hold a good conversation, often turning it on its head with a propensity towards silliness. He would make what we were speaking about into a joke if he felt that it was becoming too deep and, therefore, 'dull'. But he was open and fun to have around.

Martin I got to know through persistence.

He lived at home with only his mother, after his parents were divorced. He did not see his father, and probing with more questions Martin admitted that he was 'better off without him'. He in no way had Josh's affluence but he did have the same pressure from his mother to succeed.

I did not think that there was any danger in Martin not doing well; he was obviously intelligent and had a very analytical mind. Yet he was certainly still capable of joining me in my flights of fancy and discussing my wayward philosophical theories.

We ended up in long conversations and it was not long before we engaged in debates about the realities of the supernatural world. We both understood that the subject was an open book and that often the simplest of things may have the deepest roots. I was pleased to find a cohort, and knew that, when the time was right, the little people could well become part of that discussion.

Martin and I would often end those turbulent days of learning and social intrusions at the school library. It was a calm sanctuary. Small, close, yet heaving with books in what appeared to be, at my first perusal, a completely haphazard order. A little time reading the tiny hand stencilled labels on the old wooden shelves soon made sense of it all.

There was a lot of non-fiction, and many of those books covered more alluring and important subjects than the school curriculum. I remember things I learnt there far clearer than any of the sanctioned lessons.

I instinctively knew where to look for the most interesting volumes. Crouching low to the ground, and in a dark corner, I found books on things such as film, art, music and then local history. That led me along to the best row; titles about mythology... and ghosts. Martin and I would sit and read them together for a while before catching the bus. We had learnt that if we waste some time, and catch the second bus home, we could avoid sitting with *those* boys.

One afternoon I was alone there, and discovered a book that I had never noticed before. My eyes singled it out, homing in upon the title on the spine. I knew immediately that it might well become my favourite; it was called 'British Folklore'.

I slid it out from between two much larger books, and moved out into a more comfortable area to take a closer look, the book treasured in my clasped hands.

There, on the faded dust cover, between the washed out artwork of a mermaid, a unicorn and a knight fighting a dragon, was a strange tiny man with dark skin. It was portrayed squatting upon a toadstool, dressed in tight green clothes and wearing a small, pointed red hat. He was quite an ugly fellow, with unkempt hair falling around his face in matted strands and a squashed, pig nose. But I knew what it was supposed to be; that it was a piskie.

There was some doubt as to whether anything in the text would have a basis in reality however, as I had also noticed, in one corner, the typical image of a fairy. Seeing that pretty ethereal female with its butterfly wings, delicate body and thin elfish face meant that the book might be more fantasy than fact. It was disappointing, yet at the same time relieving. If the little people knew that I existed, if they knew I was now making the woods my playground, I would be much happier if they did not look like that squat faced man.

I had been staring at that cover for a while, but then broke the spell it had on me, looking up and almost physically taking a deep breath to gain some stability.

I decided to take the book straight to the desk.

There stood the usual small, plump man who worked at the counter. He dressed in an appropriately brown, wrinkled suit, arranging cards in a small tin drawer. It seemed that he wanted to look important, and pretended to be all the more busy when he saw me coming, trying not to look up at me lest it prove that he was not involved in his work. He even held the cards close to him as if he thought I might want to peek at them.

His hair was dark and greasy looking and, as his head was lowered, I could not help but stare at it. He had bald patches where it was thinning, with long strands stretched over the gaps.

I stood there for some time, just waiting for him to acknowledge me.

Eventually he grabbed the book from my hands, opened it up, and shut it again, thrusting it back to me while I watched dumbfounded.

"Reference only," he said abruptly, in a voice too highly pitched for his frame. His tone expressed some annoyance at my ignorance of library rules and of how I had interrupted his solitary work.

I wanted to argue, because I had clearly seen names on the book plate. But I guessed that now the book was so old, they wanted to preserve it.

The little man refused to even look at me.

Eventually I moved away, taken aback by the rudeness of it, feeling a little angry and wronged. I kept staring down at the book with a real need to have it.

Martin and I would usually sit and read in the tiny dark study area with its few tatty desks, but it was certainly underwhelming. Those old desks were obviously ancient relics from school history, engraved with a thousand names, insults and declarations of loves. It wasn't really a place for a scholar like me to study the metaphysical world.

So I just opened the book where I stood, cupping it in my hands, hoping that Martin would soon show up.

The inside was yellowed with the torn library stamped paper I knew I had seen, still adhered to the left hand side.

The first stamp was dated as 1958 and it had last been taken out in 1979. No doubt it had survived the years needed to promote it to reference only status. But I could guess that it might well have been standing there on the shelf for all that time; uncared about for the last six years. Maybe interest in such things was waning, giving way to the technological age. Back in 1958 it had been popular.

I stopped my musing with a jolt in my head as I read one name written there from that year: Annie Penrose.

Sharply I turned, feeling too uncomfortable to be there with that thought, and I almost walked straight into another boy, a large heavy built body blocking my way.

"Adam!"

It was Josh.

"Sorry Josh, err... I was waiting for Martin."

"Yeah, I know. Little swot's doing some errand for the teacher! Anyway, he said he'd have to meet you at the bus stop. You gettin' that out?"

I looked down at the book I was now holding up to my chest as if I were shielding myself from his interruption. I was embarrassed by the cover and its title, thinking that perhaps Josh might think it childish.

"Apparently it's not for taking out," I explained.

Josh held out his hand.

"Give it 'ere," he said.

I passed him it and together we both looked over at the greasy little man working behind his desk, paying us no attention.

"I'll be able to get this out for you," Josh assured me. "You just get off to ya bus stop."

I was glad that he had come to my rescue again. He truly was a friend now. And I was also glad to see Martin hurrying along the road from the main buildings towards me. The library was right near the school gates, and the bus stop just outside.

"Sorry Adam," Martin said out of breath. "Did Josh find you?"

"Yes, it's ok Martin. He's getting me a book out."

We both looked round at the library door where Josh was now coming out with a huge smile on his face. As he got nearer to us he opened his bag, producing the book, and handed it to me.

"Cheers Josh, how come you're allowed to take it out?"

He leant back on his stance with his smile growing even larger.

"You do know that he's probably stolen that don't you?" Martin said quietly.

My heart skipped, yet it was really quite pleasurable.

Josh just grinned, and Martin's expression was of disapproving acceptance to his friend's rogue actions.

"It's yours now mate!" he announced.

At that point a long silver car pulled into the side of the road, and Josh's attention went to that. It was his ride home; an expensive, new looking, shiny car driven by a smart looking man that was his father.

"See you tomorrow!" he called as he made his way to its passenger door, still grinning uncontrollably.

I looked at the book in my hands, and I too smiled. It was probably not much of an injustice. I would treasure it more than anyone, and getting home to read it was all that I now cared about.

I wanted to immerse myself in that book and replace the school day thoughts with those more mystical and favourable. I doubted that my mother would even remember a book from all those years ago, but to think that she might once have had an interest in such things certainly pleased me.

There was, as I'd hoped, an entire chapter entitled 'faery folk'. As well as listed facts there were also short stories which were supposedly based on true accounts passed down through generations. I read them with my mouth gaped believing every single word, delving deeper and travelling further into that strange world with each story I read.

Through the written word, and by Grandpa's word of mouth, I was now becoming quite an expert. I would have been a very good pupil if I could have adopted the same passion for things like mathematics and science.

I realised quite quickly that there was a lot Grandpa had neglected to tell me about these creature's darker side. Things which he had only hinted upon were there in black and white. And the more I read the more I began to feel a sinking dread in my stomach, the kind of feeling that one gets from a fairground ride, dangerously enjoyable.

I read one passage after another, of people, not only children but grown men or women, being lost to the faerie world. It did not seem particularly awful to be taken by them, because their world sounded quite wonderful with food and wine and dancing, yet there was something very sinister about it. The idea gave me a funny feeling which I could not quite explain.

Perhaps that was the danger I faced by walking in those woods. Those were the whispered warnings spoken by the trees themselves. I risked being taken, living a breathing dream, a life out of place and wrong.

It gave me the shivers, yet enthralled me just the same. The idea that if the faeries favoured you, you could gain a kind of immortality at their pleasure. That hundreds of years in their world, to us were mere days. But it always ended badly in the stories, with the person returning to their own home where their previous life had long left them behind. From the time passed their families were gone, they were forgotten, and at that point, they turned to dust.

At least Grandpa had taught me many things that would protect me, and the book had taught me some more. By reading those things I was now prepared, aware and ready for anything that might come to pass. I would appease them and I would appeal to their better natures. I would not eat any faery food or take any of their drink. I would be safe.

But I did think that perhaps I might even want to be taken by them. To have that experience, to discover a world beyond our own, the underworld, the hidden dimensions. How amazing to know that those things were real, right under our noses, cloaked in the secrecy of myth.

Life was wasted in the stark secular realities of school. I knew which life I would rather choose, and how important I felt that all this had chosen me.

I might be growing older, but I would not have to give up the magic of childhood quite yet.

* * *

I could not get out of bed fast enough when I awoke to bright sun and the realisation of it being Saturday morning. I was not yet a teenager so did not feel the need to lounge in bed when there was so much on my mind. The word boredom seldom made sense to me, because the world was full of things you could do. Boredom is not really a lack of interesting pastimes, but the lack of interest in any of them. At twelve years old I was excited by every possibility and every unknown. At that age my enthusiasm for life, or at least for my free time, was an alarm clock that would allow me to waste none of it on too much sleep.

"Hey slow down!"

My father caught me running down the stairs, and then physically held me still to prevent me from barging straight into Grandpa's room.

"Your grandpa has the nurse in with him Adam, just go get your breakfast."

Thwarted, I resentfully followed my father's orders. He sat with me at the kitchen table reading his newspaper and drinking his coffee as usual. I was yet to see Martin actually deliver the paper. He must have done his rounds very early indeed.

"You going walkabouts today then Adam?"

"Probably," I said sulkily. I did, of course, very much want to go back to the woods that day, but I also wanted to speak with Grandpa, I had been waiting for that all week.

"Your mum's gone into town."

I metaphorically kicked myself when I realised it was not as early as I'd hoped and that my internal alarm hadn't realised the importance of an early start. The lounge clock mocked me and my mother's horrible washed out looking ornaments smiled at me sarcastically. I had always disliked them and I wondered how Grandpa felt about it, especially as his chair faced them all. Figurines of little girls and ladies in some kind of glossy white china, light blue dashes of paintwork highlighting parts of them in an attempt to make them less dull; it did not work.

As usual my grandpa's table was cluttered with his things including the tape player which I was itching to have a play with. I knew that I could not risk mucking about with it while he and my father were there. I could get away with helping myself to a sweet though, the bag miraculously having been filled again.

I sat on the edge of the sofa and popped it into my mouth, realising then that I could almost hear what was being said from Grandpa's room. I tried to suck the sweet as quietly as possible, so as to still listen. There was a familiar warmth to the taste which was definitely growing on me.

The voice I could hear was Grandpa's, and it sounded as though he were annoyed about something. The nurse was answering him but her voice was soft and quiet. I crept out into the hall to listen more intently.

"These days," Grandpa was saying, "they won't just let ya die. They wants to keep ya alive with ya insides rattling like a baby's toy."

"You may not want to take the pills Mr Penrose, but I am sure your family would rather you did."

The nurse was right; I wanted Grandpa to stay alive for as long as possible, forever. I wanted that with all my heart.

I felt sad to hear that Grandpa was fighting against the idea of taking pills, and that he wanted to be allowed to die. I was far too young to understand that concept, to realise that he was struggling each day and had probably just grown tired of it all. I only hoped that the nurse would continue to battle his stubbornness.

"And what's in these pills then?" he said, ignoring what the nurse had said, "goodness from the earth, or more 'orrible chemicals."

"Quite honestly I do not know..." the nurse sighed, "but isn't everything from the earth, in a manner of speaking?"

I heard what I guessed to be my dad pushing off his chair, the squeaking of wooden chair legs on shiny floor. Knowing that I was eavesdropping I quickly ran up the stairs, slowing down on the landing and trying to 'act natural' in case I was seen.

I had to sit in my room now, still feeling saddened and not sure whether to wait and speak with Grandpa or go straight out. I heard my dad knock on Grandpa's door and go in there, but then nothing.

After a time I settled into some doodling on a pad. I drew a scribbled picture of the tree in the woods, of the mushroom ring beneath it, and then I drew the figure I thought I had seen. My mind darkened with the imagery, yet at the same time was lightened by excitement. Staring at my finished work, ideas began to fill my head, and with a few more pictures those ideas became plans, and with those plans came that buzz for adventure.

I was conjuring up a whole project which grew in my brain like vines around the woods themselves. The evolution took hold within minutes, sprouting blooms each and every way. Ideas for the camp and a proposal to form a gang, a research group... With Martin and Josh at my side we could attempt to find the truths behind the world's greatest mysteries!

I presumed a facade of ghost hunting would be for the best, something my friends might find palatable. But I knew where my true interests lie.

My brain had become itchy with all its ideas. I took up the pad and pen and grabbed my bag which lay in the corner of my room, emptying it of school books before setting off downstairs. I paused momentarily outside of Grandpa's room and my dad, having heard my eager commotion, came to see me.

"Don't disturb your grandpa," he said, "I think he's having a sleep."

We were both looking at the closed door.

"Is he ok?" I asked, keeping my voice low.

"His blood pressure has gone up apparently. But it's alright Adam, he's ok."

* * *

I tried not to worry, but despite a head in the clouds of exciting plans, my heart was hanging low.

The weather did not help. Typical for an English weekend the sun had not held out, and there was a drizzly rain which felt as though the very wind were made of moisture. There were dark clouds in every direction. If it stayed as it was, or even improved, then the day could be saved, but darker, solemn, fun spoiling clouds were rolling in from the ocean ahead.

I was heading towards Martin's house, and that donkey which always watched me pass was right up by the fence. I took a moment out to trudge up the banking through long wet grass to go for a closer meeting.

The animal did not move away but raised its head a little as if to greet me. I put my hand out slowly and touched it upon the soft furry part above its nose, stroking it with the tips of my fingers. I think the poor thing had been rained on for a while, yet had no choice but to stand out there in the open regardless. Its course grey hairs were darkened.

I smiled and looked right into its eyes; black and beautifully shaped, as though wearing the makeup of an Egyptian queen with long dark lashes. From that I decided that it must female, and she did look very gentle and kind, those eyes sad and thoughtful. I felt her long pointed, soggy ears and her thin wiry mane.

"My name's Adam," I said. The donkey, of course, made no response. So I patted her again, hand flat against the course grey hair on her muscular neck. And then I left her to carry on that solitary life.

Martin's house was not far into the main part of the village. I knew my way around now. The village was so small that I had seen what it had to offer on the surface, but it was scratching beneath that which interested me. I was going to take Martin on that journey with me.

I hesitated at the garden gate, nervous because it was

the first time I had actually called for him. I knew that his house was number 23 and those iron numbers were clearly nailed onto the worn rotten wood of the gate.

I liked the way his garden stood out from the others by not trying to stand out. Yet despite being young, I also realised that it probably did not please the neighbours so much. The two houses beside it boasted their lushly green, neatly cut grass, Martin's garden was mainly dusty gravel, the greenery coming from the weeds which protruded from it and the few trees around the mesh fence which kept it secluded. It looked old and forgotten, but perhaps intentionally so, not succumbing to the peer pressures of next door.

I was staring maybe too long. I had not noticed the twitching of yellowed net curtains, the preface to my first meeting with Martin's mother. She now appeared, standing in the half open doorway staring at me from out of the dark shadow.

"You looking for my boy?" she asked me without a greeting.

The manner in which she secretly peered at me from the end of her wild unkempt garden made me think of a witch that did not want to be disturbed. She did have long straggly dark hair with some streaks of grey throughout it, but she was not exactly a hag. She was probably my mother's age, though not as pretty. And was dressed in white, not really what I would expect a witch to wear.

"Martin's not 'ere," she said, as I had been too slow to answer.

I was about to rectify my impolite silence, but she was already closing the door. "He's out 'n' about."

She had seemed rather wary of me and couldn't wait to shut the door.

Josh's house was up a long drive near that end of the

village. I could catch a glimpse of the big white house briefly as we passed on the way to school. After that the drive became nothing but the surrounding countryside and winding roads which distanced us from all other civilisation.

His house was right next to the church and I wanted to look around there at some point, and more importantly the old graveyard which circled it. Perhaps that was something our 'gang' could do together; seeking mysteries among the ancient dead. Walking in those places, healthy, young and alive in the sunshine had never seemed morbid to me, it had seemed somehow quite beautiful.

I had always been fascinated by the gravestones, trying to read the names that time had taken hold of, lichens covering the grey in yellows and white, growing over the indented words. It was time continuing and nature constantly living despite the death beneath. I used to take rubbings of them, paper pushed against the stone and scrubbing over it with a crayon. I guess I had never really thought that perhaps it wouldn't hold so much serenity if I had ever actually known death, if I had lost someone, if the name on the stone was Grandpas'.

Without really having taken notice of where I had walked, I had reached what I dubbed as the 'roundabout to nowhere', because the road ended and turned back at the coast. Lost in my head, trudging along the path surrounded by the houses of living people, I did not feel anywhere near as alive as I did when striding through graveyards. Within the ancient woods or amongst buildings of age I think I must have felt more grateful for my life.

I don't suppose I understood that way of thinking back then, but it is certainly true. Perhaps even at that young age I shared Grandpa's philosophies. Why *should* we be frightened of the cycle that is life and death? It is part of what we are. Everything dies if once it has lived. Though no one alive even knows what death is, and no one who has not yet died can tell you that life is all we have.

Filling my head with ghost stories over the years already made it impossible for me to believe that death was just an ending. And if every religion throughout the world and throughout history believes that we go on; then how can there not be some truth in that?

But we are not supposed to know. I think we would go crazy if we knew the half of what was going on in the world.

My head was full of thoughts, but only now do I actually understand what they were. I simply knew that I was trapped in melancholy, walking dreamily along the coastline. Perhaps the landscape was weaving a spell upon me. I was so close to death myself, if I were to merely take a few steps in the wrong direction.

I knew that some people, especially of my age, would not give a single thought to any of those things, refusing to open their minds or their eyes to see that which isn't directly in view. And was it unavoidable to lose sight as you grow older? It angered me that my own mother had once read that book on folklore, yet seemed to have conveniently forgotten all of it.

But Grandpa could still see well enough. He knew, as I now did, that the boundaries are never that clear, and many strange things happen, to very ordinary people. I wanted to investigate those hidden dimensions. I wanted to uncover things that would shock the whole world!

Until then I had all but forgotten what I was doing, what my plans had even been. I had almost forgotten that I was supposed to be finding my friends. I was nowhere near Josh's house now. Without even thinking or instructing myself to do so I had begun to head towards the woods. I would pass the place my family lived to where the faeries dwell, to where I belonged.

Perhaps I wanted to be alone. Perhaps I needed the trees to subdue the gloom which had now begun to germinate.

I had not even noticed the wind picking up over the coastal hills, or that the rain had stopped to give way to the spray. And for a moment I had not even noticed the two very recognisable figures on the cliff ahead.

"Hey!" I called, and then worried that I might have startled them. They were both so close to the edge. But they turned with a wave as I made my way up towards them. My sudden return to normality had probably surprised me the most.

Martin was wearing his usual burgundy coloured coat. As well as being far too large for him, and making him look much bigger than he was, I noticed that it was also inside out. The lining was showing, lightly coloured, and you could see the pockets hanging loose, unusable. I stared a moment, looked at Josh, but we said nothing. I presumed it was an unwritten rule that no one was to mention it.

"I tried to call... I'm heading to the woods, ya wanna come?" I always feared that my childish excitement was too overwhelming for Martin. But Josh never put a rein on his.

"The woods, yer sure, why? Which woods?" Josh asked at once.

"By my house... Old Bob's... You ever been there?"

Both of my friends looked confused and shook their heads. I could read in their expressions that they probably did not understand the need to go to such a place.

"I want to set up a camp in there," I grinned, and then let the smile fall away. I sounded like a child.

I had already begun to wonder if it was all such a good idea. But both Martin and Josh were happy enough to follow my lead. I looked back at my motley crew a few times as we trudged over the dark green and muddy field. Martin with his coat inside out, Josh looking far too tidy but thankfully not appearing to be bothered that his clean white trainers were getting filthy.

I was proud to show off the woods, just as if they were my baby, my creation. What they were was my discovery and that which I had more knowledge of than the two of them. This was my domain, shared with the little people in mutual respect. I was sure that we would all be safe, and welcomed, but I had remembered to put stale bread in my pocket, just in case.

Ahead of us those fields stretched on and the only break was that dark patch of trees to which we were heading. They stood out through the low cloud and grey sky, an ink blot on the dull canvas landscape.

I had not realised it but at some point Martin had slowed down to a stop. For a while my friends had been beside me but now it was only Josh and I.

We turned around in unison to see Martin stood stock still in the middle of the field, staring ahead. It did not seem as though he was catching his breath, it was something else. He looked paler than usual, dark clouds closing in from behind, the breeze pushing his dark hair forward, but Martin not moving with it.

"What's up?" I called back from where I was, having to raise my voice. I felt the wind catch me, and the gust throw moisture against my face. The sun had decided to stay away, hiding behind a veil not yet ready to begin the onslaught of summer.

"I don't feel right about that place," Martin answered, his voice was as quiet as ever yet it drifted towards me, taken up and delivered by the breeze. It made me feel vulnerable, so I marched back closer to him. What he had said stumped me for a moment, but it felt more important that I remove the obstacle to my future plans and speak with him about it.

"It's fine," I said, feeling as though I were lying. "Today's just gloomy, makes it seem strange."

I found myself holding the sleeve of his coat, tugging at it a little to practically pull him on. His eyes were focusing on the ominous patch of trees, and now I too felt the eeriness that the dull day cast upon them. But I did not want to think of Martin's fear as an omen. I knew that they would welcome me again, that they would be tame after the offering I had made to them.

He made a noise, a humming sigh, and he managed to force his feet into moving again.

"Just trust Adam," Josh said with a smile and a mischievous tone. And then followed me on, but Martin was still keeping a few steps back from the pace, as though he had become my shadow, or I had become his shield.

The dark bleak clouds continued to threaten, taking away even more light as we closed in, as if the sky itself had lowered its head to mourn. We all looked up and almost witnessed the exact moment that the rain broke through, rushing forwards as the huge drops came down, to use the woods as shelter. They may well have felt more benign to Martin then, as they suddenly became very useful.

It was drier inside with the roof of leaves and branches. Although the rain was now pelting down hard, within the woods it was merely dripping.

I continued to lead, parting the best route through the brush, holding back some of the long twigs so that they did not spring back at my friends. It might have been darker amongst the trees, but to me it felt far less dour, it was alive, tingling with the fresh new water. You could practically hear the ground drinking in the rain and the snapping sound of buds opening up into flower. I had been longing for that moment all day.

"Follow me," I said after giving them a moment to acclimatise to the other world we had entered. And I made a forwarding gesture with my hand, smiling and trotting off along the path I now knew well. I was heading to the wood's best exhibit, the camp that I had found for us all, once hidden but now found.

Josh appeared to be looking forward to seeing it. On the way I upped my hand a little by telling him it was haunted in there, trying to keep my voice down so as not to scare Martin further. Of course, only I knew what I really meant.

Although I was excited about sharing the camp I soon began to regret my decision to take my friends there. Looking back at the stragglers I started to feel somewhat embarrassed. The way in which Josh was speaking so loudly, stomping clumsily through the sacred place was making me cringe. He even proceeded to pointlessly pull leaves off their branches as he pushed through the thickets.

And Martin was not as respectful as his usual demeanour would suggest, stepping on flowers without even looking. I was a little ashamed, and growing ever more nervous of what they might do next. The woods required dignity and it was my job to ensure we showed them no disregard.

I was worried the whole time, that my friends might completely 'spoil relations' between myself, and *them*.

I kept up my pace towards the camp, but continued to stop occasionally to see them both ambling towards me, their mannerisms continuing to make me recoil. Perhaps not everything is better shared. Maybe some things are only precious when they are yours alone?

I guess I had opened myself up to jealousy. The woods were mine, and I did not want them being there to make it any less my own. Selfishly, it was only the camp I wanted to share, and not the surrounding setting which I held such reverence for.

How could I expect them to understand the delicacy of nature, or the hidden creatures which dwelled secretly around those foundations? They saw the place as nothing more than a bunch of trees to frolic amongst, and perhaps it was safer to let them think that was all they were.

Both my friends were now quite a way behind me. I had hurried forwards, turning my head around regularly to check on them.

On seeing the bowl of milk ahead I quickened my pace and checked again that they would not see what I was about to do. Crouching down I attempted to steal my emotions on seeing it almost gone, having been drunk, either by some woodland creature or by the faeries themselves.

Very quickly I held the bowl to my nose before tipping away the remainder of it and discreetly hiding the evidence into my bag. The book I had been reading confirmed a belief. The little people were known for spoiling food and turning milk sour. Sure enough, there was very little left in the bowl, and what was there had smelt foul and sickly. It was hardly even liquid anymore, more a kind of thick mush which now clung to the leaves I had thrown it amongst.

Martin was catching up and I hoped that he would not have seen what I had just done and start to ask awkward questions. I also hoped that the smell of that stuff had faded away. As a diversion I went to him instead. I pointed in another direction, and lead my friends off towards the great tree, the centre of it all.

"It's great in here don't you think?" I said, not really expecting an answer, but rhetorically speaking in appreciation. "You feel better now you're actually in here?" I then asked, directly addressing Martin. This time I did want to know how he felt, looking back at him with more intent.

"It's nice enough... but..." His eyes were darting about as he walked beside me. "It feels like something's watching me, like... I don't know."

I had a big grin on my face as he spoke, and I could not hide it.

"What?" he asked of my expression.

"I know," I said, "I knew you'd feel it!" It felt invigorating.

But Martin appeared to grow quite anxious as we stood still in the shifting lights of the woods. I was glaring at him, trying to understand his unease with enthusiasm in my eyes.

"Martin often thinks he can sense things," Josh spoke up as he came closer.

"Really?"

Martin was squirming under my scrutiny somewhat.

"He's sensitive aren't you mate?" Josh teased.

"I'm *A* sensitive," Martin corrected. "That's what my mum calls me. She thinks she's a medium, 'in touch' with the spirit world."

"Cool!" I could not help myself.

"It's not," he said bluntly. "I don't trust her at all. She reads people's fortunes for money. But I *know* things exist."

I was excited now; it was the perfect opening to my pitch for the club. Martin would be a great asset if he could perhaps sense if somewhere was strange or haunted just by going in there. He might know where *they* were, where they were hiding. I was listening with my mouth agape and I didn't want to let it drop despite Martin now becoming quite agitated by the conversation.

"It scares me."

He seemed to shrink further into that massive coat, looking straight up at me, meeting my eyes even though he had been trying to avoid them. Big green dark eyes which told of deep knowledge he might rather not have. But his voice was very much that of a child.

It was obviously reassurance he wanted, and not my eagerness for mysteries. I felt bad to have pushed him, yet I so desperately wanted to ask more questions. Now I was worried that he might be too afraid to join in with my plans at all.

My mind worked through ways that would help persuade him and not scare him from it. Yet for the time being I had to be unselfish; the caring friend.

In silence we took up walking again until the tree was upon us.

"This tree is the wise man of the woods," I announced, standing with my hand on the bark, displaying it as act one to the whole piece.

"An oak," Martin said, but he only shot a brief glance at me. I did not really have their attention. Martin was standing some way back amongst a crop of dying, faded bluebells and Josh was meandering behind him.

For perhaps different reasons to my own, Martin seemed to be losing himself in the place. There he was, his feet lost in the sea of foliage, looking up through the branches despite drips of rain still penetrating through the mesh cover above us. And there was I, admiring the oak tree again, its age, its wisdom, holding both palms against it as though some of its knowledge might flow into me.

I side stepped around it, still holding its body, wasting time to wait for Martin to come yet enjoying that moment. I was happy to be alone. For some reason I felt they were both a million miles away. I was lost in my own bubble.

Below me something caught my eye, not a movement, but something out of place. I shot my attention down at my feet to see it. A slice of bread.

I stood with my hands still firmly on the tree, staring at it, my focus perfectly clear and unmistaken. Of course I first thought that it might be the bread I had brought there myself, but I knew sensibly that it wasn't. That was still in my pocket, broken up, and crumbling.

The oddness of it came lucid and with uncomfortable clarity into my consciousness. I was lost within my head, bending my knees and slowly lowering myself to the ground, curious to check that what I was seeing was solid and legitimate. Yet I was frightened of what I might discover.

I crouched beside it; I physically poked it with the tip of my finger, only to find that it was soft and very real. It was not even stale. It was light beige coloured, and looked perfectly fresh and edible.

First peering my head around the tree to check where my friends were, I gave it my full attention. Stabilising myself with a hand on the moist dirt ground, I quickly opened my bag with the intention of taking the bread as a specimen.

I may have been crazy, but I truly believed that *they* had left it there. I even contemplated that it might have been placed purposely for me to take, that they wanted me to have it. Faery food, perhaps there to tempt me, to take me into their world just as I had read.

I *was* hungry, but I would not eat it. I was too clever for them. To me this was a piece of evidence, a puzzle for me, as the self appointed leader of the group, to solve.

I grabbed up the pliable slice of bread to discreetly tuck it away from sight, and as I did so I heard a noise. It was faint, and distant, but an identifiable sound. It was the gentle single ring of a tiny bell.

On hearing it I rushed to my feet, zipping the bag up and attempting an air of composure as I came from behind the tree to join back with my group. There stood Martin with a bluebell stem in his fingers, looking down at its flower, robbed of its former glory, yet Martin was enchanted.

Time ceased, but only seconds passed. I was unnerved by the whole chain of events. And at that point I truly felt the need for their company.

"The camp's not much further."

Martin dropped his bounty upon the ground; picked from the earth and now left dead upon it. I felt a strange sadness as I saw it slowly fall, now lying limp amongst its living clan. In my head I heard Grandpa's words of distaste about the way human beings take from the world. But it is not because we are abominations of nature, it's because that *is* our nature.

I could not tell Martin that I felt so bad about it, or chastise him for doing that. I had two options, I could join Grandpa in my discord or I could accept it as it was. I think I have struggled with that choice all my life.

And so we joined back up and carried on through what was a more thick set part of the woods. It was even darker there with shades more of brown than of green. To me, it felt that the ground we walked on was very old, as though the trees at the beginning of the woods were the children to this, the formidable deep rooted wise men of bark. Not so much that each tree had a great age, but that perhaps the very earth where they stood had been important for many more years, and seen many things. Perhaps the little people spent more of their time in that part of the woods, in the seclusion of dense darkness.

The rain took up hands with the feelings of awe and murkiness and increased its power. We could hear it suddenly battering down hard upon the canopy, and despite the number of trees which mingled their branches above us, the huge drops were coming through and we were now getting quite wet. It fitted my mood, though I really wanted to snap out of it.

I led the way quickly to the camp which was close ahead, and without having time for any grand introductions I parted any weeds and vines that were hanging over the entrance to allow Martin to run in, and I followed in the hope of gaining its shelter. Josh was last in, standing outside for a time to admire what I had found.

"Now *that's* a camp!" he exclaimed, suitably impressed. And then, almost as if he knew exactly how to get to me in my current mood said, "I'm glad *we* found it!"

He took no more time in contemplation and was stepping over the tangled web of bramble to get in through the door, looking around the interior with real interest.

"We'll need some of my dad's tools," he said surveying the situation, "break down all the mess." He was touching the walls as if he were a builder checking the craftsmanship.

Although there was not much room for the three of us with so much growing inside, it felt almost warm, and safe. It was noticeably dark but the rain seemed unable to get to us there.

Martin had his face up at the glassless window, trying to lean through it, though it was a little too high. It appeared to have captivated his imagination as much as it had mine.

We hadn't much choice but to stay in there a while, protected from the downpour, so I decided to 'bite the bullet' and took the opportunity to tell them my plans. I skated over talk of little people or indeed any of the things I had witnessed. I merely explained how ghosts had intrigued me for as long as I could remember and that no one seemed to investigate it or try and find proof. I said that is what I wanted us to do.

The idea, I said, was to delve into mysteries rather than spend our lives in the mundane. It was to fill our heads with things that were not so secular because that always made the world seem so much richer and full of wonder.

My pitch started off restrained, purposely reining it in as I knew that it might frighten them off. But as my eagerness increased I could sense my intensity becoming a bit much for Martin.

Perhaps it *was* all too much, and the noise and excitement from three teenage boys was a violation.

"I'm not sure you would want to go around finding the truths to all of that, if you actually knew the truth," Martin said. His serious tone sometimes chilled me. It sometimes seemed like an older person was living in his head.

But I knew by now that Martin's will was bendable and all he needed was encouragement and persuasion. I could deliver both of those attributes to the gang.

Josh was a willing recruit.

"So ya wanna know 'bout ghosts now do ya?"

Martin actually put his hand over his face and shook his head. I had never actually asked but Josh had started now, and I had realised that there was never any stopping him.

"Have you seen that house opposite mine?"

Martin let his hand fall and his flushed face was suddenly ashen. He said nothing but looked imploringly at Josh while he spoke. It was obvious that such talk made Martin uneasy.

"No," I said at last, "haven't noticed it."

"It's haunted," Josh said without a hesitation, as if he knew for sure.

Martin hugged himself as though he had suddenly become cold. Standing huddled in the camp there was a chill, but it was the conversation which was freezing him.

"I've never liked that house," he said, looking at me, "And I don't think any of us should mess about with it."

I ignored Martin's words. He no doubt knew me well enough to tell what track my mind was working on.

Josh continued. "It's no secret why that house has had so many people come 'n' go... It's 'cause no one wants to stay there. No one can put up with living there.

"Story goes that a young girl, good-looking, raven haired, curvy body..." Josh had a smirk and a glint in his eye. I would have presumed the story he was about to recount was just for fun if Martin's reactions were not there to take stock of. He must have heard the tale before, maybe many times, but he was definitely finding it unpleasant.

"She went mad, they said. For weeks people could see madness in her eyes that wasn't there before. Like it was a disease, widening her pupils' 'n' paling her skin. It was real gradual, everyday getting worse."

Josh was enjoying the fact that he had me as a captivated audience. He was putting on a spooky voice, which although a little comical, had me enthralled.

"One afternoon she came out of the house making merry hell, screaming and crying, throwing a fit. And she was yelling 'n' ripping at her own clothes. Everyone started coming out their houses to see what was going on, and she was stood there, naked as can be, thrown all her clothes off and standing there crying and staring at the house."

He left a dramatic pause and searched with his eyes... then stared right at me for the finale. "Turns out she had murdered both her parents, stabbed 'em to death and the blood was stained on her pink dress. Seems that once it was done she had come back to her senses, seen all that blood, and couldn't bear it. She wasn't mad anymore, she was as sane as we are, like something had made her that way... that house. But the grief and guilt was enough to send her back to insanity. She hung herself in her cell before the case was ever tried."

I had clung to every word, and every word was spoken slowly and clearly so that it echoed around the woods and my head, playing out in my imagination. It was quite a story.

"Take no notice of him Adam," Martin said, "there's no reports of any of it, it's just a folk tale."

Perhaps Josh had been allowed to watch too many video nasties, but it had certainly got me thinking.

"Is that right?" Josh challenged his friend. "Well, I never knew them, but the family who moved into the house last said you could hear crying, every night, real quiet so that you would have to question what you 'eared, but they were pretty sure and pretty scared. And they didn't know anything about the girl or the murders either. And the noises were getting worse, there were bare feet running on the floorboards and the slamming of doors despite the fact that their real doors never moved.

"They just couldn't live there anymore. The man's hair had gone grey over a month, he looked like hell, never slept, spending every night in fear of what noise would startle him next. And he was getting irrational, going *mad* some people were saying, it was wrecking their marriage. So they left and got a house down the street... been empty since then 'cause no one can live there."

"It's probably condemned." Martin said logically, though his arms were still around himself as though the whole thing made him shiver.

It was all very creepy, and standing there, in the camp, within the woods, just magnified every emotion.

At least I now knew that Josh was interested in it all.

My intention would not be to search out the truth behind the ghostly noises, trying to disprove them, saying that it was just a creaky floorboard or bad pipe work. I wanted only to indulge my wish that life was not all it seemed to be. I was interested in finding more things that proved that there was, in fact, more to it, rather than explaining it away.

"We should definitely check out that house!" I announced, ignoring the obvious recoiling of my only other group member.

"Yes, definitely," Josh agreed. "I'm up for that. So what's the story of this place? Is it really haunted?" he challenged, leaning back with a smirk.

I felt a lump in my throat stopping me from speaking. I couldn't really follow his great story and my thoughts were trying to form a suitable cloaked reply. I could only think to tell them what Grandpa had said about Old Bob. I embellished however, telling them that at night Bob still roams about, lost and looking for home.

"Is that so? Well I bet you wouldn't dare stay here all night to find out?" Josh said.

"No, that's a stupid idea," I quickly answered defensively. I cannot begin to tell you how awful the idea sounded to me, and Martin obviously felt the same.

"If we're supposed to be looking for proof we should all do it," he carried it on. I could tell that he was actually quite serious. His face was straight.

"No way my mum would let me," Martin said, turning to face us both now. And Josh's eyes then went straight to me. I was not as quick to think of an excuse.

"Me and you then?"

I felt physically sick at the thought of it, scared to even consider doing such a thing. Not only would it be completely black in there at night; so dark that you would be unable to see your own hands; but I actually knew what might truly lurk in there once the sun had gone down. There was no chance I would ever be persuaded to do it, yet I had to think of a way to evade Josh.

"No," I said eventually, "it's dangerous, seriously, you could get hurt."

"Oh ok, I get it. Well if you two are too chicken I'll just have to do it on my own."

Martin and I could not believe that he would stay there a night completely alone, we all looked at one another, an exchange of mixed thoughts that none of us actually voiced. I personally just hoped that he would not go through with it and that, in time, he would forget the whole idea. His attention span was certainly much shorter than that of Martin and I.

Already he had bored of the discussion and had wandered outside the camp. I could hear him kicking things about out there and it made me uneasy, but I was glad of his absence.

Martin looked at me, an innocent face that made me feel instantly wrong for having told those haunted wood stories.

"Not all of that was true," I whispered to him. "My grandpa told me someone disappeared here that's all." I shrugged my shoulders to soften the blow of my deceit but I now believe it was not that which bothered him.

"Well something's here," he said, looking back out of the window.

I stood there, feeling that I was on my own inside my mind, feeling anxious. But I was not alone; if I were I might have enjoyed the time of contemplation, but worrying about my two friends just put me on edge. I wanted to head back.

Martin said that he would call Josh through the window, just for the fun of it, and I watched him put his head back through the frame. As soon as he had done that though, he stepped back away suddenly as if something had pinched him. And he stood with me in the middle of the tower, his face had fallen, a brief humour had now become fixed and serious. He stood unmoving with his eyes still trained on that glassless opening.

"What's up?" I asked him with a slight nervous laugh.

"I saw something," he said blankly.

I did not speak, just going through a list of possibilities in my head. But anything was possible with such limited information. We were both quiet and both looking out onto the wood through that little window, wondering, and feeling a strange unease.

It could have been nothing, it could have been an animal, yet I knew Martin well enough to believe it was more. I desperately wanted to know, yet at the same time, I kind of wanted him to forget it. We spoke no words.

Suddenly Josh jumped in at us scaring us half out of our wits, making some stupid noise that was supposed to resemble a ghost. He found our shock most amusing.

"Scared ya?" he laughed. "Hey what's up?"

Although he had startled us, we were keeping silent with eyes firmly fixed at that gap.

"Martin?"

CHAPTER SEVEN

With the rain calming back down to a drizzle, we decided to make our way home. We had probably outstayed our welcome, and I would be glad to go, and get my friends away from the woods.

Martin had promised to lend me some books so I walked back with them across the far side of the field rather than head back to the cottage.

I could see how he drifted towards the coast unintentionally, his body falling heavier on his right side so that he would have to physically align himself back to the path. It made me laugh a little, putting me in mind of someone who'd had too many drinks making their way back from the pub. I supposed it was habit, because he always liked to look at the sea. From where we walked it was just out of view with the brow of the cliffs and the white of the clouds hiding it from us.

Josh made his exit at the crossroads, grinning from ear to ear. He had been pacing ahead already, fired up by all that we had seen and spoken of.

"I'll see ya soon... We'll break into that house and find some real evidence!"

I could not help but worry that I had just unleashed a monster.

The rain had already flattened my hair as though I had just stepped out of the bath, and halfway to Martin's house it started to get heavy again. We had to speed up our strides with salvation not far away and I was now nearer his home than my own.

It would be worth it; the dreariness of a wet Sunday looming into mind meant that I could really use some new books to read.

We laughed as together we began to run, the rain now

coming down so hard that it was impossible to ignore. Trying to stay dry while the elements did all in their power to soak us to the bone was becoming ludicrously funny.

We had no cares anymore. We skidded round the corner and down the drenched street, Martin swinging his gate wide open and I, immediately halting my laughter, as I stood at the end of the garden path.

His mother was there, door open, towel in hand which she threw over her son as he stepped into the entrance. He was still chuckling, but something about that woman's stern face, made me uneasy.

Martin was gone, lost into the house, and his mother and I were eyeballing one another across the distance, my face damp and drops dripping from my nose. I could not read her thoughts, I wondered if she was reading mine.

"You staying or coming?" she said at last. It was matter of fact, but there was no animosity, it was an actual question. Though I guessed it was phrased in order of preference.

"I need to get home Mrs. Kendall, Thank you. Martin is just..."

And he returned into view. I had the sense to walk a little up the path and take the few books from him. And he smiled at me before making a retreat.

I stood on the path as the rain soaked me cold, opening my bag to deposit the books. There was little point in rushing. The rain was beginning to let up again but my thin jacket was already dark green rather than its usual light colour. I was sodden, right through to my T-shirt, and I was shivering and feeling clammy, the temperature of the air warmer than my body.

I looked down at the open bag, having favourably forgotten the disquiet caused when putting that slice of bread inside. It was still there, and so were the confused emotions. It was still a mystery.

Walking back alone, the despondency I had felt so deeply earlier that day was back with me, sucking my will like a vampire. Only occasional drops of rain hit me now, but they had finished me off already. The sky was as dark as twilight, and there was a gloom to the fact that no sun had shown its face for hours, and it would not be long before the night took its hold.

The day had been both fun and strange, and for some reason my emotions had been intensely raw. I had been feeling melancholy overshadow my thoughts, and it was melancholy in the true sense that there was serenity in my sadness. I was maudlin for the whole state of the world and the whole human condition. Though I didn't realise that I had been coherently thinking of anything.

I was completely rooted within my body, in tune with the fact that I was human. I did not care about time, future or past. I did not care about the weather. I was experiencing nature's forces with my soul somehow both at peace and at odds with the earth on which I walked. In an almost dream like state I allowed my feet to move with no instruction, following the pattern and journey instinctively known. Lost in the present I moved on to the place in which my body must dwell.

I turned my head to see the donkey I knew would always be there. That darkened, mud drenched field seemed a harsh place to be alone in. And as always she had that same constitution which I now shared, of general, sombre contemplation. Perhaps she knew more than we did.

She was staring away from me, unmoving yet with her eyes obviously focusing upon something.

Silence was a voice that whispered. The light changed, a speck of sun piercing through a tiny gap of cloud as the rain became droplets. Mist or perhaps even steam from the earth and drying rain was hazing my own view as I strained to look, yet something had caught the attention of that animal, something else moving within its field. And it was that something to which I now focused towards, adjusting my eyes to see it and make sense of it. A twisting shadow by the horizon; spinning perhaps, slowly yet also with some buoyancy about its progress.

The grey backdrop of moist air, dispersing mist and dark sodden ground was surreal, making everything feel out of place. But this thing I watched was of its own, something from an unfathomable dream.

Devoid of sound it twirled, a circle bobbing low and high above the flattened soaked grass and around through the mist. Not quite close enough to make out distinctly yet the shapes it was formed of could surely only be those of people... of tiny dancing circling people.

With my heart holding its beat and with my breath stopped I squinted and stared, and that donkey stared also. We watched together, the spinning, slowly ever spinning people; featureless, smooth, thin and unclothed. They seemed to be joined by the hands and gently kicking up the mist into clouds that surrounded their dancing, obscuring them, and then revealing once more.

It should not have been, yet I swear that it was. And this anomaly had not only violated the animal's field but was also infiltrating every sense of my own psyche. We watched it together, we shared the moment.

For what felt like long minutes, yet may well have been a mere glimpse within seconds, I was in the same world as the donkey. We had both lived through those moments, there together, eyes drawn into the desolate field. And although now the brow of the hill, the mist and sky, had taken that vision away as though it were never there, I knew in my soul that I had seen it.

It felt right. It felt justified.

And I had experienced it by myself, yet not alone.

* * *

"What's the matter boy? You've got a face like a white washed wall."

I had entered the lounge still held within a daze, still dreaming, but my grandpa had been looking at me for a while before he spoke. To some degree I had seen him sitting there, yet I did not feel quite in the same room or the same time. I think that somewhere in my head, I was still lost within the mist of that field.

I stood unmoving and he sat forward on his chair, examining me, that voice I had heard from somewhere close, full of concern. Through glazed eyes I could also see that same emotion in his expression.

I think I had heard my mother say "You need to get yourself dry Adam... go on..."

But memories were so vividly replaying in my head that concentrating on the moment was proving a struggle. I had not even thought about how wretched I must have looked.

Later, during dinner, my grandpa continued his intent scrutiny. His stricken face was completely readable; deeply worried for me. I think that he must have known something had happened, and no doubt he wanted to ask. But the evening went by without a mention.

I myself had never been so quiet. Twelve years old and already run out of things to say, or rather, of ways to avoid those millions of untold declarations. I took myself to bed early that night, after my first taste of Cornish pasties. I was tired and my head was buzzing so loudly with thoughts that I needed the quiet and seclusion to hear them coherently.

It was always very quiet in my bedroom.

The weather was calming down from its day of turmoil though the breeze still whistled outside. Occasionally it sounded as if it were whipping through the house, playing tunes with the pipe work. But even when the wind blew stronger those natural sounds did not really break the air of silence, but became part of it.

Some nights I used to think the branches of the trees in Grandpa's garden were all tuned to different notes with the sole purpose of giving the wind an instrument with which to sing. It was a peaceful song, soothing the harrowing feeling of disquiet which had taken space in my mind.

I knew that I would not find sleep easily so decided to look at the books Martin had lent me.

They were in the same bag as that bread... I took them out carefully so as not to disturb my evidence. And I looked down at it suspiciously, suddenly feeling the shivers and throwing the bag gently into the corner.

I was pleased to find that one of the books was not just about ghosts but entitled 'mysterious creatures'. I lay in bed, turning the pages as though they were heavy weights, occasionally eyeing the bag that was lying there, with *that* inside of it.

I almost felt it looking back at me.

Soon my lethargy began turning to intent as I sat up to read further. The section on faeries was short, and I knew much of what was there already, but I had been made alert by stories of little people within the mines. It did not tell me much, but I knew that Grandpa could tell me more. It was duly added to my mental list of questions and to my encyclopedia of faery lore knowledge.

Sleep was threatening with every blink but I feared the

dreams my addled mind might throw at me. That evening had opened my eyes and I was not sure if I would ever be able to peacefully close them again.

It was then, with some shock, that I turned the final page of the chapter.

I was confronted with an artistic image depicting a scene so like the one I had witnessed, that it took me back there with an unwelcome jolt. My eyes widened as I stared at it. Semi-light and dark shades of paint showed grasses and foxgloves parting the way for the group of little people hand in hand in a perfect circle. The wind was amongst them as they were seemingly portrayed in their dance of moving just as I had seen them, around and around.

Such an image would not have even been within my psyche till now, proving to me that I could not have imagined it. The recognition was astounding. It was just as I remembered, though clearer without mist or warping from distance. They were just people, drawn with no wings, so quite unlike the typical Victorian fairy images I had seen over and over. The only wings in the picture were those of a bat flying above them in the twilight sky.

I looked long and hard, and the more I looked the more it drew me into that connection. It was so frighteningly real, and so very close to accurate. But I knew that, at last, I had witnessed something tangible. I wondered; had the painter himself seen what I had seen?

And then it was only after I stole my eyes away from the image that I saw the words beneath, words of warning which struck yet another chord.

'*Never enter a fairy ring*'.

It was late. I crept out onto the landing, feeling quite shaken, but needing to use the toilet. Clawing for the light switch I noticed a faint voice. It came not from my parent's room, but from downstairs. And I knew that my mother and father had come up to bed some time ago.

I stood in the darkness and I listened, wondering if I had been mistaken.

But it was Grandpa. For some reason he was still awake, and was in the lounge speaking to himself.

Strange though it was, I really wanted to go down and speak to him. I had to fight with the urge. And I knew that it would have to wait until morning.

I did not expect to manage sleep, yet sleep I did as dreams certainly found me.

They were worse than I had dreaded and definitely not the normal dreams of a child. And they were more than nightmares. It was not that I felt I was there, within the world my dream conjured, but rather that it was not even my own mind that concocted its imagery.

As I tussled, twisted and turned, something was playing within my brain, something was painting for me a dreamscape that I had no choice but to experience, and the brush man was extremely skilled in showing to me the most hideous of forms.

When morning came I did not feel energised by a night of rest. I felt that my mind was even more disturbed and my body was aching as though I had physically played out each one of those dreams.

For the first few moments I was unsure if I was actually awake, and that if I was, had I in fact just lived through hours of strange activity? I had to reacquaint myself with normality, with my room, and with myself.

I leant forward to open the curtains and allow the light in. Briefly I saw the woods, until I moved away and they fell from my view. But I swear that they were getting closer.

I felt an urgency to go and check on Grandpa. I had things I wanted to chat with him about anyway, but those dark thoughts of death still prevailed.

I put my clothes on as quickly as possible, but as I lifted my legs into my jeans I felt each muscle tense as though they had been worked too hard already, and my arms were painful.

Carefully rolling back the sleeve of my pyjamas to see why my forearm felt so tender, I saw a real bruise, navy blue, two marks and pale skin between. I knew it was *them*. This was the final affirmation.

After a struggle I was finally dressed and made my way down stairs. I did not understand the shock that was in my mother's voice when she saw me. "Adam what's the matter with you? Look at your hair... are you ok?"

I guessed I looked tired, dishevelled, I certainly felt that way. But I did not know the extent of it. I lifted my hand and felt at my hair, ruffled and knotted. And as my arm lifted I felt sharp shooting pains up my spine as if I had spent the entire night unnaturally twisted. I winced. Perhaps I had caught the flu by getting so drenched with cold rain.

"I'm fine," I lied, wanting only to get in to see Grandpa.

I knocked at his door, heavier than I had meant to, and waited a few seconds. I heard nothing, no nurse today, no rustle of book pages or bed covers. I did not usually hesitate in going in, but I was nervous and I just stood there, lost in the stillness. I did not like the silence of it. I wanted to see and hear him, alive and well.

When I hastened my entry, I found him lying there, not sitting up as usual, but lying with his face up to the ceiling. And so I began to shuffle towards the side of his bed, a little afraid, but wanting so badly to be close to him.

I wanted to tell him everything, I wanted to understand. Speaking with him always felt both relaxing and thoroughly intriguing. Our chats ignited dormant feelings, and explained things I had never even queried. Today however, I had a thousand questions.

I was cheered then by his sudden squirming movements inside the sheets, like a caterpillar struggling in its chrysalis. He made a few bear like grunting noises to demonstrate his efforts.

"Grandpa? Sorry, did I wake you up?" Though I was actually relieved.

He made more noises as his head came up like a turtle from its bed shell and he struggled up against the headboard, pulling himself on to shore.

"Sorry boy... Late night," he said, sounding more like Grandpa than any of the animals my mind had just likened him to. "Glad you woke me. Was 'avin' an 'orrible dream."

"You too?" I asked.

He was sitting up now, in the middle of the bed. His wispy white hair, which barely covered the sides, stood up in thin strands as if he had rubbed a balloon on his head. I also noticed more stubble than usual, white sharp points of hair about his tanned face.

I was holding onto the side of his mattress, rocking and leaning over. My whole body was feeling so achy that I was hoping to sit up beside him.

"Shouldn't give 'em any credence," he said. "What bloody use are they?"

I shook my head noticing that he was looking at me as though that were an actual question. His top lip was protruding over the bottom one, pursed as it waited for his voice to come again.

I pushed myself up the side of the bed a bit more so that I was bent right over, shifting my weight about.

"Come up 'ere on the bed lad," he thankfully said, tapping the empty space. "Tell me about yours."

I got myself comfortable under the covers beside him as he made comfy movements next to me, smiling and giving me a sideways, mischievous look as we purposely knocked shoulders. And there I sat, staring at the bump my feet caused in the bed-covers deciding on what to say.

The visions from my nightmares had faded so that they were just beyond my grasp. I could not recall any of it or even imagine why they had been so affecting.

I shrugged, "Can't remember now," I admitted.

"Probably for the best," Grandpa said, "let 'em go... they is meant for sleep."

But I saw a hint of understanding in his eyes, as if he knew already.

He put a hand on the cover where my leg was and with a pressured friendly grip he softened me towards the next discussion. "It's yesterday my questions are with young Adam... Something 'appen did it?"

I squeezed up my lips as if to keep my mouth from opening as he continued looking at me over disarrayed eyebrows.

I had so much going around in my brain that I did not even know what was going to come out first. I remembered my bag upstairs, still holding that questionable gift. I pictured myself standing by the field, with that uncanny apparition dancing through my head. Yet it suddenly did not seem right to speak about any of it.

"Grandpa... are you ok?" I asked, not expecting those to be my words. Yet the question was obviously closer in my mind than I had realised.

Grandpa knew exactly what I meant by my tone and the fix he had on my leg tightened, using the firm feeling of his physical self to heighten the words in his reply.

"I'm alright boy..." he said, smiling with his lips closed and face creasing. "I'm old but I ain't that old. Ya Grandpa ain't a goner till 'es gone. I'm feeling skwith but not yet ready to be sleepin' forever." He paused a minute, and perhaps seeing the sombre look on my face he tried to lighten the mood, but still to find his answers. He let go his grip and then patted the same spot, pushing on the discussion. "Still going ta those woods is ya?"

"Yes, I think I understand it all now," I said proudly, and not wanting to be a burden. "So I'm not that scared anymore. I'm growing up Grandpa."

He smiled yellow teeth at me and slapped his flat hand hard on that leg again. My limbs were still aching but I did not have the heart to tell Grandpa that it had hurt me. "Adam, you'll never grow up lad, no one does! Ya might get older 'n' a little bit wiser, but I tell ya Adam..." He got close to me and whispered, "inside even I'm still a frightened little boy."

He moved himself back away with a quiet chuckle and I smiled back at him, his secret safe with me. Grandpa and I kept our chats to ourselves.

"So what 'ave ya been up to in there then?"

"We've got a camp in there."

And I pleased Grandpa's curiosity for a while by speaking about my friends for the first time. I was restraining so many other things, but the more I spoke the more I talked myself out of telling him any of it. I was excited as I told him of Martin and Josh and a filtered version of my time at school. He showed some recognition at their names but was letting me rattle it all off just nodding and making the odd responsive grunt.

I told him about the camp, and he said that he did not know of it or what it might be. We were mentally walking together through the woods, and we came to the oak tree.

"Oak is it?"

"Martin said it was."

"Judith Kendall's boy?" he asked, and I acknowledged. "Dare say he's right." Grandpa nodded with lowered eyelids. "There's faery folk in old oaks." He had left his eyes closed but now slowly opened them in emphasis. "They is special. All trees are special but oaks is the all-fathers, just as the earth mother is the ash."

"Ash Cottage!" I said, far too loudly, suddenly remembering.

Grandpa made a low noise in thought. "Yes this place has that name. That big tree out back in the corner, that's an Ash... And the woods is full of 'em too. Ash trees are for healing. So long as that tree stands out there and as long 'as this cottage has that name then the house will protect us. The earth mother keeps us safe in 'ere."

I certainly hoped so. I was enjoying the woods too much not to keep going. But I knew what was out there now, and I did not like the idea of anything following me home.

"Used to 'ave a nice name plaque but no sign will ever stay," he continued in a tone expressing bewilderment. "Read into it what ya will. I put one up, 'n' days later it's gone, just disappears. So I don't bother. But it's 'Ash Cottage' sign or no sign."

I could tell by his face that, although a logical explanation might be available, it was the illogical one that was most likely.

"What were you trying to tell me, about the oak?" he pushed me on.

I had actually forgotten the thread of the conversation, and Grandpa seemed keen to put me back on track. His trail of thought was leading right into the depths of the woods.

I had to tread carefully, choose what to divulge and what to keep hidden. But reining in excitement about bizarre events is not that easy for a twelve year old boy. "I think the faeries want me to stay there." And then I realised what a bold statement I had made and buttoned my lips, unsure if I was even going to explain further.

"Yes..?" he prompted excitedly.

"They left food there for me," I whispered.

And he quickly changed his expression. "I 'ope you haven't eaten it?"

I violently and expressively shook my head. He must have known the laws about eating their food, but now I was becoming his well trained apprentice.

"Good," he continued. "But ya took it?"

I gave a cautious nod, and felt a little ashamed.

"Hmm. Well you can't trust 'em Adam. They makes things wrong, glamour them up. If I were you, I'd take it back. I don't want them in me 'ouse... don't ever take gifts from the wood folk."

I felt my stomach sink, but really my gut instinct had been telling me that from the start, and I had chosen to ignore it.

"I 'ope you's all being careful in there? You keep on their right side Adam. Take heed what I say boy."

I nodded again in the way I would if I was being told off, though I don't think he meant to sound harsh. But perhaps I *had* gone further with all this than I should have, and more than Grandpa would have liked. I knew how fun and interesting he found the subject, but he seemed to be getting all the more serious.

I considered slowing the pace, and certainly I had to at least be seen to tow the line. I would probably need to keep more things to myself from now on.

"I will," I said, "but I know quite a lot about it all now."

"That so? Well I lived 'ere all my life 'n' still know nothing... No man does. And what ya read in books ain't nearly the 'alf of it."

Now he did sound harsh, but the subject of books allowed me to ask a question less personal to my experiences, and closer to his.

"I read something about mines," I said, "what was it you wanted to tell me? Was it about the knockers?"

Not surprisingly there was clear recognition in his expression. But the despair that seemed to fall over him and sink down his shoulders was unexpected.

"You got me on a subject now Adam," he said, slowly shaking his head and finally resting his gaze upon his table of strange objects. It was no relation to the things there, but perhaps that altar of precious earthly relics gave him courage, and made him feel some kind of peace. He was looking at it as though gathering his energies. "You'd be an old man ya self if I told you every story from my mining days." And then he turned back to me and took a breath.

"The mines was tough, but... knackers ay? Hmm," he said with a sigh. "All us lads knew about them but if we 'eard their knocking we turned our ears, pretended it wasn't 'appening. No one really knew if they were trying to 'elp us find a good lode or tryin' to lead us to disaster, but we weren't stupid enough to take a risk.

"We do what we can to placate these creatures but who knows how they think, whether they think at all, or whether they work by basic instincts with meanings long lost. I reckon they don't like people mining the ground, disturbing them.

"Maybe they are the ghosts of ancient dead, like some say. Their cairns could have been desecrated in the name of progress, years before my part. We should have left it all well alone. The underworld is theirs."

"Must have been scary down there Grandpa."

"I tell ya Adam, I'm lucky that I'm even sitting 'ere on this bed at all. I swapped a shift with one a the Bevin boys, and you ain't supposed to do that. He was younger than me, and he want at all superstitious. I don't know how fate works... why it chose to keep me safe. Could be he just had plain bad luck or he might 'ave passed some woman on the way squintin' 'er eyes at him.... But I reckon he followed the tapping of a knacker... Anyway, if I'd been there that day I wouldn't be 'ere now, and neither would you, or ya mother. One decision changed my whole life, and gave me more of one, but that poor lad, he didn't make it."

I could hear emotion in Grandpa's voice, how it sounded croakier than normal, but I watched his face and it was hard, poised. There were no signs of tears restrained, but I guessed he had done all of his crying over that, or lived such a hard life that he had slowly grown accustomed to such things.

"No it want the nicest of places Adam. But us lads used to have a time." He seemed to be trying to pick himself up from a darkening situation, thinking of what to say next, but his conversation got no lighter. "We would sing to keep our minds busy. I remembers like yesterday, that sound of monotone voices echoing through the bal. I can still 'ere it now Adam, to be honest, it haunts me."

He started to rub his squinted eyes with his fingertips and I guessed he was getting tired. We had been speaking for quite some time and the subject had grown heavy; while the things I had kept to myself hung over me like a weight of my own.

But I had resolved to take its burden, rather than fuss Grandpa with any more of it. Of course it was a constant fire in my mind but Grandpa would either dowse it or use his bellows; I decided that, for a time at least, it was burning fine just the way it was.

"Sorry Grandpa," I said, but he struggled to smile. "I suppose mum will be in soon."

"I expect so Adam yes." He sounded quite drained but was trying to come round.

I swung my legs straight out the side of the bed without giving it any thought, forgetting how painful they were, or perhaps not expecting them to still hurt after the rest. I made a wince, and then, as I struggled to get up my own weight felt unbearable. I felt as though my bones were rusted, my limbs like lead. I wondered if old men like Grandpa always felt that way.

Each tiny step sent such shock waves up my nerves that I could not stop myself from making small whining noises. I was trying to leave the room inconspicuously, but the shortness of each movement was probably very obvious.

"Adam..." his voice was leading in its tone. I was anticipating that challenge.

I turned on the spot to see his face, questioning, eyebrows rising.

Only then did I realise why I was trying so desperately to hide the pains I was having. Somehow I knew that it wasn't the flu which I was inflicted with. I had put two and two together and made a magic mystical number. Somehow, by my own accord, and with nothing to back up my supposition, I believed that it was all a punishment dealt out by the little people.

"What's the matter lad? You feeling sore?"

I nodded, and kept my mouth shut, eyes wide and hoping to keep my silence. Grandpa's voice had a warm hearted tone, but he soon lost that and went straight to his words of warning.

"I knows you been hilla-ridden last night boy, I think we both 'ave. I can't trust that they don't have designs on you. If it's ya legs aching they may well have worn 'em down, might have had you dancing all night, round and round, if only you could remember. Don't upset 'em boy... I'm not joking anymore Adam, you take care... They play games, but they ain't playthings."

I nodded with no words that could further release me. I whimpered, and left, tail between my legs. Grandpa had a way of sobering my thoughts when it came to the discussion of little people. He was right to believe that I sometimes took the matter too lightly.

"And get rid a that faery food," he added grumpily.

That conversation with Grandpa had taken a very different tone. I had held back, realising that he was not a child like me, but the older, wiser guardian that I should perhaps have respected more. I worried that things were changing between us. And to think that it could be true; that I might not have spent the night simply lying safely in my bed; gripped my guts tight with further, nervous uncertainty.

Grandpa was right; I should not have brought that food back with me, to where I was usually safe, perhaps endangering myself and everyone else in my family. Perhaps doing that had allowed them to follow me home... Perhaps they now knew where I lived.

I could hardly bear it to be in the house a second longer, and the fact that it was up there unsettled me. It was like a dirty secret waiting to be discovered by the wrong hands. I did not expect anyone to go into my room, and certainly not to check my school bag, but the 'what ifs' froze me. It was possible that my mother might have been in there already... And had I not left the bag wide open?

I would have rushed straight up the staircase, if my limbs had allowed such an energetic movement. I would grab that bag and set off, to return the gift as unwanted.

But one foot on the steps in sudden decision and I was stopped by my father peering out of the lounge doorway.

"Have you had any breakfast yet Adam?"

I shook a weary head, and his finger silently beckoned me, telling me that I had to do just that.

Normal life seemed to want me, but so did *they*. I was pulled in two directions, and I felt my mind splitting. I could see that bag in my room while I ate crumpets and jam, I could hear it while my parents chatted and tried to get me involved. That festering corpse of evidence was there, left unattended, and I could feel it drawing my body away from staying in the living room any longer than I had to.

As I had assumed however, the weather that day was still terrible. The rain was not so heavy as the previous day but the outside world was certainly uninviting. The idea of trekking to the woods was not very appealing either, walking all that way with my legs like crumbling bricks. The camp, brought to mind, was no fun on my own, and I hadn't the energy to call for my friends.

It was almost as if this was what the little people wanted, to keep me alone with their favour until my mind went insane with its presence and I would perhaps succumb to its allure. Perhaps it *was* the faeries exercising my limbs over night, just as Grandpa had proposed, making me dance with them to their arcane rhythms. Perhaps it was an initiation.

While I still owned that gift there was a link between my world and theirs. I really should never have taken it.

My fleeting ideal, that it could be the start of some mystery museum, was simply childish. It was dangerous to have possession of something that was theirs, and to anyone but myself it would not serve as any proof to their existence. It was just a slice of bread wasn't it? I was gaining nothing from owning it, and it was eating me away.

I got up without a word, to do what I had to do, feeling my legs stiffen and refuse to be used. At some point my mother had left to see to Grandpa and it is possible that my father had been talking the whole time but I had not heard a single coherent word. He could not help but now speak to me more directly.

"Adam what's up with you, you seem to be away with the fairies?"

I was nearly sick, mumbled a reply that I was ok, and struggled to pull myself as far away from prying eyes as I could.

Lying there in the corner of my room, incongruous yet seemingly benign, disguised as a mere school bag, was the cause to my disquiet.

I stood at a distance and tried to out stare it, to tell it that I was not afraid, but it looked ever on, threatening yet unmoving.

I gritted my teeth, stomped over to it and grabbed the damn thing, putting the strap over my shoulder as I always would and leaving to do what I must do. Literally marching to the beat of my own drum, down the stairs, coat on, door open.

"I'm going out," I called into the house, and did not wait for any reply, with a half heard voice complaining of the rain completely ignored.

I did not cease my pace until I had gone round to the side of the house. There I came face to face with the woods; a sheep in wolf's clothing? Or simply a wild animal, misunderstood.

The trees swayed in the winds, looking back at me beyond the showered emotionless space of grey field. Silent of answers.

I think I already knew that I would not be going there,

and in fact, my second idea seemed much more fitting. I turned and began heading the shorter distance to the donkey field.

The rain was steady but the sky was a lighter shade of grey, almost white as though the full covering of cloud had used most its reserves already. No light on the horizon, no clearing where the sun might try to cheer the atmosphere, but the sombreness did show signs of ebbing.

Get this job done, I thought, and we will be on our way.

I was a trooper, steady paced down that road, rain drops splashing off my head, a martyr with humankind on my side. We dominated this world through intellect and progress, through speech and communications. We could not be held back to times where these primitive creatures had any sway.

My legs may ache but maybe it was nothing sinister at all. Maybe it was just growing pains, as humans are want to grow, in height and in power. Grandpa may have said they were things to be weary of, but I could only allow them to be things of fun; because thinking of them in any other way scared the hell out of me.

It was not long before I saw her; dampened hair, head down to shield herself which always made her seem despondent to her plight. Poor thing, always there, at mercy to the elements. She was the only other living creature that knew what had happened that day before. That late afternoon, with faded light and murky senses. She would vouch for my sanity if only she could. My true friend, the donkey I had yet to name.

And friend she was now, as we had shared things together, and she was actually coming over to the fence as I approached. It made me feel better to have a confident, and to not be completely alone while I carried out my duty. That field held memories now, and its eerie quiet still whispered into my ears.

"Hi there donkey," I said, quite cheerfully as she was such a welcome sight. Lifting my feet up the bank I came closer to stroke her nose.

As I touched her she shrugged her head away back over from the fence and lowered it again. It felt momentarily like rejection, but I knew it wasn't personal. She was just an animal.

I caught sight of her tail and felt immediate worry for her. It was a mass of knots, not even knots really but more like badly fashioned braids. I looked as close as I could without climbing the fence, stepping up on to the first rung and leaning over. I would have liked to think it was merely tangled by rain, but thought it more likely a child of the owner had once done that to its tail and left it to grow into such a state. I racked my brains to remember if it had been that way before.

The poor thing was trying to move it and it seemed stiff with all those soaked coils. I was annoyed to think that people were not looking after her well enough. If she were mine I would brush it, and to be honest, I thought with firm fortitude, that if it didn't improve I would go into that field and sort it out myself.

I whispered over to her, "How are you after yesterday?" Half an eye peering over her sodden mane to the field beyond, and remembering, wondering, with both fear and desire, if I would see that whole spectacle again.

The donkey was slowly walking away. A car passed, wet tyres on the road, lights on against the weather, travelling too fast. I watched it over my shoulder but the donkey was not at all interested. She would have seen little else from the field but cars passing and the odd few people on the path. But yesterday we had both seen something much more unusual, and it had us both transfixed. The scene was clear, a video cassette in my head, playing itself back, over and over.

Now the field was empty but for the donkey. The setting was similar; misty again, soaked in drizzled rain. But although something could easily have been hiding over the distance, there had been a different feel to it all that day before. When I had seen their dancing my mind was dancing with them. On this day my mind was focused.

With heady determination I unzipped my bag in one swift movement and put my hand down into it. I was ready to remove that slice of faery bread and dispose of it, to throw it far into the field, give it back to them, back to where they held their revelries. Let the rain pelt it to mush and ravens peck it away to nothing.

I saw it in the dark bag, and put my hand in, gripping it between my fingers but instantly knowing that something wasn't right. The texture was wrong, and not because it had become hard and brittle as it would if it had gone stale. My fingers had pushed right into it, and my nails sank into a spongy consistency.

Quickly pulling it out in revulsion and with some trepidation I held it in front of my eyes.

What had once been bread was now nothing but a rectangular slab of dirty, mould covered fungus. In my surprise I was frozen, staring at it, thick, yellow, mottled and filthy. I should perhaps have examined it more but I had seen enough.

I threw it, I threw it as hard as my young arms were able and slung the putrid thing across the field. I yelled, partly in exertion and partly in my disgust and hatred for their horrid trickery.

I *knew* that it had been bread, and I knew that this was *their* doing.

The air made from drizzled rain was disturbed for but

a split second by my movements. And now all became still again.

There it was, a nondescript speck on a distant piece of wet turf. It was not mine anymore, I had returned it to them, and in the form they would know.

I stood catching my breath, looking at it and feeling the anxiety slowly leave, though contempt was burning behind my unblinking eyes. My heart pounded hard in my ears, the rain gently soaked my paled face.

Another car passed and again I turned to see it, and surprised to then see it stop on the side of the road not much further ahead. I watched as a door at the back came open and a head showed itself around it, looking back at me. It took a few seconds for recognition to crack my shell, so trapped was I in the moment. But it was Josh.

"Adam! You wanna come back to mine?"

I had to think, to go back to being Adam the boy and break myself out of life's ominous interval. My eyes briefly dragged my sight back over at the field. I could not see that thing now, could not even find the spot where it lay. It was hard to believe that any of it had even happened.

I had probably thought too long.

"Yeah, sure," I found my answer.

CHAPTER EIGHT

All children, as they come of age, have decisions to make about life. But choosing which world to spend their days in does not usually come into the equation.

I sat in that car, telling myself, life should be about this. It is about friends, the warmth of the car's over compensating heating system, and the loud music they played as we travelled. It's about looking forward to seeing someone else's house, to play on their brand new Spectrum computer. It is family.

Josh's father was driving, his mother in the passenger seat, and his sister next to him at the other side. He had not even mentioned a sister but her presence was certainly felt. I found it strange that he was throwing insults at her in a banter they were obviously both used to, but without realising how very attractive she was. I was embarrassed by the fact that I could not help but notice.

A few years his senior, she was wearing a lot of bright makeup and a baggy jumper top, the arms of it stopping to reveal her wrists covered in multi coloured rubber bangles. Although I did not spend much time thinking about girls I made up for it in the back of the car as we travelled that short distance which felt as if it took forever. I was too hot, squashed in at the side, and worried that everybody would be able to read my thoughts.

Strangely, that car journey full of people felt much more surreal than my encounter outside alone.

* * *

I suppose I did spend too much time thinking about

existential matters for a twelve year old boy. And thought that perhaps I should try having the same kind of fun that everybody else took for granted. Though it was hard. Once you have had a taste of something so rich, every other taste becomes bland.

I could not stop thinking about faery glamour, about what the little people might have wanted of me. And every day that I walked home from the bus stop I would pass that field, and I would stare across it, scanning the views to the horizon, wondering if that vision would ever dance its way back across the land.

Those weird dreams kept returning, and my health did not improve. I spent most of my time feeling lethargic, as if I was managing only a couple of hours sleep a night. And I could not tell anyone, because I knew that no doctor could help me. I completely believed that the little people had caused my sickness, probably because I had taken that bread. And the insult caused by returning it seemed to be preventing me from healing. But nothing else happened.

I had to try and just get on with being a boy, despite no longer having the carefree mind, or the energy of one.

My gang of three had our fun at the weekends and I went to school, I did my work, and even excelled somewhat in certain subjects such as English. Whenever I was on my own I still indulged my love for nature, or I went out with my family.

For some time I just juggled my life that way, trying to keep it all safely in the air.

My dad was happy enough; working hard and boasting at how clever he was to be 'selling houses in the area that no one else seems able to'. My mother had finally settled in and she and Grandpa did not seem to be 'at each other' quite so much. He and I were close despite the fact that I was now keeping things from him.

I never did tell him of the things I had seen or that had previously happened. If he asked I would say that all was quiet, that *they* were my friends now.

"Friends don't always do what ya want them to do young Adam..." he had said.

And he was right.

Although we used the camp regularly, it was nowhere near as much as I had first planned, mainly because I purposely discouraged it. On occasion my friends and I would meet there only to 'regroup' and then go on to somewhere and something else. I guess, as far as they were concerned, there was not much to do in the woodland. But to me it was still a haven, and my place to fully experience and to give thanks to the world.

I admit to feeling protective over the place, as if it were my home that I had lovingly and painstakingly restored, and it did become a spiritual home for me. I still felt that my friends being there was not quite right, that they were stepping on toes so to speak; or perhaps literally. I preferred spending time there alone, sitting in the camp when no one was there and no one would see me.

I could stay there for hours, feeling perfectly safe, where the only sounds were those of birds and breeze. I wanted to trust that all animosity had been misunderstanding, and that the faery folk and I would be in mutual peace. I did feel relaxed there, and the beauty and the quiet cleansed my spirit of the mixed up day to day world. I connected to a part of my being that most twelve year old boys would never have known existed.

There was many a magical moment savoured in that state of being, where I felt absolute freedom to be myself. Moments spent just walking through the hanging branches, stroking the moss that grew upon them as though it were the fur of an animal, and feeling the texture of veined leaves between my fingers.

In the deepest parts of the woods I could lose myself. The dark shadowy canopies that blocked the sun would once have made me afraid but now just reignited my respect.

And they had begun to repay my esteem with gifts. No more was I given sinister offerings of glamoured bread, but single feathers which seemed to fall directly at my feet. Sometimes I would see them fall, slowly drifting to the ground caught in an ark of breeze. And then other times they would just be lying in front of me when I gazed to the ground, yet I would attest that they were not there beforehand.

I gathered them and displayed them in my own room, wondering if that was how Grandpa had come by his own collection. I was now a wise old man of the woods, growing a beard of ivy and dressing in armour made of bark.

I had even become quite an adapt story teller. My friends and I would read one another spooky stories in the dark, as if we were around a camp fire, although there were never any real flames. We would sit in Josh's huge garden, imagining we were out in the wilds.

Some of the stories were from books, but some we wrote ourselves. I wanted to tell them my own story, the truth to it making it the spookiest tale I knew. But it was a bad idea to involve either of them in those matters. Remembering how disrespectful they sometimes appeared to be of the woods themselves, I dreaded how they might act towards the hidden people if they got wind of their true existence.

That thought was quite a portent, and I do not know how much I must blame myself.

I never actually told them anything.

With the nights getting warmer and summer on its way, Josh actually suggested that we all go to the woods one night with a real fire. But I swiftly led him away from the subject and on to something else. I loved the woods but being in there at night was not a desirable prospect. He still maintained that he planned to spend the whole night out there sometime, reminding me of his idea as though it were a threat. I'm sure he liked seeing the horror on my face.

It now seemed that my friends were more actively focused on the idea of mystery seeking than I was. But I was being sly; setting up this whole front of a 'club' to hide my real purpose. Ghosts did interest me, and Josh's story had rekindled that love of the subject, but I could not lie to myself. There were very few mysteries to seek, other than the biggest and closest kept secret of that place, and that was mine to keep.

I could never tell the others. Martin might be quietly concerned to know what I knew, but Josh would just laugh at me. Ghosts are one thing, but piskies and faeries? That was far too unbelievable.

Our sights were set on that haunted house.

It stood out like a sore thumb. I had never noticed it before Josh had spoken of it, but now its presence was ominous. Its white paintwork was tired and peeled, the garden overgrown yet most of it dead. The windows were boarded up with wooden panels as I was aware that sometimes they are when a building is left uninhabited over a long period of time.

Perhaps Martin had been right that the only reason no one lived there was that the structure was unsound. But it did have a feeling to it, perhaps more of neglect than anything else. It was sullied, and to that end it felt somewhat sad.

It whispered tales of when it was once loved, but now life had abandoned it. I had only a little belief in the story of the house's history and the ghosts that now wandered its empty rooms, but despite that I would not cross the road to look any closer until I was with my 'gang'.

Josh lived in that huge house to the other side of the road, obscured by the trees at the front. Behind it I could see the church steeple visible over more trees at the back. You could see the church yard from some of his windows.

I had wondered if having those graves so close bothered him. But his healthy attitude to scary places seemed to stretch so far that he was quite happy sharing their space. Maybe he did not really believe. Maybe he sought proof for that very reason. But to me it seemed that we had just the right mix of personalities to be a proper club of mystery seekers, or as it turned out, a poisonous cocktail.

We were just kids, a motley crew, 'little people' up to mischief.

All three of us wore jeans and a T-shirt yet still managed to look very different from one another.

Underneath that coat Martin always wore, his T-shirt was tight to his skinny frame, too small for him in fact, and although white it was a bit grey from over washing. Mine was also white but had red on the shoulders, while Josh tried to be more individual. Although white, his T-shirt was adorned with some kind of glossy coloured monster design.

Martin and I had also done next to nothing with our hair while Josh's blonde locks were, as always, combed and sprayed into place.

The 'coolness' factor was even more obvious as that hierarchy seemed to go up by training shoe size.

Martin's were flat black plimsolls, mine were normal as far as I was concerned, once white with coloured stripes, but now covered in mud. Josh, who had certainly taken to caring about how he looked earlier in life than we had, wore trainers which looked massive on his feet. They were startlingly white and far too conspicuous for sneaking around old houses. But that was what we were now about to do.

We set out with no real plan to speak of. Martin protested the whole time, saying that we would get caught, and becoming quite anxious of the whole idea. Yet he tagged behind us never the less.

Josh was the leader on that particular 'mission' mainly because he had access to a camera. He also knew the most about the place, or at least thought he did. He was the confident one, walking ahead of us and talking the whole time, perhaps a little over excited. I of course, was there for strictly professional reasons.

Perhaps agreeing to investigate that abandoned house was only to throw my friends off the scent, or maybe to break them in gradually to my overall cause. But I had now become truly interested in the possibility that it was haunted.

The house was detached but quite close to its neighbour which meant being quiet so as not to be seen. There were also two cars parked on the road and someone could come out to one of them at any time. Swiftly we crossed over and snuck around the side which we knew would lead to the back garden.

The gate was off its bottom hinge and threatened to fall off completely to which Josh was laughing and Martin and I simultaneously had to hush him up. Then we moved on, stepping silently over ground covered in dry strips of white paint and shards of glass and wood.

Bushes had overgrown and hung down from the side wall, darkening the pathway so that it felt like we were entering some forgotten cave.

It was a relief to come out from that and into the open, straightening our bodies in that enclosed garden of long grass and nettles.

We stood there making our own sign language to try and explain what we should do next. Unfortunately the windows at the back were also boarded so that was the first stumbling block. I knew as well as Martin that if we were seen trying to prise them off that it would look like vandalism. Plus the house next door had windows which overlooked the very spot that we conspicuously stood, clear and unhidden in the sunshine.

Josh went ahead and started pulling at the boards and looking about, camera in hand, quite ready to use it. Personally my heart was pounding; I cannot vouch for how the others felt. The supernatural qualities had stepped aside and the fear now was much more about risk. We would be in big trouble if we were caught.

Martin seemed to be faring the worst and was keeping well back, hardly really taking part, but he had special skills which made him, in fact, the most important asset to the mission.

"Do you feel anything Martin? You know…Do you feel it might be haunted?" I whispered, trying to get his attention. But he just stood, staring at the house with his arms crossed, eyes darting over its brickwork as if he was afraid there was something crawling across the walls. His eyes found me at last, those huge green eyes framed by worried eyebrows.

"Yes," he said, a little choked, as if he had been crying. And he slowly turned back to look at the building with that one word sticking into me, my breath stopped.

I wanted to quiz Martin further, but I suddenly

worried because I could not see Josh. He had disappeared, and I was not sure for how long he had been gone.

I jolted my head about me, and the garden was empty but for myself and Martin who had not even noticed, his head now up, staring at the roof.

Then, looking back around, I became aware that the house's back door was a jar, and I could not remember if it had been before.

I felt very alone, no one was with me on this, but I began to edge slowly towards it. What horrors my mind then conjured I do not remember but I'm sure it was stewing up a long list of outcomes. I was watching that door intently as it moved in tiny increments, back and forth with the gentle breeze. I feared having to go in there, the unknown, what was yet to be revealed. And I feared for Josh who may well have been foolhardy enough to go in there on his own.

I paused at the door and tried to peer into the darkness without getting any closer, without touching it, cocking my head on its side. I felt my arm involuntarily rise in readiness to open that door, though I knew that I did not want to do it. I wanted to call for Josh but could not bear to raise my voice. I looked back at Martin, shocked to be suddenly eye to eye with him as he was watching every movement.

"You feel something?" I pressed him in a loud whisper. And there was a pause, a dead silence before he withdrew that hypnotising gaze and looked about himself again. I watched him frozen in time with my body twisted on itself.

"I feel we shouldn't be here," he whispered back.

Suddenly there was a commotion, a noise, which took a few seconds of confusion to reveal its true nature. It turned out to be Josh running towards us from the side of the house with a huge smile on his face, giggling hysterically.

"Quick!" he said to us as his running brought him nearer to our paralysed bodies. "They saw me!"

And with that we all ran, and we moved through the side alley much quicker than we had come. We 'bottle necked' at the gate, jostling each other through it as the fear turned to childish amusement.

We were all laughing by the time we got across the road and were hidden in the driveway of Josh's house; even Martin. We were catching our breath and grinning at one another. Martin and I had no idea what had just happened, but for a few minutes there it did not matter, we were just relieved it was over. We were simply a group of friends on adventures, as boys our age should be.

"You got seen, by who? What?" I asked, as I was the first to calm down. "Did you get a picture?"

"Yeah, I got one!" Josh smiled.

Apparently he had found that he could squeeze up the other side of the house, and from that little alcove he had found a window that wasn't boarded up.

"They looked right at me!" he said, still catching his breath, but grinning wildly.

We all laughed again through heavy breaths, except Martin.

"Well, no one's supposed to be living there," Martin said accusingly, and I knew what Martin was thinking, and so was I.

"How quickly can you develop that film?" I asked, taking the leadership role back now.

"Well, there's still ten shots left," Josh said looking at the camera in his hands. And then without a further thought, Josh had held up the camera and taken a picture of Martin and I standing there together.

I still remember that photo. Martin looked shocked, and at the same time, as though he had just been devastated by something. And I just looked ruffled in that picture, with a flushed face, gaping mouth, wide eyes and incredibly messy hair. I think that is the most natural and telling photograph I have ever seen of anyone.

We used up the rest of the film by posing in silly positions and pulling faces in Josh's room. I suggested that we take some shots in the graveyard despite Martin's protests that ghosts don't actually hang around in graveyards. But no one seemed to be moving from the bed and my ideas fell on the deaf ears of two boys who had become boys again. They had done their quota of mystery seeking for the day, but I could not turn it on and off as easily as they seemed to. I wanted to see those pictures so desperately.

Josh said he'd do it next time they were in town, now shrugging it all off and putting on a heavy metal music cassette. In the end I just had to go with the flow of childish banter and singing along to songs I did not know the words to.

Josh kept breaking into fits of mimicking the music with an imaginary guitar and making Martin giggle. But my heart was not in it, not with that camera sitting there on the desk, and with answers hiding inside its black plastic casing.

That whole week was an agonising wait for those pictures. For three days school continued, each day passing without that big reveal. Josh kept promising that it would be the next day, and it wasn't. I was losing hope of ever seeing them. Until Thursday came, and Thursday just happened to be my birthday.

* * *

I had not made any hints for presents that year, my enthusiasm for it all waning now that toys had dropped off the list. I would have liked a pet, a cat preferably, but my mother said they were too much trouble. I decided that I either wanted a computer like Josh's or a library of books like grandpas'. I guess that made sense really, to continue as a boy, or grow to be an adult.

"So what day's ya birthday master Adam?" Grandpa asked, but I became bashful.

"It's on the twentieth," my mother answered for me.

"Ah! Day before the solstice," Grandpa said. He read our blank faces without patience, "Midsummer!"

"Not that we've even had any summer yet," my dad joked.

"We will," Grandpa smiled knowingly, "you mark my words, the sun'll remember how to do its job. And this year midsummer 'appens to fall just after young Adam ere's birthday. Good day for being older I say."

"What's a solstice?" I asked.

"It's what all those hippies 'caused a riot about the other week," my dad said, trying to be smart.

"From where I stand it was the police 'caused all that," Grandpa corrected. "The solstice has been celebrated for centuries. I got a book somewhere I could lend you Adam, got all that in it... It's really 'bout the planets movin' about an' all. But that'll make it the longest day of the year. So we calls it midsummer. In some parts 'ere they celebrate with bonfires on the hills. Plus, as far as old Shakespeare's concerned, it's the time when the faeries are abroad and having their most fun!"

My mother's face dropped and so did mine. Dad noticed his wife's disdain and gave her an enquiring look, leaning his neck back. He stayed that way for some time.

Grandpa knew he had accidentally spoken out of turn and he looked at me for support while the silence echoed in the room. It was suddenly most uncomfortable, and got worse when my father made his mocking comment.

"Come on Ann, it's just a bit of fun that. A bit of mumbo Jumbo."

She actually threw down the magazine she had been attempting to read and walked out of the room not looking at any of us or saying a single word.

I woke on that birthday with only the slightest hint of the usual excitement. Certainly that feeling was getting less each year that passed. But I did not grieve my childhood because I actually welcomed my age. Although my body seemed to have felt the ravages of time already, feeling sore most mornings, my mind was constantly learning. I hoped that I would grow up to be a good man, wise and caring about the world.

Grandpa was my role model now; I wanted to be like him. I did not really admire Josh and his wealth of gadgets and fancy clothes. My dad seemed more interested in him than me, asking what his dad did for a living, what car he drove, how many rooms their house had. But to me it has always been more important to have wealth of the heart, and a mind that was enlightened.

Still, I was bound to get some presents if I rushed myself downstairs.

"Ah the birthday boy!" my father and mother spoke practically in unison.

Grandpa was in the garden as the weather had taken a turn for the better. He stood staring out with his back to us, leaning on his Zimmer frame. I watched as he began to slowly turn himself about in tiny increments as soon as he heard the ruckus. He was smiling, squinting, and shuffling towards the door as quickly as he could.

I wondered, then, if I should actually have asked for a

particular present... a wheel chair for Grandpa, so that he could come with me over to the woods... I would have wanted that most of all.

"Happy birthday master Adam!" my grandfather said when he was close enough, in the way in which a street corner Santa Claus might call merry Christmas. "May there be many more, till ya as old and ugly as me!" And he managed his way into the room. "So, you one a these teenagers now then?"

"Yes I'm afraid so," my mother answered. "Thirteen today." And I bowed my head as though ashamed of it.

"Ah, in my day you was a man at thirteen and a teenager never! 'Orrible things teenagers, seems that's where it all goes wrong... not wantin' to offend ya of course."

My dad stood behind me and put his hands on my shoulders.

"Well we've got a good kid here. Sure he won't fall foul to the 'orrible teens." From his pronunciation I could tell without looking that he was smiling one of his cheeky grins.

I rushed through breakfast as I was allowed to open my presents before I left for school. My mother argued when I said I was ready because she maintained that I needed to do something with my 'messy hair' which admittedly always seemed to be tangled. But I had managed to fight her hands off when she tried styling it without my consent. And with that battle won we all headed to the lounge where on the couch, in the space I would usually sit, were a good few neatly wrapped gifts, and one not so neat.

"Open that one first," Grandpa said with an unreadable smirk. He was pointing to a small gift that looked as if the red wrinkled paper had been merely wrapped around something and then kept down with a single strip of tape. Obviously it was from Grandpa, and that made me smile straight away.

I believe he had always sent a card in the post on my birthdays with a pound note or two inside, but now I was at his house I was getting a real gift from the heart. I was excited all over again.

I swiftly unravelled the twist of tape that had been spun around the sides, my smile not leaving despite eyes upon me in anticipation of the reaction. The paper gone and there was a white bag, and instantly my heart fell into my stomach with the realisation.

I looked up and I saw the humour in everyone's faces, especially Grandpa's and it was only a second or two before I felt that amusement infecting me as well. A great big paper bag filled with the glossy striped sweets that I had been periodically stealing from Grandpa over the last few weeks. He started to laugh loudly like an actor on cue. And I turned with a cautious smile.

"Well, I know you like 'em," he said, and gave me an over exaggerated wink.

Although I felt a little embarrassed, I soon found it funny. He did not mind at all that I had been helping myself and so I gave him a big hug.

"Your real present's on me bed," he said in my ear, and my eyes widened as I stepped back from him. There was some deep emotion in his face.

"Go on Adam," my mother said softly, gesturing to the pile of gifts.

"We'll have your big present ready for you when you get home," my dad announced, "but I've got to pick it up on my way back from the office." And he attempted a Grandpa wink that really was not working for him.

I felt very loved and very lucky from the presents I received. They were bought for me by a family that actually cared to know my character.

Among other things now forgotten I got a handheld

electronic game 'Dungeons and Dragons'; a maze game which appealed to me a lot. A personal cassette player, although I had no tapes to play on it. And a pair of walkie-talkies to which my mother joked would probably work better than Dad's mobile phone.

I still had Grandpa's 'real present' to see, and I really wanted to know what he could possibly have thought to buy me.

"Can I?"

My mother and father looked at one another from their seats as though communicating their decision telepathically. They gave a nod.

I had to be quick so that I did not miss the bus, yet I still savoured the moment.

There on his bed was something wrapped that I instantly knew to be a book. Grandpa had not even used tape on this one, simply laying the paper over the top, but the book inside was amazing and I physically gasped.

It was bound in hardback, brown card and cloth like many of his other old books, and the imagery upon it was gold gilding. I picked it up and held it on my palms, feeling its weight, and sensing its age. In the centre of the cover was a gold tree and above that the title in the same shiny finish 'A Midsummer Night's Dream'.

I had wonder written all over my face. I knew this was special, and I knew with what grace it had been given to me.

Seated on the edge of his bed I carefully opened it.

It was old. The age was apparent from the thick yellowed paper and brown marks of foxing about it. On one side a darkly colourful image of a beautiful maiden asleep amongst the flowers, on the other were drawings of what I knew were obviously pixies. And between those two mischievous looking little people the date was marked; '1908'.

I knew that I had to take care of that book, and when I turned the pages I did so gingerly and with the respect it deserved. Guards of tissue paper covered mounted colour illustrations; pictures of the woodland realm, intricately drawn faeries, majestic figures and all the fruits, flora and fauna of the forest. I was reading a few words and looking intently at those images. It reminded me of what I loved most, the woods themselves.

Half the way through I saw an amazingly well painted scene, but one which made me shut the book quickly. It made quite a loud, but somehow satisfying noise, and something fell out of it. For a moment I worried that I had damaged the inside but then realised it was just a book mark.

I bent over to pick it up trying to not feel so unnerved by the picture I had just seen; a mushroom fairy ring with dancing little people around it, some coming out of the tree itself, and the words beneath '*Come now a roundel and a fairy song*'.

All the text in the book was strange but that only made it seem even older and more mysterious. I felt very blessed to have it.

What had fallen was a long plain yellowed cardboard marker with a red ribbon attached, upon which Grandpa had made an inscription in ink:

'*To Adam, on his most important birthday. A good young man, and a true seer. Remember: When you are young your eyes are wide open yet you go through life blindly. When you are of age you can see it all yet often close your eyes. My wisdom is this; keep them open.*'

Sitting there, in the silence and dusty shadows of Grandpa's room, I felt something had just happened that would always be with me, and with that, I felt a deep love for him. My lip quivered and a tear was threatening the duct of my eye, but I wiped it before it came.

"Come on Adam you're gonna be late!" my mother called me.

I took the book to the lounge with me, not really wanting to let it out of my sight, and before I was finally whisked out of the door I managed to whisper to my grandfather.

"Thank you Grandpa, it's very special."

When Josh came into school that day, he at last had the packet of photographs with him. But he didn't seem too excited.

I had been waiting around outside and showing Martin my new game, keeping out of the sunlight in order that we could see the moving black characters on the screen. Martin was watching attentively but then flippantly said that I should just make a map of the maze so that I didn't keep falling into the traps. But of course that would have defied the whole point in playing.

Josh waved the envelope of photographs aloft as he walked towards us, just as the bell rang for the first class. Foiled again! And he scrunched up his face in resignation.

More waiting. Two whole lessons with my mind travelling far from the subjects in hand. I was thinking only on what might have been in those pictures. And then, it was finally time. We were all rushing, my little gang quickly ducking into the form room, looking about us in case anyone was to see us. A secret meeting for members only.

We noisily pulled up chairs to sit around a single desk as Josh produced the envelope again.

"Did you actually get anything worth seeing?" I

whispered impatiently.

Josh put a finger up and waved it with a smile on his face. I was already annoyed that he had got to see those pictures first, and now he was really playing his hand.

He pulled them out of the envelope, face down, drawing out the moment. But his smile was over to one side of his face and I could see he was keeping from saying something.

"What?" I asked again.

I think he was trying to tell me but found it hard. So he fanned through the pictures and then laid one down, face up. It was semi-black with a strange white mist across it. But it was not a ghost.

"I must have moved too quickly," he said, defeated.

We stared at the shot, at the darkness, at the light reflection from the window glass, and into the motion blur mist. I saw nothing, and it was hard to not feel disappointed.

"It's alright," I said, in order to be friendly.

"But I did see someone in there," Josh swore.

We had passed it around, each of us examining it closely. Abstract though it was, it was our only evidence.

"It's creepy," Martin said.

"It's nothing," Josh negated. He was annoyed at himself, I could tell.

But Martin handed it back to me, and pointed at a swirl in the mist.

He was right. There did seem to be something there. I could actually see a face, with eyes so dark that it appeared to have none, but with a definite whiteness that made up the head. I could even make out something black below the eyes which could have been a drooping mouth. If that was a person their expression was tortured, and I was sure that if it was a human face then it was not of any person alive.

Martin shivered and took up his characteristic stance of hugging his own body, while Josh snatched it back to look.

"There's nothing there!" he mocked.

But I too felt a little uneasy to think that we might have really photographed a spirit. The ghost of a mad girl who once murdered her parents in a fit of insanity; and there she was, staring straight back at us.

"I will take this home for verification," I said in a mock detective voice. But I was hiding a growing anxiety. I did not quite feel at ease with that picture.

It was an instant continuation of the morning's festivities when I arrived home that day. My dad was even there, back from work early just for me. And a cake and candles, and a huge present sitting right in the middle of the lounge with bright paper loosely around it.

As a child you expect all that on your birthday, at the age I was, and with the extra weeks of my recent maturity, I was almost uncomfortable with the attention.

Perhaps it is also symbolic that my questions about the photograph were much closer to the forefront of my mind than wondering what that gift was.

"Open your present then," my dad said, noticing that I was hesitant.

"Yes go on Adam," my grandfather spoke up, "it might suffocate!"

"Shhh," my mother said in a comical manner and smiled at me.

True enough, now that we were all quiet for the first time, I could hear snuffling noises from underneath the paper. Could it be they had actually bought me a cat? And had I left the poor thing there in its large carrying box, in the dark under that wrapping?

I returned my mother's smile with a grin and pulled

the paper away.

But it was a cage, and the snuffling turned to a scuttle which meant that I did not even see the creature which had obviously just made its escape into the tiny red plastic house. I don't know if I had time to think of hiding my disappointment, and I can't remember saying thank you.

"Gone in its 'ouse," Grandpa said. "Little creatures don't like bein' on show."

I was staring into the cage, on my knees beside it trying to catch some glimpse of my new pet. There was a short list of animals that it could have been. I did not know which it was, but a cat was definitely off the cards.

"It's a hamster," my father said. "I know you wanted a pet. Something you can look after."

I guess it was obvious that I was somewhat underwhelmed.

"Make sure you gives it a name," Grandpa added. "Everything should 'ave a name, like this 'ouse does. Names make things yours. And did ya know," he then whispered straight at me, "that if ya find out the name of a faery, should one ever become a nuisance, it will keep you from harm."

I looked to my mother, expecting some negative reaction, but she did not take up the bait. Her ears were closed and we were all concentrating on the emptiness in that cage. It was my father who now seemed the most perturbed.

"He's in there somewhere."

But the little animal never emerged.

I eventually decided to carry the cage upstairs to my bedroom and place it on a free shelf. The poor thing was no doubt too scared of all the noise and movement to show its face, and I thought it best if I leave him in peace for a while.

I myself had to return to the 'party'. But the whole birthday goings on had prevented me from talking about the photograph and I was worrying that I would not be able to mention it to Grandpa until the next morning. However, early that evening, my luck changed.

The adults were using my birthday as an excuse to get a little merry and for some time both of my parents had disappeared into the kitchen. I set my attentions to Grandpa, who noticed my eyes and held his glass of whisky aloft.

"Cheers master Adam," he smiled.

He took a small sip and then put his arm back down to the chair. He then appeared to purposely tip his glass to the side, and spill some on the floor beside him.

"And there's a drop for you good fellow," he said quietly, to no one.

It was possible they had all had a little too much booze but now I was safely alone with my grandpa I took my opportunity. Urgently I located where I had dropped my bag and found the photograph, hurrying to Grandpa's side with it clutched in sweaty hands.

He sat up to attention looking bewildered at my rushed and pressured actions. But I was sure that I had but a short window in which to broach this with Grandpa or have to wait the whole night wondering.

I whispered, "Grandpa, quick, look at this, what do you see?"

He held the picture between the tips of his shaking fingers and pushed his head back against the chair to distance himself from it, then moved in, to look slowly closer. He looked at my eager face, and then back to the photograph, then lowered his arm.

"What is I supposed to see?" he asked, confused.

I looked behind me to the kitchen. They were still in there, moving about, preparing food. I kept my voice low.

"We all think there's a ghost," I said openly.

"*We* being these friends of yours?"

"Yes, it's like a club we have. We go out seeking mysteries."

Grandpa looked up at me with knowledge in his face, "But it ain't mysteries you're seekin' is it Adam? It's the answers to the ones already there."

"I suppose so." And there was a pause. I expected Grandpa to take another look at the picture but he never did, he simply leant further towards me over the arm of his chair. I was prepared now to hear his wisdom, to hear his tales of dark creatures of another world, of how modern technology might solve those age old riddles.

"You should ask ya'self boy. If ya even *wants* to find the answer to a mystery... 'cause then it ain't no mystery anymore is it... it's something else entirely." And he scrunched up his brow.

I gave that a second to sink in but then had to say, "But it looks like a face."

"What looks like a face?" My father had come in and put a couple of plates down on the coffee table. I became anxious and was not sure how this would turn out. I did not expect what actually happened; Grandpa leaning forwards and passing my dad the photograph. I was mortified.

He started to examine it in a similar way to how Grandpa had, then sat down to continue his scrutiny.

"Think he means in the white bit," Grandpa said stretching out his finger, curved as though to point to it across the room. "Looks like a face."

Now my father began looking at the picture with his nose practically pressed against it, and then came away with a smug expression.

"Ah, I see," my father said as if he knew. "That gentlemen is a mix of shadows and reflections. That's what most 'so called' paranormal pictures of ghosts are."

Timing it badly for us all, my mother then came in with the food on a tray.

"Sit down Adam," she said so that I would move out of her way. And on relinquishing herself of the plates she stood straight with hands on her hips.

"Did I hear the word ghost used in my house?"

"Still my 'ouse actually Annie, I ain't dead yet," Grandpa corrected. My mother turned to face him.

"Well ghosts are still a banned subject."

"Actually," my father took hold of the situation, "I myself am not talking about ghosts but about science. This here," and he held the picture up in the air, making me cringe. "This is a classic case," he continued. "People see faces in things because faces are the first thing we learn as babies. We can't help it. There's an actual word for it, starts with a 'p'" And then he started mumbling the letter 'p' trying to draw something out from distant memory.

"Plonker," my mother joked.

"Ha-ha," my father said, not wishing to be put down when he was on one of his information out-pours. "Where was this taken Adam?"

I hardly dare answer, but all eyes were on me. "Josh took it, at an abandoned house opposite his."

My father's expression changed, but I was not observant enough to know why.

"He said there was someone there..." I went on, over defensive, "and he knows the story of that place..."

"That house," my father interrupted, "has just been sold... by yours truly. It was probably the new owners in there, they're going to do it all up. So you tell your... friend, to stay away. The last thing they need is kids sneaking about." He sounded a little angry and the fact that I was involved was probably clear. "It's out of bounds ok?"

I nodded. Surprised at how annoyed he sounded.

"And so is all this talk," my mother said and sat back with a plate on her lap. "Zip it, and eat!"

"The night is young!" my Grandpa chortled, and then there was silence but for the purposeful clatter of cutlery upon plates and the chewing of food.

My birthday might not have technically been the longest day of the year, but for me, it had gone on long enough.

I went up to my room not long after our meal, feeling dejected, but with the intention of relaxing and reading my new book. When I got up there however, I straight away knew something was amiss.

The hamster's cage door was open.

I could only imagine that I had knocked the latch when I was manoeuvring it into position.

The little shredded paper nest inside the plastic house was empty but for an indent in the middle where its body had been. And there was little doubt that my birthday present was now on the run somewhere in my room.

I immediately thought to slam shut my bedroom door and got down onto my knees to start searching, walking on all fours about the room to look in all the nooks and behind all my things. I tried not to panic but I didn't want to get in trouble for losing the hamster before I had even seen it.

At length I realised that I could hear something. It was a kind of scratching noise, like it was trying to get out of somewhere, or get in. I finally traced the sound to under my bed. The offending article was an old shoebox. Slowly I dragged it out, and took off the lid.

There he was, looking up at me, quite affronted because I had suddenly decided to pull the roof off his new found home. That delicate little thing, sniffing the air to check all was safe. He looked so helpless and lost in his unfamiliar surroundings. His tiny front paws were poised over his soft white belly as he stood there erect on flat back legs. So innocent looking with jet black shiny round eyes.

It did warm my heart, observing its minute movements, I felt almost guilty for taking such little interest in him.

I reached in and picked him up in a cupped hand. Luckily he did not try to bite me, but did squirm a little. He had no weight at all and felt like tiny fragile bones wrapped in a brown fur coat.

"Awww I'm afraid your adventure is over for now little guy," I said to him quietly. And put him back into the cage. He was mine now, my first ever pet, and I would care for him as best I could.

Until fatigue took me over I was lying in bed looking through that special antique book. I did not really understand the story because the language was so old, but the fact that it was about faeries kept me looking through it, and at the pictures.

"How would you like the name Cobweb?" I asked my hamster quietly across the room. It was a name from the book, used for one of the 'fairies', and from the shuffling I heard from the cage I took the answer to be yes.

The faeries themselves were winged in the pictures, yet not really whimsical. They had a menace to them, a mischievous darkness. I understood that was why I liked them so much, that their allure was that thin line between light and dark. The little people, and those represented in the pictures within the book, were both pleasant and repellent in equal measure.

With eyelids hardly refusing to let me see further, I hesitated on the penultimate illustration. It was of two faeries peeking around a bedroom door, a baby asleep in a crib, and the words beneath:

'*Almost fairy time*'.

* * *

Perhaps I should have explained to my new pet that night time is for sleeping.

No sooner had I drifted off than a noise woke me.

The room was hazy with the greying navy of twilight through my curtains, and my hamster was wide awake, running like crazy on its wheel. I squinted as I levered myself up on my elbows, looking over to the cage. It was rattling with the repetitive spinning, stopping only for a second before starting up again. I dropped back down and grunted with annoyance and fatigue, pushing my head hard against the soft pillow so that it might cover my ears.

I lay there hoping that it would soon stop, wishing that the hamster had something better to do, yet worrying that it hadn't. In my semi-awake state I began to imagine letting him out again just so that he could be happier roaming my bedroom, and so that he wouldn't disturb me so much.

I watched my digital alarm clock show the changing minutes and that infernal noise went on and on, becoming one with the usual white noise, becoming a noise with no meaning. And then sleep found me again.

The next time I woke was to a very strange feeling, facing those illuminated digital numbers, 11.59. And no sooner had I realised that I was conscious, those numbers changed to 12.00am. My birthday had passed, and the solstice was upon us.

The room was dark now, and it was silent and still. Everything before my eyes was as it should be, yet slightly askew, and there was a buzzing in my head which made no sound. The faint moonlight filtering through the curtains cast abstract shadows upon the walls, straight lines in all directions forming shapes which my mind transformed into monsters.

I knew that I was awake, yet at the same time felt trapped within a dream. It was a sense that I had woken into another world, a contrasting reality, one that was always there, yet I should never have been awake to witness.

I thought that my senses had begun to adjust, but shivered as I saw the curtains make a pulsation. At first I guessed there was a breeze, but then I saw something. Something ran across the room.

It was quick, made my heart skip and forced me to twist my neck up to follow it. Seeing it only briefly and in such a confused tired state, I could not be sure of what I had seen. There was no noise, yet what I thought was that it had run along the floor, across from my bed, only to be lost into the dark corner at the edge of my wardrobe.

I turned my body straight so that I could see in that direction and as I did so my head fazed and I was close to sick. I saw only shadows, the objects in the room causing patches of complete black, blotting out places where things could hide. I stared into those shadows, holding my breath, hearing only the strong beats of my heart.

The feeling of unease was engulfing me. There was a thick atmosphere in the whole room yet it was most focused at the spot I was now fixed upon. That jet black corner where the wardrobe met the wall, and where I swore that I had seen it run. I knew that I might have been mistaken and yet something was causing that creeping feeling, the feeling that something was there... creeping.

I closed my eyes tightly only so that I might again open them and make better use of my sight, up onto my elbows and staring, unmoving. I feared what it might be, my imagination intent on feeling that fear. My heart was thudding in my ears while up my spine I felt the tight grip of tension.

I was in that position for some time yet attempting to check around me with small movements of my head and eyes, not wanting to draw any attention to my presence.

The curtains were inanimate, everything was still. My senses were heightened so that I would hear any slight noise there may have been. But now fully awake my thoughts began to manage attempts at reason. And eventually my shoulders sank with relief as panic subsided and logic came back to me with an injection of realisation. I felt my muscles finally relax and I almost laughed.

It seemed so obvious now. My hamster must have somehow got free of its cage again. The damned thing was more trouble than it was worth.

I sighed deeply. So glad was I to have reached that conclusion that I forgave the poor thing all of its sins and started to rise out of bed.

The movement must have startled it as I then saw it run from whence it had been and dart beneath my bed. It was much clearer this time, for although I was no longer intently watching for it, I had been looking straight in its direction. It was too dark for definition, but I had no doubt whatsoever that some small black shadow had moved towards me along the floor, making no sound, and had now gone out of sight below me. I guessed it wanted to be in that shoe box again.

I would be lying to say that the uneasiness had completely lifted, it lingered, it played with my natural human caution of the darkness and of anticipation. But I now had the gumption to switch on my bedside lamp and take some of those dark thoughts away. It was not bright but one side now had enough light to further investigate.

It was the middle of the night and I was too tired to go chasing around after the thing, but I had to make some effort to do so.

I leant slowly over the edge of the bed so that I would be able to see under it, even if at an inverted angle. I was taking care not to startle the creature, moving ever so smoothly, no sudden movements, and now my line of vision was beginning to see passed my mattress to the objects underneath. I saw shadows, I saw the boxes... I saw something...

The sudden, loud noise of the hamster's wheel made my heart painfully pound and I leapt back up onto the bed and crouched upon it.

Instantly, I pulled my knees up to my chest to form a protective ball as my eyes shot straight to the cage. There was the hamster, as it always had been, the door shut tight. It ran and ran in a spinning circle so much so that the metal bars rattled and my vision could not keep up with its incessant turning. Yet at the same time, I saw again, that black shadow, though this time I also felt it.

Despite the light it was still black, a dark orb which I saw in my peripheral vision, dashing across the foot of my bed. Its slight weight caused impressions upon the sheets, the notion of tiny feet, quickly scuttling. Although it was fast I followed its movement as it was lost beneath the curtains. And with that those curtains moved as I had seen them move before, undulating ever so slightly, then coming slowly to a stand still.

I have no idea how long I sat in that position. Cold

fear had gripped me paralysed. I could not bring myself to move and check the window. But something had been there, something had been in my room, and that something now, had left in the way it came.

The noise of the hamster on its wheel was driving me out of my mind as I felt unable to move or make any attempt to stop it. The cold of my bare legs and the discomfort of my posture seemed unchangeable and so I experienced it and I sat with it and I waited for it to leave me.

I was too scared to see behind those curtains, too afraid to comfort myself by allowing the sleep I was being deprived of. And so I just sat there with my eyes wide and alert, thinking about it all, coming to conclusions much needed. But all I could think was that it was *them*. They had come into my house, despite no wrong done to them. Perhaps they had been coming every night. But midsummer was no excuse. My security was breached and my privacy was invaded.

I had stayed sitting that way, alert to any tiny fluctuation of light and sound, until the sun made enough illumination to force those shadows into retreat. I watched them slowly drifting away, repelled by the light through the curtains, until the walls became only walls, and the objects were their natural form again.

Only then did I allow myself to fall back onto my bed, to rest, and drift back to the vulnerability of sleep.

CHAPTER NINE

My mother woke me, literally shaking me into consciousness.

"Adam, come on you don't want to be late for school."

I could not remember turning off the alarm, but I guess I had at some point. Considering it felt like I'd had about ten minutes sleep, staying in bed and being late for school would have been fine by me. The events of the night before were fresh in my mind, and yet felt distant. They were lodged somewhere between dreams and thoughts, trapped within a mind that might never feel clear again.

I groaned as my mother opened the curtains to employ the sun's help in rising me, and then left the room.

I just lay there, staring at the closed window.

I could feel the ever present voice of the woods. Kneeling at the foot of my bed and staring out there, it could easily be mistaken as benign, but I knew... I swear they were getting bigger day by day, not simply moving closer but *growing* closer, tree by newly grown tree. It seemed that I did not even need to crane my neck to see them anymore. Soon they would fill the whole field.

I had to pull myself away, drag myself downstairs, start another day. Thirteen years old but with a body that felt as wrecked as Grandpas.

I took my new book with me, hoping to ask him a few questions if I could find a moment. And when I reached the lounge I slumped down on the sofa with it beside me, feeling unable to get as far as the kitchen.

"What's wrong with you Adam?" my mother said huffily. "I hope you don't think you're having a day off school, just because you're tired? I expect you've been up all night reading this?" And she lifted the book in emphasis, as though it were nothing but garbage.

Grandpa was watching from his chair and obviously did not like the disdain she showed his gift either, or the way she was speaking to me. "He's more than tired Annie, your Adam's not been well for a while... He's been blighted."

"Poppycock, he's fine, aren't you Adam? And why did you decide to give Adam this anyway dad, out of all the wonderful books you could have given him?" She had put it down, but was still scowling at the cover.

"His birthday fell over midsummer!" he said, exasperated, "And you saying Shakespeare ain't wonderful enough? Huh." Grandpa sounded truly offended and my mother tried to ignore it and eat her toast.

"It's really special mum," I defended.

She managed to return my comment with a smile, but it was cloaking annoyance. Rather than continue the argument she had raised she went back to the kitchen, at the same time swapping places with my father.

"It means a hell of a lot to me that book," Grandpa went on. He did not want to let it drop even though my mother had now left. "I kept it all this time, waiting for someone special to pass it on to, and 'ere 'e is... your boy. I don't 'ave a true heir do I Annie?" he raised his voice but with no response.

My father seemed to have taken an interest in the book though.

"Got to be worth some money that Finn. It's an antique."

"Argh, money ain't important, objects lose their worth when ya buy them for their value in money. Besides, didn't buy this one, was a gift, a christening gift funny enough. Only good thing to come from being baptised against me will."

My mother came back in and shoved a bowl of cereal on my lap. "Dad you were a baby, I'm sure they didn't force you kicking and screaming," she smiled, trying to hide her previous animosity.

"When I was a baby kickin' 'n' screamin' would have been all I was doin'!"

Grandpa was laughing but I was not really engaged in the moment. I was thinking how the book truly was a piece of him, a piece of his history, and he had given it to me. I would treasure that book, as a constant memorial to Grandpa, and as a mark of my becoming a man. I thought that perhaps, one day, I would even be able to pass it onto my own child.

Thirteen years old and I was already thinking of all that was ahead, and all which had passed. Life had unfolded before me, and it had in fact begun to unfurl the moment I stepped foot upon Cornish soil.

* * *

I did not even want to stay home that day, as sick as I felt. What I planned was to 'minch off' as Josh would have put it; to act normal, as though I were going to school as usual, but then go straight over to the woods. I wanted to have it out with them, settle this matter, and make sure nothing like it ever happened again.

Eventually picking myself up from my paralysed state, I moved swiftly while making constant checks over my shoulder. I took a bottle of milk, a bowl which I thought was least likely to be missed, and a slice of bread. This time the bread was in fact quite stale, so I presumed that it would give me more powerful protection. And then I went back through the hallway, not wanting to be seen for I knew that my expression would look stern with my focused, serious intent. I had tunnel vision upon my rebellious task.

"Hey Adam," my dad noticed as I passed the lounge, trying to make conversation as though I had any interest in general life. "You named that hamster of yours yet?"

"Cobweb," I answered with no emotion.

And barely hearing or caring about the chatter between them all, caused by my reply, I left.

I worried about that hamster; poor thing, trapped in that cage, spending its whole life in such a tiny space. It aimlessly clattered that wheel all night because it wanted to be able to move, to run in the wild. Part of me wanted to whisk it away with me, take it over to the woods and let it go. But it had been born into a closeted safety and would have no idea how to survive in the big bad world. It was a creature of nature, but had no idea how to live in it.

My room had the only window with a view of the woods. If I was quick enough I could rush over there and no one would be any the wiser. I could be there all day, so close, but completely unknown.

Missing one day of lessons meant nothing in the scheme of things, and I did not feel in a fit state to participate in those social mores. This was more important. There were choices to be made which could affect my whole life, maybe even the whole world.

Not for the first time was my goal to claim back a place I loved, a place of natural beauty as well as mystery, that I would not allow to be spoilt for me.

Perhaps *they* thought that *I* was spoiling things for them, that human beings always had done. People had for centuries taken all for themselves, chopped down the woodlands and built houses roads and towns through their land. I knew that years ago the world would have been covered in trees, perhaps full of little people. And perhaps human beings did have a lot to answer for. But I was not like everybody else and they would see that eventually. They could share their home with me and I would respect it, bring them gifts, and be their friend.

But perhaps they did not want that. Perhaps their ways would always be off kilter to our own. And we all have deep set prejudices of things that work so differently to ourselves.

I just wanted to understand them.

I think that the little people knew I was coming. They had taken the summer and made some half hearted attempt to hide the woods from me, almost lost in that engulfing fog. Rain the previous night seemed to have turned to steam that billowed up from the ground. I imagined that the clouds had come down to surround those trees, taking their grip and ready to lift the whole woodland into the sky, out of my reach. It looked surreal; it was as if I were still dreaming.

The mist hung over in the distance, above and all around, coming from nowhere yet like smoke from some cold internal fire. It silhouetted the trees and made them appear far away, somewhere from another world. But the sun was looming not far behind them, and the warmth of the season would soon ruin that particular illusion.

I myself was closing in, not faltering in my persistent walk, over the field and towards that wall of trees. Their tricks with the elements, playing with my mind were wasted now, and soon enough I was upon them as always.

Once inside it felt instantly magical and more ethereal than perhaps it ever had. The fog rolled low over the ground, retreating far away through the throng of trees. But where I stood was clear. It smelt clean from rain and even fresher from its touch with the mist. The old trees were making new air of which I was taking the very first honoured breaths.

But I was sure that the whole place was alive with those creatures, full of them, as if they were all around me. Though I did not feel any malice. Perhaps they were just fascinated by me. Perhaps I was of a different breed than they were used to.

Looking around me I saw only a place of awe, and realised how much greener everything now seemed; the moss, the ferns and plants. It was almost glowing with the colour.

The bluebells were gone but other flowers had begun to bloom around the wood's edges. The trees looked healthy; their twisted branches were curves and patterns of feminine delicacy and masculine strength. Every nook had a thousand feasts for my eyes, different in every inch, no spot more perfect than the next. To me, every part of those woods was special.

No wonder they were so protective of it, they'd had that place to themselves for so long and I was just a stranger. They did not know me or my intentions.

But I was making my offering to them as I had always done, pouring the milk into the bowl and whispering under my breath. It reminded me of an old horror film where people chanted incantations, yet this was real and it was my life. I felt powerful and although childishly saw some humour in it, tried to remain serious because I believed completely in what I was doing.

I wondered if Grandpa had actually spent time in those woods, doing exactly as I was. I knew that he once enjoyed his time roaming the countryside and I felt bad for him that he had lost that part of life. It occurred to me that his questions about my adventures might be intent on seeing through my eyes, as I knew how much he missed it.

Perhaps if I could find the faeries and actually speak

to them, convince them that I was a friend? Were they not supposed to grant wishes? Well I had my wish ready. I would have them conjure up that wheelchair and I would struggle, pushing Grandpa along over the fields. And there we could share some precious moments together. And he could see again, the parts of the world that were left untouched. He could remember.

Sitting in the woods, resting upon the roots of a tree, it was my thoughts that were the enemy, not the faeries. Worry was a word that I was now old enough to understand.

I worried for the world. In the short time I had lived there, Grandpa had installed within me his same enthusiasm for nature, and a deep, bias love of it. Perhaps those sensibilities were genetic. But now I found it hard to understand why some people did not seem to care. Surrounded by all that beauty which I beheld around me, all the plants and birds and especially the trees, I actually felt the anger of the little people for what the human race was responsible for.

I heard even more about what was going on outside the cottage doors than Grandpa ever did, and it made me feel sad that I had no power to change anything. I was still a child but I was trying to be a good person. That day, I voiced a pledge strongly in my head, and I promised to never harm anything in nature's kingdom again.

Perhaps that is a promise no human being can keep.

The day was peaceful but slow. I was surprised how much longer a few hours seemed to take when there was nothing to occupy you but your senses and your thoughts.

I went around the entire wood, systematically pointing to each tree and giving it a name; whatever was the first thing to come into my head. I do not remember many of them, but I gave the great oak the most important name; I called it Oberon.

And then, finally, I made my way around the village via the coast, so that I would end up travelling the road I always would if I had actually gone to school.

I felt a little guilt about my day to myself, but perhaps I needed that time to take stock, to recover. And I really did feel that my work there had been important. I was living under Grandpa's roof so if I had made the mistake of allowing the little people in, I had a responsibility to at least try to keep them out.

I actually believed that a mere boy could tame the untameable.

The rain had come again, so fine as to be mist, or maybe the mist and rain had become as one. Visibility on the road was bad and being able to see only a little way ahead had an eerie feel. Cars came into existence by way of a distant drone, followed by the piercing of their headlights.

That bad weather felt as though it had always been and always would be. Despite a few good days it was the rain I remember. I imagined how awful a world would be if the sun forgot how to shine and the climate was forever in chaos with wind and rain a constant rather than a change. I imagined how depressing it would be, how the personalities of the people might change in reflection to the dreary surroundings. I wondered if a world like that might be the perfect place for the little people to inhabit.

I could not wait to have the summer, and the long school holiday. Six weeks of freedom to look forward to, or of boredom for a child unless it was active, unless it had some adventure to partake in. For my friends and I, with our collective imaginations, there would always be an adventure somewhere.

But we could never have guessed how our particular adventure would end.

At the donkey field I turned to see her, but saw nothing but that haze of grey moisture.

For a moment I worried what else I might see. I tried to shake it off, staring into the mist for some basis of normality, yet wondering if I would ever feel truly normal again. There was less visibility than ever, yet out there was a shadow. It was barely there, perhaps just the breaking up of the foggy covering, but I saw it, and then I did not. Something was moving, but only as the mist moved.

I heard the echoing voices of the sheep behind me; hollow in the silence. Some of them were standing there by the fence, staring at me, as though they knew something. They held their ground as I turned, but when I stepped forward there was a sudden movement and the muffled rumble of thumping hooves as they ran clumsily away into the white. Only one of them remained. Whether it was too afraid to move or purposely checking my intention I did not know, but it seemed to be waiting.

Its black eyes looked right through me, interrogating my soul, unnerving me. I could not help but wonder what it might be thinking. Like all animals, it seemed to have wisdom for which no one gave them credit. And then I wondered if it might not be staring at me, but at something unseen in the field beyond.

I gulped, and spun back around. With an unhinged logic I worried if I could have sent the entire world into turmoil by throwing that thing away there. I climbed the fence to prove myself wrong.

Slowly moving forwards while the drizzle soaked my skin and the fog parted as I walked. I could not see more than a few inches ahead. I could hardly even see the ground, looking down to see my footfall, hearing a noise and looking up, only to see nothing there.

I looked about myself and found I was lost in a cloud. All was white and I could not see anything in front of me or behind. I circled on the spot I stood and the fence I had used as entry was nowhere to be seen. I feared getting lost. I feared seeing that vision.

And then the noise again, a snuffle, an animalistic snorting.

I panicked, my heart jumped and landed in my stomach, and I ran. I hoped that I was heading back from whence I came, and that something would come into view to save me from my self induced terror. To add to that fear I was sure that I was being followed. I was sure something else, which could see better than I, now tracked my movements.

As I ran my feet sounded like hooves on the soft ground and the thing behind had even heavier steps. It's probably just the donkey, I thought. I probably scared it. And yet the thought was not strong enough to stop me from running, or to keep the fear from my heart.

The dispersing moisture gave way to the fence in what may have been a short time, but was too long for my nerves. Clumsily I climbed it and landed on my hands on the other side, my palms now filthy with wet mud. I stared at them as I got to my feet, ready to rush home, standing and finding myself face to face with the field, almost completely empty of mist... completely empty.

And at that point the sole sheep turned its back, and slowly went off into its own misty field, to join its brethren.

I used to pass that field each day, and each day the donkey had been there. Now there was nothing. The fog had withdrawn towards the sea and the view was open, giving no sign of her.

I remembered how I had seen her lately, how worried

I had been about her as it seemed that she was perhaps getting old. I knew that she was being fed and looked after, but she had not seemed that well as the weeks went on. She had been getting thinner and I could see ribs through her old grey fur. She had hardly been roaming the field at all.

It did not seem at all right and it made me feel very strange. I touched my hair, remembering the tangles in her tail that I had wanted to help her with. My own hair was a mess with them, my body feeling weaker than ever. I could not help thinking that maybe coincidences have a more arcane origin.

I feared now that I would never see her again.

Perhaps it had something to do with *them*, perhaps it was all somehow linked. Looking ahead over the distance of empty grass and recalling that vision. It was never far from my subconscious, it lived inside my brain now, finding its own nook in which to fester. The feeling it had invoked often came back as if I were reliving the whole experience, freezing my body and my mind, threatening to replay. Yet I never did see that illusion again. I saw nothing but the empty field and the white haze of the sun.

The fact that I could not just 'make it happen' was my proof. I had truly seen those dancing figures, they were physical, and it had all been real.

But that reminded me to be forever vigilant.

I checked my watch, and the timing was good. With confusion and sadness now my usual state of mind, and my heart a thumping lump in my chest, I dragged myself the rest of the way home.

* * *

Having to juggle the strange juxtaposed with normality

seemed to be my everyday life in those days. At home everything was going on as it should do, the TV playing, my father watching it, mum busying herself in the kitchen and Grandpa reading a book, sitting on his chair. But I had lost all interest.

During the week I had to try and get on with things as though I was an ordinary child, but there was much more to my life now. I did not think it fair that I had to put myself on hold over those five long days of normality, and I skipped school quite regularly after that first time.

I missed being able to chat to Grandpa as I chose. Of course we still had conversations, but it was hardly ever private and therefore the subject matter was somewhat stilted.

I had to be content in listening to him chat about the world with my father, old times with my mother and nature with us all. But no matter what everyday conversation he was having, Grandpa had a knack of linking it somewhat to the spiritual. He was a devout man, but his devotion was to the world itself, to the things upon his altar, not to any unseen creator.

I remember that Grandpa had once said how the world would have been a much better place without religion ever playing a part.

But he was as spiritual as a man can be when following no doctorate outside of his own beliefs. He loved the world and was moral because he was inherently good, because he wanted to be so, not because he was afraid of any God.

"Nature is my church," he had said.

I had not given much thought to religion before, but I had started to follow his lead.

The stories of Christmas and Easter that I was confusingly force fed at school since a young age had always seemed like nothing more than stories to me. I never thought them to be any different to the tale of the 'Three Bears' or 'Hansel and Gretel'. I think the same now. If the bible is proof to the existence of Christ then Grimm's fairy tales proved that Rumpelstiltskin once lived and bargained for a young girl's first born child.

Grandpa enjoyed watching the natural history programs on the TV, even though he still maintained he hated the technology. He used to get upset sometimes, although tried not to show it. I remember him mumbling to himself about the fact that so many animals were becoming endangered. He tried to not let anyone hear as he swore about 'peoples' under his breath, but I always heard him.

Because of his age he had witnessed a lot happen in the world, a lot of changes, and it was no secret how despondent he felt seeing its slow decline. He had become disillusioned with it all and had seen enough of all the bad things that wore him down.

"I'd rather of been born about eight thousand BC..." he said once, then paused a second before explaining his joke, his own made up acronym; "before crap!" I remember that it made him laugh for a good ten minutes.

My father did not seem to notice the signals and would continue to read stories out to him from the newspaper.

"Every day there's something else in here about this, AIDS illness Finn. It's getting a bit scary," he said, ignoring Grandpa's multitude of subtle hints. To his detriment, Grandpa always had something to say.

"If I was to be a merchant of doom," he said with a sigh, "I'd say it was the beginning of the end of the world."

"Well it seems to be mainly gay men... that's who they say caused it."

"Well I'd say that's propaganda... trying to victimise

folk. I don't know the whole story, but far as I can see, neither does anyone. They give ya a bit of information then a bit more, then they change it and take back what they said. Give it a year, and then, if we're not all lyin' dead, see what they 'ave to say then... if ya must."

Grandpa was a little impatient about it all, yet in his wisdom, had learnt to be objective about things.

We looked at each other across the room in a poised comical expression, waiting for my father to speak again. He didn't, and we shrugged our shoulders together, both took a sweet from out of our own individual bags, and popped them into our mouths at the exact same time. We then chuckled at our performance like a couple of children up to no good. It made me muse that perhaps the faeries were also locked in a perpetual state of infancy, or maybe even worse; adolescence.

* * *

While Grandpa might have been ahead of his time, the rickety old bicycle he had in the shed was not; in fact I think it was a museum piece. But I did not have a bike so had pestered my dad about it from the moment I had seen it in there. Eventually he found time to pull it from under the debris to see if it was road worthy.

It was definitely somewhat of an antique, and even had an old corroded bell on the handle bars. It was brown, almost gold and the frame was thin and more than a little rusty, but it worked ok after a little work. If I had been the sort of boy who worried about being part of the 'in crowd' I would never have allowed myself to be seen on it. As it was, my friends were the only two kids in the village, and we were all a bunch of misfits.

It was a set of wheels and I could not wait to get going, despite my feet hardly reaching from the saddle to the ground. I just enjoyed the freedom of the air rushing over me as I rode, wobbling the whole way, but with hardly any traffic it mattered little. And I remember instinctively increasing the speed of my pedalling every time I travelled passed that ominous empty field.

But nothing untoward had happened for quite a while and I was thankful that I had at least found some equilibrium. The milk I brought to them on my weekly visits was obviously working to keep up the amiable relationship between man and woodland spirit. I had not been disturbed during the night again, except by my hamster, and I had not seen any visions. My mother had not even complained of losing anything else, other than the odd half litre of milk.

I thought that I was doing fairly well at keeping my lives separated. My truancy had not been noticed and I just got on with things. But my parents often asked me questions, and although I know they were just chatting, I always saw it as interrogation. I had kept everything my secret and I now had a lot of them.

They asked about my friends and about what we were getting up to.

"That's Judith's boy ain't it?" Grandpa had said to my mother when I mentioned Martin.

They stared at each other for an uncomfortable time with nothing else spoken. I was looking at my mother and I could see her face cracking as though she wanted to say something but remained stable. Then I looked over at Grandpa sitting back in his chair, partly as though scolded, yet also with some air of pleasure in his face.

The atmosphere was often thick with those tensions and I could not help but notice.

I only strived to make sure that none of it was because of me.

"Anymore nightmares lad?" Grandpa whispered across the room, as sometimes he did when my mother was not in there.

"No," I said truthfully.

"Good boy Adam."

The coming of July had brought with it the true onset of summer, and when it came it was completely noticeable; quite unusual for England.

We finally had whole weeks where there were no clouds and very little of that disorientating mist. I did not spend much time indoors. It was bad enough being at school, staring out the windows at the brightness beyond, so when I was free from that formal cage I made sure that I felt my freedom.

I would take rides on my bike and would track down Martin somewhere on the cliffs, for he was never indoors either. And Josh would tag a long, often being the one who chose what we were going to occupy ourselves with.

Gradually I allowed our escapades to gravitate back towards my beloved woods. I know that I was being complacent, but I wanted to be there, and I wanted to be with my friends. I guess it was selfish, but naively thought; if I am supposed to be a seer, then I should know when there's something to worry about. Things had been stable so I presumed that we were safe, relaxing my opposing stance, simply for an easy life. I was just a kid and I didn't want to spend my whole life in opposition. But this failure to uphold my position was yet another nail in the coffin of my mistakes.

My friends seemed to have lost all fear of the place. Josh, undeterred by the debunking of his 'ghost' photograph, always took the camera with him to investigate. Though I myself had all but abandoned any grand ambitions of finding substantial proof. Still, he would show me the pictures he took, and looking closely into the leaves and undergrowth, I could see faeries in every one.

We even took the walkie-talkies into the woods, having childish banter from one to the other, and trying to scare each other. Our ghost stories had evolved into gory murders by mad axe men, and headless horsemen riding through the trees.

One day we were having our usual fun but I could tell something was going on between my other two friends. They stood before me about to make a presentation.

Josh nudged Martin who looked around with objection as though the slight contact had been painful. Josh was smiling, Martin was not.

"We wanted to ask you something," Josh began, sounding more serious, and coughed to clear his throat for courage. "You know you said the woods were haunted?"

Just the mere mention of that made my heart drop. I was on edge with anticipation hoping that the conversation was not going to go the way I feared. I kept quiet.

"Well, Martin was gonna write a story about it for us, so he was doing some research, he had some books didn't ya Martin..." The whole time he was speaking to me he was looking at Martin, and Martin was looking at me. He sounded uncomfortable as he spoke, yet at the same time enthusiastic. "Well... Don't laugh, but he reckons it isn't haunted, like, not by normal ghosts. Well... Martin..." and he nudged Martin again who this time looked Josh right in the eyes with a concerned expression. "Tell Adam what you said," Josh urged.

Martin turned slowly back to me, and his face was deadly, blankly serious.

"I think it's fairies," he said.

In the silent seconds that froze us there I may have smiled. But now I was nervous. It was undisclosed comprehension that foreshadows were coming to fruition.

With Martin having certain 'powers' of sixth sense I had often wondered whether it was actually pointless trying to keep anything from him. I knew it was more than possible that he already knew everything that I was trying to hide.

I felt exposed, but it was inevitable that this would eventually come to pass, and although unwanted, it was not completely unwelcome. It had been forced upon me, but my dark little secrets had been hidden long enough.

"I knew you'd laugh," Josh said to try and fill the gap and hide his embarrassment. I was not laughing. "It sounds stupid but Martin has found loads of stuff about it, and they're supposed to be real, especially round 'ere. They are a bit like ghosts."

I was almost glad that Josh had taken an interest and my smile may well have fixed in place, but I felt tense, and could not truly decipher the thoughts I held inside. I was tense.

"Some hauntings might actually be these things instead," Martin said with huge eyes looking up at me, perhaps wanting me to speak. But I could not find the words.

If my mind had been quick enough to push away my shock and pride I should have told them what I knew; that faeries are no less threatening than spirits. In fact, they could be much worse.

"Well, I'm definitely gonna stay in the camp one night," Josh went on, intent on sounding serious. "All night like I said I would. And I'm gonna see for myself."

Despite that revelation, my normal life went on. But

apparently, in the real world, that world I hardly cared to keep in touch with, things were no more settled than they were in those other realms.

My father's conversations from over his newspaper were as regular and undesirable as ever. He liked having a man in the house to discuss all those current affairs. But it was a routine I could tell my grandpa often went out of his way to avoid.

"Hey listen to this then," my father said one morning, oblivious. Even I could feel myself recoil at the thought of hearing more sensational misfortune. "Front page news. Greenpeace have had a ship sunk, not very peaceful!"

"Told ya the boat was already sinking!" Grandpa quipped. He always appeared to use humour to nullify the impact, just as I used the fact that I was only thirteen.

"Sharp as a tack your father isn't he?" Dad smiled.

"Yes," my mother scowled, "sharp in all the wrong places... A man died dad."

That only made my grandfather pause for a second of thought. "Well," he said, "I give 'em their dues, they certainly got their 'earts in the right places. Doin' more than I am. They's out there tryin' to make peace while I'm sittin' 'ere on me arse just moaning about it."

I did not understand the politics behind how the world had become as it was, but out of the mouths of babes comes logic 'why can't we all just get along?' Even though my grandfather was in his seventies, I know he believed in that same impossible sentiment.

There was a brief taster of 'peace' when July 13th brought the whole family together around the TV set to watch a piece of history being made.

It was a warm Saturday but rather than go outside to enjoy the weather we were all glued to the live band performances beamed to us by satellite in the name of charity. Martin and Josh were watching it at their houses too, and it was spoken about at school for days.

We all knew what it was in aid of, having been force fed that knowledge through the television and on the radio that last Christmas with the 'feed the world' song played over and over. But despite seeing those images of people, and so many children starving in Ethiopia, it all seemed a million miles from my life. I could hardly believe it was even true that such things went on. And if it was so bad, I did not understand how giving a few pounds of our money could be any help, or why it was up to mere pop stars to try and make a difference.

Grandpa was attempting to concentrate on reading while my parents and I enjoyed the show, but he kept looking up and shaking his head. He was trying to keep his opinions to himself, but that never worked for Grandpa.

"Bloody shame," he said, "It's doin' good I know, but should never 'ave 'appened in the first place. Ya can't run a world on charity. As it is, it's run by greedy powers starving us of every right we 'ad... so that's our choice!"

It seemed too immense to get my head around, and I was far too young to change the whole world. All I could do was protect and make peace with the little corner that I lived in. And I tried to live in the way Grandpa preached, to remember that every footfall leaves a print.

* * *

On the last day of term Josh made his announcement. He had decided that on that very night he would stay in the woods... that he would keep to his word, and keep his vigil.

It was hot, almost unbearably so, and the heat can do strange things to your mind. But although I would like to put it down to momentary insanity, it was already in Josh's nature to follow through with things no matter how unreasonable they may be.

He was perhaps the happiest of us all to have weeks without school and had already got an idea for adventure firmly stuck in his head. He came towards me with Martin on his heel; big smiles, grand plans. As I waited there for the bus and watched them draw closer I was blissfully unaware of what was going through their minds. But the peace I had found was soon to be gone forever.

I had screwed up my brow and pursed my lips, almost wincing under the strain of what he had said, yet trying to think of an apt answer. I had still hoped that the idea was an idle threat, but now the time had finally come.

Martin covered for my silence. "I've already tried to talk him out of it," he said shrugging his shoulders, "but you know what Josh is like."

Josh grinned. His stubborn attitude would not break down, and we knew it.

"So," he said to me. "Can I borrow the walkie-talkie?"

I nodded before even wondering why. I knew there was no way they would work from the woods to my house over the expanse of field between them. Josh anticipated my revoke.

"I know it won't work when I'm far off, but... I need some kinda contact."

I nodded again and was still trying to think of a few words of warning, considering whether or not to let them know something of what I experienced there. I probably should have at least given some advice. But it did not even sit well with me that they knew as much as they did. More than anything I was afraid that the little people would not take kindly to having Josh in their homeland during the hours in which were most sacred to them. I had divided loyalties.

The chance for speaking came and went, and time took away the thought of words, but not my concerns. Josh had left in the car with his father, still smiling at the concept of his night to come, and I was very quiet on the bus ride home.

Josh arrived at my house just before nine. It was still warm but evening had subdued the sun and the cooling was welcome. Summer's twilight evenings came with a magical, pleasant atmosphere, and I was sure that Josh was in that frame of mind. But the serenity of the semi-light and the gentle tepid breeze could be but a cloak of glamour. To me there was nothing that could completely hide the feeling of foreboding.

I imagined that they already knew he was coming, but I did not know how they would react. They might be at peace with me, but I was not sure how they felt about the most rambunctious of my friends.

I was glad that I was not the one to be spending the night there but my concerns were not founded simply in fear, it was deeper than that. I did not really imagine Josh coming to physical harm, but that it was more likely his soul which was in jeopardy. With those imaginings came an overshadowing of dread, yet held too many possibilities to even grasp a one.

Josh carried with him a bag and was excited to tell me everything that he had with him for his overnight stay. He had certainly brought his courage but I doubted that he truly believed in it all as I did. Perhaps to him it was a story he could find the root of, an explainable list of phenomena that he would be the one to unravel. Or perhaps he just did not know enough about these things to know that there was a reason to be afraid.

I handed him one of the walkie-talkies as we stood on the doorstep. All the while I was looking over to the side, to the field where he would soon be walking. It was fairly light, and he also had a torch, yet they had their ways of cloaking the senses. I could not see the woods with the angle of the house, but I knew they were there, I felt that they were there.

Time was passing. The moment for me to stop him was fast slipping through my fingers. I felt guilty that I would let him do it alone, but not guilty enough to go with him. I am glad that he did not ask me to.

Perhaps to ease my guilt slightly, I decided to step out with him, to see him off from the fence. I wanted to see what he was facing, but he would be facing it alone.

There were no houses or street lights to give any luminance to the barren field or the total blackness that was the patch of opposing woodland. I watched them throb and undulate as the clouds shifted the darkness into different shades of shadow moving over the surface of the field. It was as though something there was always awake; flickers of light in amongst the trees which were there for the briefest of moments, and gone with no validation. They could all have been slight shifts in my viewpoint, the dappling, dwindling sun making patterns upon the ground, breaking through tiny gaps in the distant branches. But I did not need to see to be a seer. I knew what was there.

"Adam…"

"Josh?"

"Just go back in! I'll be fine."

I had not realised how obvious my unease had become. I was just staring, thinking, making prayers to unknown gods. I could hardly believe this was going to happen.

The false calm could not disguise the descending darkness and I had been physically fidgeting with my

urge to be inside. I wanted nothing more than to shut
the door on the night, and despite the guilt, on my friend
as well.

I followed his welcome order, and left him to his fate.

From my bedroom window I watched him walk across
the field.

The waning light seemed to grow a little dimmer with
every few steps that he took. A silhouette which at first
looked like my friend became just a shadow, just a
distant figure as he got smaller with his distance over the
grey grass.

The trees he headed for were black, and the spaces
between them were disappearing. My forehead was
pressing upon the window glass, the curtains drawn
about my head so that I might see. Inside my room was
light and life. I felt blessed to be safe. It was his
decision, not my fault, but perhaps I should have told
him?

My mind was batting that back and forth until
eventually I managed to console myself with the
thought, and realisation, that knowing Josh, he would
have done it anyway.

The walkie-talkie crackled and I heard a voice. I held
it close to my ear as I watched the figure move in the
middle of the open field. I could just make out that he
had it held up, yet I could not even tell whether he was
facing me. The voice was Josh but it was very faint
through the sounds of static.

"I can't really hear you," I said through it as loudly as
I felt I wanted to. "I think that's about as far as it
reaches... good luck Josh."

It crackled again, the figure moved, and then I heard
him.

"I'm going in..." And I saw his torch come on, making
a thin stream of light, a doorway opening into the woods

themselves.

It was impossible to not think about my friend all that night, to not imagine what he might be doing, thinking, seeing.

I spent the entire evening in my room, unable to concentrate on doing anything other than lying on my bed with my thoughts.

Perhaps in honour of Josh's quest I lay with my curtains undrawn and the light off, staring over and up into the dark blue sky. Occasionally, feeling unsettled, I would sit up and look over there, to the blackness, to where I knew that he still was. But I could see nothing and had no way to know what he was going through.

He was probably not terribly afraid, but even if your imagination is limited, darkness can do strange things to your mind and senses. I doubted very much that he would actually be able to sleep there in the camp. It would not be very comfortable, even with the sleeping bag he had taken. Every noise would be sure to startle him, the flapping wings of a disturbed bird, the screeching of an owl. All of those unfamiliar sounds of creatures lurking, cracking twigs beneath tiny feet. I wondered if he knew enough of nature to console himself of their earthly origins. I wondered if anything would happen to him that was not so benign.

I almost wanted him to find something, to see something that would substantiate all of my ambiguous experiences. But I dared not think what that would be.

CHAPTER TEN

I had drifted off to sleep at some point, but was no doubt half awake as I became aware that I could hear my grandfather speaking. My hamster was running in its wheel again, and I was trying to 'shush' it from across the room, so that I could listen to what he was saying.

It was definitely his voice, softly spoken, and ascending from the lounge. It seemed that his sentences were strangely long, with very few breaks, and no answer from anyone else. But I was getting annoyed at Cobweb's constant movements that were keeping me from hearing the words properly.

Looking at my clock I saw that it was only eleven o'clock, but Grandpa was the only one still up. I silently rose from bed and tip-toed onto the landing, being as quiet as possible and pricking up my ears. From there I could hear him, strange though it was. He was speaking to himself again...

"Perhaps Annie should've never come back 'ere, I'm surprised she did really. Adam's still so young. But I think I teached him well enough, things is quiet now. I do think they must 'ave lost some patience over time though. Didn't know they'd still be so active to be honest."

I continued to listen, half expecting a friend of his that I had never met to join in the conversation. But after a while I could tell that there really was nobody else there.

I did not want to continue standing alone on the landing, but I felt that I had to or Grandpa might stop speaking. Perhaps he was just thinking out loud, but I was very interested to know his thoughts.

"But I knows theys always 'ere," Grandpa went on. "Kinda nice to know they ain't gone anywhere, even if they are getting teasy. Guess I'm a silly old man, jealous that I ain't ever seen 'em me self. Foolish maybe, but I thought it was 'armless to tell Adam everything I told 'im."

I gasped, and immediately, I heard a heavy click. Straight away I put the facts together and realised that Grandpa had been taping himself, speaking on the recorder beside his chair. My thoughts were quick, formulating a future plan, and to hide my reaction I was loudly stepping down the stairs with a fake yawn as I entered the lounge.

"Ah young Adam," Grandpa was acting too, but he had more experience. I did, however, witness his hand leaving the machine by his side. He lowered his voice. "Havin' a bad night?"

I nodded, still continuing to stretch back my arms to complete my charade.

I felt a little guilty.

"Not been 'avin' nightmares again have you?" he pressed.

I shook my head. Words were on the tip of my tongue.

"Nothing much happening of late?"

I knew what he meant, and I think the shake of my head was this time rather hesitant and rather telling. He beckoned me over to him, and once there, he whispered in my ear.

"D'you know where ya father's toolbox is Adam?"

I did, but was obviously confused as to what he might be saying.

"You might feel better if yous 'elp yourself to one of his nails."

I squinted my brow as I moved my head away from Grandpa and he gave a knowing nod.

"Keep ya safe," he said, tapping the side of his nose with a stretched finger.

It was comforting to have seen him that night, brief though it was. At that time I really needed some assurance and I was glad that he could see into me like one of his over-read books. Taking a nail from the toolbox, a trinket of faith, was an easy way to gain enough confidence to see the rest of the night through. But I was not planning on sleeping.

I sat waiting on my bed. I stared at the reflections of my room in the glass of my window. I listened to every sound. I heard the toilet flush, the clicks of lights switched on, lights switched off. I heard Grandpa's door finally close.

My own mission was about to begin.

It involved waiting a little longer until I knew he would be asleep, and then creeping back downstairs. It involved moving slowly over to Grandpa's table while remaining in the seclusion of the dark, ejecting the cassette from his player and taking care not to make a sound. But the panel for the tape holder came up too quickly and it rattled loudly.

I stopped moving for a second to insure that all was silent. I was still, waiting in a frozen position in the grey light. I stayed that way long enough to know safely that no one had heard, and then I removed the cassette, and made my retreat.

I was faster as I went back up the stairs, the urgency to listen to what was on that tape, too tempting to keep me from hurrying.

I had not even used my personal cassette player much so I knew that the batteries would hold out. Josh had leant me a couple of his cassettes but I did not really like them, and no music had interested me enough to yet buy any of my own. This would put the technology to good use.

I set myself up, sitting on top of my bed, back against

my white headboard and putting the semi-circle crown that was the headphones onto my head. The parts which cupped my ears were made of soft orange sponge and were comfortable enough. My bedside lamp was on, my room was in shadow, but Grandpa's voice might well keep me from the fears I had for Josh, and for myself.

I put one hand in my pyjama pant's pocket and took a grip of that nail, then pressed the play button on the player.

A slight whirring sound but otherwise only silence. I let it rewind back for a few seconds and pressed play again, to check that I would hear my grandpa.

"I think perhaps they are like spoilt children sometimes these creatures," it was him, and I knew exactly what his subject matter was. Now I hoped that the whole tape was going to be about them, and that the uncensored version of his theories might give me the greatest of insights.

"They can be bullies," he was saying, "but maybe because we 'ave bullied them for centuries. We might not know it, but we is the bullies."

I stopped the tape and thought for a moment, pondering, and then rewound it again. It was quite a wait but I let it reel all the way back to the beginning. I sat there, hearing the spools turn, becoming impatient, and finally, it clicked to a stop.

I might be about to learn the truth, but I wondered if I would be able handle it. A deep breath and my finger pressed down on the play button once more.

I heard that whirring sound, then some rustling as if of papers. I heard a cough, and I knew it was Grandpa. He began to talk, sounding a little tentative at first, but he had my full attention.

"Right... I reckons us old folk have a duty to pass on

wisdom 'n' my Annie stopped listening many years ago, she don't wanna know... well, this 'ere tape thing I'm speaking on will listen and one day someone can 'ear what I have to say and what I believe."

"Finn you want a cup a tea love?" Another voice came from the background, a lady. Grandpa coughed again, and the cassette made a loud snap sound where he had obviously stopped the recording. I decided to stop the tape too, as I felt the need to think.

I knew that the distant voice was Grandpa's wife, it was not my mother. There she was, a lady that was no longer even alive, recorded forever. That imprint of the past had not been erased simply because her life had been. I wondered how it would feel to hear that voice again if I were Grandpa, but to me right then, it felt a little spooky.

I started the tape again.

"Err... Well my Hilary probably wouldn't approve too much of all this either, she'd think I'm a silly old man, but I've got stories to tell..."

And I listened to those stories.

The first part of the tape was full of Grandpa piecing together parts of folklore and explaining them how he saw fit. It seemed almost as if he were dictating for the text of a factual book.

Most of it was similar information to that which he had told me face to face, although perhaps a little less cryptic than our bedroom lessons. He said about how there were mistakes in other people's stories, 'Chinese whispers' throughout the years changing how those stories are told, and reiterated how you can only really know if you experience it yourself.

And then he told of the weird things that had been happening in his house, of things going missing and of food going stale. He said how he would protect himself from them, 'just in case'. Yet he also said how he had never seen anything with his eyes, but plenty with his gut.

He recounted more about his mining days and told a story he had never spoken to any of us about. He said on the tape that a work mate had once uncovered a tiny tool from out of a rock. He described it as 'a miniature pick, no bigger than ya little toe, fashioned by expert hands.' And his voice sounded dumbfounded by the recollection, exclaiming 'how do you explain that away?'

And then he began to speak of my mother.

I tightened my grip upon the nail in my pocket, which was making an indent upon my clenched palm.

"Annie don't wanna be near me anymore 'n' it ain't nothing I done, it's what this place is and what it represents. Maybe one day she'll forgive the place, but it's 'erself she'll need to forgive first.

"I never said all what I'm gonna say to no one and I'm sayin' it now only to this contraption... Hilary's gone out a while so she won't even 'ear. I'm 'oping young Adam will hear all this one day, make up his own mind. I doubt his mother will ever tell him any of it. Up to me to do this I think, imparting my wisdom from generation to generation."

I did not stop listening but my mind was going crazy with all of the information, hearing my name being spoken, and having no idea at all what was yet to come.

"She, my Annie, she used ta love my stories of faeries when she were small, just as I loved my father tellin' 'em to me. We were rough as rats my family, 'n' I only had one book to me name. I treasured it, but without 'em my head was still filled with the wonder of tall tales. My father spun a good yarn, people seem to be losing the art of telling camp side stories. But only later I found out some of 'em may well 'ave been true.

"I know he filtered 'em, some of the frightening bits taken out, at least till I was a bit older, so I did the same for Annie. Beings a cheel, I suppose I softened 'em up quite a bit. You know, sugar and spice and all things nice, is what little girls are made of. Think I might of liked a boy, not that I'd ever tell Annie that, but slugs 'n' snails is more my speciality.

"Still I turned my hand to the fairy tales that she liked. The faeries had gossamer wings and fluttered about doing good turns for people. Not really faeries of course.

"But her imagination blossomed seeing old paintings of delicate little ladies and gentlemen dressed in fine clothes among the flowers. I taught her that nature needed these creatures to 'elp it grow, because she liked all that, and I think it was my way of teaching her to care. 'Course nature don't need no 'elp from other worldly beings, has its own creatures for all that. Nature has a magic of its own. There ain't no faery dust... just dust.

"Well, she played in my garden, losing herself in it, hidden safe under the shade of the trees, protected by the ash. But her age got theirs attention. Things was 'appening and I knew they were abouts. No 'arm of course, but I 'ad to keep an eye.

"I built them a little house that looked like this cottage and she was happy playing with it, pretending that the faeries came to her for tea. Said they were there and singin' her songs. She didn't even need 'er dolls 'cause she had the faeries.

"I'd 'ave liked to believe it, that they were makin' use of that 'ouse, but I knew she hadn't really seen 'em. Even when she played in Old Bob's wood, coming back telling me about mushroom rings and the place being full of little folk, I knew she hadn't actually seen anything, probably not even felt 'em. I just 'ad a feeling that Annie want no seer.

"Her sensibilities were to play make believe, making food for the little people, even taking real food and leaving it there for them. Certainly no 'arm in that, I thoughts. Be good to them and they is good to you.

"I've no doubt they was coming, interested in 'er, but she didn't notice, couldn't see, even if they was staring her in the face. I don't think she was too happy that she never really saw anything.

"Course it never was real faeries that she believed in, it was those picture books, and my stories.

"She was just a child but she wanted to grow up. Liked to play mummy and that was what she was doing with that house I made. Got more of a chance later, making friends with a local girl, Judith Kendall.

"She was a strange one she was. I think Annie took her under her wing 'cause she felt sorry for her. Some kids though, they don't 'ave any friends 'cause they really don't invite them. I could hear them talking and she was real odd, nice one minute, then pushing you away with spite the next.

"Anyway, turns out she had a little sister, only just four years old and I know for fact it was 'er that Annie liked best. She was a dolly for her to mother, old enough to say a few words, and that made her a good playmate. Judith might have been her age, but it was little Esther that was the better friend."

I had to stop the cassette player, almost involuntarily. There was already a lot to take in.

So Martin's mother and mine had played together as children? Just as their sons were now doing. What comes around...

"She mothered that kid, and its own mother didn't seem to mind. I myself would never have let a ten year old girl take my little one out, but that woman did. She was no good, but not really to blame I suppose. My Annie was responsible enough. Brought her in my garden and me 'n' my lady, rest 'er soul, looked out for 'em both. Annie thought she was in charge of course, and we let 'er believe that and play mummy for a few hours. They'd have their tea parties, Annie feeding Esther too much cake.

"Would 'ave been ok but the thing is, young Esther seemed to see things. It made Annie annoyed I could tell, and I knew why too. Annie thought that Esther was seeing faeries, and I dare say that's exactly what she was seein'. It made my one jealous. That was Annie's undoing.

"I had no idea till it was done, but Annie took Esther to the woods with 'er one day. I'd never 'ave let 'er of course. But I know what she was up to, hoping that the faeries would come out to see 'er little friend and she would see them as well.

"Annie only told me all this 'cause we put 'er through the mill about it, the little girl had apparently given 'er the slip and run off. Took her quite some time to find her again and she was perfectly well but ummin from scrambling about in the dirt at the bottom a some hole. Crawling in the mud in her flam new yellow dress.

"I don't know what she'd been up to, what she'd seen and done in that time but I certainly have my theories. I remember that little girl was always singing a pretty tune, real pretty... too sweet. It 'ad no words but I always thought it meant something...

"Anyway, my Annie got in trouble for it all and was told she was never allowed to take Esther out again.

"She didn't have a chance as things went, 'cause the girl went missing.

"It was a terrible time for us all, days 'n' days of not knowing nothing. But the village was buzzing with fear and rumours. Annie got the blame and I had to swear blind that she ain't done nothing. Far as I know she were innocent, but who knows? Was all such a mess.

"I had to keep her at home so she didn't get bile spat at her. She was in tears of course, but soon after that, went completely numb. It blighted the village for her, and for us all at the time.

"The papers were full of it. People thought the worst, thought she'd been taken, kidnapped or murdered. There were miserable news reports with photos of young Esther making it all ten times worse for everyone. And she were never found no matter how much they searched.

"The whole village was over the fields walkin' in a long row, eyes to the ground, police in front, checking for any tiny clues. Our community was broken but we were glued together through it all.

"For years after that, when I went on me stanks, I'd be 'alf afraid I'd find 'er little dead body, see a little flash of yellow fabric in the dirt. Feels bad to think of it even now, that she could still be out there somewhere. But I 'ave other theories of course. Part of me thinks that she *is* out there, but it ain't just her body. I didn't tell no one, would have been a laughin' stock. But I knows how the faeries like children.

"She could be in those woods, neither in their world nor ours, flitting between them, perhaps completely unaware of time and space. Neither 'ere nor there.

"She might pass back through sometimes, not even knowin' it, not even rememberin' the life she 'ad. But she can't ever come back now... To come back to this world now, she'd probably just die from the trauma or go out of her mind.

"Anyway, far as the village was concerned it was a human tragedy best forgotten. Doubt Judith ever got over it, losin' her little sister. Certainly tainted everything for Annie, made her grow up even quicker.

"As the shock wore off, people round 'ere started makin' jokes and talkin' of the little folk 'avin' something to do with poor little Esther. Annie got upset about all that, was like she could never get away from it I suppose. And no doubt she thought I'd been lying to her all those years with my pretty stories.

"She hated it all now, knowing the darkness in it. What happened to Esther made it too real, too dark even for me, not that everything can be blamed on the little folk. But Annie never wanted a single word spoken about it again, wanted to fill her life with what she convinced herself was reality.

"My Annie turned into a bit of a madam after that. She's lived a prosaic life, went to school and studied hard. She said she hated living in a small village where everyone knew everyone's business and that she wanted to live in the city and get some highfalutin job. She did just that in the end, but I'd already lost 'er as much as we'd all lost little Esther."

Grandpa coughed, heralding the end of his recounting, and then he continued to ponder on it all, coming up with other interpretations. I think, deep down, he really did believe it was to do with the little people.

Darkness and tiredness were causing my eyelids to grow heavy and forcing me to give up to sleep. But my mind was forever changed now. It spun with all that I knew, things that could never again be unknown.

I had managed to stay awake to hear the end of that which was so important. Now I lay myself under one thin sheet, still dreading something happening that my unconsciousness would be unable to fight. But Grandpa's voice went on speaking into my ears. And as I drifted off, it was Grandpa I could still hear, reading me his bedtime stories.

* * *

There was a phone call at two in the morning, which my father answered.

I woke, sweating from the lingering heat, and run a hand over my face, propping myself up and listening.

A loud thud beside me was the tape player falling from my bed. Memories interspersed with the present.

My dad did not sound at all pleased, his voice coming from the hallway as I tried to wake myself enough to hear the words.

"No Josh, he's sleeping...I'm sure it can wait till morning...Calm down lad..."

I had managed to swing my feet over the bed and shuffle onto the landing. The light was too bright and made me squint and hold a hand over my eyes. My father saw me there and looked up at me as I came down the stairs, his face confused and tired.

"Hang on Josh, he's here."

He handed me the phone, but certainly did not seem very impressed.

"Get rid of him will you?" he whispered to me, and went straight back up to his bedroom.

I lifted the phone receiver slowly to my ear, fearing to hear whatever was going to be said and not awake enough to deal with it.

"Adam, I'm at home, I had to go. I couldn't sleep there, I was too psyched. I saw something. It was brief you know but I saw it, through the camp window.

"Damn, I left your walkie-talkie in there. Sorry mate, but it started crackling and it distracted me for a second, and at the same time... I saw like a shadow of someone. So I looked out really quick and it moved in the trees.

"I can't explain but there's a feeling in there, and I just knew... There was someone in there I'm sure of it.

I just keep thinking about it, 'cause I know it's not right, you know? I mean, it's weird isn't it? We never see anyone else in those woods.

"But Adam, I think it was a little girl, really little, real young, I mean she had to be, she was tiny, and really thin. It was just a shadow but I'm bloody certain I saw it... I saw her Adam. But what the hell would a kid be doing in the woods at that time of night? I mean..."

I could hardly cope with hearing those words, and he would have gone on rambling like that for hours if I had not spoken to calm him down. Yet my mind was about as calm as a tornado dancing with a hurricane. It was not just me now, both my friends had seen something there, and perhaps with good reason.

"It's ok Josh," I said, "maybe you did see something, I have too."

"Really? You think there's a girl living in the woods? Like a wild child or something?"

"I don't know what to think, but I'm glad you're ok," I said, realising my relief that he was no longer still out there. "We'll talk tomorrow."

I was about to put the phone down, but he quickly added one thing that would prevent me from getting any more sleep that night.

"I think I got a photo."

I had put the phone down before anything else was said that my brain could not handle. I had no words to express how I felt now that my closely personal experience had suddenly become something much larger and involved us all. Josh would not let the matter drop now, I knew that, and I also knew how it would spark the interests of Martin. It was the three of us now, not just me, and my peace had shattered.

To further, and terrifyingly enforce the belief that life had just changed, my sleepless night did not seem able to keep away dreams.

With all that Josh had said, and all of its implications on my mind, there was no way that sleep would find me, but something did. Somehow something found its way into me, forcing nightmares upon me while I lay awake, twisted and sweating.

I had crawled back inside my bed with the vain hope that I might rest, but the heat of the room, and the heat of my mind prevented any moment of calm. I remember the minutes passing and at no point did I lose time or consciousness. I know as clearly as I know that I exist; I was not sleeping.

I lay on my back, and then on my side, tossing and turning, watching the illuminated red digits of my electric radio clock, seeing every minute as it changed.

From the corner of my eye I saw the curtains move ever so slightly, just as I had seen before. I held my breath, anxious that something was there, that something was about to happen. I was completely on edge, but tried to rationalise that the curtains probably often moved, and that I only noticed because I was looking. The half open window making a draft.

But after a few moments of calm, they did it again.

This time I forced myself to leave the comfort of my sheets, to check, and tentatively move the curtains apart to see outside. I saw the darkness, I saw the taunting trees, I saw my own eyes staring fearfully back in the reflection.

I was becoming tired of being frightened, and so over tired that I perhaps could have hallucinated. But after all that had happened to me, how could I believe in any rationale?

It must have been three am. I had been lying awake for about an hour. The faery time of midnight had passed me without event, but it had no doubt found Josh. Now it was there with me.

Perhaps the house stood in their way; the cottage built on an ancient faery road. Perhaps they had always come through there; the first abode that they came to should they travel from the woods. Or perhaps, as I suspected, it was me that they wanted.

Again I saw a slight wave of the curtains, their movement subtle but apparent. They lifted below, as if to let something pass from behind, then gently fluttered to a stop.

I watched this, tired, but awake, my line of sight direct enough to see that motion. My eyes were wide against the room's darkness, they flicked about their sockets and did not blink. I was looking for it, because I knew that it was there, I felt that it was there. I was waiting.

And what I felt was a shifting in reality, a shift between the sounds and sights of my room, to a room the same, but different. It became too quiet, too filled with shaded shadows, too thick with atmosphere for the day's heat to account for. It was as if the thing which had surely entered my room brought with it more than its presence, but also a piece of its own world so that it might dwell in mine for a time. And time was no aspect because time, it seemed, had stopped.

I turned my head, eyes quite adjusted, seeing through the murk, my hamster at its bars, sniffing the air.

And with the instant panic that ensued I tried to sit up and challenge this thing, my brain suddenly enraged, but my body giving no response. Nothing, no movement. I could not move an arm nor a leg, not even, though I struggled, a single finger. I tried to call out but I had no voice. I could not even move my eyes inside my skull anymore, staring straight up at the ceiling unable to even close them. I was completely and desperately paralysed.

Yet my mind was completely active, it was on fire, and at the forefront of it I was asking this invisible entity one question over and over, because I actually believed it might have been my only chance of salvation. I asked it for its name.

I heard a thousand whispers but the voices were neither mere sounds nor speaking true words. My entire body felt cold, frozen in a clenched state, a perpetual flinching as a weight slowly increased the pressure from above my bed covers.

I needed to know what it was, and yet, I almost wished that I could just pass out, shut it out, end the torment. There was no way I could make my eyes look to see as the covers began pressing closer against me. That weight on my chest was taking my breath. I continued to struggle yet my body did not obey. Something was bearing down upon me, and with it a buzzing in my head, taking all other sounds away.

The darkness filled my eyes with its presence, getting deeper and richer and heavy with black oscillating shadows. I thought I might die. It was becoming that unbearable. I kept asking the question but now I was losing hope that I could do anything to save myself. My only real hope was that this thing would just leave, that the ordeal might, at some point, come to its own end.

It was a living nightmare, yet I remember having coherent thoughts. I remember how I prayed and cried out with no sound, wishing that my parents would know something was wrong and come to my aid. Surely the whole house would awaken to this. Surely in my anguish I could not be alone.

And yet I knew that this experience was mine, for me to deal with, to put up with, to suffer. Alone was exactly what I was.

And then it faded.

Even though I had not been sleeping, my normal senses seemed to return to me as though I had suddenly become awake. A continuous sharp and tinny noise became the basis of reality, the unworldly state I had been trapped in drifting away. The darkness, that had for a time become deeper even than black, now immediately retreated, leaving only that sound; confused snapping whispers.

A veil had been lifted. The weight was gone as though never there, and I was not even short of breath as I instantly sat straight up in bed, the paralysis leaving no remnants. My heart pounded hard in my chest as the only physical reminder, though my mind was recalling it all too well.

And the noise persisted.

Within a few seconds my head was clear enough to locate that the sounds came from across the room... the walkie-talkie lying upon the shelf top. It was crackling and popping quietly to itself as I sat there looking at it with the memories of my ordeal becoming lost as a dream, yet leaving shaken emotions hanging over me.

I shivered as if gripped by cold and switched on the lamp. Immediately I saw that the feathers I had gathered and displayed were now strewn about the floor. They had obviously been disturbed by something. Something had obviously, physically, happened. And it took me a moment to realise, distracted by commotion, that although some of the feathers seemed to be merely randomly fallen, there was also a definite circle.

The crackling static stopped. And I held my breath.

A reprieve and then it briefly came again. But now within that mess of noise I could hear something else. It was a voice, rising out yet almost hidden beneath the unclear sounds. It seemed to be whispering, words that occasionally rose in volume, yet were completely indecipherable.

Until it shouted. One word, above the constant mumbling. A clear voice that sounded like no voice I had ever heard, returning me to total, unwelcome consciousness.

It had said but one thing, answering that question I had asked over and over... To keep me from harm.

Like a parent calling to its child, it said a name...

'Esther'.

CHAPTER ELEVEN

After the indistinct amount of time it took me to find courage enough to move, I managed to reach the walkie-talkie and switch it off, slowly and thoughtfully putting it back down.

I sat there on the edge of the bed, looking down at the feathers, so long that after a while I did not even see them anymore. My memories of the turbulent night were replaying as I kept hearing that voice in my head, saying that name. It was indescribable; nothing with which to compare it, no way to even decipher its gender or age.

But although my brain was occupied with thoughts it did not allow me to ignore that my body was now feeling sorer than I had ever known it. It felt as though I had been in a vicious fight... and I had not fared well.

I did not want to make an appearance downstairs that morning, but knew that could look worse on me. I kept quiet but I know that the anguish on my face was obvious and readable. I feared that they would know everything.

My father had got up from his chair and started to inspect me, my mother looking on, concerned. Grandpa must have still been in his bedroom.

"Has someone at school had a go at you?" my father asked. "You can tell us you know."

"You look like death Adam," my mother said over Dad's shoulder.

I flinched when he tried to touch me, he moved a hand towards my face.

"What is it Adam?" my mum asked her questions again, her voice sounding desperate as she and my father gave a look to each other. "I didn't notice that last night."

Notice what?

I felt fragile and did not like the scrutiny, backing away from both of them.

I had no idea how bad I looked. But when I went to see Grandpa, he almost immediately motioned for me to take a look at myself in his dusty mirrored wardrobe. Although my hair was still not that long it was twisted into thick strands, a little like ill-conceived dreadlocks. I also had a slight bruise on my right cheek and a small scratch. My eyes were red where they should have been white, and dark below them, suggesting that I had not slept in days.

Grandpa knew straight away something was going on, and although he was acting very reserved, he was only waiting until I was ready to unload my burden. We had only been speaking in single words and grunts, but now that I had become fully aware of my physical appearance, I was ready to talk.

"Something happened to me last night Grandpa."

"I know Adam, I think even ya parents have noticed this time. I want to know everything, but I got a bad feelin' that you tellin' me what 'appened ain't gonna make me worry any less," he sounded completely sincere, looking up at me with his head down, as if peering over spectacles that he did not wear.

I deserved his disdain. I knew that I had done wrong.

I crept up sheepishly onto his bed and hardly dare say what I now knew I had to.

"I had a nightmare," I started, "but I was awake."

Grandpa pursed his lips and was nodding as though he already knew what I was going to say, but I continued. "There was something on top of me. I couldn't see it, but I know. I couldn't move... and I heard things..."

Grandpa gave me a moment while he was thinking of

what to say, scratching his chin. "My first question would be what ya done? But I guess you want ta know what they as done to you?"

I was not sure that I did.

"Well, you've got their attention alright. Sounds to me like you got the stag now boy. No messin' about. Was this the first time? Anything else ya ain't been telling me?"

I could physically feel the colour drain from my face.

Grandpa still had a sympathetic manner but I could tell by the shortness of his speech that deeper down he was annoyed. He had a right to be. I had gone against his wishes, and against unwritten laws, or at least my friends had. But I had started my confession now.

"I'm scared Grandpa, I've got bruises all over me."

He lengthened his eyelids with an inquiring squint as I showed him one of my arms.

"Pinched," he said, as though he had suspected it. One word inducing a thousand more nightmares.

"Adam..." he looked me dead in the eyes in order to prise out the truth, with a hand on my shoulder as a notion of support. "What on Earth 'ave you done to upset them?"

I knew this was a good question, but it was one I did not want to answer.

They would not have done those things to me unless I had made them angry. But it was not me, it was Josh. I wondered then if he had been given similar treatment, or if either he or Martin had ever experienced the things that had been happening to me over the last two months. I felt selfish to have never asked. I felt that I should have called Josh straight away that morning before caring about myself.

Being so set on keeping everything secret could well have caused me to miss answers that were right there in front of me. I was agitated as I sat there, not only to have been put on the spot by Grandpa, but because I now had the urge to know more about what Josh had seen. Only then could I make any of it right again.

But only Grandpa would know how to help me; I did not want a repeat of the previous night. In the light of that day I may well shrug it off, forget how bad it was like any child does. But this was more than getting back in the playground after a grazed knee, this would not just go away on its own. Come the dark I would be thinking on it a fresh, and fearing the loneliness of my own bed. I had to continue my conversation.

Glossing over any previous undisclosed encounters, I told him about my friend spending the night at the woods.

"And he says he took a photo of it," I finished.

Grandpa's face dropped. It was sudden, apparent, but almost as if he had been trying to keep it from happening the whole time. Now it appeared that the pain he had tried to hide overcame him and creased him up, showing in this expression. It almost shocked me to see it. I felt that I had crossed a line with him, that he would no longer think I was the 'good boy' he wanted to believe I was.

"Adam, these is secretive creatures, if they finds out you been spyin' on 'em it'd be dangerous for you an' your friends. Ya can't capture something like them on one of your modern contraptions... didn't I tell ya all this an age ago?" He sounded as if he was restraining anger, confounded, at a loss. Perhaps all this time he had thought me an equal, and now realised that I was but a child.

"Adam I mean it, ya pushin' your luck now boy. Better fit you don't ever go back there. Stay away now, play somewhere else."

My mouth had dropped open. Grandpa was the most

animated I had ever seen him, fidgeting with emotion.

"I know ya like the woods Adam, so do I, but that's not the way to enjoy 'em. Round 'ere we've learnt to respect their privacy. Maybe I told ya too much, got ya all wound up excited. I suppose I just wanted to share 'em with ya... thought it was important 'cause it's all getting lost and I reckon knowin' it shaped me, made me who I am, made this place what it is.

"It's a passion speakin' to ya, like it's always spoken ta me. Nature has an ancient language but we still 'aven't learnt it Adam. You can 'ear it in the streams, the wind itself, if we could only understand it... You can't forget how wonderful it is to know all this. That every hollow could be a doorway, every leaf could be a shelter, every mushroom grown from their footprints.... The whole countryside is dripping with things unseen and without ya even knowing it, that's part of why ya feel so much for those places. And yet ya ain't really listening anymore... it's like you've given up on seein'."

He slowly shook his head, overcome it seemed by his own emotive words. But his displeasure had changed now, from closeted annoyance to something closer to sadness. I had a dread fear that he was going to say he was 'disappointed in me', I didn't think he could say anything worse than that.

"Most folk don't care about all a this anymore," he went on while I remained silent, lump in my throat. "I suppose I wanted you to care..."

I tried to interrupt, to say 'But I do'. I cared so much, too much. But Grandpa put up a hand wanting to continue.

"I know Adam, I know... and most folk 'ave gone on with their so called civilised world while I've stayed put. I might be a wise old man or I might just be a fool. I'll certainly never stand as long as those trees, and never 'ope to know what they know. But it's almost like it don't matter anymore, yet it matters same as ever.

"From where I stand I can see the bigger picture, the whole landscape view. And it seems those others are the ones who 'ave gone on blindly, exploiting everything as they go. I see it and it cripples me more than me stroke did. I was just trying to show you Adam, not to forget like they 'as. I want you to know about nature, about the old ways, the old tales, and the little people that never forgot.

"Me 'n' you Adam, we knows that they's still around. Probably laughin' at us humans now they are, with that deeper wisdom of theirs, quiet in their knowledge.

"Sometimes I reckon they might be more 'elpful things if we treated 'em right. They used ta be ya know? Used ta help in the fields, 'elp with the housework. But now I reckon they got every right to be aggrieved at us, play their tricks, be malevolent when they please.

"Maybe I should 'ave kept me trap shut. Probably just as well other peoples don't believe 'n' don't remember, 'cause if they knew about the little people they'd exploit them 'n' all."

He looked at me even deeper than before, softened his voice and spoke slower, a plea to my nature not yet mature enough to truly comprehend. And yet, I knew these things already.

"I ain't chastising you master Adam... just thinking loud I suppose. You are from these times and it ain't no ones fault. But I don't want you to make the mistakes of modern folk. Leave it be now, forget about it, play with ya electric toys 'n' let the people of the woods rest easy and left in secret.

"It's time we moved on... both of us."

I felt an ache, deep down, like my entire stomach was full from the weight of that ache. It must be what it is like when a partner tells you that they are no longer happy, and that the relationship does not work for them any more. I worried that it was all over. My moments sitting on the bed with Grandpa may never be able to happen again. My eyes stung with tears I would not allow to fall.

I knew that I had hurt Grandpa, and I knew that it had hurt him to speak to me that way. He was fighting with his own dreams to have to shatter mine. But I could not help but be a child.

When I left his room that morning, giving Grandpa my slow disheartened nod, I knew that my agreement was impossible. I had seen too much.

He would never be able to 'forget about it' or 'move on' any more than I. The little people had fascinated him all his life, and now they were in mine, and I knew they were fascinated by me too. They would never leave my consciousness. And being only thirteen, it was no wonder that my thirst for adventure was rarely that well considered.

But I will perhaps try and give myself these excuses until the day I die.

Grandpa had told me to 'go and sort myself out', but that we'd chat again later 'about nicer things'. He was trying to make me feel better, but I did not know what to say to do the same for him.

I spent the next hour or so trying to make myself look human again while my thoughts tried equally to tidy themselves. I had a bath and examined the bruises, the pinches given to me by unseen fingers, punishments for my indiscretions towards the good people. I did not remember receiving a one.

My hair was a struggle but I made the best job of it that I could.

I felt better once I was clean and dressed but the gravity of Grandpa's words could not be so easily washed away. I know that he thought I had pushed it too far, crossed an invisible line... But when you cross a line you may as well continue forward because there really is no way of going back.

As I came back down the stairs I could hear arguing. It was the bitterness that often raged between my mother and Grandpa however this time it seemed to have been stepped up a notch. Half way I stopped to listen.

'Shut up about bloody faeries dad! This is serious. This is real life!"

"Ya son is real life ain't he? Even if ya don't like all this, it's 'appening. Even if ya don't believe it's 'appening it's bloody happening to Adam."

"In his head dad, because you've put all this in his head as you always do. I warned you about..."

"Warned me? Warned me about telling a kid stories? You used to love my stories Annie."

"And look where that got me!"

There was a cold hush.

* * *

Childhood is fleeting. Even while you are living it there are things which make it a much darker place than they would have us believe from the Saturday morning TV shows. Mine already had an ever changing shadow cast firmly over its innocent joy, of my own making, with one thing after another reminding me of that creation.

I passed that field, my donkey friend gone forever, nothing now but empty grass. Even though the grass now looked fresh and green, rather than logged with rain or a mess with mud, with the sun shining high, I was not fooled. Life is just another glamour, hiding its true character.

We try and shrug off the feelings caused by hopelessness, we pretend that our brains are just making us think the worst, though deep down we know that what they are thinking of is the most likely. No point hoping for the best and then being crushed, best to invert that train of thought so that the future can only be better. She was gone, and I knew that I would not see her again; I never did.

My rocky relationship and differences with the little people might be irresolvable, but my other relationships were equally important. I had to keep hope for them.

It was Josh that I had to go and see, but it was Martin that I needed. I wanted his support, unable to shake the feeling of loss after what Grandpa had said. I had not truly lost him, but I did think that we were not quite so equal anymore, that perhaps he did not like me so well, and that made me sad.

If I wanted to talk of the faeries and the woods, I would have to seek my friends.

I did not even try knocking on Martin's door. Too many times I had been made to feel somewhat of a nuisance by his mother, simply by taking a friendly interest in her son. Martin would be on the coastal paths as usual, exercising his freedom.

The day was hot again, it was the summer holidays, and time was ours. Though perhaps freedom is not always better than being on the rails. Trains are less likely to crash than cars, and without rails, how do you know if you are on the right track? But I always knew which track to walk to find my friend. There he was, not too close to the edge, kicking a stone in front of him.

We stood there together, quietly speaking, somewhat restrained even though our minds were full and wanting to spill over. His calming presence helped me feel at ease, and to slowly trickle out every recollected experience. I let my guard fall because I simply needed to off load my fears onto another. It might have been selfish, but I could not live with it a moment longer. Martin simply listened, and stared at the ocean.

He had heard from Josh as well, and when I finally asked what he was thinking, he looked up at me with those huge dog like eyes. It made me realise how often he must have been asked that same question in his life. He was so often quiet, so obviously lost in his own world. At least I hadn't offered a penny for his thoughts, he would certainly have heard that one before.

But he had been standing there contemplating it all, coming to his own theories.

"There wouldn't be anything without our minds," he said. "Our eyes can't actually see anything, it's our brain that tell us what's gone through them, that's all. We wouldn't even know the world was here, without having senses. We wouldn't even know that we were standing on the ground."

He looked focused at me then, waiting for response. Confused only for a few seconds the line of his words soon straightened, but then twisted. It became to me as awesome a concept as the chats we'd had about the never ending universe. Compounded if mused on deeply, but completely coherent enough to hit you with insecurity and make your whole existence feel quite unsafe.

He added one more line before turning, "That's why they say about having a sixth sense... because that might be all we need, to see everything that is always there."

"But maybe faeries can cast spells over our vision!" I proposed. "Maybe they can get in between the signal that travels from eyes to mind... make us see what they want us to see."

"Either way," Martin said to close, "if Josh has managed to get a photograph of it; it isn't a faery."

* * *

Something was askew. Even Grandpa's cottage, although lit brightly white by summer sun, was cast in foreboding shadow. Hopelessness was an atmosphere which for some reason had now gripped the world. It was not so much my thoughts but everything around me.

A cackling laughter, croaking and chattering was filling the otherwise thick silent air. I stopped ahead of the house and looked up to its source.

A throng of black ravens were gathered on the roof, stretching their wings and squawking like a coven of witches concocting evil plots. A conspiracy.

I felt that they knew something, that it was by no accident that they chose my roof to roost upon. They were right above my bedroom, beautiful, fascinating, but holding with them that surreal displacement.

It was hard to believe that only I could feel it, but I was trapped within my own unease.

Even the house itself had a cold atmosphere to it which I noticed the moment I stepped in through the door. It was so warm outside and although there was a lack of light in the hallway which always made it cooler, this did not account for the feeling. I feared, knew, that it was formed by *them*. I feared that my whole life was governed by their will.

But I tried to reason that the feeling might still be resonating from the frosty discontent between Grandpa and my mother. I hoped more than anything that it did not last.

He was sitting on his chair as I entered the lounge, not asleep, but having a 'doze'.

I rushed up to him and gave him a hug, which as

usual, he was hesitant to reciprocate. Eventually however, I felt his large manly hand flat on my back, and the gentle tap of it.

"I'm sorry Grandpa," I said, and I meant for everything.

"No need for sorrys boy..."

I straightened up and smiled at him. I so wanted us to begin again.

"If ya read 'Midsummer Night Dream'... That ends how things should end... restore amends."

He looked at me with warm but yellowed eyes.

"I'm sorry I got you in trouble with mum."

He made a dismissive movement with his hand.

"Ah 'eard us did ya? Well, she's all bite and no bark!" then he started to laugh. "I can 'andle ya mother... same as I did when I had to change 'er dirty nappies," and his laughter only increased. The smile I gave back was a little strained.

"I was just stickin' up for ya Adam, 'cause you weren't doin' so great today. She says it's all in yer 'ead."

"Actually Grandpa," I said, excited to be able to speak of these things again, "me 'n' Martin think all life might be in our minds!"

"Hmm, well, that's not bad thinking young Adam. But our minds can't be very nice places these days if that be true."

Still wide eyed and eager to speak, I could physically feel the anxiety of the recent tumult break down. The lump in my chest dissolved and I truly believed that everything would now be alright again. "We should all start thinking better thoughts," I said smiling, "and work to make the world beautiful again."

My words might have been overly positive, but I had finally found something to say, something to make Grandpa happy. He looked up as if taking in what I said, basking in it, with a smile that looked truly peaceful. Perhaps he felt pleased that I had listened to him, at least sometimes.

"Where is mum anyway?" I eventually asked.

"Gone to some garden centre with ya father. She don't like ta leave me she says, but 'cause she's in a huff with me it's suddenly ok! I'll 'ave to wind 'er up more often!

"Yeah, a garden centre? I ask ya, why d'ya need to buy things that grow? Things grow anyway, without spending money on different things that grow!"

I felt at ease with him again, and dropped myself down on the sofa. We managed to enjoy each other's company for a while, without my parents being there. Putting everything aside, and trying to forget; we had a warm and pleasant Grandfather to Grandson chat, without any mention of the hidden people.

But it was hard to pretend that everything was normal. Sitting and eating my evening meal in the lounge, eyes constantly checking, feeling secrets hanging in the air.

No one knew that I had uncovered it all, not even Grandpa. I had managed to return the cassette tape safely to its player.

I kept catching the eyes of my mother. I now saw something in them that I had never seen before, something I did not know, her darker story, hidden behind a mask of normality. At least I now understood some of the friction she had towards Grandpa's faery stories. A psychoanalyst finally uncovering that deep seated core issue.

I feared that I would suddenly scream out my own confession.

"Stop gawping and eat your dinner Adam," my mother said.

I shut my mouth that I had not even noticed was open, and realised that I would have to step up my facade if I were to keep my thoughts as private.

Although my mother was obviously still holding grudges, Grandpa certainly did not seem to be feeling any pressure from their earlier argument. He ate as he always ate, as if he was afraid that the food might somehow escape.

"What's wrong with you lately Adam?" she asked me suddenly. I never did find out exactly what Grandpa had told her so did not even know how to cover for him. I did not know how to cover for myself.

I shrugged.

"You hardly even grace us with your presence anymore... you're always out, you always seem tired and scruffy... just look at your hair..."

I touched my head; it had been too difficult to brush out those knots.

"You need it cut Adam, there's something wrong with it... there's something wrong with you. You've changed."

It was her own insecurity speaking, but I probably did not understand that then. I just took it as an insult and made an excuse to leave the room.

It is never nice to hear somebody say that you have changed; it somehow suggests that you have lost yourself, something that people saw as 'you'. It sounds negative.

But I was better for my change. And I had certainly not lost anything of myself. I was finding deeper sides to me, finding parts that I never knew existed. Though now the longing to carry on exploring those sides was close to clouding all others.

My room was thick with that same uncomfortable atmosphere when I returned there. It was cold, certainly not in temperature but with an altogether lack of feeling. Perhaps the coldness came from me. My warm chat with Grandpa had not defrosted the chills I was getting.

My bed no longer looked like a cosy haven but a platform for more nightmares. And the feathers were still there on the floor.

Maybe that was all the feeling was, the eerie presence of the feather circle causing a change in perception. I looked down on them, somehow knowing that touching them would be sacrilegious, yet also feeling disgust. I did decide to remove them, putting each one back in a pile, but it was a struggle to do so without feeling a strong pressure all around me to leave them be.

I then found myself trying to lean backwards out of my window to see if that gathering of birds were still there on the roof. I could not see at that angle, and I could not even hear them. Perhaps they knew the sun was losing its hold.

Turning myself about as I pulled my body back I saw, briefly, the woods to my right. It was but a fleeting glimpse but the image burnt itself into my eyes. I saw their silhouette in the darkness of my eyelids when I blinked.

A sudden squawk made me slip and hit my head on the window frame, trying to get myself back inside. And straight away, I closed tight the curtains.

I was not looking forward to that night.

* * *

I was surprised that my next conscious thoughts were of morning.

I must have needed sleep so badly that I blotted out even fear to give me the strength to get through the night.

I actually felt quite rested, having had no repeat of the injuries inflicted upon me previously... But perhaps *they* were waiting for me to make the next move.

My father was the one to step up the game.

I had eaten breakfast with my parents as normal, but my father had not been reading his paper, and now we were in the lounge, with the TV turned off. I could see in his face that a discussion was imminent. I dreaded what it might be about.

"I know this is a bit out of the blue..." my father began to address me, "but I've been offered a great opportunity at work Adam... And I've accepted." He paused very briefly, taking a breath, "I'm going away for a while."

He did not even look at me now, he had his face pointing to the floor and feet splayed in front of him. But then he stole himself to look up and smiled as best he could. "I'm going on a business trip, to sell a big house to a big client, it could make us a lot of money... I'm very lucky really, they must think I'm worth it..."

My eyes were burning wide and I wanted to shout but I sat silent. I wasn't sure if I had any words of protest, or whether I was just glad that the conversation was not about me.

"It could be as much as a month..."

A month? Words now came to my mouth, but were dry of sound.

"I'm going to Australia!" he announced, trying to make it sound positive, hoping I might just think it exciting.

And I would probably have accepted it fine, if it wasn't for his next lines.

"I need you to be a man right now, stop all the silly talk and keep out of trouble. Do you think you can hold it together, help your mother?" He searched me with eyebrows raised over pleading eyes.

I was still silent as I left my father's line of sight, head turning and eyes finding Grandpa's chair; currently unoccupied.

I stood up and went over to it without wanting to stop myself, yet knowing that it had huge significance. And although I never had before, and perhaps no one but Grandpa ever had; I sat straight down on it.

Both my mother and father seemed frozen as they watched me shuffle myself back, put my elbows down on the arm rests, and smile smugly.

I might not literally be the man of the house, but my father was putting me in charge.

"Good," my dad said, "It's settled. I've got to leave tomorrow morning, ok?"

I nodded, but I was silently aggrieved with him. It is more than just two letters which separate the word career from the word care.

But he had no idea how important this time was for me, how much was going on in my life. All the problems I was having juggling priorities and the things I struggled with in my mind. My father could not help me with those spiritual things. For that, I had Grandpa.

But I did wish that he could be more sensitive, and realise that money was not the best way of looking after us. The pseudo importance of his position did not impress me at all.

Perhaps my mother pressured him more than I realised. But it was probably worse for her. The thought of being alone there with only Grandpa and I for a whole month must have been quite daunting. And not forgetting whatever else was lurking around the house and garden.

I waited to check that the conversation was definitely over, and then I left the room. My father's suitcase was already packed and propped up near the cupboard in the hall, with paperwork and his passport sitting on top of it. He probably felt guilty, but he would have also felt pride. And he was not willing to discuss any objections.

* * *

Fuelled with subtle anger and at determination to lead my own life; I decided that I was fit enough for another encounter with the trees.

You could say I was foolhardy, a glutton for punishment perhaps, but children are quick to forget, quick to forgive, and capable of a bucket load of optimism. Yes, even me.

Although I spent a lot of time moping about the lot I had been given, I was still trying very hard to not see every shadow that followed my steps. The woods are just the woods, Grandpa had said, and the little people are only the little people. They were like a naughty dog that looks up at you with doleful brown eyes, so that you can't be angry with them for long.

I did half expect the woods to be alive with revelry, but they were silent.

I stood on the trodden path, sun-light brightening everything as I looked around at what was nothing but trees and undergrowth. Yet I would always know there was more. I stood only moving my head to look about me, the rest of my body rigid, waiting to face something, but becoming lulled by the veil of tranquillity.

My temper was quickly fading, taken by the woodland's breeze. When you close your noisy mind in a place like that, and listen, you know that even silence has a voice. The birds sang the song of quiet and the wind hummed along.

We do not think of those natural sounds as breaking the peace, only human noise can be accused of that. Even though nature has its music turned up loud, it doesn't annoy the neighbours.

I was almost ashamed to be human. I would not be surprised to find out that we were in fact aliens, and that we never belonged. On our true planet we might be a helpful part of the eco-system, but we do not seem to fit into this one. The little people and all of Earth's creatures would have trembled in premonitions of horror the day that they watched us fall from the skies. They had every right to their vexation.

I felt more akin to Oberon. I wished that I could be as great and wise and at peace as that tree. I sat on the ground opposite and looked it up and down. It was truly magnificent, the thick trunk with wrinkles in its bark like an aging man, bright green moss growing as though in fanciful decoration around it, the old man's soft whiskers.

The tree could have spoken, it could have creaked and stretched open one of its thick ridges and that could have become a mouth with which to impart its wisdom. In such a place I could well imagine such enchantment.

He was like a symbol of God to me, and just like Grandpa, nature was my only place of worship. Yet as with any God, he did not speak, he was inanimate, completely solid and motionless. Though this God lived... I could prove it.

After a time I stood up and looked about me, still hoping for answers. I only wanted the smallest of signs; a feather dropping in front of me, a flash of sunlight through a breeze parted leaf, anything that might give me any clue as to how to go on from all this. But the woods would not help. No little bearded man wandered towards me to engage in conversation, explaining their reason. I had read about such interactions between the human and faerie realm, and I knew that it could happen, but only the vaguest of things ever happened to me. Those opaque visions and encounters were merely adding to the puzzle.

Agitation took over me once more, knowing that my questions were an ever growing list, nothing getting any clearer, growing out of all control.

But there was some movement ahead; I became aware of it then. There was a noise that could only have been something large travelling through the woodland, parting brush and snapping twigs as it came.

The first explanation to strike me was not that of anything preternatural, but a little excitement in thinking it might be a deer. I had never seen one. Perhaps that would be my sign, a symbol of hope. Yet it seemed to be making no secret of its approach. It came towards my clearing with quite some haste.

I held my breath and as the shadows between the trees merged to show a shape of its form, I soon realised why there was no secret to be kept.

It was Josh.

I held my heart in a show of exclamation, trying to hide my true anxiety. I hoped he had not been watching me. He was trespassing on my private time.

"You scared me," I said. I was actually quite affronted to find him there on his own again, as if I believed that he should have asked my permission. But I also felt a twinge of guilt that I had not even been back in contact with him.

"Just me," he said, sounding uncharacteristically dour.

"What are you... why are you here?" I stuttered.

Josh handed me the walkie-talkie he had just retrieved from the camp. I wasn't sure I wanted it back.

"Well, I wanted to see in the light... where I saw her."

Perhaps it *was* Esther he had seen, and she had in fact died there. Perhaps she did haunt those woods. Or perhaps she was between worlds as Grandpa had suggested. I had little doubt that Josh had seen something, but I think I believed it even more than he did.

"You ever been right back near the edge of the woods? There's a tree uprooted, probably from the storms back in February... Dunno. But it's made a massive hole, I'll show you."

I had seen it, and paid it no mind other than to think it quite sad. Now I was being forced to notice. Josh wanted me to follow him.

Through one of the darker shaded areas he increased the pace, seeing the goal ahead. A tree, ripped up from the ground was lying across the others behind it. The spot it had been growing for years was now a huge hole of dirt and stone.

Josh stood there with one foot on the angled trunk as though it were his prize, a hunter's kill, the vein like roots hanging down from its wound. But it was the wind that had destroyed this magnificent piece of nature's construction. Nature is as equally capable of destroying itself as we humans are.

"I'm gonna dig it a bit more, make it harder to get out of... Get some bait of some kind... What d'ya think?"

I did not want to think, because I already had.

"Is this not the perfect trap to catch ourselves a faery?!"

Josh announced his plan almost as though it were a natural progression. You see something unusual, you capture it. I was horrified at every word.

But talking in the sunshine of that clearing, those ideas began to sink too comfortably into my mind. They found a place amongst all other childish adventuring. A place which was not quite so clear of right and wrong, a place which may have been a little dark, but not really due to an absence of light. And despite myself a smirk of a smile flickered on my lips. If it was to work, I would finally have my proof.

"Then what?" I had other questions, but that seemed to be the most pressing.

"Well, I haven't really thought that far... d'ya think it will work?"

I walked up to the edge of the hole and looked to the pit below. It was already quite treacherous, but the scheme sounded far fetched. "No," I said, kind of for effect. I wanted to slow things down. "What does Martin think?"

"He says it's a bad idea," Josh shrugged off, now pacing up and down the thick trunk, keeping his balance with splayed arms. The tree did not give way to his weight by even the slightest of movement.

"Martin think's everything's a bad idea," I joked, though now it was nerves forcing me to speak. I should have known better than to put down my friend like that, or negate his intuition.

I was a little lost in the moment, but looking down there again, I suddenly felt quite sick. It was black, wet dark dirt with stones jutting out of its crumbling walls.

"I know it's not that deep," Josh said, "but I've figured it all out. Anyway, they're supposed to be little people right? I got plans." Josh was defensive of his idea, yet also somewhat flippant. He was trying to make the tree trunk bounce. "I'm gonna cover it with twigs 'n' stuff.... Is there something faeries like to eat? Cause we could put that right in the middle.... then... wham!"

I looked back up at Josh who now jumped down from that tree, landing on his feet, and started coming towards me, smiling like a child.

My mouth moved without proper consultation with my brain.

"Cake," I said softly, lost in incoherent thought.

"Err?"

"Faeries like anything baked..." I could hardly believe

I was answering. It sounded like I was actually endorsing his ridiculous plot.

"Done! So you're not going soft on me, like Martin is?"

I wished he hadn't said it like that, it made it impossible for me to then issue any warnings without sounding paranoid or cowardly. But he did not know how stupid he was to mess with those things. He had no idea. But I should have.

The sideways smile on his face spoke of a mind spinning, of dares, and of double dares.

I kept quiet.

"I'll call for you tomorrow," he said, not allowing me any time to construct a protest. But I had no intention of actually helping him. In fact, I would get out of it at all costs.

The whole thing was infantile. It was not scientific, lacking any real logic or care, and that made it dangerous, for lots of reasons. But it was his plan, not mine. Let him walk that path, if that was his choice, and I would watch, but I would not follow.

Though his enthusiasm was infectious, and I could not help but find it all interesting, childish exuberance can become out of hand.

Human's always have a knack of going too far.

Was it progress? Was this not what all pioneers do, in order to gain knowledge? People always want to benefit from the results, even if they don't agree with the method.

But there was no point arguing with my own gut feelings. I knew it was wrong, because I knew without a shadow of doubt that I would, and could, never tell Grandpa.

* * *

I hadn't completely forgotten the whole thing, but I had certainly put it to the back of my mind, and had a night of fairly untroubled sleep. But I woke to commotion.

There was yelling, arguing, my father mainly, with my mother obviously trying to calm him down. And my name was mentioned, my name was shouted in a manner of annoyance. I was sitting up in bed listening, the heat of the day already at full force, and it was only a matter of minutes before there was a banging of my door, and then the red faced vision of my father entering.

"Adam, have you seen my passport? Tell the truth 'cause this is serious." He was trying to speak slowly and coherently but was suppressing an obvious urge to yell at me.

I slowly shook my head, barely awake but having joined the waking world long enough to remember where I had seen it the evening before.

"It was on your bag," I mumbled. I certainly knew that I had not touched it.

He left me and went back through to the landing, then I could hear him stomping heavily around the upstairs of the house moving things. I had to get up and find out what was going on. I was wearing pyjamas though felt overdressed in the warmth that held the whole house close in dense oppressive pressure. I could imagine my dad sweating and boiling up with his impatience.

"Dad," I said as I found him in their bedroom. He barely looked at me, his head in the chest of drawers. "It was downstairs."

He stood up straight now and glared down at me, his jaw jutting out from clenched teeth. He did not say anything and actually pushed me out of his way as he left the room. My mother was out there and I could hear him whisper loudly to her, spitting aggression and then the thumping of his feet as he went down the stairs. Tentatively I stepped out to see her.

"Sorry Adam," she said softly, "your father has lost his passport. Are you sure you haven't got it?"

I shook my head and felt close to tears. The atmosphere was so thick with tension.

I did not like that I was obviously being blamed for something I knew better than to interfere with, yet I could see why they thought it. I had not wanted him to go away, and without his passport, he would not be able to.

There was a loud bang downstairs, my father slamming another door. Then stomping feet and he appeared at the foot of the stairs, looking up at us.

"You realise this is it? If I don't find it in the next five minutes I can wave goodbye to my fucking job."

There was a huge lump in my throat and I expect my mother felt the same. Hearing him shouting like that and seeing him so angry was really quite frightening. He hardly ever lost his temper and to witness his character turn so abruptly was scaring me.

He came up the stairs again and both my mother and I stepped back out of his way, but he was going into my room.

"Dad!" I could not help but protest that he would do that, and following, I saw him looking under my bed and pillow and throwing my things around in desperation. I was impotent to stop him, afraid of what he would do next.

"If I find out you've taken it Adam," he said turning back round at me, but he did not finish his sentence.

The next thing I knew was that he had gone downstairs again and my mother had followed. I stayed in my room, keeping away from the fall out. I know that Grandpa was doing the same. I remember his door had opened only a crack, probably so he could peer out to see what was going on, but he saw it best to keep out of it.

My dad's five minutes were definitely up and I had no desire to go down and complicate the situation. I waited it out, my stomach in knots. I felt sick and incredibly stressed. My father, no doubt, was in a state far worse. I did not want to know.

It was only when I heard the front door knock that I felt any urge to join the world again.

It was Martin and Josh, but I did not get down there fast enough. My mother was already speaking to them. I joined her side but she did not leave us, rather turning to me and whispering loudly.

"You're not to go out today Adam, your father has said."

I screwed up my nose, but could tell that it was not negotiable. My friends stood on the doorstep as though they were being the ones that were told off, while I shrugged and sulked back into the house.

Before they left I heard my mother speak with an enquiring voice, "Martin..." I listened from the end of the hallway. "You coat is inside out."

I rushed back up to my room and watched my friends for a moment from my window as they drifted off together over the field.

I knew what they were doing, and was secretly pleased that I could not go with them. Josh was carrying a spade which I hoped that he had hidden from my mother's sight. And Martin wore his coat which my mother could not help but notice, even though it must have been about 23 centigrade in the sun that day.

"Careful of those piskies." I whispered under my breath.

I was soon summoned into the lounge in order to be 'spoken to' or more truthfully 'spoken at' about the missing passport. My father tried to tell me calmly that this would really jeopardise his career and that he did not know what was going to happen to us now. He was obviously devastated. He explained that being out of work 'in this day and age' was no joke, that our future would be 'uncertain'.

But I was a child and living in the present made more sense to me. That is a healthy concept to live by. Enjoy life as it comes to you, see what happens, see what grows from a handful of unknown seeds.

I'm sure Grandpa would have agreed. But age usually changes all that.

Anyway, it was irrelevant. I had not taken his passport. And now the present moment had grown very uncomfortable.

I simply allowed my father to have his lecture, kept perfectly quiet, and when I could be excused, I left to be with Grandpa who was now hiding out in the garden.

He saw me coming and shuffled slightly around, lowering his head with his mouth closed tight. It was like we had both been sent out and told to 'think about what you've done'.

"I didn't take it," I told Grandpa.

"Didn't think you 'ad," he said, looking out over the sunlit garden. "Not your fault. Just all a huff 'cause his dream didn't come true. But sometimes that ain't what dreams is about.

"Don't worry Adam, something new and bright always grows from the ashes."

I forced a smile, but did not stop to chat. I felt too solemn and my thoughts were too preoccupied. I think Grandpa was happy to be on his own.

So I walked down the path, sun at my heels, the thick summer shadows and the fence of fruit trees shielding me from the sight of Old Bob's wood. I knew my friends were there, and although I could not see them I pictured the scene being played out. Martin might well make his protests but Josh never let an idea drop. Only I could put a stop to it.

Perhaps I should have run over there and sabotaged the whole thing. But I did nothing other than sulk and wander about in the bottom of the garden, feeling very lonely.

I sat on the ground by Grandpa's model cottage, down low with nature stretching up above me, engulfing and welcoming me in. The warm sun kissed my skin and the light dazzled through the green. I looked up and managed a smile. I was thinking of a sentiment, probably taught by Grandpa; that with all which is about us we are never really alone.

At length, I looked down at me feet.

Sitting as I was with my knees up in front of me, I saw something beside me on the ground. I had not seen it when I sat down, but it was almost right up against my hip with only a thin dusting of dry dirt upon it. A little navy blue book... my father's passport.

I was strangely calm, though obviously confused.

Slowly I lowered my hand to lift it, patting away the dirt, holding it in front of me and gingerly turning over the cover. There, sure enough, was the small photograph that proved it was my fathers'. I could almost hear my mind ticking over. My brow creased. The sun reflected from the gloss on the picture and with squinting eyes I shut it and lowered it back to the ground.

Grandpa? I wondered.

I left my hand rested on it, and tried to think.

How it had got there was only part of the issue. Giving it back to him now would not look good for me; they would believe even further that I had taken it. He had already missed his plane and his appointment; and certainly had no qualms about telling us a thousand times how disastrous the whole thing was.

I looked down at it lying there under my fingers and despite the hot sun; dark clouds seemed to form.

I hardly even remember instructing my body to carry it out, yet there I was, sitting as I was, eyes checking that no one could see me, quickly pushing dirt back over the passport so that it would stay lost forever.

I remember a glance at Grandpa when I went back inside, now sitting back on his armchair; his rightful place. But I saw no recognition of the deed.

I told no one, even though I half expected it to be written all over my face. When I went up to bed that night I took its memory with me, and I wished for *them* to take it away.

CHAPTER TWELVE

The strangest and most vivid of dreams bewitched me.

It felt so truly experienced that I still find it hard to believe how it could merely be a figment of my sleeping mind. It means so much looking back on it, and remembering it so clearly despite the years which have passed. I do not know what I experienced but something was happening to me, something intense, during every long hour in which I supposedly slept.

They say that the faery folk can take you away, and I actually believe it is possible that, for a time, I was in their world.

I walked through the woods, over trails I knew well and had walked many times in the waking world. It was daylight and I saw clearly the sun as it had been for weeks, bright and warm, rays through the branches. I heard each footfall, every snapping twig and I heard the songs of the birds. There was no purpose and no thoughts but to take in the wonders around me. It was like my own personal heaven.

I simply meandered through, marvelling at the natural beauty that was nothing short of astounding without the need for perfection. The woodland's mixed mosaics of different shapes and colours, contours and angles that no architect could ever replicate.

I recall those vivid images, glorious sights too unique for human imitation. And in those moments, for however long that part of the dream played out, I felt a complete peace and connection to it all.

But then the mood dramatically shifted. The woodland was cast in shadow. Looking up, as I remember that I did, the sky over the tops of the reaching trees had suddenly turned to dark navy, the colour of dusk. And with it a wind travelled over me, coming through the trees that were ahead, caused by something which my eyes now found, a distant shadow.

No sound accompanied it, in fact all sound had ceased. But the feelings invoked were loud in my ears, ancient awe and untouchable power, and that distant figure was the source.

There on a higher peak, within a clearing to which my line of sight could easily make out, was the thick and murky silhouette of a man.

He stood facing me, yet featureless in the black. And, entranced, I stared, for I knew that this was not a human being but something more, something which belonged to the woods and to them alone. He was unmoving yet alive, with twilight shining darkly behind him, the line of his imposing shape shifting like gentle smoke. Both broad and tall and hooded it seemed, yet with horns growing from each side of his head like the antlers of a stag, like the branch twig fingers of the trees that surrounded me. He was part of it, and I was not.

In my gut was something resembling fear, yet I knew that the being was not evil. He was a warning... he was silently telling me to turn away.

I was afraid that my mind would be unable to cope with seeing it further, so completely humbled was I by its presence. And so I followed that instruction, and I ran.

He did not follow. I doubt that he so much as moved. Perhaps he did not have to move; perhaps he was like the old trees themselves. My belief now is that he was in fact the very god of those woods and I was blessed to have seen such a vision, dream or no.

I remember that I kept running for an age, never wanting to stop, though I felt no shortness of breath.

Around me the woods were as they should be, yet

seemed to be on an eternal loop as I reached the end only to begin again. And each few steps that fell became the rotation of a day. As I saw the trees whisk pass me I also witnessed the light of the sun between them rise and set. It was as though twenty four hours was over in a few seconds as I ran through day and night with the impression that I was actually growing older with every sunrise. I was no longer thirteen, but the man I would be.

Amazing though it was, there was no questioning to any of this, for who questions their sleeping delusions until they wake? But I can recall only a handful of dreams that I have had from my entire life. This one I remember distinctly, as though it were truly lived. It was momentous.

And I remember *her* clearly. When she came into my vision she took my soul so completely that I may well have become lost forever in those woods from that moment on. She was the very ideal of beauty in a creature so exquisite that she too must have been something greater than human. And it was only when I saw the figure of her, running a short distance ahead of me that I stopped, and I watched.

Fascinated and enchanted I saw clearly that ethereal female. Her body was completely naked, skin bronzed, almost like gold, and shining in the light which had paused now in its twilight state. She was slender yet with the frame of a grown woman, moving as a wisp, weightless over the ground. She was aware of me, and she turned her head about with a chaste glitter of a smile, her face long yet unequivocally attractive, dark hair floating slowly across her back as though it were flowing underwater.

This creature was also of the woods, I knew that, but so entranced was I that I cared not of her motives or origins. I had to follow her as once again she set off through the undergrowth. I could not bear to lose sight of her; I needed to see her, I wanted her. And every now and then she stopped and turned. Although bashfully, she bade me to keep on her trail and I would do just that. Until it came to pass that we found ourselves in the clearing, at the great oak I named Oberon and with one more turn and one more smile she moved towards it.

I believe she waited for me to come to her, standing with her back to me, arms held above herself, stroking the trunk of the tree with the palms of her hands. I was mesmerised, transfixed to that image within the falling darkness.

She was caressing the tree, it was unquestionably provocative, and I remember longing to watch, to see and to know. I slowly moved nearer, though feeling an urge to move faster. And when I was near I saw the bark come open, without noise, splitting apart from her height to the floor. And only then did she cease her intent stroking, and turn around.

Before me was a woman that was more than a woman, her naked body now grey in the shadowed light. Such exquisiteness in a form almost human, that I was aghast to be a witness. I felt honoured to be there with her, feeling an attraction that was unchallengeable. Her eyes were a kaleidoscope of changing colour. I stared on at the lost galaxy inside of her. I was like the merest of moths invited to take in the most intense of flames.

And then her arms were snaking around me, her hands touching my back just as she had that tree. And slowly, ever so slowly, as if the trance might be broken by anything too sudden, she drew me closer. I felt my body against her, pressed upon her breast, my lips almost touching hers. Gradually the thick black darkness began to envelop us both. The tree was enclosing around us as she moved back and inside it, taking me with her, taking me inside...

And then I felt myself being dragged, lifted as though by my hair, pulled up from beneath the weight of tangled branches, claw like twigs, roots and dirt. My body was breaking free and I both welcomed the rescue and resisted the escape. From the warm woodland womb I was reborn against my will.

I gasped, breath coming as though I had been holding it, my heavy eyes flickering open.

I felt disorientated and ashamed to be so abruptly shocked awake, sucked back into my aroused body.

I darted eyes around the room, almost surprised to be there.

I awoke from my chrysalis, and things were changing.

* * *

I had the feeling that I had lost time, lost something important, and I sat straight up.

I looked at my clock but it gave no help. The red luminous lines that usually made up numbers were flashing in abstract shapes, lines lit up in a pattern which told me nothing. Perhaps there had been a power cut. Perhaps I had lost days.

I gave it a knock with a clenched fist and the numbers instantly reformed to 4.18am. I knew it was wrong, because the room was hot and bright. If the clock was right then it would have been a while before sunrise.

As I brought my fist back away I realised that my hand hurt a little, and I opened it up from its clenched state. The nail I kept for protection rolled across my palm. I had obviously been holding it all night while it embedded itself, blunt into my skin.

It had not kept the dreams away, and I had awoken feeling unsafe, as though a cord had been cut sending me drifting into unknown space.

I think that somewhere in my subconscious I had been aware of things happening in the house, movements and speaking. But rather than a sudden noise I believe that it was now the acute silence which had woken me. Things were not simply still, they were hushed.

That same emotionless, cold ambience I had been feeling of late was now strangely palpable.

I had an urgency to find the cause to the unsettled feelings, although in the last two months the gambit of emotions I had been through rarely had an obvious Earthly source.

I dreaded what *they* might have done and my mind was making me see everything before there were things to see, feel things that might not have been happening. I descended the stairs with resolute anticipation that I would have to face something unpleasant. My mind casting shadows in the sunlight...

Before I reached the bottom my mother came directly out from the lounge and asked me if I would 'come in here a minute Adam...' She seemed abnormally dour, speaking with a voice so low it could only just be heard.

Her manner concerned me.

I would have liked a chat with Grandpa but she was keeping her voice down so low that I considered he was sleeping and not to be disturbed. And so I followed my mother to the lounge where she had just disappeared back to. I looked straight up at the clock, surprised and confused that it was after nine.

In the living room both my parents were sitting in silence, and that chill was there, gripping tighter than ever. The sun shone brightly through the window behind my father, who sat in shadow looking as equally solemn as my mother.

It was obvious that they had something significant to discuss with me.

Presuming the matter of the lost passport was finished with, I wondered what else I had done wrong; wracking my brain to think of a recent deed bad enough that would give them such a fixed, sombre demeanour. I wondered if my truancy from school had come to light, or if Grandpa had noticed that I had taken his tape. But the feelings of guilt were a mask for deeper emotions. I knew it was more. Their look was not simply serious, but actually sad.

They did try to smile at me, but it was laboured. And I truly began to worry.

"Adam..." my mother spoke in that same soft voice. I stood stiff in the doorway. Once more, she strained herself to raise the corners of her mouth, an act of a smile. "It's your grandpa."

My eyes had widened, I swallowed my own heart and it pulsed in my stomach. I could not wait and I could not look at them... I rushed to his room.

"Adam!" my father called, and I know that he had stood up making an attempt at a protest, but it was too late because I was at Grandpa's door. Neither of them saw fit to follow me.

As soon as I was in there I felt the source of that silent, lifeless atmosphere. I stopped just inside the room and it washed over me; that strange cold aura which seemed to be there simply due to the lack of anything else.

The room was more than still, the sun strained at the closed curtains, denied entrance, the grey light filtered through but even the dust hardly dared to move. Besides me the deer skull looked wisely on from its altar through empty bone hollows, but it was lifeless.

And I knew intuitively that the human shape lying under the bed covers was no longer my grandpa.

He had gone, I knew it.

He may lie there, as he had always done, but he would not suddenly sit up and animate... would not be full of excitement chatting to me about nature and folklore, laughing at my mother's expense, he was not with us anymore. My grandpa had died.

I was choked, as now I feel again, with sudden sadness, but I could not quite equate it. I felt the need to look at him, to check that it was really happening, that I was in reality and not still trapped in a horrible dream.

I hesitated of course, standing there and looking about me, experiencing that off kilter atmosphere soaking me cold, fearful. It was perhaps my own emotions that I was afraid to face. I was only thirteen and I had not been taught how I was supposed to feel. I had not been broken in gradually, learning about loss from the death of a hamster. Cobweb was still alive, leading its pointless existence. I had left him upstairs, running on the wheel as usual, always running as though it might blot out all else.

That was what I felt like doing. I wanted to get out of there, run from it, from myself... And yet, I stayed.

Stepping slowly up beside his bed I purposely averted my eyes from his face. I was waiting for my courage, and when in slow increments that prevailed, and I finally saw him there, it all made sense.

I had been quite right in my feelings. Grandpa was lying before me, but there was something that was not there, the most important of 'somethings' was gone.

It is not true that the dead look like they are resting, that they are merely asleep. He did not look lost in deep happy dreams. His face had fallen to one side as though he had always been a painted portrait, never dried. And it shocked me just how much he still looked like my grandpa, how anyone would recognise him as such, but that he really was not there at all.

Now I could never deny it. That stillness, inhuman in its completeness, was more than a mere lack of movement, more than being devoid of breath. I did not know where he was, but he was not with us anymore.

What was left was a shell. He did not need that body now. It had done its job, aged, deteriorated and failed. I was not surprised really, that he had now chosen to shed it. And it was no surprise that because of his leaving I was now left with a gaping hole of wrenching sadness. Because he had also left me, he had left me behind.

Death, and my facing death for the first time was not the problem; it was the total absence of life that I was finding hard to stomach. That I would never hear him speak or feel the strength of his huge hand upon me again. No more moments.

It was at that point that I found my tears, they came now very easily, as acceptance found my grief. A time I had feared was there in the present, and the finality of it hit me hard.

A little whimper grew and then came in waves, one overlapping the next. I was soon choking on them, my lips quivering, my mind thick with sorrow, despair and injustice. My cheeks were washed with that sadness as I stood before him, fingertips on the side of the bed to keep my balance. I could still see his face through squinted watery eyes.

I remember that time spent stood there as though it were yesterday. Some things are never forgotten, some so bad that you cannot forget them no matter how much you would like to. But I made a vow, and have kept to it, that I would not forget a single moment of the time I had known Grandpa.

I will never forget him.

After a while my convulsing grief began to subside. I tried to calm myself and with my voice almost lost to the remaining sobs, I mumbled my words.

"Goodbye Grandpa," I said, very low, knowing he could not hear anyway. And I pulled up the white sheet over his head, as I knew that was something you were supposed to do.

Within seconds I was in the arms of my mother, crying again, smothered by her consoling love for me. Yet she had her own personal grief.

"It's ok Adam..." she said, stroking my hair as I cried gently, very few tears left to shed, but plenty of pain still heavy in my heart. "I'm glad he had you in his life. He was young again, for a time."

Each of us had our own thoughts and we sat with them, together in that living room, waiting for time to change things. But that day would be very slow. Every second of the clock audible, clicking onwards and sensed as an age. The time would be spent feeling bad, for Grandpa's sake.

"But he was fine yesterday."

"I'm sorry Adam. We think it was another stroke. A big one this time. The doctor is on his way."

Death is shocking, even when time has not been so harsh, because death is always sudden. It is suddenly over.

The sorrow was thick, weary and unshakable. I was too young to be going through that, my emotions travelling through bitterness, soon followed by stronger denial.

I wondered if maybe Grandpa was not truly dead at

all, but out there, with the faeries. They could do that, I was sure, take a soul and leave the body. Perhaps he was happy to finally be invited to their kingdom, those that had fascinated him all his life. Now, without the restrictions of his aged body, he was enjoying their parties, dancing round and round, joining the roundel. Grandpa was still full of life, he was just sick of this one. His soul was vigorous, his spirit tireless...

But when someone you loved dies it does not have the dark enchantment of Halloween stories, it is just dark, it is bleak. It is not something happening, but something that will never happen again.

As much as I tried to convince myself of something positive, it was the sickening grief which stuck in my chest.

"The pain will pass Adam, in time."

They were wrong. And as they seemed to be more concerned with funeral details than emotions, I owed it to Grandpa to feel the pain all the more.

This was not just going to fade away. The initial shock may well pass, but the loss would never be lost. In the past, being a child meant that no matter how intent I was on feeling bad about something, eventually I would start having fun again, whether I liked it or not. Eventually, my old life and my old mood would begin to creep back. I'm sure that would have suited my parents better but I knew that this was not going to be like that. I was not a child anymore, and I wanted to feel it. I wanted to be in mourning and devote the rest of my life to feeling bad.

I guess that is another vow I have stuck to.

It was all too much for me, that unspoken gloom. Sitting there in a house now missing its vital essence, its heart. I knew that the atmosphere of cold lifelessness would not be shifting any time soon. I just wanted to run away.

And so I did get out of there. My parents understood. 'Yes, clear your head'. But they did not realise how full that mind of mine was.

Even the weather was disrespectful. The sun should have known not to shine; it should have retreated behind the clouds for sullen contemplation. But while our lives are in crisis our neighbours are happy. Outside the world still turned and people went on with their days completely unaware that for one incredibly special man, all days were over. I hated everybody in that instant. I hated the world.

I could not even take solace in the sanctity of the woods. They had been tainted, and I was not sure if they were now my enemy. What if *they* had taken Grandpa from me, stolen him against his will?

I stared over there and the horned god stared back, towering over the tree tops, a shadow becoming part of the black looming clouds.

I took my bike, and I rode the other way.

I remember pushing forwards, pedalling violently, my legs in a constant rhythm, rising and falling with barely any instruction. I had no destination, yet I travelled on as though time was just out of reach. The land moved passed me, faster than ever before. I went through the whole village, saw visions of memories come and go. And I know that I was being reckless. I know that Adam Briggs was somewhere there inside of me, but the body riding that bike had been taken over... moving dangerously over the roads... close to the edge of harm... But I was already broken, whatever was to happen now, I did not care.

* * *

For the next few days after his death I stayed in my room, shutting out the rest of the world, going through everything in my mind. I guess I thought the same thoughts over and over, only rarely coming to any revelations. But I thought of little else.

Early one afternoon I heard a knock at the door, and listened for what might transpire. The phone had been ringing a lot, and my parents had been making arrangements I did not really want to hear yet listened to anyway. They had been calling people to let them know, and I had to hear it said, again and again. I was certain that the news would have spread fast around the nosey village population.

I heard mumbled voices, my mother speaking to someone on the doorstep. I strained my ears to pick out words, expecting condolences spouted by a complete stranger. But I was quite sure that it was Josh's voice, though he was speaking unusually softly. Perhaps he had already heard the news.

I had given my mother strict instructions not to let anyone disturb me, and felt on edge, hoping that she would remember.

I think I picked out Josh asking my mother to give me something, and her replying 'yes, of course'. Then there was a pause before she slowly shut up the door and came back through the house. But she did not come to speak to me.

Eventually I decided that I had spent enough time in solitude. My mind had stopped looking for resolutions some time ago. But the important thing I *had* realised was that missing Grandpa was selfish. I know that he would not have wanted me to be so constantly forlorn. And it was not really Grandpa that was suffering... It was me I was feeling sorry for.

All I was doing now was berating myself; searching

every dark recess for memories of mistakes, the kind that wake you in the middle of the night reminding your quaking body of the things you have done wrong. All those times I let my instincts overtake reason.

But the little people were leaving me be, so perhaps they thought I had suffered enough. Perhaps they even respected my grandpa. He was their voice for a new generation, he had taught me to see, and I had promised once, to keep my eyes open.

Yet I had turned my back.

"Feeling better Adam?" My father asked me when I finally showed face. I shook my head and nothing was said.

We just sat there together, trying to be normal, trying to move on.

Grandpa's empty chair haunted me. I could not keep from looking at it. The dark patch on the seat and the same shiny black markings where his head would have pressed were now an expression of sadness. It just proved there was someone missing.

"Maybe he's still there," my dad said, giving a nod to the armchair as I stared. "Maybe he'll hang about the house, looking after us all."

My mother was not in the room, which given the topic, was for the best.

But I thought on that for a while because it gave me some warmth. That *was* Grandpa's wish. And if he was now within the realm where the faeries dwell, then he may, from there, be keeping an eye on me, to protect me from their more malignant natures.

* * *

The funeral was on a suitably dark and wet day, the perfect weather for it, breaking days of irreverent sunshine.

My mother had silently tied my black cotton tie, but she was not quite finished getting ready herself. Her hair was still tied up in a ruffled mess, and the make-up she had only recently applied to her eyes was smeared from a few overwhelmed tears. I had truly thought that I was the only one who really loved Grandpa.

I loosened the knot from my collar a little, brooding as I watched her with interest from the doorway. Why, if she was supposed to be so distraught, did she still take such an effort with her appearance? Perhaps she actually believed that her late father would be there, attending his own funeral to see her one last time. Or perhaps a woman is always a woman, no matter what else is going on.

I wanted to admire myself in a full-length mirror, and I knew that there was one on Grandpa's wardrobe. I had not been back in there since that morning, and I had some trepidation about entering that shrine; a time capsule of his existence, accumulated through the years. I suppose there was some slight belief that I might see his ghost, or feel his spirit. Yet it was only inbuilt unease; I would actually have relished a relationship with him alive or dead.

But it was not quite like that.

Straight away I noticed what had happened and was sickened, shocked and felt the violation of it all. There were cardboard boxes stacked in the corner to my right and his bed was stripped down to its mattress and frame. The curtains were wide open and the room well lit, despite the day being duller than usual. It was practically free of its usual floating dust. His books were no longer on the shelf, and worst of all, his altar had been desecrated, completely removed. It was as though all of Grandpa's character had been purposely expunged.

It was obviously my mother's doing. I would not have been surprised to find that those things had been literally thrown away. I feared more than anything that his deer skull was now lost completely or had been damaged, disrespecting all that Grandpa stood for.

Not for the first time during this whole episode did I feel anger towards my parents for not caring as much as I did.

I stomped over to the wardrobe. The mirror had been wiped; it shined, clean and devoid of anything that gave it style. I had, however, never looked so smart, or as sinister. The look reminded me of pictures I had seen of vampires, white shirt, black trousers, shoes and tie, a sophisticated looking gentleman with a dark secret. It made me smile to see myself dressed like that and it fitted my frame of mind perfectly. I showed my teeth to the reflection; and although not sharp, my mood was biting.

Emotions were high and we were rushing to get into the long black car that was parked outside on the road. It was raining hard and I remember the driver had been standing outside waiting. His suit drenched and drips of water falling constantly from the rim of his hat.

As soon as we were safely in the car the blank faced man stepped in to drive it, not saying a single word. This was obviously the etiquette, and it seemed right somehow. I did not speak either, knowing that it was definitely not a good time to broach the subject of Grandpa's room.

I was sitting by the window, almost squashed against it by my parents next to me, watching the tiny waterfalls slide down the glass as the normal world drifted slowly by. The huge car pushed on through the puddles almost as if the torrential rain was actually preventing it from going any faster. But we were only going as far as the church near the end of the village.

From inside that warm protective bubble we passed the sodden field where my donkey should have been, but I could see nothing but the rain streaming down against the window. Houses were interspersed with thin trees growing out from the dark earth and my mind was taken to the woods. I wished that it could stay there. I did not want to go through this, feeling sad and out of place in the austere adult world.

Nearing the church the car slowed even further, and my father whispered to us, an attempt to lighten the mood. "Just no one mention that the old man was pagan!"

I did not understand, but I do now. My mother was not amused.

The funeral was for everybody else, not for him, and I knew that he would rather not have had one at all. But I suppose Grandpa was the only one of us that was not actually in attendance there that day.

I imagined his voice saying 'no point in making a big deal, I'm too dead to care.' And 'do what ya like with me body, I ain't using it anymore.' It made me smile, and I believed that his voice would always be in my head now bringing humour to the dark times or making them all the more exciting.

If it was pleasing my mother to do it in the traditional way, if it made her feel better then I guess there was no harm. Grandpa *would* have wanted that.

To see that his life had obviously impacted on so many people was quite heart-warming, although the church itself felt cold, dour and unfeeling.

There was quite a crowd; friends from the village, old people Grandpa must have known at different points in his lifetime; though I did not know any of them. And then there was the family, some so distant in connection that I had never even met them before. Most of those I did know made some comment as to how tall I had grown, marking the fact that they, too, were not exactly frequent visitors. But it did make me feel kind of proud to see them all there.

It felt so final now though. His last send off, and that's it, no more.

The music of a cassette tape filled the otherwise lifeless church. The words 'thanks for all the lovely delights...' threatening stinging tears in the ducts of my eyes as it took me back in time to when Grandpa must have enjoyed it himself.

And then, abruptly, the music was stopped. There was a hollow silence with a few tearful sniffs before the minister began his speech.

I was sure that Grandpa would rather have heard his Bing Crosby song to the end, and so would have I. The lyrics spoke much more deeply of human life than the words then spoken by that holy man. He was talking of what a shame it was to lose Finn Penrose in the overly tuneful voice men of God always seem to have, but I doubt he had ever laid eyes on my grandfather. I actually began to find the whole display rather distasteful and spent the time thinking of Grandpa in my own way, ignoring the pomp that went on around me.

If I had known what I know now, I *would* have told them he was pagan.

We were the last of the mourners to leave the church. I could not wait to get away and yet was also scared to continue my life now completely without him.

I was admiring the architecture, though I never understood how people could find churches comforting. To see that huge image of Jesus tortured upon a cross, a reminder of man's inhumanity. At that age I did not understand all of the ideology, but even now that I understand more, it is still equally disturbing.

But there in front of me my dad had stopped. He was looking up, examining a stone carving. It was a male face made of leaves, wise, intriguing, yet slightly ominous, it's tongue protruding.

"That's a greenman!" my father exclaimed with intent interest.

"What?" my mother asked bluntly.

My father dropped his gaze and turned back to us. "It's a nature god, isn't it Adam?"

I was secretly impressed, not only that it was there, but perhaps even more that my father knew what it was.

"Well I'm sure dad would have approved," my mother said.

And with it the heavy malaise seemed to be somewhat lifted, and my father went up in my estimations. Maybe it meant that Grandpa *was* there that day, perhaps he always would be, because a little piece of him was now within us all.

* * *

It felt strange that it was all over.

To my parents, it was a fresh start.

"We have to throw some things out Adam," my mother said the next morning, as challenging her about Grandpa's room was the first thing I did. I did not want to lose any more of him. "Clinging on to all those bits and bobs won't bring him back," she argued.

"No," I said angrily, "it will keep him here."

After that they continued to clear his room, but I was asked if I wanted anything before it would be thrown out or sold. They knew that I was not in a good state to be argued with.

My mother had put the skull from the long dead deer in the back garden, not quite knowing what to do with it, and being too squeamish about it to decide. That faery cattle relic would have pride of place upon my own altar.

"He was an odd man my father," Mum said at one point, with a curious humour. "When I cleared the bed there was a knife under his pillow, not a weapon, just an old stainless steel kitchen knife."

"Was he paranoid about intruders?" my father asked, and I kept quiet.

"God knows what he was thinking. All his clothes were tidied away, and he would always ask me to help him do it if he was struggling, yet everyday I used to find one single sock under his bed... like he'd left it there on purpose. There was a layer of salt underneath too... like it had been sprinkled there... a pile of crumbs by his chair..."

My father was listening with his eyebrows up. "Do you think he was starting to go senile?"

"No, he was always a little eccentric," my mother went on nonchalantly, but I was becoming angry. She must have known what it all meant, yet she had a smirk on her face. "I had noticed things were going missing since we got here... now I might know who was behind those magical disappearances!"

I tried to button my lips yet words broke past the barrier. "He was protecting us!" I shouted in defence, "you know that. It was to keep the faeries away."

My father laughed instantly, almost too quickly, as though he were nervous. My mother looked like she had been stabbed.

But my outburst was misdirected and I said no more. All I cared about was that it was proof. Grandpa really had believed that they were real. And just as I, he had been pulled in two directions; the urge to indulge his passion for them, and his gumption to exercise caution.

I did not know if things would settled down now, or get a thousand times worse.

Another night had passed without event and it was to nature that I was rudely awoken.

The birds never stop singing no matter what tragedies might be occurring in the human world and the wind played its usual whistling woodwind instrument that was Grandpa's creaking trees. Now, rather than a melody, it all sounded more like the wail of a banshee crying in pain. I was in pain, but it was too late for a banshee to herald death, for death had already come. She should go and bother someone else.

I tried to block out the sounds with my pillow, and ignored the sunshine which beckoned me outside. The warmth and light were trying to persuade me into celebrations of the world, but I had turned down my invitation to that particular party.

The next thing I was conscious of, now early afternoon, was the door being knocked.

My mother answered, and it was Josh again. I decided to go down, and my mother left us to it.

"Hi mate," he said in a sigh, trying to give me a smile, "I'm sorry."

"Me too," the words choked in my throat. My mouth was dry. The new, broken version, of me had neglected both the idea of talking as well as taking regular drinks or eating much food.

"We all liked your grandpa," Josh said, "he was nice... the wise man of the village."

"Really?" I perked up a little on hearing Grandpa being spoken of in such a revered way.

"Well, apparently. Or can men be witches?"

I had to try and tune back into what was 'usual', but even Josh was not his usual self, I could tell.

"Martin and me haven't been too well Adam, are you ok... well, apart from..."

"Yes, I guess so," I answered, looking down at my own pyjamas and imagining what a state I probably looked.

Josh shrugged, somewhat uncomfortably. He was ready to change the subject. "What did you think of the picture?"

It took a while for me to put a few things together in my brain and come to any conclusion. But my mouth and mind were not quite in synchronicity.

"What picture?" I asked.

"I gave it to your mum the other day," he said, struggling to make any real exclamation. "I got a picture of the girl... the faery."

"She never said..." I realised; and I had neglected to ask. "I haven't seen it."

Josh's attempts at photo evidence did not exactly have a good reputation, so even if my mother had looked at it she might not have known what it was. It was possible she had just forgotten, or perhaps she had thought it best not to disturb me with anything. But I did think it a little strange. Maybe she did not know how important it might be to me, or perhaps she did? I know that she would do anything to prevent encouraging further talk of faeries in her house...

"She never gave you it?"

I shook my head, still feeling dazed by all this sudden intense interaction as well as from the glaring sunlight.

"I hope she hasn't lost it, it's the only copy, it proves what I saw."

I was confused, the world of faerie never a million miles from me, but now right up close to my face again.

Everything came flooding back.

Josh craned his neck to the side of me, and I turned around. We had both heard something coming from the back of the house; crackling, snapping noises.

"You having a bonfire?" he asked.

And my heart, already held from its beats, thudded once, hard against my chest. That was exactly what the sound was, and I knew what they would be burning.

"Josh, I gotta go."

And I actually slammed the door in my poor friend's face. Suction caused by the back door being open took it swinging from my hands too quickly. He was trying to say something else, but I was rushing to get out there and find out what was happening. I had to make sure none of Grandpa's things were being surrendered to flames.

"What are you doing?" I challenged.

I was out there in an instant to see that a clearing had been made at the start of Grandpa's garden. There was the bonfire structure piled knee high with kindling twigs and old paper work, the flame already blazing in its core as my father now moved back from it a little. On the path beside my mother's feet were a few boxes which I knew would contain items once belonging to my grandfather, ready for the sacrifice.

And then I was aghast to see that the guy on top of the bonfire was Grandpa's own wooden model cottage.

I only stopped for a moment to take it all in, and then I was lunging my hand towards that model.

"Adam! Stop!" My father caught my arm in mid flight, gripping hard and pulling me back roughly.

As I stumbled backwards and away the flame suddenly took off and engulfed the whole frame, reaching up to Grandpa's replica model, and instantly blackening the sides. I had nearly been burnt, but now I had been forced to see that special thing destroyed.

I shook the arm free from my father's grasp and stared at them both with harsh watery eyes.

"Why are you doing all this?"

"We need to move on Adam," my mother tried to reason in a soft voice.

"You're ruining everything."

"Adam," my mother tried to take my hands and I moved away. "I want to make the house feel like ours that's all, clean it up a bit."

"No you don't... you want to forget... you want to forget Grandpa ever existed and you... you want to forget Esther!"

My mother's face instantly drained of all colour. She actually shook with nervous fear, she was beside herself. My dad comforted her, shielding her from my tumult, even though he did not know her like I did.

"Why should we even stay here then?" I went on, my anger on a roll. "There's nothing for us now. You hate it, Dad's lost his job, and I've lost Grandpa!"

I started to stomp back towards the house knowing that I was completely on show, tears welling up that I would not allow them to see. I knew their eyes were on me the whole time, but I did not turn around. I heard the cracking of wood in hot fire and the fury burnt hot inside my head.

"I hate you!" I called over my shoulder. I could not believe I had said that, but true enough I heard the words come out of my mouth, and it was the truth of them which shocked me.

I had never felt anything but love for them.

If they hadn't changed, then perhaps it was true, that I had.

CHAPTER THIRTEEN

I was a teenager now, and had begun to act like one. I was agitated, moody and felt that everything and everyone was against me. Whether the little people still made that list I was not sure.

I could not remember any horrid nightmares yet I knew that it was not normal at my age to be waking up everyday with so many aches and pains. I was always sleeping longer than I should, yet never feeling rested. The days of my life were passing me by, and my mind was addled with both despair and apathy.

I walked around the house in a grumpy daze.

"Adam?" my mother almost caught me at the bottom of the staircase, held tight to my arm lest I fall. I was like a zombie, staggering down to answer the phone, almost certain that I knew who was calling.

Her face was stricken with concern as I rocked in circles in the hallway, standing unsteady while I tried to gain enough balance to pick up the receiver.

"Adam what are you doing?"

I could not answer. I just stood there teetering on the spot with my lips making silent words, looking imploringly at my mother. And then I went to pick up the phone once more, my thoughts trailing ahead of me.

That was when it started to ring.

The ringing was still reverberating in my ear drums long after my friend had spoken at the other end...

It was Martin.

I was actually surprised it was not Josh, as Martin hardly ever called. He spoke quietly, barely audible, but he sounded deeply serious. He said that he and Josh would meet me at the gate that afternoon, because we *had* to go back to the woods.

My mouth was sticking to itself when I opened it to speak, and I realised that the words I wanted to use were unwise with my mother standing so close. I was waiting, hoping that she would eventually drift away, but her eyes remained fused as she stood to my side.

My brain was still dizzy as thoughts swirled and I tried to stop at one long enough to be read. But I knew it was best to withhold all questions, and I thought of something to say that might later help my cause.

"How are you felling now?"

"Not too good, must be something going round. Josh has it too, what about you?"

"I've been feeling a bit... drowsy," I answered, and I actually heard his expression drop. "But," I said steadily, "we have to go."

I tried to keep calm, but remembering that other world now hit me like a brick. I tried to put on an act of sanity so that my parents would leave me be. I played the game, the family lunch. I tried to buy into the ideals of my father, the 'let's spend some quality time together, make the most of some free time until I find another job'.

But when I felt that I had done my bit, and things had settled, I announced in steady monotone that I had to go out.

I had turned into a robotic emotionless version of myself and my parent's worry for me was obvious and understandable. My mother had been keeping a close watch on me. Most of the time the expression on her face made me feel that she was actually afraid of who I had become. But she was keeping me prisoner in that house which no longer felt like a home. My true nature was being subdued while I was constrained within a normal family life.

I could not cope with that restraint any longer, not by them or by enchantment.

I told them that I needed fresh air and that I needed the company. I was persistent.

And very reluctantly, at length, they had allowed me to go.

Despite the fact that I still felt trapped in that trance state, my mind was working overtime. And despite my complete lack of energy, my feet were walking with purpose.

I was heading back into the wilds once more.

My friends were waiting.

"So what's really going on? Is it the trap? Did you..."

"We made it yes, but we haven't been back there." Josh stated. "So much going on, with you, your granddad, and then this sick bug."

I was quite sure it wasn't as simple as that, but I certainly had a sickly feeling.

"But Martin had a vision last night, didn't ya mate?" He was looking down at Martin with some respect. He actually sounded quite sensitive.

"It was this morning actually," Martin corrected, "about an hour before sunrise."

I know now, that was one of *their* times. But Martin did not seem to want to explain much further. He just said that 'it's time we checked.'

Side by side across the field; Martin, Josh and I, a group of mystery seekers walking forwards in order that we might go back, our adventure about to come to its end.

At first I did not think we would find anything. The dark and harrowing feeling creeping over me was that we might have angered the little people simply by our intention. But Martin seemed very uneasy, and very absorbed.

The world was quiet and still, taking in a deep breath yet to exhale. It was not long since it had rained, but now the clouds were withdrawing and the sun was at full force, drawing us ahead. The freshly watered grass looked lush, the woods which loomed closer were captured in a spotlight. Directly behind us was the dull attempt at a rainbow, the half arch barely visible with faded colour printed upon the milky sky. It was all part of the show.

We had seen it, ignored it, and were looking forward with focus to those woods. They were becoming so brilliantly illuminated by the sun that it was as though they wanted to be seen, that they wanted us there, masquerading as hope.

"I think my mother knows something," Martin said, the only one of us to dare speak, or the only one who could not bear his own thoughts. I wondered if she might have told Martin things, like Grandpa had told me. Or whether her mouth was as fastened by fear as my mother's was.

"Your mother is paranoid," Josh answered spitefully, our progress keeping up its pace.

Perhaps we were all worried, but our concerns were unclear. We all knew that the plan was flawed from the start, yet now we were each desperate to check that place, and make sure that it was really impossible.

Amongst the trees the captured rain was still dripping, almost as though one remaining dark cloud was hovering there and squeezing out its last drops. Inside there was movement and noise, everything rising, expanding and contracting. Nature continued to take its own breaths, but ours were held.

The three of us were together but alone. There were

no words that really needed to be spoken. We simply walked as though in procession. The ground cushioned our footsteps, and the wood beneath our feet snapped easily and without much sound. But my anxiety was growing too much to remain steady, and my heart raced at a speed too great to relax.

Without even consciously thinking to do so, I trudged forwards ahead of my two friends. Behind me they quickened their steps and tried to keep up.

"Hold on," Josh called, but I was lost.

My mind was racing and imagining the best and worst scenarios of what we might find. I was hoping there would be nothing, that the trap would be completely untouched, the offerings rotting and nibbled by the rodents which crawled through there each night. But the next minute I imagined seeing *her*, one of the wood's own good people that Josh had photographed against her will. We would gather together around the hole as she looked up at us, hungry and afraid. She would speak, pleading with us in a crystal glass voice. 'Help me and I will do anything that you wish, I will give you your heart's desires.'

My only wish would be that none of it had happened.

The little people were not naive, they knew all, and they would know what we had done. Faerie revenge would be harshly dealt for an insult like that.

It was within reach, and close to where it lay we met up once more, joining back into the line we had formed. I was tired after the walk, my head swam, but I really needed to get there, and I wanted to be first.

It was Josh who paced forwards, and he was there at the site a split second before me.

"Oh fuck…"

Straight away he stepped back from the edge of the

hole with a hand clasped over his mouth.

I hastened my final steps towards the fallen tree and soon saw what had caused his reaction. I fixed still on the spot, staring down. I could not move or speak, and I don't even have the words now to say how I felt, though I remember it clearly, and every day I live I feel it still.

I put a hand in my pocket, holding on to that nail which I carried with me in the hope that it might somehow save me from this. Behind me Josh was mumbling words under his breath and I believe that Martin was with him, but in that moment their world had instantly detached from my own.

I stood transfixed and paralysed within the bubble of my existence. It was both suffocating and crumbling about me as I stared down at the sight, so dark, yet lit by the sun.

My eyes seemed filled with the black dirt, the vision of falling embers, and tattered dying dreams. I saw a child, lying below, twisted and broken in a puddle of filth. She was solid, real; clothed in a frilled yellow dress now covered in the muck of rain and mud. Her skin was ashen, her body cold and curled, left forgotten in the bottom of that foul pit.

It has never left my mind, how could it? I will always remember her, bent up, wearing that soiled and soggy dress, once pretty, now macabre. Her neck was wrenched to one side and her eyes completely open, staring blankly ahead at the instrument of her death. Our trap, our fault, our hideous and heinous crime. Our one foolish action which has lasted forever.

I had envisaged something going wrong but even in my dark imagination I could not have come up with anything so awful.

Why had Josh dug it so deep? Why had I let him? We should have listened to Martin...

He was the only one of us yet to see it, unwilling to join my side. His hesitation was insight, seeing the suffering of his friends and knowing that this would change everything. I think he understood what was happening, perhaps he had already known. But the longer he could keep from seeing it, the longer he could remain a child.

As I backed away myself Martin at last walked slowly up to take my spot. I could not take it any longer, it was suddenly completely real and painfully sobering. Even the lethargy which gripped me let up its grasp to make way for that one raw thought. I forgot everything but that.

Josh and I stood apart, completely silent, our eyes finding each other briefly and then averting our gaze, watching Martin. He teetered on the edge for the briefest moment, and then his steps came slowly backwards while his eyes still stared on. His preservation soon drove him quickly away, and he held on to a tree to keep himself from collapse, falling then into a crouch beside it.

He was the only one of us to cry, soft dry sobs which caused wheezing with each breath. It was the only sound cutting the deathly atmosphere. But we left him to suffer alone. Neither Josh nor I so much as moved to give any assistance. We could not help each other through it. None of us could even bear to interact with the other at all. We each had our own private hell, and our own personal demons that had to be faced.

Shadows formed thick and black. Clouds engulfed the sun. And suddenly a violent rain shower was upon us.

We moved back under the trees, the pit in front of us never leaving our sight, still lit in broken sunshine as the rain fell hard upon the clearing.

Martin saw my eyes find him. His bottom lip was falling and shaking, his mouth said my name, imploring me as though I were able to make it all better. I looked at him, felt for him, but could do no more.

For completely different reasons to those of Martin and Josh; I felt that this was my life over.

"Let me think," I broke the silence, though only really talking to myself. I ran my hand over my head, lost in confusion. I was sure that they were waiting for my instruction but I felt frozen, unsure if I could function at all...

"There's nothing to think about," Josh spat back, "it's a girl. We've actually killed a girl."

I could not bear him speaking, and I could not give him my time. My mind was full with things my friends could never hope to understand. I knew those woods, I knew their story. I knew that there was no reason for a mortal girl to be in those woods, so young, so tiny, and so vulnerable... I knew who *she* was.

"Adam, what have we done?" Martin spoke again, he could not take it, he needed people to be talking; he could not accept the silence; he needed answers and solutions immediately. But I was trying, beyond all possibility, to keep calm, to decide what I could say, and what it was best to keep quiet.

With my knowledge I felt that it was all up to me. But my impotence at how to help my friends was making it all far worse.

Surely the woods would know that I meant for none of this to happen? My friends knew no better, they understood nothing. It was Josh who had stupidly thought all of this was a good idea, making the hole deeper, disguising it, ineptly trying to catch a creature he obviously had no respect for... catching a faery... and breaking her neck.

"I'm not going to jail for this," Josh said, and took determined strides forward, looking down at it as if it were merely a problem to now solve. The rain was pelting him hard, his styled hair flat within seconds.

I shot a glare at him while my stomach was tight and throbbing. I felt only anger for him now.

"We've got to tell someone," I heard Martin say, and I immediately forced myself back to the sympathy of the situation. He was truly crying now, sobbing in uncontrolled fits, "we've got to explain. We didn't do anything, it's just a hole."

"No Martin..." Josh yelled back at his friend, trying to act tough through clenched teeth, "we've got to cover it up."

Martin recoiled. It was killing me to see him so shattered. He was under that tree, hunched up as if trying to make himself smaller would keep the full impact away. It wrenched at my heart as his eyes searched both of us for reassurance we could not give.

"That's just what we've got to do." Josh had calmed his voice now, and it had a strength that was frightening. He stood fast and looked on it with a scowl as though he was forcing himself to grow accustomed to the emotions. We already knew that this would be with us forever.

For a stolen minute I looked up through the trees and watched the clear rain drops as they fell down upon me. I imagined being lifted up, taken away from it all, but it was only the slightest glimmer of peace. What we had done was below, part of the ground on which we stood.

I held my face tight in my hands, hoping that darkness would take it all away, hoping that it would all be gone as I then wiped the rain from my skin. But as I took my hands from my eyes I saw ahead of me that same imprinted scene. Josh was still standing there, and he was making a pile of loose dirt with the side of his foot. I held my breath as he paused for a moment, and then finally I saw him give it that one more push, taking that one more step, allowing the soil to fall down into the grave.

I could hardly believe that I was living through those moments. It was all so abhorrent and so harsh. He was covering a little girl with the rotting muck from the woodland floor. He was burying our crime. But it would always be there, in that spot, over the perpetual years, decomposing as the leaves after autumn, becoming forever a part of it all. It would tie us to those woods forever.

"Wait!" My voice broke free; I had not even expected to make it come.

They both turned to me; beseechingly.

"You don't know what you're dealing with..."

"And you do?" Josh screamed through the summer torrent.

I hated him in those moments. Perhaps I have never truly forgiven him.

"Just... It's not as simple as you think. We need to stop... sit down and talk for a minute."

It would have been too much to expect them to believe that this girl had already been lost to the world decades before. To them any supernatural element had been stripped the moment they saw the harsh reality of a body broken by the cruelness of our trap. But I had to at least try to say something, or all of our lives had ended that day.

Josh came up to me, his hands on his hips, squaring up into my face as though he wanted to fight. It seemed the dynamic of our relationships had become drastically altered, tested to a measure that no friendship could survive.

"After today," Josh spat, "we don't need to talk. Because this never happened... ok? We bury it, and we forget it."

I doubt he was as strong as he seemed. He knew as well as we did; there was no forgetting this.

The air was thick with words that came to the surface and stopped on our lips. We had to settle this now.

"Seriously Josh... just stop. That isn't a girl."

Martin got up and came over to my side. I had not lost him yet.

I actually think that he would rather have faced the consequences than hide a crime, but he knew that there were three of us in this, and we all had to agree. We were thirteen; we had our whole lives ahead of us. Even Martin could see that it was imprudent to allow one mistake to condemn us.

"I'll never speak of it again," Martin said, a quiet voice, but with complete integrity.

"Swear," Josh said heartlessly. He was still the only one of us standing in the rain, as if he wanted the punishment.

I had lost all control, the conversation had been ripped away from me, and now everything was on Josh's terms.

"We all swear Josh," I said with agitation. "Best we don't speak at all."

No doubt he felt my animosity towards him but he did not care. He gave an assured nod, though without really looking at us, and immediately marched back away. With feigned strength he returned to his work.

He fell down on his knees, cupping his hands, hastily pushing more dirt to the edge.

His mind was obviously set on self preservation, the urgency to just get it done; tapping into a part of his brain that should always have been dormant; should never have been so cruelly woken.

"For Christ's sake help!" he exclaimed.

And we animated to his attention, going to his aid because, whether we liked it or not, his strength was to our benefit.

But as soon as I was there I lurched forward and grabbed him. I did not remember actually instructing my arms to reach out or my hands to grip, but there they were, pulling him back away.

"Josh... look!"

He was affronted, brushing me away and probably ready to take a swing at me, but this was important.

I pointed frantically down into the hole... it had been filling with rain water, but the rain had ebbed off now, the sun was bright again, and I was quite sure...

"She's not there!" I declared, feeling a moment of respite. I could not see that body at all.

"It's under the bloody water," Josh discounted, "let's just get on with it."

And I will never know because the moment was lost. Josh had already started to shovel the wet dirt down inside. I was certain then, but now all is opaque, time has hazed my clearest memories. And it was impossible to begin with.

We could not reverse time, and so we went forwards.

We had to finish what we had begun, because we had started this the moment we began making games out of things that never were toys.

So we did it, together. Although we were broken inside, and none of us could bear to think about what had happened, what we might have done, or what we were doing. We filled in the hole.

I could hardly bear to breathe during those moments but took my first gasp of new air once that hole was no longer visible. It was but a mere, soggy dip below the roots of that angled tree. But that would never be all that it was to us.

Our eyes that found each other were all fixed wide, amazed that this had happened at all, unable to feel any relief that it was over. I was appalled at the skill we had used; sickened to think that human beings must all hold an instinct to conceal such sins.

But we were done.

Though it was not yet over.

"Let's just go," I said, breaking a long silence, and we took our leave, never looking back despite the urge. And when we had enough space between the trees to do so, we ran from that scene, finally leaving the woods through the exit we had always used.

We practically fell upon one another on our way out, hurrying as though followed, so desperate to be away. We could not wait to be free of it. But then we looked ahead, and the familiarity of the field was gone.

All was white with the thickest fog that had ever fallen. It was as though the world itself had been erased, and all that remained was the three of us, and the ground on which we stood. I almost wished that to be true.

We looked at one another in bewilderment.

Although our thoughts had been consistently dark, the clouds had not been as persistent. The rain had stopped a while ago and we had felt the sun bright and hot through the trees. But now it was gone, there was not even sky, just a plain expanse of blank nothingness.

The fae were angry.

It was another trial and we had no choice but to go on. Our steps were blind, kept steady. I was walking in front, my head stretched forward ahead of me so that I might try and place my feet before they fell. I knew the route, I had travelled it enough, but in that mist I could have been anywhere. There were no landmarks to see, no sound to follow.

Martin and Josh appeared to be relying on me to see us safely onwards. They stayed close, yet we could only just see each other.

I don't know how they felt in those moments but all

the while I was wondering if we would ever see our normal lives again, and how long we had really been away. I believed that we were already lost, our bodies and our souls. I knew about the wrath of the little people and I believed that we were being punished. The haze around us was not low cloud but a veil pulled over our eyes to disorientate, to keep us from escaping, to prolong our agony. It was the world of the hidden people over which we had trounced. It was their ways we had slighted. Now it was us that were hidden, bewitched and blinded by their command of all things natural. We were being led astray...

"We're being pixy-led," I said assuredly.

Martin made some exclamation and looking back through the mist I saw him manically feeling at his face, spluttering. His distress caught Josh's attention and took their minds away from my hasty comment. I felt them too, cobwebs that came from nowhere and made no sense to be in the middle of that empty space. But I worried more that it was not empty, whether we were alone or whether other things were now circling us in the cover of haze. Anything could have been out there.

Fear led us to move quicker, to walk on relentless, and finally we saw the stone wall. It just suddenly rose up from the ground at our feet. The most welcome sight. The end of our trial.

I had no idea where the gate was, so we hurriedly climbed, urgently wishing to escape the fog soaked field.

Immediately ahead of us the veil was lifted and the mist almost instantly dispersed. The sun once more pierced the clouds from the sky and cleared our view as though we were only just able to fully open our eyes.

There we were, our path lit, dangerously close to the edge of the cliff.

Just a few more steps and we would have been

amongst the rocks and the ocean below us.

Hearts in mouths we all moved rapidly backwards, clinging on to the wall behind us. We were in shock and yet relieved. We were alive, and now we were safe. We could keep to the border and follow it home.

As we looked back at the field we had just walked it was as clear as it always should have been, as though the mist were never there. The spell had broken. The woods laughed back at us. Our secret whispered.

My guts had tied themselves into a knot and I swear that they have stayed that way ever since. Even the sight of the village was unable to wash away that unclean stench of guilt. Our deed was in every word unspoken, in every face we saw; strangers looking at us as if they knew, as if they were all our judges.

Had we changed? Was our crime imprinted upon us like some physical scar? Would our families even recognise us now?

It seemed impossible that we could just continue our lives, pretending everything was normal. Nothing would ever be the same again.

I hardly cared for Josh, but if this was it, if we were to keep our silence, then I had to choose Martin some poignant last words.

I touched him affectionately on the arm, a numb farewell, with a carefully conceived whisper, "Things aren't always what they seem to be Martin." And he looked at me, bewildered, yet I believe that I saw a glimmer of recognition in his eyes.

I can only hope that he understood.

* * *

So that is how it all happened, as far as my memory allows. And although I have tried to shut it out, I have never managed to.

That was how it ended. A life once had.

Everything from that point on has been acting out the sort of existence that is expected of us.

I had to forget to remember, but in doing so I also lost the things most important to me. My love for the countryside was brushed aside, my friends were strangers and my most stable of influences was gone, assigned to a place in the back of my mind.

I had been bludgeoned with so much unwelcome stimulus that I wanted nothing now, nothing to ever happen to me again.

To keep my sanity, I put my character in stasis, and I have not really been Adam Briggs for some time.

Each day felt stolen; a dark cloud threatening its final storm. But I know now that we all need the occasional shower. I could not truly close my mind after being so enlightened and a secular existence would never be able to compare. But the adventure was over, it had reached its terrible finale, the train we rode had derailed and for the rest of our lives we would pick pieces of ourselves from the wreckage.

Clearly I had left the old Adam somewhere in the woods. I was not the same boy I had been a mere few hours before, but for better or worse I had been losing him for some time.

The old Adam would have most likely eaten dinner with his parents, but I could stomach nothing. I could not even tell the difference between hunger pangs and that nervous twisting anymore. When they spoke to me, I heard their words in a different part of my brain, processed my answers through a filtration system that over the next few years would mature and become second nature.

I remember my mother complaining that I should not have gone out, that I was not well enough. But people get over sickness and I would never get over this.

Things simply got worse as time went on. It felt as though I were constantly waiting. I could hear the clock ticking, whether there was a clock there or not. I was waiting for the feelings to pass, for the memory to fade, but I had a long wait ahead of me.

I could not sleep anymore, though reality had become just as surreal as my dreams.

I glared over at the woods from my bedroom window in daylight and in darkness, checking that they were there, checking that they were undisturbed.

I became erratic, pacing the house, wandering from room to room, picking up a book or a magazine, reading two lines only to put it down again. I would sit in a chair, then stand and stare out of the front window. I would go and lie down but my mind would slowly creep back, dragging that dark cloud over me once more. I would tire of the house and go out into the garden, only to hate what it had become, the work my mother was doing there. I would circle it once and come back in again.

It had not gone unnoticed. My parents had seen my behaviour change and I could see them examining me and giving me curious side way gazes. They hardly spoke to me anymore but my name was always on their lips. They could tell that it was more than teenage angst, that something serious was going on with me. But it seemed that they had no idea how to deal with their new son.

I needed my grandpa.

I was sure that everybody knew, but they were saying

nothing. Paranoia had become a constant and unwelcome companion while I waited for my dark secrets to be revealed. I would torment myself thinking of it, deeply thinking for hours on end; what if it were a human girl? Thoughts of how the girl's parents would be broken, not knowing where she was nor even if she was alive. Thinking that I was a killer, that I was inherently evil.

My mind was perfectly capable of keeping me in darkness, but our crime never came to light. It did not reach the news, and no one ever asked any questions.

My father had obviously noticed me picking up his newspapers and that I had now started watching the broadcasts with him everyday. It was out of character, the serious intent on my face not right for a thirteen year old boy. They definitely *did* know something, but they would never guess what that something was.

I kept it away from them, but they knew I had a problem, and presumed it must be mental. My mother actually asked if I needed to 'speak to someone' and that she understood it must be hard for me.

Maybe I should have taken her up on that. But I could not see how I would be able to tell a psychologist the truth and not be locked away for life. I had to deal with it in my own way, though I had no idea how to keep on living.

I never saw my friends again. They were so important for a time, now completely abandoned. There was no point trying and I'm sure just seeing their faces would have sparked unwanted, aggravated memories. There was nothing we could say to each other that would not just be a covering for the real thoughts. Our silence was our tomb, our secret resting there as sure as that girl's body.

Of course I thought of them.

I used to watch Martin deliver the paper each morning, though I did not let him see me. I was worried for him. I wanted so badly to help him through it, but I doubt I could have found words that would be of any comfort. I would have choked on those words if I were to try and tell him that everything would be all right.

I hope in time he came to his own conclusions and his own resolutions. I hope he can remember me without pain.

We all had our own torments. I was not the only one in turmoil.

It wasn't just my issues that were causing tensions in the house, my mother had plenty of her own.

"I think it was Dad, he doesn't like what we're doing," my mother said following my father into the kitchen from the back garden. He was bleeding from his hand, holding it up while it dripped down his arm.

"Oh Ann don't be silly..." he huffed in agitation as they both fought over a plaster, trying to get it covered up. I watched from the corner of my eye, sitting in the lounge.

"Thom this house was his, not ours. It will never feel right here. And it will never be ours."

My mother seemed to have found her own dark place. But I was more concerned that she was right, that Grandpa *was* unhappy with all they had done.

"Well what *are* you doing?" I confronted, staying in my spot but raising my voice. "If it's not Grandpa then it's *them*, it's the little people. They probably took Grandpa in the first place."

Both of my parents turned to me and stared. I was standing up now, about to go in and have it out with them.

"Just stop all this Adam!" my father said with unrestrained anger. He was seldom that quick-tempered and it was probably the stress of the moment, but those moments were becoming more frequent.

I was momentarily struck dumb by the sight of devastation in the garden, and walked over to the window to see it.

The whole front part seemed to have been indiscriminately stripped of its flowers and bushes while the trees had been trimmed right back to the point of looking quite sorry for themselves. They looked more like sticks than trees, their dignity cut away, standing in a desert of bare dirt. I thought that my mother must be crazier than I was. I turned my back in disgust.

"They took your passport too."

Perhaps everything *was* the fault of the hidden people. And what point was there in hiding tiny morsels of truth, when there was a massive lie which I would always have to conceal?

Each day I continued to sit on the floor in front of the television watching the news, my breath held and my heart clenched, listening to the headlines and half expecting to see a photo of that dead body or a search conducted in the woods. But there was nothing. No one seemed to have missed her and it was becoming obvious that they never would... because they already had.

It was her, it was Esther.

I thought on what might have been happening all along. That wild creatures only attack when they feel threatened or when they are protecting their young; they thought that Esther was theirs. But we had released her, and I wondered if by that train of thought I might forgive myself.

Children can be cruel, but they are also innocent; and nature is the same. They had no more right to keep her in that state than we had a right to play with things we did not understand. We belong in our own worlds.

But guilt and resolution were constantly batting between one another, and I was 'piggy in the middle'.

I knew that *they* would never let me forget it.

I guess I felt that I had let Grandpa down. Peace was broken, and his house was a mess. I had tried to be at one with the little people but I had fumbled in the darkness of their light. I had failed.

When it comes down to it; I was just a boy and I suppose a boy also has to make his own mistakes. We can try to rectify them, or we can turn our backs.

It might have seemed irrational, but I wanted to stick rigidly to my promise and allow no more violations of nature. I suppose it was my way to 'restore amends', but it was another straw to break the back of my already dysfunctional family.

I was chasing a moth about the house trying to get it to go out of a window. But every time I chased it onto a wall, and drew nearer to it, the creature would take flight and head towards me, making me duck under its path. Then I would have to begin the pursuit once again.

"Stop trying to get it out the window and just squash the damned thing," my father had said coldly, not so much as lifting his head from between the pages of his newspaper.

It riled me up terribly. "You can't just kill things!" I shouted.

It was beautiful, like a bird. Pure white, with a body of fur.

It lifted off from its spot and hovered before me as though in slow motion. Its wings moved as fast as ever and I could hear the air move between them, while all other sound ceased. And as I focused on it I swear there was something on its back, not mere markings, but something on top. A little person mounted upon the creature as though it were a steed. For the briefest of moments I saw it clearly, but then it quickly moved away. I threw open the door, and it was gone, leaving only doubt.

The floodgates had opened and my beliefs were spilling out. I told my parents what I had seen, ranting how those things were everywhere, knowing that I should have kept quiet. But they just tried to make excuses for me. It was Adam being over sensitive.

But being sensitive is not an illness, if anything, it is a cure.

They could not deny that strange things had happened about the house. Things were going missing, the electrics were tripping off and creatures were making the place their home. Everyday there would be another plague of insects to remove, every night the garden was full of hedgehogs, up to five of them at a time, staring at us as we looked on through the window.

I ran out into there one morning, yelling and in actual tears because my mother was killing ants with a kettle of boiling water.

"Adam... they're just ants."

"Nothing is 'just' anything," I protested, possibly being the most animated I had been in some time. It seemed so barbaric. "They could be faeries... Some of them get smaller and smaller and end their days as ants..."

"Adam!"

I saw my mother's hand lift as though she were about to slap me and then managed to restrain herself. She would never do something like that. I knew then that things were very wrong.

I stomped away in disgust, objecting to everything that she was. How could she pretend that those things weren't real, after having first hand experience?

Sometimes it is the skeptic, putting their head in the sand, who appears the most deluded.

All of this had to come to a head at some point. We were all going insane.

I had overheard more than one conversation about it all while I was supposed to be asleep, but I remember the most important one, a decision being made that would change my life again.

"Maybe it's a blessing that you lost your job Thom, I've really needed your support with all that's happened and with Adam now the way he is."

"I'll find something soon. And Adam, well, he's just thirteen."

"You think he's normal? You think he's happy?"

It was becoming heated, though I could tell that they were trying to keep their voices low. It was no use. Wide awake and with the rest of the world deathly quiet, I heard it all.

My father was trying to shake it off but the discussion was set to go the distance.

"I thought I could do this Thom, coming back here, but I can't. This place is strange, it's not right, never has been," her words perhaps as much a shock to her as they were to my father and I. "I don't really want Adam growing up here, I really don't. It will just make him worse."

"What are you saying? You want to leave, move already? We don't have much money saved, and we can't even sell the place... It belongs to our son!"

I did not hear what my mother said next, I was too shocked by what my father had revealed.

And then I heard sobs in her voice, and my father was consoling her.

"We don't need anything but to be safe. Adam's right, there's nothing here for us. Let's just start again, pretend none of this ever happened."

My mother had never sounded so vulnerable or so honest. My heart opened for her a little and I thought that perhaps she was right. That would be for the best. Perhaps I should try to understand and follow her example from then on.

My mother's way of coping had always been denial, and I had always been at odds with her about it. But in light of all that had happened, and how it had affected me, her stance now seemed perversely sensible.

But choosing to repress an important aspect of your character is ultimately impossible.

We can try to put things behind us, but we cannot help but be shaped by our past. In the end, it will build our future.

THE FINAL CHAPTER

Human beings are the only creature on Earth that are ever at odds with their own nature. We are the only ones that want to run from ourselves.

But my only fear was that *they* would follow.

I was relieved to have the chance of escape, to leave the scene of the crime. Let it stay hidden in a story of my past. And I would start my adult life again, amongst the concrete and technology. In time I would recondition myself back to living in the environment of the town. Though I knew that after the enriching experiences of the countryside, it would not be so easy.

I had spent my time with trees as my roots, and my head had blossomed with stories. I did not really know what was real anymore, and though it had grown out of all control, reading those thousands of tales about the little people from all over the globe proved that it could not just be brushed away. They were 'everywheres'.

But I guessed that I would be safe from little people in the overpopulated, civilisation. Humans had claimed those areas for the modern world, building over their land, taking away the natural habitat from a now rare species. I wondered if those I had encountered were the last remaining colony, and they too might be close to extinction. I wondered what loss that might be to the world, and if they were more important than any of us realise.

It was certainly possible that all the British faeries would have retreated to Cornwall. The land is cut away from the rest of Britain by the great river Tamar almost as though it might just float away, trapped in its own bubble of the past. It had taken time to tune into the pace of that life, but now that I was on its wave length it was all being taken away, and we were leaving.

But I don't think my heart ever left there.

I missed Grandpa, and I knew that by leaving his home I would have all the more to miss. It seems impossible now; that I could have turned my back on all that he stood for. But although I would like to blame my parents, it was a mutual decision. I was old enough to realise that sacrifices have to be made, and some things just have to be.

I was sad, of course, yet to make sure that I bought into the concept of avoidance I left my most prize possession behind. It was a wrench of will but I lay 'A Midsummer Nights Dream' beside Grandpa's old chair, so that he could read it when we were gone, and when the loneliness of the empty house made his spirit hanker for the past. But perhaps I knew that it was not gone forever.

I felt no urge to visit his grave... he was not there.

And I did not need any 'one last look' at the haunts which now held my memories.

In my mind they would always stay the same. And it seemed hard to believe that those places and people would even exist without my eyes there to see them. They would be waiting for me to one day return, and I would instantly recognise them all.

But things there were already changing.

The haunted house which once scared us and sparked imaginations was now very different, much less malignant with its boards removed and the garden cleared. It was being cared for now, with life inside its walls. It would be Grandpa's house that now remained abandoned.

And the woods had evolved, and always would continue to do so. I could not look at that swaying patch of deceivingly innocent trees without remembering a thousand emotions. I knew what lurked there, and what lie beneath its soil. Yet I also knew its beauty. I had a distinct connection that would never be completely severed, but I knew that I must not continue to follow the path I had trodden.

Nothing could be the same as it was.

Lost in my thoughts, I had been staring back at the cottage, and I felt a hand upon my shoulder.

"You'll see it again," my father said.

And eventually we drove slowly away.

I stared longingly from the back window of the car, watching the house grow smaller, and then in only a moment, we turned, and it was gone.

We moved on as the mist of the morning hovered above the level of the sea, a shroud which might lift in hours, or days, or might last forever.

The woodland we passed through, the memories it evoked, drifted away and were left behind. Open fields and road made it clear that while we may feel attached, even trapped by a place, there is always distance to help us forget.

The further we drove away from the village, and from Cornwall itself, the more like a dream it all seemed. With each mile the idea of faery people ever being real was becoming close to imaginary once more.

Perhaps I had been in a coma for those few months, dreaming every amazing experience. But I knew that could not be any further from the truth. In the time I had been there, amongst those old trees and walking the ancient land, I had felt alive. It was being away from there which would make me feel the most catatonic.

I was beginning my semi-life, in which I would find no pleasure at all, my emotions always sleeping.

I had no choice but continue to live, despite my total

disinterest. But in truth, for me to lead an ordinary life like that was to be as good as dead.

* * *

That is really the end of the tale.

Though of course there is more to the story.

I continued to turn the pages of my book, hoping that one day I would see a change for that character. And there was always that special bookmark which Grandpa had given me, keeping my place in a land named Cornwall.

I was right that there would be no little people to be found in the population of the town, but I was still not safe. They *are* everywhere. I found them sure enough, because they were living and breathing full lives within my head.

I constantly looked for them. I searched under every stone, in every hole. I looked for them in every noise and searched my understanding over every coincidence and every unusual event. I kept finding them, over and over again, but only ever in the confines of memory and fear.

So eventually I did succumb to some psychology to help me weed them out. But weeds are just plants with a different name... aren't they?

Surely not everything was so tediously explainable?

Over time I began to feel physically better, but my spirit was suffering. A life without dreams, but where dreams would be my only memory of life.

The great storm of '87 made me remember the wild powers of nature, and I pined for some feelings within me to be shaken up.

Deep down I knew how wrong it was to try and tame

something that was once wild. But all I could think of was that I had left those feelings in Cornwall, and I saw that place only in my mind's eye. I saw every tree ripped from its roots, the homes of the hidden people destroyed forever. And our crime in the flattened woods would be exposed for all to see.

I felt neglectful that I was not there to protect it or to uphold the old ways. And of course those woods were still there, whether I could see them or not. It began a growing anxiety that our grave would be discovered, that it would be obvious. I had irrational images in my mind of that girls' arm protruding from the dirt, or the whole area being infested with wriggling maggots. Or what if Martin had gone mad and dug her up? What if he was sitting there in front of the hole crying with the bones in his arms?

Every morning I would have to shake it all away so that I could continue as the Adam I was trying to be. But who was he really?

No psychoanalyst could really understand. This was well beyond their training. And do they really know our minds well enough to tell that there are truths kept from being spoken?

My dreams knew the real me, the unfettered Adam. They were vivid; hacking off limbs, the grisly imagery of burying those body parts in black dustbin bags. And then I would dream that someone finds one of those dirty, black gloss bags, filled with rotting flesh, and then another and another as though I had killed and killed again. Sometimes I would wake drenched in sweat with that anxious feeling that *they* were there, that they had found me, or that I had really killed someone and that I was going to be found out.

The true horror was realising, as the sleep slowly gives way to reality, that some of that was memory and not just flights of fancy.

I was a lost cause, an anti-person. I now began to embrace the dark clouds which perpetually lingered over my head; because only they gave me stability. I kept to a plateau, a cold numbness.

That was my only true defence, to go on like that with only a small hope in the back of my mind that one day I might decide to live again. But that decision is not as easy as it sounds. Fear always held me back. My conditioning to a temporary mediocre existence was powerful enough to be permanent.

Meeting Tabby was the storm which shook up my resolve. That was when I first began to take an interest in reading my story again. My first true breath after many years with my head under the muffling of water.

My time with her has definitely given me something to live for. But even though we have had a good life together up till now, I know I have still been holding part of me back, and have never allowed myself to be truly happy. I was wrenched back into life, but I am always afraid of those smouldering embers returning to full flame; now more than ever.

I guess it was quite a romantic chapter.

It felt right from the start, and I did not feel that I needed a list of failed relationships just to get one right. Any mistakes I was going to make I made with her, and we solved them together.

The moment I set eyes on her I had no doubts. It wasn't simply love at first sight; it was recognition; because I remembered her from a dream.

Tabby was the new girl at school. And I knew how she felt, though it was even worse for her, joining the school at the very last term. The hierarchy of friends and foes had long been set already so to fit in at that point was practically impossible. The best she could have hoped for was a solitary year, but she got more than that; she was immediately picked upon. Her refusal to conform to archetypes was dangerous, but to me it showed strength, and an attitude similar to my own.

Tabby would never have just blended in or been overlooked. She had a strong personality which meant that to most of the other girls she was a threat. A large part of it was jealously, because she was much prettier than any of them.

She did not even have to try. She had a fresh face with wonderfully shaped lips which the others would have had to buy expensive makeup to achieve. And she did not follow their fashions either. Her hair was almost red, and ginger hair always seemed to be the cause for teasing at the best of times. But she also wore it long and with some of it in braids, tied at the ends with little plastic beads.

I noticed her straight away. To me she was beautiful, and I saw her as a kindred spirit. I had a strong urge to speak to her, but Adam Briggs did not do that sort of thing.

For some time I observed the dynamics from a safe vantage point, and it was still frightening to watch. I saw how the general bitchiness soon became actual violence. She must have felt so alone, and completely victimised at a time when she most needed to concentrate on things much less trivial than popularity.

"Bloody tree hugger, bloody hippy cow..." There was one girl more vocal than the others, and was leading the pack as I had seen so many times before. Then she decided to lay a hand on Tabby, the other two followed suit, pushing her back and forth.

I had a clearer view than most, sitting up a small bank under a single tree where I often had my lunch, left in peace. But I could also see clearer because, unlike everybody else, I did not turn a blind eye.

I stood up to get a better idea of what was going on as they started making noises at her, imitating a cow's voice; 'moos' with pushes and spiteful faces. I felt sick to my stomach.

I could feel myself struggling with my decisions, but ultimately I knew that I would do something. I remembered how much I had once needed help; a sensitive in such an insensitive situation.

I began to stride towards them.

For a few moments I did not know what I was going to do, but then it just seemed to play out.

The girl's saw me coming and stopped, looking at me with surprised and confused faces. I stepped in between them all, ignoring the bullies and looking straight at Tabby. Although I could not find any words my eyes made a connection which showed her my intention.

Firmly I grabbed her hand, staked my claim, and gently pulled her back from whence I came. She seemed surprised too, yet smiled shakily and willing followed as I manfully led her away and up the banking.

We were up there, alone. They did not follow.

"You ever actually hugged a tree?" I asked her, making reference to the mocking I had heard hailed at her on more than one occasion.

"No," she said, her Scottish accent soft and feminine and somehow mystical. "They just call me that... only 'cause I'm a wee bit of an eco-warrior."

I smiled strongly at her, a determined and almost happy feeling. I was hers from that moment.

As I expected, the three girls were still staring at us, so I decided to give them something to watch.

I gave one more smile to Tabby and walked over to the tree, gently putting my arms around its trunk. I moved in towards it as close as I could, pressing my left cheek to its bark and closing my eyes.

It was not exactly soft but it softened something within me, my guard and hard exterior instantly broke down. It was like being a child again. I was being mischievous, defiant and close with that nature so long deserted. Memories played out in my mind, all those wonders I had been needlessly vilifying.

I would never have thought that it could feel so peaceful and still, despite being surrounded by the hell I had been living in.

I took a deep breath, taking in the scent of the smoky wood, and all that I knew was me came flooding back to mind with the freshness of new air. It might only have been a moment, but for those few seconds everything else was blocked out and instantly unimportant. As my lips rubbed close against that tree I once again knew what life was about.

Somewhere deep inside me, I was still the man that boy had been.

When I opened my eyes I saw the wonderment in Tabby's eyes, and she smiled so openly at the spectacle and marvel of what I was doing. Shaking her head at herself she came directly to the opposite side of the tree and she too gave the trunk a massive and happy hug. The grin on her face was completely infectious and our eyes were now on each other.

"It's a subtle vibration you know," she said, ignoring the whole strangeness of what we were doing, "that makes us feel so connected."

I guess there is some inexplicable sixth sense which helps us see the soul of one that is right for us. And although I had to discreetly lean over to check her back, making sure it was not horribly hollow, I knew that Tabby was *her*.

Our souls were as one from that moment on. And while we felt that pull of the Earth, we were completely and for always in a world of our own.

I know full well how a single event can change the course of everything. Without it, who knows how my book would have ended. But I always thought that Tabby would be safer by only knowing half the story. I wanted to ensure our happy ever after. So we were together for well over a year before I even made mention of the little people.

My mouth just ran away with me, unsettled and paranoid over a patch of flattened grass.

"It's *them*," I whispered.

I actually believed that after all that time, they had finally caught up with me. I was a frightened child.

But Tabby is a clever woman. Not only did she know a little about folklore from living in the countryside herself, but she always knew how to make me happy, and how to diffuse an uncomfortable situation.

She asked me about them, about my beliefs, and then she softened the whole conversation with dark humour.

"You actually saw them Adam... That's amazing."

"Yes, I suppose I'm lucky."

"You're lucky they didn't put out your eyes."

Tabby has never been quick to judge. Perhaps, at first, she just thought I was just quirky, but she was ok with that. And so I felt able to tell her more, which ultimately brought us closer than ever.

I spoke to her about Grandpa and she said he sounded really nice. Said 'sounds like he had his head screwed on'. I wish she could have met him.

She was interested when I mentioned he was pagan, and liked how he had taught me to love all nature and worship only that. She said that she had spent most of her life, desperately trying to 'find herself', and had done her time with almost all the religions and spiritual paths. But then she realised... None of that is really finding yourself, it's just finding them.

Yes, Grandpa was on the right track, but now I follow my own path. You can take something from all that people teach you, take the pieces that fit your own puzzle. But we have to be ourselves, and when we are, and we are still loved, then you know it is true.

Tabby and I were in love, and many years have passed, and that love is as strong as ever.

We may have once travelled different roads, but we had always wanted to see the same sights.

Sometimes it feels as though nothing can hurt you, and nothing ever will again. Even old fears become a comfort. You just wake up and feel right with the world; you feel completely connected to it. The sun seems to light things more beautifully, the music you listen to touches your soul, and even the birds sing a sweeter tune. From that point I began to feel that way every day, despite it being years since I had even caught hint of such a feeling.

Cynically I would have said it was stolen happiness. To feel so happy is merely forgetting to feel bad. But of course it was the wisps of love, and happiness is a reaction. My day to day life at last had contentment, and that is all we can ever hope for.

Tabby was an air of clarity. She taught that I should just 'be' and not drive myself out of my mind by thinking around every single thing I did or felt. I might have spent forever searching for the meaning of life if I had not met her. Now I know that there really is no meaning other than to experience that life, and to be alive.

* * *

Of course there was too much water under the bridge for a dry spell to last.

How she has put up with me all these years I do not know.

Sometimes I think I have never grown up, never grown out of my fears and neuroses, that sensitive and nervous disposition. I have been the cause of any argument, and I have been the one that threatened our peace... not *them*.

I never stay in a job; no company I have found work with does any good for the world. I have relied on Tabby far too much. I have made her move from one crappy town flat to another, always finding excuses, always expecting her to just follow. Even I did not understand my reasons.

Eventually the noise of living around people drives me mad, though there is little doubt that it is the noises in my head that I run from the strongest. Voices berating me for all I have done, and all I cannot do.

I say that I want to live somewhere quiet, but then I fear that I would hear those voices even more. I want to live where there is at least one tree, just some view of greenery, and yet, not too much. Constantly looking for somewhere perfect, though perfection does not exist, and I need to look inside myself if it is peace I am after. I used to appreciate imperfections, now they just nag at me to be improved.

I own a cottage.

It was always Grandpa's wish that I live there, and yet it has stood empty. I could never steel myself to go back there, or to even rent it out. I guess I was frightened of what I had inherited.

For years I have hidden from myself. I thought I could change. And I have always believed that some things are meant to be for that time only, and then you move on, while there are other things which are definitely supposed to last forever. Where the cottage fitted into that I have never understood, but in some deep way, I missed the place.

My first taste of real life was there. That love of the countryside, and with it, my love for all nature has become intrinsically linked with any fond memories of childhood. I don't think I could ever feel similar pangs of nostalgia for a graffiti covered wall.

But the draw to be there also repelled me. Those conflicts were always present.

I would constantly find reasons to remain trapped in my guilt.

A pile of rags in the middle of a field should not have been enough to send blood pumping hot through my veins, but anything could have been *them*. It could mean that they had found me.

Tabby argued that superstitions are often formed through fear and they cannot be believed. But my philosophy was Grandpa's... to take precautions, just in case. Though I was driving myself mad with it all, and dragging her with me.

I always fought against her rationality; I always found ways for her to be wrong.

People see what is in front of them, I look behind. People see the trees swaying as though dancing to their own melody. But I know their tune.

"These things may exist," she said, as always, inexplicably calm, trusting and patient. "But they are not out to punish you. You are nay bad Adam, and they are not our enemies. I think the problem is that you have always treated them as though they were."

Her words struck a chord, but it has taken some time

to resonate.

It may well be the moral of the story, but I will always question.

I sit here, shirt sleeves rolled up, a winter mixture sweet in my mouth, speaking to a cassette tape unsure if I even have an audience. But maybe I need to have words with myself.

I am a man now, and I have responsibilities.

Tabby is expecting our child.

To my shame my first reaction was not to be overjoyed but was closer to fear. To be honest, I have never been so terrified. I know that I need to provide for my family, care for them, keep them safe. But I have only ever known one way.

She could have perhaps forgiven the bells I put up at every door, but as usual, I let things go too far.

It is hard to know how to be a good father, and sometimes it is our impotence that drives us to do certain things. We will all over compensate, some of us become martyrs, and some of us go temporarily insane. I can well imagine why Tabby was becoming impatient with my irrational antics.

She caught me in the act; leaning over the new cot, tying steel scissors to every line of the mobile which hung over the place where our child would one day be sleeping.

"What the hell are you doing now?"

"I'm trying to protect our baby...from *them*."

"Adam come on, this has to stop. Please, for our child's sake, stop worrying about faeries."

I had hardly even looked at her, never ceasing the frantic twisting of knots, while my mind twisted with them. And then I slipped, and a pair of scissors fell down into the crib, sharp and hard onto the bare wood.

Tabby and I stared at one another; a realisation that did not have to be spoken. My anxious tension had reached a peak, and the burden was too much to bear. I felt my face heat up and force tears from my eyes.

I promised that I would change. I told her everything. I told her about my past. I told her about the cottage. I planned for our future. But I lied that I knew it would all be ok.

* * *

Our baby was crying in the next room. It was dark, I could just see my love shifting beside me and groaning. We were so tired, weeks with little sleep. New parents; trying our best, floundering in our lack of knowledge, our struggling emotions.

The child's cries were unearthly, sounding more like a dying swine than a human baby. That sound began quietly and then filled my head, a fretful, tortured noise.

"See to her would you?"

And into the corridor I would go, the din so loud it made me wince. I would see my bare feet upon dusty wooden floorboards, hesitantly moving through the haze of grey semi-light.

And then I would push open a door, into a room where the only thing inside it was the cot, rocking side to side as though the strength of the child were able to send it off balance. I would feel true fear as I went slowly towards it, the sound now painful in my ears.

But I felt the duty of a father, struggling with those wavering emotions, not really wanting to see what I knew would be there.

Lying in the sweet soft covers was the emaciated, wizened creature which appeared to be human, yet I knew was not. Its little mouth opening and closing in its thin face, like a fish gasping in air, its eyes similar, white and staring at nothing. And that noise, a crackling whining which I had to make stop.

I would lower my arms to lift the baby from its crib, unwillingly bringing it towards me to give it the comfort it would never accept. And I would hold it against my chest and feel its movements cease.

When finally I stole myself to look upon that child in my arms, wrapped in its blanket, I saw nothing but a lump of hard and dirty wood, crudely carved. An effigy... of my child.

Not my child.

* * *

They may have left me alone for all these years, but if there is one thing they have, it's time... and this could be what they were waiting for.

They steal children.

They know I have agreed to return to Cornwall, to live in that cottage.

But if their revenge is merely to force upon me these reoccurring nightmares, then I will take it, suffer it, and as always, try to make it right.

I am sorry that I cannot change what has already been done.

But learning from Tabby has made me wake up to myself.

I can have me my dreams, and my life. They don't have to come true. Sometimes that's not what dreams are about.

And to be honest I'm actually looking forward to going back.

Saying those words means a lot... helps me understand how I feel about it all; frightened, mixed with suppressed excitement. My life tends to be like that.

Now my pain is more to realise how much of myself was wasted on those fears. And now Tabby has pains in her belly, the baby kicking, the baby wanting to come into this world.

My only hope is that I can help make sure the world is a good enough place.

* * *

There is a saying of not being able to see the woods for the trees; somewhere along the way I lost sight of what that means. It was always the woods that I saw.

But now I understand.

If I am guilty of anything then it is a guilt I share with everyone. I have been ignorant. And I am sorry. I am sorry for the mistakes of all Earth's people.

But we all need to forgive if we are to move on.

Tabby tried to explain to me, "We can't worry so much about the world that it stops us from living in it Adam. I know it's always been grand scale ventures that have damaged the planet, but believe me, it will be small caring gestures from ordinary folk that soothe it better in the long run."

She might be right. It is never too late to restore amends.

Just please don't take my child.

Let them grow up in the countryside and love it as I did, but see it with fresh eyes, a clear mind and a heart with no fear. It is a beautiful world.

We are all born innocent. We have no enemies. We know only love. It is living this life which taints us.

But if we just try. Keep learning. Don't close the

book. Then why should we be afraid?

That is all we can do.

We have pushed blindly forwards but I understand now that what has always been is important to keep in our future. It is up to some of us to keep looking back. We are not children anymore.

But my childhood was different to those of today. It was a time when kids still played outside and had real adventures which were connecting us to the world, not the World Wide Web. Children nowadays don't seem to have the imagination to entertain themselves like that, because they have too much else. When your choices are limited you make more of them than there is...

Perhaps that was all I did. Perhaps everything that happened as I grew up became over inflated and now seems to mean so much more than the sum of its parts. Or maybe I can now see its deep intricacies.

Believe what you wish, but learn from my lessons. I have grown up.

Now I am the one afraid of the old ways being lost. As you get older it is hard to not sound like your parents, and then your grandparents, saying how it was 'better in my day'. But maybe it was, maybe it always has been. The human race should be growing wiser with each generation, yet we forget. Important things we have learnt are thrown out for the new, moving ever further from the way human beings started out.

Perhaps one day we will see it all clearly again. We will all be seers.

I want that for my child.

I will make sure it happens.

I promise.

There is a change on the horizon... I can feel it... I am

part of it.

There are things I now know, things I can teach my child, and that they can teach theirs.

You don't have to believe that those mystical things exist. You can see the world and see the magic that is in it, you don't need to see the magic before you see the world.

But do not turn your head away.

Keep your eyes open.

Our worlds are not so separate. They are different, but always connected, and we have to try our best to live them together. If it seems that we have to walk on egg shells, then so be it. Perhaps we always should have treated the world with that level of care.

Nature is not just 'out there', it is inside of us, and so we have to let it in.

It never was my enemy.

And if we all understand that, then we can grow, and our roots will be sound.

So I will make one more vow, I will make a bargain... To the little people, the faeries, and all those hidden things, if you let me keep my child, then they will grow up to be good, a new generation that will change this vicious, needless cycle.

I will teach them to abide nature's rules... the ways of the woods... I will teach them wisdom, and I will make sure that they understand. We each have a place.

I will teach them to tread softly, to leave no mark. To not spy, but to delight in all they see. I will teach them never to pick blue bells, and to carry no nails, no stale bread...

The horseshoe attached to the front door of the cottage was a sign of a war still raged. It is time it was removed.

In our house we will call you only 'the good people'

and you will always be welcome.

Just let me have my child.

I know now what is important.

If we are ever going to be at peace with the Earth on which we walk, and which we share with all other living things... We have to remember.

THE END

Made in the USA
Charleston, SC
01 September 2015